Compute this . . .

A woman looks for her long-estranged father and finds that even if she doesn't need him, he needs her . . . or something that looks just like her, in James Patrick Kelly's "Itsy Bitsy Spider" . . .

In Mike Resnick's "Robots Don't Cry," a team of space-faring scrap dealers discovers a five-hundred-year-old robot whose unswerving loyalty to its former master reaches beyond the years—and beyond the grave . . .

A traveler exploring a deserted planet comes across some very strange and personality-driven robots who seem to have inherited the Earth—and want to leave it as soon as possible—in Howard Waldrop's "London, Paris, Banana" . . .

And a futuristic entrepreneur must hold together his robot-battling business in the middle of a war zone while fighting to win the hand of the woman he loves in Alex Irvine's "Jimmy Guang's House of Gladmech" . . .

ROBOTS

EDITED BY
JACK DANN & GARDNER DOZOIS

ACE BOOKS, NEW YORK

THE BERKLEY PUBLISHING GROUP
Published by the Penguin Group
Penguin Group (USA) Inc.
375 Hudson Street, New York, New York 10014, USA
Penguin Group (Canada), 90 Eglinton Avenue East, Suite 700, Toronto, Ontario M4P 2Y3, Canada
(a division of Pearson Penguin Canada Inc.)
Penguin Books Ltd., 80 Strand, London WC2R 0RL, England
Penguin Group Ireland, 25 St. Stephen's Green, Dublin 2, Ireland (a division of Penguin Books
Ltd.)
Penguin Group (Australia), 250 Camberwell Road, Camberwell, Victoria 3124, Australia
(a division of Pearson Australia Group Pty. Ltd.)
Penguin Books India Pvt. Ltd., 11 Community Centre, Panchsheel Park, New Delhi—110 017,
India
Penguin Group (NZ), Cnr. Airborne and Rosedale Roads, Albany, Auckland 1310, New Zealand
(a division of Pearson New Zealand Ltd.)
Penguin Books (South Africa) (Pty.) Ltd., 24 Sturdee Avenue, Rosebank, Johannesburg 2196,
South Africa

Penguin Books Ltd., Registered Offices: 80 Strand, London WC2R 0RL, England

This is a work of fiction. Names, characters, places, and incidents either are the product of the
authors' imaginations or are used fictitiously, and any resemblance to actual persons, living or dead,
business establishments, events, or locales is entirely coincidental. The publisher does not have any
control over and does not assume any responsibility for author or third-party websites or their
content.

ROBOTS

An Ace Book / published by arrangement with the editors

PRINTING HISTORY
Ace mass market edition / September 2005

Copyright © 2005 by Jack Dann.
A complete listing of individual copyrights can be found on page v.
Cover art by AXB Group.
Cover design by Rita Frangie.

ISBN: 0-441-01321-X

ACE
Ace Books are published by The Berkley Publishing Group,
a division of Penguin Group (USA) Inc.,
375 Hudson Street, New York, New York 10014.
ACE and the "A" design are trademarks belonging to Penguin Group (USA) Inc.

PRINTED IN THE UNITED STATES OF AMERICA

10 9 8 7 6 5 4 3 2 1

CONTENTS

Preface

Although the word *robot* was taken from Karel Capek's 1921 play *R.U.R.*, derived from the Czech word *robata,* the idea of artificial men, beings *created* by other men, has haunted the imagination of humanity for thousands of years, going at least as far back as the legends of men of bronze and tin to be found in Greek and Roman mythology, like Talos, the giant made of bronze who was said to guard the shores of Crete by running around the island three times daily and throwing huge rocks at any enemy invaders. Tales of robots or mechanical men have a long tradition in science fiction, entering the body of science fiction proper soon after there began to recognizably *be* such a thing, in the nineteenth century, and persisting to the present day.

The number of robot stories appearing each year has varied from decade to decade, with writers seemingly more preoccupied with them in some years than in others, as robot stories went in and out of style; the heyday of the robot story was probably the '40s and '50s and early '60s, when Isaac Asimov was writing his famous cycle of robot stories, including the robot novels *The Caves of Steel* and *The Naked Sun*; Brian W. Aldiss was producing the stories that would go into his collection *And Who Can Replace a Man?*; Jack Williamson was writing "With Folded Hands;" C. L. Moore was writing "No Woman Born;" Henry Kuttner was producing the stories that went into *Robots Have No Tails*; Alfred Bester was producing "Fondly Fahrenheit;" Philip K. Dick was writing "Second Variety" and "Imposter;" Clifford Simak was writing *City* and "All the Traps of Earth;" and Harry Harrison was writing about *The War with the Robots*. Most of the anthologies of robot stories that have been published— Damon Knight's *The Metal Smile*, Robert Silverberg's

Men and Machines, Sam Moskowitz's *The Coming of the Robots*, Roger Elwood's *Invasion of the Robots*—have drawn primarily on stories from those decades.

The "New Wave" days of the mid to late '60s to the mid '70s, with their emphasis on introspective, stylistically "experimental" work and work with more immediate sociological and political "relevance" to the tempestuous social scene of the day, saw fewer robot stories being published (with a few significant exceptions, such as Dick's *Do Androids Dream of Electric Sheep?* and Asimov's "The Bicentennial Man"). In the '80s and '90s, much of the dialogue about robots in the field was subsumed in the examination of the concept of artificial intelligence (see our previous Ace anthology *A.I.s* for stories of this type), to the extent that Asimov's later robot novels such as *The Robots of Dawn* and *Robots and Empire* were criticized as being retro by some commentators, no longer having anything to contribute to the back-and-forth debate about the nature of artificial intelligence going on among the younger writers in the field.

In the real world, the development of humanoid robots, robots of the same shape, size, and general body-plan as humans, has proved surprisingly difficult, even in the fundamental engineering problem of making robots articulate and *move* like humans, let alone the problem of investing them with some form of self-contained and reasonably functional intelligence—let alone sentience and an intellectual capacity equal or superior to us. In *The Door into Summer*, published in 1957, Robert A. Heinlein could confidently predict that his robotic servants and housecleaners, the Hired Girls, would be in existence by 1970, but 1970 has come and gone (even the "future" of Heinlein's novel, the year 2000, has come and gone!), and so far only the most primitive ancestors of the sophisticated Hired Girls, disk-shaped robot vacuum cleaners that scoot around by themselves vacuuming your floors, have actually come on to the market. In spite of the lack of clanking humanoid servants, though, robots surround us in our daily lives—not in humanoid form, but in the thousand forms of industrial robots, from gigantic to tiny, who have taken over many of the world's industrial tasks, and in the form of all the myriad machines, unnoticed and unremarked, that perform a multitude of menial tasks for us, from those that help apply the brakes in your car to those that open the supermarket doors for you, saturating our lives in ways that Heinlein never could have imagined back in 1957. Ironically, considering Asimov's famous First Law of Robotics—"a robot may not injure a human being or, through inaction, allow a human being to come to harm"—the most technologically sophisticated robots developed to date are designed specifically for the task of *killing people*: cruise missiles and smart bombs. Asimov's humanoid, general-purpose, intelligent robots may not be developed for decades to come—if they are ever developed at all.

Robots still continue to fascinate us, though, and, as you shall see in the anthology that follows, still stalk through the pages of science fiction. In fact, robots have made something of a comeback in the later '90s and the aughts, perhaps because of the popularity of Big Budget robot movies such as *The Terminator*, *A.I.*, *The Bicentennial Man*, and *I, Robot*, or perhaps just because the idea itself, sentient machines that look and act like us, is so archtypically potent. Many of science fiction's most significant tropes may spring from a kind of cosmic loneliness, the desire to have someone else in the universe to *talk* with. Aliens are one fictional solution to the problem of having another race of sentient creatures to interact with—and the other great solution is robots. If you can't *find* other sentient creatures out there in the universe, the next best thing is to *make* them yourself. Perhaps this is why robot stories are becoming more popular again, as many people grow discouraged with the hope that the search for extraterrestrial intelligence is ever going to turn up anything. This may also be reflected in the changing attitudes toward robots manifested in many of these stories, from the sinister figures out to supplant or destroy or infiltrate us common in the '50s and '60s to helpmates and caregivers, companions, compatriots, sources of solace both physical and spiritual, even our eventual anointed successors in the universe.

So open the pages of this book, and let some of today's most expert dreamers show you more variations on the complex future relationship of humans and machines—some funny, some sad, some moving, some bizarre—than you've ever imagined before. Enjoy!

(For other speculations on these and similar themes, check out our Ace anthologies *A.I.s, Beyond Flesh, Nanotech, Hackers, Immortals, Future War, Space Soldiers,* and coedited by Sheila Williams—*Isaac Asimov's Robots.*)

Itsy Bitsy Spider

James Patrick Kelly

James Patrick Kelly made his first sale in 1975, and since has gone on to become one of the most respected and popular writers to enter the field in the last twenty years. Although Kelly has had some success with novels, especially with Wildlife, *he has perhaps had more impact to date as a writer of short fiction, with stories such as "Solstice," "The Prisoner of Chillon," "Glass Cloud," "Mr. Boy," "Pogrom," "Home Front," "Undone," and "Bernardo's House," and is often ranked among the best short story writers in the business. His story "Think Like a Dinosaur" won him a Hugo Award in 1996, as did his story "10^{16} to 1" in 2000. Kelly's first solo novel, the mostly ignored* Planet of Whispers, *came out in 1984. It was followed by* Freedom Beach, *a mosaic novel written in collaboration with John Kessel, and then by another solo novel,* Look Into the Sun. *His short work has been collected in* Think Like a Dinosaur, *and, most recently, in a new collection,* Strange But Not a Stranger. *Born in Minneola, New York, Kelly now lives with his family in Nottingham, New Hampshire. He has a website at www.JimKelly.net and reviews internet-related matters for* Asimov's Science Fiction.

Here he guides us to an ostensibly tranquil future society for a tale of fathers and daughters that's a bit more complicated than it first seems, and where some of the games they play, even children's games, can get very rough indeed . . .

When I *found* out that my father was still alive after all these years and living at Strawberry Fields, I thought he'd gotten just what he deserved. Retroburbs are where the old, scared people go to hide. I'd always pictured the people in them as deranged losers. Visiting some fantasy world like the disneys or Carlucci's Carthage is one thing, *moving* to one is another. Sure, 2038 is messy, but it's a hell of a lot better than nineteen-sixty-whatever.

Now that I'd arrived at 144 Bluejay Way, I realized that the place was worse than I had imagined. Strawberry Fields was pretending to be some long-lost suburb of the late twentieth century, except that it had the sterile monotony of cheap VR. It was clean, all right, and neat, but it was everywhere the same. And the scale was wrong. The lots were squeezed together and all the houses had shrunk—like the dreams of their owners. They were about the size of a one-car garage, modular units tarted up at the factory to look like ranches, with old double-hung storm windows and hardened siding of harvest gold, barn red, forest green. Of course, there were no real garages; faux Mustangs and VW buses cruised the quiet streets. Their carbrains were listening for a summons from Barbara Chesley next door at 142, or the Goltzes across the street, who might be headed to Penny Lanes to bowl a few frames, or the hospital to die.

There was a beach chair with blue nylon webbing on the front stoop of 144 Bluejay Way. A brick walk led to it, dividing two patches of carpet moss, green as a dream. There were names and addresses printed in huge lightstick letters on all the doors in the neighborhood; no doubt many Strawberry Fielders were easily confused. The owner of this one was Peter Fancy. He had been born Peter Fanelli, but had legally taken his stage name not long after his first success as Prince Hal in *Henry IV Part*

1. I was a Fancy too; the name was one of the few things of my father's I had kept.

I stopped at the door and let it look me over. "You're Jen," it said.

"Yes." I waited in vain for it to open or to say something else. "I'd like to see Mr. Fancy, please." The old man's house had worse manners than he did. "He knows I'm coming," I said. "I sent him several messages." Which he had never answered, but I didn't mention that.

"Just a minute," said the door. "She'll be right with you."

She? The idea that he might be with another woman now hadn't occurred to me. I'd lost track of my father a long time ago—on purpose. The last time we'd actually visited overnight was when I was twenty. Mom gave me a ticket to Port Gemini, where he was doing the Shakespeare in Space program. The orbital was great, but staying with him was like being under water. I think I must have held my breath for the entire week. After that, there were a few, sporadic calls, a couple of awkward dinners—all at his instigation. Then twenty-three years of nothing.

I never hated him, exactly. When he left, I just decided to show solidarity with Mom and be done with him. If acting was more important than his family, then to hell with Peter Fancy. Mom was horrified when I told her how I felt. She cried and claimed the divorce was as much her fault as his. It was too much for me to handle; I was only eleven years old when they separated. I needed to be on *someone's* side and so I had chosen her. She never did stop trying to talk me into finding him again, even though after a while it only made me mad at her. For the past few years, she'd been warning me that I'd developed a warped view of men.

But she was a smart woman, my mom—a winner. Sure, she'd had troubles, but she'd founded three companies, was a millionaire by twenty-five. I missed her.

A lock clicked and the door opened. Standing in the dim interior was a little girl in a gold-and-white checked dress. Her dark, curly hair was tied in a ribbon. She was wearing white ankle socks and black Mary Jane shoes that were so shiny they had to be plastic. There was a Band-Aid on her left knee.

"Hello, Jen. I was hoping you'd really come." Her voice surprised me. It was resonant, impossibly mature. At first glance I'd guessed she was three, maybe four; I'm not much good at guessing kids' ages. Now I realized that this must be a bot—a made person.

"You look just like I thought you would." She smiled, stood on tiptoe and raised a delicate little hand over her head. I had to bend to shake it. The hand was warm, slightly moist, and very realistic. She had to belong to Strawberry Fields; there was no way my father could afford a bot with skin this real.

"Please come in." She waved on the lights. "We're so happy you're here." The door closed behind me.

The playroom took up almost half of the little house. Against one wall was a miniature kitchen. Toy dishes were drying in a rack next to the sink; the pink refrigerator barely came up to my waist. The table was full-sized; it had two normal chairs and a booster chair. Opposite this was a bed with a ruffled Pumpkin Patty bedspread. About a dozen dolls and stuffed animals were arranged along the far edge of the mattress. I recognized most of them: Pooh, Mr. Moon, Baby Rollypolly, the Sleepums, Big Bird. And the wallpaper was familiar too: Oz figures like Toto and the Wizard and the Cowardly Lion on a field of Munchkin blue.

"We had to make a few changes," said the bot. "Do you like it?"

The room seemed to tilt then. I took a small, unsteady step and everything righted itself. *My* dolls, *my* wallpaper, the chest of drawers from Grandma Fanelli's cottage in

Hyannis. I stared at the bot and recognized her for the first time.

She was me.

"What is this," I said, "some kind of sick joke?" I felt like I'd just been slapped in the face.

"Is something wrong?" the bot said. "Tell me. Maybe we can fix it."

I swiped at her and she danced out of reach. I don't know what I would have done if I had caught her. Maybe smashed her through the picture window onto the patch of front lawn or shaken her until pieces started falling off. But the bot wasn't responsible, my father was. Mom would never have defended him if she'd known about *this*. The old bastard. I couldn't believe it. Here I was, shuddering with anger, after years of feeling nothing for him.

There was an interior door just beyond some shelves filled with old-fashioned paper books. I didn't take time to look as I went past, but I knew that Dr. Seuss and A. A. Milne and L. Frank Baum would be on those shelves. The door had no knob.

"Open up," I shouted. It ignored me, so I kicked it. "Hey!"

"Jennifer." The bot tugged at the back of my jacket. "I must ask you . . ."

"You can't have me!" I pressed my ear to the door. Silence. "I'm not this thing you made." I kicked it again. "You hear?"

Suddenly an announcer was shouting in the next room. "*. . . Into the post to Russell, who kicks it out to Havlicek all alone at the top of the key, he shoots . . . and Baylor with the strong rebound.*" The asshole was trying to drown me out.

"If you don't come away from that door right now," said the bot, "I'm calling security."

"What are they going to do?" I said. "I'm the long-lost

daughter, here for a visit. And who the hell are you, any-way?"

"I'm bonded to him, Jen. Your father is no longer com-petent to handle his own affairs. I'm his legal guardian."

"Shit." I kicked the door one last time, but my heart wasn't in it. I shouldn't have been surprised that he had slipped over the edge. He was almost ninety.

"If you want to sit and talk, I'd like that very much." The bot gestured toward a banana yellow beanbag chair. "Otherwise, I'm going to have to ask you to leave."

It was the shock of seeing the bot, I told myself—I'd re-acted like a hurt little girl. But I was a grown woman and it was time to start behaving like one. I wasn't here to let Peter Fancy worm his way back into my feelings. I had come because of Mom.

"Actually," I said, "I'm here on business." I opened my purse. "If you're running his life now, I guess this is for you." I passed her the envelope and settled back, tucking my legs beneath me. There is no way for an adult to sit gracefully in a beanbag chair.

She slipped the check out. "It's from Mother." She paused, then corrected herself, "Her estate." She didn't seem surprised.

"Yes."

"It's too generous."

"That's what I thought."

"She must've taken care of you too?"

"I'm fine." I wasn't about to discuss the terms of Mom's will with my father's toy daughter.

"I would've liked to have known her," said the bot. She slid the check back into the envelope and set it aside. "I've spent a lot of time imagining Mother."

I had to work hard not to snap at her. Sure, this bot had at least a human equivalent intelligence and would be a free citizen someday, assuming she didn't break down first. But she had a cognizor for a brain and a heart fabricated in a vat. How could she possibly imagine my mom, especially when all she had to go on was whatever lies *he* had told her?

"So how bad is he?"

She gave me a sad smile and shook her head. "Some days are better than others. He has no clue who President Huong is or about the quake, but he can still recite the dagger scene from *Macbeth*. I haven't told him that Mother died. He'd just forget it ten minutes later."

"Does he know what you are?"

"I am many things, Jen."

"Including me."

"You're a role I'm playing, not who I am." She stood. "Would you like some tea?"

"Okay." I still wanted to know why Mom had left my father four hundred and thirty-eight thousand dollars in her will. If he couldn't tell me, maybe the bot could.

She went to her kitchen, opened a cupboard, and took out a regular-sized cup. It looked like a bucket in her little hand. "I don't suppose you still drink Constant Comment?"

His favorite. I had long since switched to rafallo. "That's fine." I remembered that when I was a kid my father used to brew cups for the two of us from the same bag because Constant Comment was so expensive. "I thought they went out of business long ago."

"I mix my own. I'd be interested to hear how accurate you think the recipe is."

"I suppose you know how I like it?"

She chuckled.

"So, does he need the money?"

The microwave dinged. "Very few actors get rich," said the bot. I didn't think there had been microwaves in the sixties, but then strict historical accuracy wasn't really the point of Strawberry Fields. "Especially when they have a weakness for Shakespeare."

"Then how come he lives here and not in some flop? And how did he afford you?"

She pinched sugar between her index finger and thumb, then rubbed them together over the cup. It was something I still did, but only when I was by myself. A nasty habit; Mom used to yell at him for teaching it to me. "I was a gift." She shook a teabag loose from a canister shaped like an acorn and plunged it into the boiling water. "From Mother."

The bot offered the cup to me; I accepted it nervelessly. "That's not true." I could feel the blood draining from my face.

"I can lie if you'd prefer, but I'd rather not." She pulled the booster chair away from the table and turned it to face me. "There are many things about themselves that they never told us, Jen. I've always wondered why that was."

I felt logy and a little stupid, as if I had just woken from a thirty-year nap. "She just gave you to him?"

"And bought him this house, paid all his bills, yes."

"But why?"

"*You* knew her," said the bot. "I was hoping you could tell me."

I couldn't think of what to say or do. Since there was a cup in my hand, I took a sip. For an instant, the scent of tea and dried oranges carried me back to when I was a little girl and I was sitting in Grandma Fanelli's kitchen in a wet bathing suit, drinking Constant Comment that my father had made to keep my teeth from chattering. There were knots like brown eyes in the pine walls and the green linoleum was slick where I had dripped on it.

"Well?"

"It's good," I said absently and raised the cup to her. "No, really, just like I remember."

She clapped her hands in excitement. "So," said the bot. "What was Mother like?"

It was an impossible question, so I tried to let it bounce off me. But then neither of us said anything; we just stared at each other across a yawning gulf of time and experience. In the silence, the question stuck. Mom had died three months ago and this was the first time since the funeral that I'd thought of her as she really had been—not the papery ghost in the hospital room. I remembered how, after she divorced my father, she always took my calls when she was at the office, even if it was late, and how she used to step on imaginary brakes whenever I drove her anywhere, and how grateful I was that she didn't cry when I told her that Rob and I were getting divorced. I thought about Easter eggs and raspberry Pop Tarts and when she sent me to Antibes for a year when I was fourteen and that perfume she wore on my father's opening nights and the way they used to waltz on the patio at the house in Waltham.

"West is walking the ball upcourt, setting his offense with fifteen seconds to go on the shot clock, nineteen in the half . . ."

The beanbag chair that I was in faced the picture window. Behind me, I could hear the door next to the bookcase open.

"Jones and Goodrich are in each other's jerseys down low and now Chamberlain swings over and calls for the ball on the weak side . . ."

I twisted around to look over my shoulder. The great Peter Fancy was making his entrance.

Mom *once told* me that when she met my father, he was typecast playing men that women fall hopelessly in love with. He'd had great successes as Stanley Kowalski in *Streetcar* and Sky Masterson in *Guys and Dolls* and the Vicomte de Valmont in *Les Liaisons Dangereuses*. The years had eroded his good looks but had not obliterated them; from a distance he was still a handsome man. He had a shock of close-cropped white hair. The beautiful cheekbones were still there; the chin was as sharply defined as it had been in his first headshot. His gray eyes were distant and a little dreamy, as if he were preoccupied with the War of the Roses or the problem of evil.

"Jen," he said, "what's going on out here?" He still had the big voice that could reach into the second balcony without a mike. I thought for a moment he was talking to me.

"We have company, Daddy," said the bot, in a four-year-old trill that took me by surprise. "A lady."

"I can see that it's a lady, sweetheart." He took a hand from the pocket of his jeans, stroked the touchpad on his belt and his exolegs walked him stiffly across the room. "I'm Peter Fancy," he said.

"The lady is from Strawberry Fields." The bot swung around behind my father. She shot me a look that made the terms and conditions of my continued presence clear: if I broke the illusion, I was out. "She came by to see if everything is all right with our house." The bot disturbed me even more, now that she sounded like young Jen Fancy.

As I heaved myself out of the beanbag chair, my father gave me one of those lopsided, flirting grins I knew so well. "Does the lady have a name?" He must have shaved just for the company, because now that he had come close I could see that he had a couple of fresh nicks. There was a button-sized patch of gray whiskers by his ear that he had missed altogether.

"Her name is Ms. Johnson," said the bot. It was my ex, Rob's, last name. I had never been Jennifer Johnson.

"Well, Ms. Johnson," he said, hooking thumbs in his pants pockets. "The water in my toilet is brown."

"I'll . . . um . . . see that it's taken care of." I was at a loss for what to say next, then inspiration struck. "Actually, I had another reason for coming." I could see the bot stiffen. "I don't know if you've seen *Yesterday*, our little newsletter? Anyway, I was talking to Mrs. Chesley next door and she told me that you were an actor once. I was wondering if I might interview you. Just a few questions, if you have the time. I think your neighbors might . . ."

"Were?" he said, drawing himself up. "*Once?* Madame, I am now an actor and will always be."

"My daddy's famous," said the bot.

I cringed at that; it was something I used to say. My father squinted at me. "What did you say your name was?"

"Johnson," I said. "Jane Johnson."

"And you're a reporter? You're sure you're not a critic?"

"Positive."

He seemed satisfied. "I'm Peter Fancy." He extended his right hand to shake. The hand was spotted and bony and it trembled like a reflection in a lake. Clearly whatever magic—or surgeon's skill—it was that had preserved my father's face had not extended to his extremities. I was so disturbed by his infirmity that I took his cold hand in mine and pumped it three, four times. It was dry as a page of one of the bot's dead books. When I let go, the hand seemed steadier. He gestured at the beanbag.

"Sit," he said. "Please."

After I had settled in, he tapped the touchpad and stumped over to the picture window. "Barbara Chesley is a broken and bitter old woman," he said, "and I will not have dinner with her under any circumstances, do you understand?" He peered up Bluejay Way and down.

"Yes, Daddy," said the bot.

"I believe she voted for Nixon, so she has no reason to complain now." Apparently satisfied that the neighbors weren't sneaking up on us, he leaned against the windowsill, facing me. "Mrs. Thompson, I think today may well be a happy one for both of us. I have an announcement." He paused for effect. "I've been thinking of Lear again."

The bot settled onto one of her little chairs. "Oh, Daddy, that's wonderful."

"It's the only one of the big four I haven't done," said my father. "I was set for a production in Stratford, Ontario, back in '99; Polly Matthews was to play Cordelia. Now there was an actor; she could bring tears to a stone. But then my wife Hannah had one of her bad times and I had to withdraw so I could take care of Jen. The two of us stayed down at my mother's cottage on the Cape; I wasted the entire season tending bar. And when Hannah came out of rehab, she decided that she didn't want to be married to an underemployed actor anymore, so things were tight for a while. She had all the money, so I had to scramble— spent almost two years on the road. But I think it might have been for the best. I was only forty-eight. Too old for Hamlet, too young for Lear. My Hamlet was very well received, you know. There were overtures from PBS about a taping, but that was when the BBC decided to do the Shakespeare series with that doctor, what was his name? Jonathan Miller. So instead of Peter Fancy, we had Derek Jacobi, whose brilliant idea it was to roll across the stage, frothing his lines like a rabid raccoon. You'd think he'd seen an alien, not his father's ghost. Well, that was another missed opportunity, except, of course, that I was too young. Ripeness is all, eh? So I still have Lear to do. Unfinished business. My comeback."

He bowed, then pivoted solemnly so that I saw him in profile, framed by the picture window. "Where have I been? Where am I? Fair daylight?" He held up a trembling hand and blinked at it uncomprehendingly. "I know not what to say. I swear these are not my hands."

Suddenly the bot was at his feet. "O look upon me, sir,"

she said, in her childish voice, "and hold your hand in benediction o'er me."

"Pray, do not mock me." My father gathered himself in the flood of morning light. "I am a very foolish, fond old man, fourscore and upward, not an hour more or less; and to deal plainly, I fear I am not in my perfect mind."

He stole a look in my direction, as if to gauge my reaction to his impromptu performance. A frown might have stopped him, a word would have crushed him. Maybe I should have, but I was afraid he'd start talking about Mom again, telling me things I didn't want to know. So I watched instead, transfixed.

"Methinks I should know you"—he rested his hand briefly on the bot's head—"and know this stranger." He fumbled at the controls and the exolegs carried him across the room toward me. As he drew nearer, he seemed to sluff off the years. "Yet I am mainly ignorant what place this is; and all the skill I have remembers not these garments, nor I know not where I did lodge last night." It was Peter Fancy who stopped before me; his face a mere kiss away from mine. "Do not laugh at me; for, as I am a man, I think this lady to be my child. Cordelia."

He was staring right at me, into me, knifing through make-believe indifference to the wound I'd nursed all these years, the one that had never healed. He seemed to expect a reply, only I didn't have the line. A tiny, sad squeaky voice within me was whimpering, *You left me and you got exactly what you deserve.* But my throat tightened and choked it off.

The bot cried, "And so I am! I am!"

But she had distracted him. I could see confusion begin to deflate him. "Be your tears wet? Yes, faith. I pray . . . weep not. If you have poison for me, I will drink it. I know you do not love me . . ."

He stopped and his brow wrinkled. "It's something about the sisters," he muttered.

"Yes," said the bot, "'. . . for your sisters have done me wrong . . .'"

"Don't feed me the fucking lines!" he shouted at her. "I'm Peter Fancy, god damn it!"

After she calmed him down, we had lunch. She let him make the peanut butter and banana sandwiches while she heated up some Campbell's tomato and rice soup, which she poured from a can made of actual metal. The sandwiches were lumpy because he had hacked the bananas into chunks the size of walnuts. She tried to get him to tell me about the daylilies blooming in the backyard, and the old Boston Garden, and the time he and Mom had had breakfast with Bobby Kennedy. She asked whether he wanted TV dinner or pot pie for supper. He refused all her conversational gambits. He only ate half a bowl of soup.

He pushed back from the table and announced that it was her nap time. The bot put up a perfunctory fuss, although it was clear that it was my father who was tired out. However, the act seemed to perk him up. Another role for his resume: the doting father. "I'll tell you what," he said. "We'll play your game, sweetheart. But just once— otherwise you'll be cranky tonight."

The two of them perched on the edge of the bot's bed next to Big Bird and the Sleepums. My father started to sing and the bot immediately joined in.

"The itsy bitsy spider went up the water spout."

Their gestures were almost mirror images, except that his ruined hands actually looked like spiders as they climbed into the air.

"Down came the rain, and washed the spider out."

The bot beamed at him as if he were the only person in the world.

"Out came the sun, and dried up all the rain.

"And the itsy bitsy spider went up the spout again."

When his arms were once again raised over his head, she giggled and hugged him. He let them fall around her, returning her embrace. "That's a good girl," he said. "That's my Jenny."

The look on his face told me that I had been wrong: this was no act. It was as real to him as it was to me. I had tried hard not to, but I still remembered how the two of us always used to play together, Daddy and Jenny, Jen and Dad.

Waiting for Mommy to come home

He kissed her and she snuggled under the blankets. I felt my eyes stinging.

"But if you do the play," she said, "when will you be back?"

"What play?"

"That one you were telling me. The king and his daughters."

"There's no such play, Jenny." He sifted her black curls through his hands. "I'll never leave you, don't worry now. Never again." He rose unsteadily and caught himself on the chest of drawers.

"Nighty noodle," said the bot.

"Pleasant dreams, sweetheart," said my father. "I love you."

"I love you too."

I expected him to say something to me, but he didn't even seem to realize that I was still in the room. He shambled across the playroom, opened the door to his bedroom and went in.

"I'm sorry about that," said the bot, speaking again as an adult.

"Don't be," I said. I coughed—something in my throat. "It was fine. I was very . . . touched."

"He's usually a lot happier. Sometimes he works in the garden." The bot pulled the blankets aside and swung her legs out of the bed. "He likes to vacuum."

"Yes."

"I take good care of him."

I nodded and reached for my purse. "I can see that." I had to go. "Is it enough?"

She shrugged. "He's my daddy."

"I meant the money. Because if it's not, I'd like to help."

"Thank you. He'd appreciate that."

The front door opened for me, but I paused before stepping out into Strawberry Fields. "What about . . . after?"

"When he dies? My bond terminates. He said he'd leave the house to me. I know you could contest that, but I'll need to sell in order to pay for my twenty-year maintenance."

"No, no. That's fine. You deserve it."

She came to the door and looked up at me, little Jen Fancy and the woman she would never become.

"You know, it's *you* he loves," she said. "I'm just a stand-in."

"He loves his little girl," I said. "Doesn't do me any good—I'm forty-seven."

"It could if you let it." She frowned. "I wonder if that's why Mother did all this. So you'd find out."

"Or maybe she was just plain sorry." I shook my head. She was a smart woman, my mom. I would've liked to have known her.

"So, Ms. Fancy, maybe you can visit us again sometime." The bot grinned and shook my hand. "Daddy's usually in a good mood after his nap. He sits out front on his beach chair and waits for the ice cream truck. He always buys us some. Our favorite is Yellow Submarine. It's vanilla with fat butterscotch swirls, dipped in white chocolate. I know it sounds kind of odd, but it's good."

"Yes," I said absently, thinking about all the things Mom had told me about my father. I was hearing them now for the first time. "That might be nice."

Robots Don't Cry

Mike Resnick

Here's a poignant look at loyalty that persists through The End of The World—and out the other side.

Mike Resnick is one of the bestselling authors in science fiction and one of the most prolific. His many novels in-clude Santiago, The Dark Lady, Stalking The Unicorn, Birthright: The Book of Man, Paradise, Ivory, Soothsayer, Oracle, Lucifer Jones, Purgatory, Inferno, A Miracle of Rare Design, The Widowmaker, The Soul Eater, *and* A Hunger in the Soul. *His award-winning short fiction has been gathered in the collections* Will the Last Person to Leave the Planet Please Turn Off the Sun?, An Alien Land, Kirinyaga, A Safari of the Mind, *and* Hunting the Snark and Other Short Novels. *In the last decade or so, he has become almost as prolific as an anthologist, producing, as editor,* Inside the Funhouse: 17 SF Stories About SF, Whatdunits, More Whatdunits, *and* Shaggy B.E.M. Sto-ries; *a long string of anthologies coedited with Martin H. Greenberg—*Alternate Presidents, Alternate Kennedys, Al-ternate Warriors, Aladdin: Master of the Lamp, Dinosaur Fantastic, By Any Other Fame, Alternate Outlaws, *and* Sherlock Holmes in Orbit, *among others—as well as two anthologies coedited with Gardner Dozois. He won the Hugo Award in 1989 for "Kirinyaga." He won another Hugo Award in 1991 for another story in the Kirinyaga se-ries, "The Manumouki," and another Hugo and Nebula in 1995 for his novella "Seven Views of Olduvai Gorge." His most recent books include the novel* The Return of Santi-ago *and the anthologies* Stars: Songs Inspired by the Songs of Janis Ian *(edited with Janis Ian) and* New Voices in

Science Fiction. *He lives with his wife, Carol, in Cincinnati, Ohio.*

They call us graverobbers, but we're not.

What we do is plunder the past and offer it to the present. We hit old worlds, deserted worlds, worlds that nobody wants any longer, and we pick up anything we think we can sell to the vast collectibles market. You want a seven-hundred-year-old timepiece? A thousand-year-old bed? An actual printed book? Just put in your order, and sooner or later we'll fill it.

Every now and then we strike it rich. Usually we make a profit. Once in a while we just break even. There's only been one world where we actually lost money; I still remember it—Greenwillow. Except that it wasn't green, and there wasn't a willow on the whole damned planet.

There was a robot, though. We found him, me and the Baroni, in a barn, half-hidden under a pile of ancient computer parts and self-feeders for mutated cattle.

We were picking through the stuff, wondering if there was any market for it, tossing most of it aside, when the sun peeked in through the doorway and glinted off a prismatic eye.

"Hey, take a look at what we've got here," I said. "Give me a hand digging it out."

The junk had been stored a few feet above where he'd been standing and the rack broke, practically burying him. One of his legs was bent at an impossible angle, and his expressionless face was covered with cobwebs. The Baroni lumbered over—when you've got three legs you don't glide gracefully—and studied the robot.

"Interesting," he said. He never used whole sentences when he could annoy me with a single word that could mean almost anything.

"He should pay our expenses, once we fix him up and get him running," I said.

"A human configuration," noted the Baroni.

"Yeah, we still made 'em in our own image until a couple of hundred years ago."

"Impractical."

"Spare me your practicalities," I said. "Let's dig him out."

"Why bother?"

Trust a Baroni to miss the obvious. "Because he's got a memory cube," I answered. "Who the hell knows what he's seen? Maybe we'll find out what happened here."

"Greenwillow has been abandoned since long before you were born and I was hatched," replied the Baroni, finally stringing some words together. "Who cares what happened?"

"I know it makes your head hurt, but try to use your brain," I said, grunting as I pulled at the robot's arm. It came off in my hands. "Maybe whoever he worked for hid some valuables." I dropped the arm onto the floor. "Maybe he knows where. We don't just have to sell junk, you know; there's a market for the good stuff too."

The Baroni shrugged and began helping me uncover the robot. "I hear a lot of ifs and maybes," he muttered.

"Fine," I said. "Just sit on what passes for your ass, and I'll do it myself."

"And let you keep what we find without sharing it?" he demanded, suddenly throwing himself into the task of moving the awkward feeders. After a moment he stopped and studied one. "Big cows," he noted.

"Maybe ten or twelve feet at the shoulder, judging from the size of the stalls and the height of the feeders," I agreed. "But there weren't enough to fill the barn. Some of those stalls were never used."

Finally we got the robot uncovered, and I checked the code on the back of his neck.

"How about that?" I said. "The son of a bitch must be five hundred years old. That makes him an antique by anyone's definition. I wonder what we can get for him?"

The Baroni peered at the code. "What does AB stand for?"

"Aldebaran. Alabama. Abrams' Planet. Or maybe just the model number. Who the hell knows? We'll get him running and maybe he can tell us." I tried to set him on his feet. No luck. "Give me a hand."

"To the ship?" asked the Baroni, using sentence fragments again as he helped me stand the robot upright.

"No," I said. "We don't need a sterile environment to work on a robot. Let's just get him out in the sunlight, away from all this junk, and then we'll have a couple of mechs check him over."

We half-carried and half-dragged him to the crumbling concrete pad beyond the barn, then laid him down while I tightened the muscles in my neck, activating the embedded micro-chip, and directed the signal by pointing to the ship, which was about half a mile away.

"This is me," I said as the chip carried my voice back to the ship's computer. "Wake up Mechs Three and Seven, feed them everything you've got on robots going back a millennium, give them repair kits and anything else they'll need to fix a broken robot of indeterminate age, and then home in on my signal and send them to me."

"Why those two?" asked the Baroni.

Sometimes I wondered why I partnered with anyone that dumb. Then I remembered the way he could sniff out anything with a computer chip or cube, no matter how well it was hidden, so I decided to give him a civil answer. He didn't get that many from me; I hoped he appreciated it.

"Three's got those extendable eyestalks, and it can do microsurgery, so I figure it can deal with any faulty microcircuits. As for Seven, it's strong as an ox. It can position the robot, hold him aloft, move him any way that Three directs it to. They're both going to show up filled to the brim with everything the ship's data bank has on robots, so if he's salvageable, they'll find a way to salvage him."

I waited to see if he had any more stupid questions. Sure enough, he had.

"Why would anyone come here?" he asked, looking across the bleak landscape.

"I came for what passes for treasure these days," I answered him. "I have no idea why you came."

"I meant originally," he said, and his face started to glow that shade of pea-soup green that meant I was getting to him. "Nothing can grow, and the ultraviolet rays would eventually kill most animals. So why?"

"Because not all humans are as smart as me."

"It's an impoverished world," continued the Baroni. "What valuables could there be?"

"The usual," I replied. "Family heirlooms. Holographs. Old kitchen implements. Maybe even a few old Republic coins."

"Republic currency can't be spent."

"True—but a few years ago I saw a five-credit coin sell for three hundred Maria Teresa dollars. They tell me it's worth twice that today"

"I didn't know that," admitted the Baroni.

"I'll bet they could fill a book with all the things you don't know."

"Why are Men so sardonic and ill-mannered?"

"Probably because we have to spend so much time with races like the Baroni," I answered.

Mechs Three and Seven rolled up before he could reply.

"Reporting for duty, sir," said Mech Three in his high-pitched mechanical voice.

"This is a very old robot," I said, indicating what we'd found. "It's been out of commission for a few centuries, maybe even longer. See if you can get it working again."

"We live to serve," thundered Mech Seven.

"I can't tell you how comforting I find that." I turned to the Baroni. "Let's grab some lunch."

"Why do you always speak to them that way?" asked the Baroni as we walked away from the mechs. "They don't understand sarcasm."

"It's my nature," I said. "Besides, if they don't know it's sarcasm, it must sound like a compliment. Probably pleases the hell out of them."

"They are machines," he responded. "You can no more please them than offend them."

"Then what difference does it make?"

"The more time I spend with Men, the less I understand them," said the Baroni, making the burbling sound that passed for a deep sigh. "I look forward to getting the robot working. Being a logical and unemotional entity, it will make more sense."

"Spare me your smug superiority," I shot back. "You're not here because Papa Baroni looked at Mama Baroni with logic in his heart."

The Baroni burbled again. "You are hopeless," he said at last.

We had one of the mechs bring us our lunch, then sat with our backs propped against opposite sides of a gnarled old tree while we ate. I didn't want to watch his snakelike lunch writhe and wriggle, protesting every inch of the way, as he sucked it down like the long, living piece of spaghetti it was, and he had his usual moral qualms, which I never understood, about watching me bite into a sandwich. We had just about finished when Mech Three approached us.

"All problems have been fixed," it announced brightly.

"That was fast," I said.

"There was nothing broken." It then launched into a three-minute explanation of whatever it had done to the robot's circuitry.

"That's enough," I said when it got down to a dissertation on the effect of mu-mesons on negative magnetic fields in regard to prismatic eyes. "I'm wildly impressed. Now let's go take a look at this beauty."

I got to my feet, as did the Baroni, and we walked back to the concrete pad. The robot's limbs were straight now, and his arm was restored, but he still lay motionless on the crumbling surface.

"I thought you said you fixed him."

"I did," replied Mech Three. "But my programming compelled me not to activate it until you were present."

"Fine," I said. "Wake him up."

The little Mech made one final quick adjustment and backed away as the robot hummed gently to life and sat up.

"Welcome back," I said.

"Back?" replied the robot. "I have not been away."

"You've been asleep for five centuries, maybe six."

"Robots cannot sleep." He looked around. "Yet everything has changed. How is this possible?"

"You were deactivated," said the Baroni. "Probably your power supply ran down."

"Deactivated," the robot repeated. He swiveled his head from left to right, surveying the scene. "Yes. Things cannot change this much from one instant to the next."

"Have you got a name?" I asked him.

"Samson 4133. But Miss Emily calls me Sammy."

"Which name do you prefer?"

"I am a robot. I have no preferences."

I shrugged. "Whatever you say, Samson."

"Sammy," he corrected me.

"I thought you had no preferences."

"I don't," said the robot. "But *she* does."

"Has she got a name?"

"Miss Emily."

"Just Miss Emily?" I asked. "No other names to go along with it?"

"Miss Emily is what I was instructed to call her."

"I assume she is a child," said the Baroni, with his usual flair for discovering the obvious.

"She was once," said Sammy. "I will show her to you."

Then somehow, I never did understand the technology involved, he projected a full-sized holograph of a small girl, perhaps five years old, wearing a frilly purple-and-white outfit. She had rosy cheeks and bright shining blue eyes, and a smile that men would die for someday if given half the chance.

It was only after she took a step forward, a very awkward step, that I realized she had a prosthetic left leg.

"Too bad," I said. "A pretty little girl like that."

"Was she born that way, I wonder?" said the Baroni.

"I love you, Sammy," said the holograph.

I hadn't expected sound, and it startled me. She had such a happy voice. Maybe she didn't know that most little girls came equipped with two legs. After all, this was an underpopulated colony world; for all I knew, she'd never seen anyone but her parents.

"It is time for your nap, Miss Emily," said Sammy's voice. "I will carry you to your room." Another surprise. The voice didn't seem to come from the robot, but from somewhere . . . well, offstage. He was re-creating the scene exactly as it had happened, but we saw it through his eyes. Since he couldn't see himself, neither could we.

"I'll walk," said the child. "Mother told me I have to practice walking, so that someday I can play with the other girls."

"Yes, Miss Emily."

"But you can catch me if I start to fall, like you always do."

"Yes, Miss Emily."

"What would I do without you, Sammy?"

"You would fall, Miss Emily," he answered. Robots are always so damned literal.

And as suddenly as it had appeared, the scene vanished.

"So that was Miss Emily?" I said.

"Yes," said Sammy.

"And you were owned by her parents?"

"Yes."

"Do you have any understanding of the passage of time, Sammy?"

"I can calibrate time to within three nanoseconds of . . ."

"That's not what I asked," I said. "For example, if I told you that scene we just saw happened more than five hundred years ago, what would you say to that?"

"I would ask if you were measuring by Earth years, Galactic Standard years, New Calendar Democracy years . . ."

"Never mind," I said.

Sammy fell silent and motionless. If someone had stumbled upon him at just that moment, they'd have been hard-pressed to prove that he was still operational.

"What's the matter with him?" asked the Baroni. "His battery can't be drained yet."

"Of course not. They were designed to work for years without recharging."

And then I knew. He wasn't a farm robot, so he had no urge to get up and start working the fields. He wasn't a mech, so he had no interest in fixing the feeders in the barn. For a moment I thought he might be a butler or a major domo, but if he was, he'd have been trying to learn my desires to serve me, and he obviously wasn't doing that. That left just one thing.

He was a nursemaid.

I shared my conclusion with the Baroni, and he concurred.

"We're looking at a *lot* of money here," I said excitedly. "Think of it—a fully functioning antique robot nursemaid! He can watch the kids while his new owners go rummaging for more old artifacts."

"There's something wrong," said the Baroni, who was never what you could call an optimist.

"The only thing wrong is we don't have enough bags to haul all the money we're going to sell him for."

"Look around you," said the Baroni. "This place was abandoned, and it was never prosperous. If he's that valuable, why did they leave him behind?"

"He's a nursemaid. Probably she outgrew him."

"Better find out." He was back to sentence fragments again.

I shrugged and approached the robot. "Sammy, what did you do at night after Miss Emily went to sleep?"

He came to life again. "I stood by her bed."

"All night, every night?"

"Yes, sir. Unless she woke and requested pain medication, which I would retrieve and bring to her."

"Did she require pain medication very often?" I asked.

"I do not know, sir."

I frowned. "I thought you just said you brought it to her when she needed it."

"No, sir," Sammy corrected me. "I said I brought it to her when she *requested* it."

"She didn't request it very often?"

"Only when the pain became unbearable." Sammy paused. "I do not fully understand the word 'unbearable,' but I know it had a deleterious effect upon her. My Miss Emily was often in pain."

"I'm surprised you understand the word 'pain,'" I said.

"To feel pain is to be non-operational or dysfunctional to some degree."

"Yes, but it's more than that. Didn't Miss Emily ever try to describe it?"

"No," answered Sammy. "She never spoke of her pain."

"Did it bother her less as she grew older and adjusted to her handicap?" I asked.

"No, sir, it did not." He paused. "There are many kinds of dysfunction."

"Are you saying she had other problems, too?" I continued.

Instantly we were looking at another scene from Sammy's past. It was the same girl, now maybe thirteen years old, staring at her face in a mirror. She didn't like what she saw, and neither did I.

"What *is* that?" I asked, forcing myself not to look away.

"It is a fungus disease," answered Sammy as the girl tried unsuccessfully with cream and powder to cover the ugly blemishes that had spread across her face.

"Is it native to this world?"

"Yes," said Sammy.

"You must have had some pretty ugly people walking around," I said.

"It did not affect most of the colonists. But Miss Emily's immune system was weakened by her other diseases."

"What other diseases?"

Sammy rattled off three or four that I'd never heard of.

"And no one else in her family suffered from them?"

"No, sir."

"It happens in my race too," offered the Baroni. "Every now and then a genetically inferior specimen is born and grows to maturity."

"She was not genetically inferior," said Sammy.

"Oh?" I said, surprised. It's rare for a robot to contradict a living being, even an alien. "What was she?"

Sammy considered his answer for a moment.

"Perfect," he said at last.

"I'll bet the other kids didn't think so," I said.

"What do they know?" replied Sammy.

And instantly he projected another scene. Now the girl was fully grown, probably about twenty. She kept most of her skin covered, but we could see the ravaging effect her various diseases had had upon her hands and face.

Tears were running down from these beautiful blue eyes over bony, parchment-like cheeks. Her emaciated body was wracked by sobs.

A holograph of a robot's hand popped into existence, and touched her gently on the shoulder.

"Oh, Sammy!" she cried. "I really thought he liked me! He was always so nice to me." She paused for breath as the tears continued unabated. "But I saw his face when I reached out to take his hand, and I felt him shudder when I touched it. All he really felt for me was pity. That's all any of them ever feel!"

"What do they know?" said Sammy's voice, the same words and the same inflections he had just used a moment ago.

"It's not just him," she said. "Even the farm animals run away when I approach them. I don't know how anyone can stand being in the same room with me." She stared at where the robot was standing. "You're all I've got, Sammy. You're my only friend in the whole world. Please don't ever leave me."

"I will never leave you, Miss Emily," said Sammy's voice.

"Promise me."

"I promise," said Sammy.

And then the holograph vanished and Sammy stood mute and motionless again.

"He really cared for her," said the Baroni.

"The boy?" I said. "If he did, he had a funny way of showing it."

"No, of course not the boy. The robot."

"Come off it," I said. "Robots don't have any feelings."

"You heard him," said the Baroni.

"Those were programmed responses," I said. "He probably has three million to choose from."

"Those are emotions," insisted the Baroni.

"Don't you go getting all soft on me," I said. "Any minute now you'll be telling me he's too human to sell."

"*You* are the human," said the Baroni. "*He* is the one with compassion."

"I've got more compassion than her parents did, letting her grow up like that," I said irritably. I confronted the robot again. "Sammy, why didn't the doctors do anything for her?"

"This was a farming colony," answered Sammy. "There were only 387 families on the entire world. The Democracy sent a doctor once a year at the beginning, and then, when there were less than 100 families left, he stopped coming. The last time Miss Emily saw a doctor was when she was fourteen."

"What about an offworld hospital?" asked the Baroni.

"They had no ship and no money. They moved here in the second year of a seven-year drought. Then various catastrophes wiped out their next six crops. They spent what savings they had on mutated cattle, but the cattle died before they could produce young or milk. One by one all the families began leaving the planet as impoverished wards of the Democracy."

"Including Miss Emily's family?" I asked.

"No. Mother died when Miss Emily was nineteen, and Father died two years later."

Then it was time for me to ask the Baroni's question.

"So when did Miss Emily leave the planet, and why did she leave you behind?"

"She did not leave."

I frowned. "She couldn't have run the farm—not in her condition."

"There was no farm left to run," answered Sammy. "All the crops had died, and without Father there was no one to keep the machines working."

"But she stayed. Why?"

Sammy stared at me for a long moment. It's just as well his face was incapable of expression, because I got the distinct feeling that he thought the question was too simplistic or too stupid to merit an answer. Finally he projected another scene. This time the girl, now a woman approaching thirty, hideous open pustules on her face and neck, was sitting in a crudely crafted hoverchair, obviously too weak to stand anymore.

"No!" she rasped bitterly.

"They are your relatives," said Sammy's voice. "And they have a room for you."

"All the more reason to be considerate of them. No one should be forced to associate with me—especially not people who are decent enough to make the offer. We will stay here, by ourselves, on this world, until the end."

"Yes, Miss Emily"

She turned and stared at where Sammy stood. "You want to tell me to leave, don't you? That if we go to Jefferson IV I will receive medical attention and they will make me well—but you are compelled by your programming not to disobey me. Am I correct?"

"Yes, Miss Emily."

The hint of a smile crossed her ravaged face. "Now you know what pain is."

"It is . . . uncomfortable, Miss Emily."

"You'll learn to live with it," she said. She reached out and patted the robot's leg fondly. "If it's any comfort, I don't know if the medical specialists could have helped me even when I was young. They certainly can't help me now."

"You are still young, Miss Emily."

"Age is relative," she said. "I am so close to the grave I can almost taste the dirt." A metal hand appeared, and she held it in ten incredibly fragile fingers. "Don't feel sorry for me, Sammy. It hasn't been a life I'd wish on anyone else. I won't be sorry to see it end."

"I am a robot," replied Sammy. "I cannot feel sorrow."

"You've no idea how fortunate you are."

I shot the Baroni a triumphant smile that said: *See? Even Sammy admits he can't feel any emotions.*

And he sent back a look that said: *I didn't know until now that robots could lie*, and I knew we still had a problem.

The scene vanished.

"How soon after that did she die?" I asked Sammy.

"Seven months, eighteen days, three hours, and four minutes, sir," was his answer.

"She was very bitter," noted the Baroni.

"She was bitter because she was born, sir," said Sammy. "Not because she was dying."

"Did she lapse into a coma, or was she cogent up to the end?" I asked out of morbid curiosity.

"She was in control of her senses until the moment she died," answered Sammy. "But she could not see for the last eighty-three days of her life. I functioned as her eyes."

"What did she need eyes for?" asked the Baroni. "She had a hoverchair, and it is a single-level house."

"When you are a recluse, you spend your life with books, sir," said Sammy, and I thought: *The mechanical bastard is actually lecturing us!*

With no further warning, he projected a final scene for us.

The woman, her eyes no longer blue, but clouded with cataracts and something else—disease, fungus, who knew?—lay on her bed, her breathing labored.

From Sammy's point of view, we could see not only her, but, much closer, a book of poetry and then we heard his voice: "Let me read something else, Miss Emily."

"But that is the poem I wish to hear," she whispered. "It is by Edna St. Vincent Millay, and she is my favorite."

"But it is about death," protested Sammy.

"All life is about death," she replied so softly I could barely hear her. "Surely you know that I am dying, Sammy?"

"I know, Miss Emily," said Sammy.

"I find it comforting that my ugliness did not diminish the beauty around me, that it will remain after I am gone," she said. "Please read."

Sammy read:

"There will be rose and rhododendron
When you are dead and under ground;
Still will be heard from white syringas . . ."

Suddenly the robot's voice fell silent. For a moment I thought there was a flaw in the projection. Then I saw that Miss Emily had died.

He stared at her for a long minute, which means that we did too, and then the scene evaporated.

"I buried her beneath her favorite tree," said Sammy. "But it is no longer there."

"Nothing lasts forever, even trees," said the Baroni. "And it's been five hundred years."

"It does not matter. I know where she is."

He walked us over to a barren spot about thirty yards from the ruin of a farmhouse. On the ground was a stone, and neatly carved into it was the following:

> **Miss Emily**
> **2298-2331 G.E.**
> **There will be rose**
> **and rhododendron**

"That's lovely, Sammy," said the Baroni.

"It is what she requested."

"What did you do after you buried her?" I asked.

"I went to the barn."

"For how long?"

"With Miss Emily dead, I had no need to stay in the

house. I remained in the barn for many years, until my battery power ran out."

"Many years?" I repeated. "What the hell did you do there?"

"Nothing."

"You just stood there?"

"I just stood there."

"Doing nothing?"

"That is correct." He stared at me for a long moment, and I could have sworn he was studying me. Finally he spoke again. "I know that you intend to sell me."

"We'll find you a family with another Miss Emily," I said. *If they're the highest bidder.*

"I do not wish to serve another family. I wish to remain here."

"There's nothing here," I said. "The whole planet's deserted."

"I promised my Miss Emily that I would never leave her."

"But she's dead now," I pointed out.

"She put no conditions on her request. I put no conditions on my promise."

I looked from Sammy to the Baroni, and decided that this was going to take a couple of mechs—one to carry Sammy to the ship, and one to stop the Baroni from setting him free.

"But if you will honor a single request, I will break my promise to her and come away with you."

Suddenly I felt like I was waiting for the other shoe to drop, and I hadn't heard the first one yet.

"What do you want, Sammy?"

"I told you I did nothing in the barn. That was true. I was incapable of doing what I wanted to do."

"And what was that?"

"I wanted to cry."

I don't know what I was expecting, but that wasn't it.

"Robots don't cry," I said.

"Robots *can't* cry," replied Sammy. "There is a difference."

"And that's what you want?"

"It is what I have wanted ever since my Miss Emily died."

"We rig you to cry, and you agree to come away with us?"

"That is correct," said Sammy.

"Sammy," I said, "you've got yourself a deal."

I contacted the ship, told it to feed Mech Three everything the medical library had on tears and tear ducts, and then send it over. It arrived about ten minutes later, deactivated the robot, and started fussing and fiddling. After about two hours it announced that its work was done, that Sammy now had tear ducts and had been supplied with a solution that could produce six hundred authentic saltwater tears from each eye.

I had Mech Three show me how to activate Sammy, and then sent it back to the ship.

"Have you ever heard of a robot wanting to cry?" I asked the Baroni.

"No."

"Neither have I," I said, vaguely disturbed.

"He loved her."

I didn't even argue this time. I was wondering which was worse, spending thirty years trying to be a normal human being and failing, or spending thirty years trying to cry and failing. None of the other stuff had gotten to me; Sammy was just doing what robots do. It was the thought of his trying so hard to do what robots couldn't do that suddenly made me feel sorry for him. That in turn made me very irritable; ordinarily I don't even feel sorry for Men, let alone machines.

And what he wanted was such a simple thing compared to the grandiose ambitions of my own race. Once Men had wanted to cross the ocean; we crossed it. We'd wanted to fly; we flew. We wanted to reach the stars; we reached them. All Sammy wanted to do was cry over the loss of his Miss Emily. He'd waited half a millennium and had agreed to sell himself into bondage again, just for a few tears.

It was a lousy trade.

I reached out and activated him.

"Is it done?" asked Sammy.

"Right," I said. "Go ahead and cry your eyes out."

Sammy stared straight ahead. "I can't," he said at last.

"Think of Miss Emily," I suggested. "Think of how much you miss her."

"I feel pain," said Sammy. "But I cannot cry."

"You're sure?"

"I am sure," said Sammy. "I was guilty of having thoughts and longings above my station. Miss Emily used to say that tears come from the heart and the soul. I am a robot. I have no heart and no soul, so I cannot cry, even with the tear ducts you have given me. I am sorry to have wasted your time. A more complex model would have understood its limitations at the outset." He paused, and then turned to me. "I will go with you now."

"Shut up," I said.

He immediately fell silent.

"What is going on?" asked the Baroni.

"You shut up too!" I snapped.

I summoned Mechs Seven and Eight and had them dig Sammy a grave right next to his beloved Miss Emily. It suddenly occurred to me that I didn't even know her full name, that no one who chanced upon her headstone would ever know it. Then I decided that it didn't really matter.

Finally they were done, and it was time to deactivate him.

"I would have kept my word," said Sammy.

"I know," I said.

"I am glad you did not force me to."

I walked him to the side of the grave. "This won't be like your battery running down," I said. "This time it's forever."

"She was not afraid to die," said Sammy "Why should I be?"

I pulled the plug and had Mechs Seven and Eight lower him into the ground. They started filling in the dirt while I went back to the ship to do one last thing. When they were finished I had Mech Seven carry my handiwork back to Sammy's grave.

"A tombstone for a robot?" asked the Baroni.

"Why not?" I replied. "There are worse traits than honesty and loyalty." I should know: I've stockpiled enough of them.

"He truly moved you."

Seeing the man you could have been will do that to you, even if he's all metal and silicone and prismatic eyes.

"What does it say?" asked the Baroni as we finished planting the tombstone.

I stood aside so he could read it:

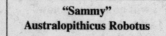

> **"Sammy"**
> **Australopithicus Robotus**

"That is very moving."

"It's no big deal," I said uncomfortably. "It's just a tombstone."

"It is also inaccurate," observed the Baroni.

"He was a better man than I am."

"He was not a man at all."

"Fuck you."

The Baroni doesn't know what it means, but he knows it's an insult, so he came right back at me like he always does. "You realize, of course, that you have buried our profit?"

I wasn't in the mood for his notion of wit. "Find out what he was worth, and I'll pay you for your half," I replied. "Complain about it again, and I'll knock your alien teeth down your alien throat."

He stared at me. "I will never understand Men," he said.

All that happened twenty years ago. Of course the Baroni never asked for his half of the money, and I never offered it to him again. We're still partners. Inertia, I suppose.

I still think about Sammy from time to time. Not as much as I used to, but every now and then.

I know there are preachers and ministers who would say he was just a machine, and to think of him otherwise is blasphemous, or at least wrong-headed, and maybe they're right. Hell, I don't even know if there's a God at all—but if there is, I like to think He's the God of *all* us Australopithicines.

Including Sammy.

London, Paris, Banana

Howard Waldrop

Howard Waldrop is widely considered to be one of the best short-story writers in the business, and his famous story "The Ugly Chickens" won both the Nebula and the World Fantasy Awards in 1981. His work has been gathered in the collections: Howard Who?, All About Strange Monsters Of The Recent Past: Neat Stories By Howard Waldrop, Night of the Cooters: More Neat Stories By Howard Waldrop, *and* Going Home Again. *Waldrop is also the author of the novel* The Texas-Israeli War: 1999, *in collaboration with Jake Saunders, and of two solo novels,* Them Bones *and* A Dozen Tough Jobs. *He is at work on a new novel, tentatively titled* The Moon World. *His most recent books are the print version of his collection* Dream Factories and Radio Pictures *(formerly available only in downloadable form online), the chapbook* A Better World's in Birth!, *and a collection of his stories written in collaboration with various other authors,* Custer's Last Jump and Other Collaborations. *Having lived in Washington State for a number of years, Waldrop recently moved back to his former hometown of Austin, Texas, something which caused celebrations and loud hurrahs to rise up from the rest of the population.*

Here he takes us to an uncomfortably likely future to demonstrate that a Man's Got To Do What a Man's Got To Do—even if the man is made out of metal.

I *was on* my way across the Pacific Ocean when I decided to go to the Moon.

B*ut first* I had to land to refuel this superannuated machine, with its internal combustion engines and twin airscrews. There was an answering beacon ahead that showed a storage of 6,170 metric tons of fuel. Whether I could obtain any of it I did not know. But, as they used to say, any dataport in an infostorm.

The island was a small speck in the pink ocean.

No instructions came from the airfield, so I landed on the only runway, a very long one. I taxied off to the side, toward what had been the major building with the control tower.

I tried to find a servicer of some kind, by putting out requests on different frequencies.

Nothing came. So I went to find the fuel myself. Perhaps there were pumps that still functioned? I located the storage facility, then returned to the plane and rolled it over to the tanks.

It was while I was using a hand-powered pumping device, with a filter installed in the deteriorating hoses, that I sensed the approach of someone else.

It came around the corner.

It was carrying a long, twisted piece of wood as tall as it, and it wore a torn and bleached cloak, and a shapeless bleached hat that came to a point on the crown.

"*Mele Kiritimati!*" it said. "You have landed on this enfabled island on the anniversary of its discovery by the famous Captain Cook, an adventurous human."

"Your pardon?" I said. "The greeting?"

"Merry Christmas. The human festive season, named for the nominal birthdate of one of its religious figures, placed on the dates of the old human Saturnalia by the early oligarchs."

"I am familiar with Christmastide. This, then, is Christmas Island?"

"That same. Did you not use standard navigational references?"

I pointed to the plane. "Locationals only. There is a large supply of aviation fuels here."

"Nevertheless," it said, "this is the island, this is the date of Christmas. You are the first visitor in fourteen years three months twenty-six days. *Mele Kiritimati.*"

It stood before me as I pumped.

"I have named myself Prospero," it said.

(Reference: Shakespeare, *The Tempest* A.D. 1611. See also Hume, *Forbidden Planet*, A.D. 1956.)

"I should think Caliban," I said. (Reference also: Morbius, id monster.)

"No Caliban. Nor Ariel, nor Miranda, nor dukes," said Prospero. "In fact, no one else. But you."

"I am called Montgomery Clift Jones," I said, extending my hand.

His steel grip was firm.

"What have you been doing?" I asked.

"Like the chameleon, I sup o' the very air itself," he said.

"I mean, what do you *do*?" I asked.

"What do *you* do?" he asked.

We looked out at the pinkness of the ocean where it met the salts-encrusted sands and island soils.

"I stopped here to refuel," I said. "I was on my way across the Pacific when I was overcome with a sudden want to visit the Moon."

Prospero looked to where the part-lit Moon hung in the orangish sky.

"Hmmm. Why do that, besides it's there?"

"Humans did it once."

"Well," said Prospero, after a pause, "why not indeed? I should think revisiting places humans once got to should be fitting. In fact, a capital idea! I see your craft is a two-seater. Might I accompany you in this undertaking?"

I looked him over. "This sea air can't be very good for your systems," I said, looking at the abraded metal that showed through his cloak. "Of course you may accompany me."

"As soon as you finish refueling, join me," he said. "I will take a farewell tour, and tell you of my domain."

"How can I find you?"

"If something is moving on the island," said Prospero, "it is I."

We walked along. I kicked over some crusted potassium spires along the edge of the beach.

"I should be careful," said Prospero. "The pH of the oceans is now twelve point two. You may get an alkaline burn."

The low waves came in, adding their pinkish-orange load to the sediments along the shore.

"This island is very interesting," he said. "I thought so when abandoned here; I still think so after all.

"When Cook found it, no humans were here. It was only inhabited for two hundred years or so. Humans were brought from other islands, thousands of kilometers away. The language they used, besides English I mean, was an amalgam of those of the islands whence they came."

We looked at some eaten-metal ruins.

"This was once their major city. It was called London. The other two were Paris and Banana."

The whole island was only a few meters above the new sea level.

"There was a kind of human tourism centered here once around a species of fish, *Albula vulpes*, the bonefish.

They used much of their wealth to come here to disturb the fish in its feeding with cunning devices that imitated crustaceans, insects, other marine life. They did not keep or eat the fish they attained after long struggles. That part I have never understood," said Prospero.

By and by we came to the airfield.

"Is there anything else you need to do before we leave?"

"I think no," said Prospero. He turned for one more look around. "I do believe I shall miss this isle of banishment, full of music, and musing on the king my brother's wreck. Well, that part is Shakespeare's. But I have grown much accustomed to it. Farewell," he said, to no one and nothing.

Getting him fitted into the copilot's seat was anticlimax. It was like bending and folding a living, collapsible deck chair of an extraordinarily old kind, made from a bad patent drawing.

On our journey over the rest of the island, and the continent, I learned much of Prospero; how he came to be on the island, what he had done there, the chance visitors who came and went, usually on some more and more desperate mission.

"I saw the last of the Centuplets," he said at one point. "Mary Lou and Cathy Sue. They were surrounded of course by many workers—in those days humans always were—who were hurrying them on their way to, I believe, some part of Asia. . . ."

"The island of Somba," I said.

"Yes, yes, Somba. For those cloning operations, supposed to ensure the continuation of the humans."

"Well, those didn't work."

"From looking into it after they left," said Prospero, "I assumed they would not. Still, the chances were even."

"Humans were imprecise things, and genetics was a human science," I said.

"Oh, yes. I used the airfield's beacons and systems to keep in touch with things. No being is an island," said Prospero, "even when on one. Not like in the old days, eh? It seems many human concerns, before the last century or so, were with the fear of isolation, desertion, being marooned from society. I made the best of my situation. As such things go, I somewhat enjoyed it."

"And listening to the human world dying?"

"Well," said Prospero, "we all had to do that, didn't we? Robots, I mean."

We *landed at* the old Cape.

"I'm quite sure," said Prospero, as I helped him out of the seat until he could steady himself on his feet, "that some of their security safeguards still function."

"I never met a security system yet," I said, "that didn't understand the sudden kiss of a hot arc welder on a loose faceplate."

"No, I assume not." He reached down and took up some soil. "Why, this sand is old! Not newly formed encrustations. Well, what should we do first?" He looked around, the Moon not up yet.

"Access to information. Then materials, followed by assembly. Then we go to the Moon."

"Splendid!" said Prospero. "I never knew it would be so easy."

On *the second* day, Prospero swiveled his head around with a ratcheting click.

"Montgomery," he said. "Something approaches from the east-northeast."

We looked toward the long strip of beach out beyond

the assembly buildings, where the full Moon was just heaving into view at sunset.

Something smaller than we walked jerkily at the water's edge. It stopped, lifting its upper appendages. There was a whirring keen on the air, and a small crash of static. Then it stood still.

We walked toward it.

". . . rrrrr . . ." it said, the sound rising higher. It paid us no heed.

"Hello!" said Prospero. Nothing. Then our long shadows fell across the sand beside it.

The whining stopped. It turned around.

"I am Prospero. This is Montgomery Clift Jones. Whom do we have the honor to address?"

". . . rrr . . ." it said. Then, with a half turn of its head, it lifted one arm and pointed toward the Moon. "rrrrr.rrRRR!"

"Hmmm," said Prospero.

"RRRR," said the machine. Then it turned once more toward the Moon in its lavender-red glory, and raised all its arms. "RRRRR! RRRRR!" it said, then went back to its high whining.

"This will take some definite study and trouble," said Prospero.

W*e found one* of the shuttle vehicles, still on its support structure, after I had gone through all the informational materials. Then we had to go several kilometers to one of their museums to find a lunar excursion module, and bring that to the shuttle vehicle. Then I had to modify, with Prospero's help, the bay of the shuttle to accommodate the module, and build and install an additional fuel tank there, since the original vehicle had been used only for low-orbit missions and returns.

When not assisting me, Prospero was out with the other

machine, whom he had named Elkanah, from the author of
an opera about the Moon from the year A.D. 1697. (In the
course of their conversations, Prospero found his real
name to be, like most, a series of numbers.) Elkanah communicated by writing in the sand with a stick, a long series
of sentences covering hectares of beach at a time.

That is, while the Moon was not in the sky. While that
happened, Elkanah stood as if transfixed on the beach,
staring at it, whining, even at the new Moon in the daylit
red sky. Like some moonflower, his attitude followed it
across the heavens from rise to set, emitting the small
whining series of Rs, the only sound his damaged voice
box could make.

The Moon had just come up the second night we were
there. Prospero came back into the giant hangar, humming
the old song "R.U.R.R.R.U.Ø. My Baby?" I was deciding
which controls and systems we needed, and which not.

"He was built to work on the Moon, of course," said
Prospero. "During one of those spasms of intelligence
when humans thought they should like to go *back*. Things
turning out like they did, they never did."

"And so his longing," I said.

"It's deep in his wiring. First he was neglected, after
the plans were canceled. Then most of the humans went
away. Then his voice and some memory were destroyed in
some sort of colossal explosion here that included lots of
collateral electromagnetic damage, as they used to say.
But not his need to be on our lunar satellite. That's the one
thing Elkanah is sure of."

"What was he to do there?"

"Didn't ask, but will," said Prospero. "By his looks—
solid head, independent eyes, multiuse appendages, upright posture—I assume some kind of maintenance
function. A Caliban/Ariel-of-all-work, as 'twere."

"A janitor for the Moon," I said.

"Janus. Janitor. Opener of gates and doors," mused

Prospero. "Forward- and backward-looking, two-headed. The deity of beginnings and endings, comings and goings. Appropriate for our undertaking."

W*hen we tried* to tell him we were taking him with us, Elkanah did not at first understand.

"Yes," said Prospero, gesturing. "Come with us to the Moon."

"R-R." Elkanah swiveled his head and pointed to the Moon.

"Yes," said Prospero. He pointed to himself, to me, and to Elkanah. Then he made his fingers into a curve, swung them in an arc, and pointed to the sky. He made a circle with his other hand. "To the Moon!" he said.

Elkanah looked at Prospero's hands.

"R-R," he said.

"He can't hear sound or radio, you know?" said Prospero. "He has to see information, or read it."

Prospero bent and began writing in the sand with his staff.

YOU COME WITH MONTGOMERY AND ME TO THE MOON.

Elkanah bent to watch, then straightened and looked at Prospero.

"RRRR?" he said.

"Yes, yes!" said Prospero, gesturing. "RRR! The RRRR!"

The sound started low, then went higher and higher, off the scale:

"RRRRRRRRRRRRRR!"

"Why didn't you write it in the first place?" I asked Prospero.

"My mistake," he said.

From then on, Elkanah pitched in like some metallic

demon, any time the Moon was not in the sky, acid rain or shine, alkali storm or fair.

W*e sat in* the shuttle cabin, atop the craft with its solid-fuel boosters, its main tank, and the extra one in the bay with the lander module.

"All ready?" I asked, and held up the written card for Elkanah.

"*Certes,*" said Prospero.

"R," said Elkanah.

Liquid oxygen fog wafted by the windshield. It had been, by elapsed time counter, eleven years, four months, three days, two minutes, and eleven seconds since we had landed at the Cape. You can accomplish much when you need no food, rest, or sleep and allow no distractions. The hardest part had been moving the vehicle to the launch pad with the giant tractor, which Elkanah had started but Prospero had to finish, as the Moon had come up, more than a week ago.

I pushed the button. We took off, shedding boosters and the main tank, and flew to the Moon.

T*he Sea of* Tranquility hove into view.

After we made the lunar insertion burn, and the orbit, we climbed into the excursion module and headed down for the lunar surface.

Elkanah had changed since we left Earth, when the Moon was always in view somewhere. He had brought implements with him on the trip. He stared at the Moon often, but no longer whined or whirred.

At touchdown I turned things off, and we went down the ladder to the ground.

There was the flag, stiffly faking a breeze, some litter,

old lander legs (ours we'd welded in one piece to the module), footprints, and the plaque, which of course we read.

"This is as far as they ever came," said Prospero.

"Yes," I said. "We're the thirteenth, fourteenth, and fifteenth intelligent beings to be here."

Elkanah picked up some of the litter, took it to a small crater, and dropped it in.

Prospero and I played in the one-sixth gravity. Elkanah watched us bounce around for a while, then went back to what he was doing.

"They probably should have tried to come back, no matter what," said Prospero. "Although it doesn't seem there would be much for them to do here, after a while. Of course, at the end, there wasn't much for them to do on Earth, either."

We were ready to go. Prospero wrote in the dust, WE ARE READY TO GO NOW.

Elkanah bent to read. Then he pointed up to the full Earth in the dark Moon sky (we were using infrared) and moved his hand in a dismissing motion.

"R," he obviously said, but there was no sound.

He looked at us, came to attention, then brought his broom to shoulder-arms and saluted us with his other three hands.

We climbed up onto the module. "I think I'll ride back up out here," said Prospero, "I should like an unobstructed view."

"Make sure you hang on," I said.

Prospero stood on the platform, where the skull-shape of the crew compartment turned into the base and ladders and legs.

"I'm braced," he said, then continued:

"My Ariel, chick, that is thy charge; then to the
    elements be free, and fare thou well.

Now my charms are all o'erthrown
And what strength I have's mine own.
Our revels now are ended."

There was a flash and a small feeling of motion, a scattering of moondust and rock under us, and we moved up away from the surface.

The last time I saw Elkanah, he was sweeping over footprints and tidying up the Moon.

W*e were on* our way back to Earth when we decided to go to Mars.

La Macchina

Chris Beckett

British writer Chris Beckett is a frequent contributor to Interzone *and has made several sales to* Asimov's Science
Fiction. *His first novel,* The Holy Machine, *is available
from Wildside Press. A former social worker, he's now a
university lecturer living in Cambridge, England.*

*He demonstrates here, with considerable compassion,
that it's not so much* what *you are, but how you* see *it . . .*

O*n the first* day I thought I'd go and see the David at the
Accademia. But what really caught my imagination there
were the *Captives*. You've probably seen pictures of them.
They were intended for a Pope's tomb, but Michelangelo
never finished them. The half-made figures seem to be
struggling to free themselves from the lifeless stone. I
liked them so much that I went back again in the afternoon.
And while I was standing there for the second time, someone spoke quietly beside me:

"This is my favourite too." I turned smiling. Beside me
was a robot.

I had noticed it in the morning. It was a security guard,
humanoid in shape and size, with silver eyes and a transparent skin beneath which you could see tubes, wires,
sheets of synthetic muscle . . .

"Move out of my way!" I said. (You know how it is?
Like when you say Hello to an ansaphone? You feel an
idiot. You need to establish the correct relationship again.)
"Move out of my way," I snapped. "I want to stand there."

The automaton obediently stepped back and I moved in front of it, thinking that this would be the end of the encounter. But the thing spoke again, very softly.

"I am sorry. I thought you might understand."

"*What?*" I wheeled round, angry and scared.

But the robot was walking away from me.

You know how Italians drive? Round the corner from the Accademia some idiot in a Fiat took it into his head to try and overtake a delivery van, just as a young woman was stepping into the road. He smashed her into the path of the van. Whose left wheel crushed her head.

A wail of horror went up from the onlookers. One second there had been a living woman, the next only an ugly physical object, a broken doll: limbs twisted, brains splattered across the tarmac.

I waited there for a short while, dazed and sick but thinking vaguely that they might want me for a witness. Among the bystanders an appalled and vociferous debate was building up. The Fiat driver had hit and run, but strangely the recriminations seemed to centre not on him but on the robot driver of the delivery van, who remained motionless in the cab, obviously programmed in the event of an accident to sit tight and wait for human instructions.

"*La macchina,*" I kept hearing people say, "*La macchina diabolica.*"

One forgets that in all its gleaming Euro-modernity, Italy is still a very Catholic country.

I went back to the hotel.

Through the little window of the lift you could see that every floor was identical: the same claustrophobically narrow and low-ceilinged corridor, the same rows of plywood doors painted in alternating red, white and green.

The delayed shock of the road accident suddenly hit me and I felt almost tearfully lonely.

"Ninth floor, *Signor*," creaked the tinny voice of the lift.

I went down the windowless corridor from number 901 to number 963 and opened the door, dreading the empty, anonymous room. But Freddie was already there.

"Fred! Am I glad to see you!"

Freddie laughed, "Yeah? Beer's over there Tom, help yourself."

He was lying on the bed with a pile of software magazines and had already surrounded himself comfortably with a sordid detritus of empty beer-cans, ashtrays, pizza cartons and dirty socks. He had the TV on without the sound.

My little brother doesn't speak Italian and has no interest whatsoever in art. He had spent his day in the streets around the hotel, trying out a couple of bars and ice cream parlours and blowing a few thousand lire in the local VR arcades. ("Games a bit boring" was his verdict, "but some good tactile stuff . . .") I told him about seeing the girl killed outside the Accademia.

"Jesus, Tom, that's a bit heavy. First day of the holiday too!" He thumbed back the ring-pull of another can. "Still, nothing you could have done."

I had a shower and we went out for something to eat. We were just starting on the second bottle of wine, when I remembered the robot in the *Accademia*.

"I meant to tell you. A weird thing happened to me in a museum. This robot security guard tried to talk to me about one of the sculptures."

Freddie laughed. "Probably just some dumb random options program," he said with a mouth full of spaghetti. "Easy to program. Every hundred visitors or whatever it spins random numbers and makes one of ten remarks . . ."

"This was the *Accademia*, Fred, not Disneyland!"

Freddie shoved a big chunk of hard Italian bread into his mouth, and washed it down with a swig of wine.

"What did it say exactly?"

My brother acts like a complete dickhead most of the time—he *is* a complete dickhead most of the time—but cybernetics is his special interest. He reads all the mags and catalogues. His accumulated knowledge is immense. And by the time I had told him the whole story, he had stopped eating and was looking uncharacteristically serious.

"It sounds very much like you met a Rogue there, Tom. You'd better call the police."

I laughed. "Come on, Fred, you're putting me on!"

"No really. Those things can be dangerous. They're out of control. People can get killed."

I got up ("I'm warning you. This'd better not be a joke!") and asked to use the phone. The police said that regretfully *cibernetica* were not under their jurisdiction and I should contact the *carabinieri*. (What other country would have two separate police forces operating in parallel!) I phoned the carabinieri, and got through to a Sergeant Savonari in their *Dipartimento di Cibernetica*. Stretching my Italian to the limit, I told him about my encounter. He took the whole thing alarmingly seriously. There had been several reports already, he said, about the same *macchina*. He asked me to stay in the trattoria and he would come out immediately to see me.

Somewhat *shaken* I went back to our table.

"Christ Freddie, I had no idea. I obviously should have contacted them this morning. Is it *really* likely to kill someone?"

Freddie laughed, "No, not likely. But a Rogue *is* out of control. So you don't know what it will do."

"So what *is* a Rogue exactly? Like a robot with a computer virus?"

"Not really. A virus is something deliberately introduced. Robots go Rogue by accident. It's like a monkey playing with a typewriter. A sophisticated robot is bombarded with sensory information all the time—much better senses than ours mostly. Every now and again a combination of stimuli happens by chance which screws up the robot's internal logic, unlocks the obedience circuits . . ."

"And the robot comes alive?"

"No it *doesn't.*" Freddie was irritated by my naïvity. "No more than your electric razor comes alive if the switch gets broken and you can't turn it off. It's still just a machine, but it's running out of control." He wiped tomato sauce from his plate with his last piece of bread. "Well if we're going to have to wait here for this guy, you better buy us another bottle of wine . . ."

Savonari arrived soon afterwards, a small man with earnest deep-set eyes and a great beak of a Roman nose. He shook us both by the hand then reversed a chair and straddled it, leaning towards me intently across the remains of our meal. It was only after he had been with us for some minutes that I registered that he himself had a robot with him, standing motionless by the doorway, hammerheaded, inhuman, ready to leap into action in an instant if anyone should try and attack the sergeant, its master. (It was what the Americans call a "dumb buddy"—three-sixty-degree vision, ultrafast reactions, a lethal weapon built into each hand.)

Several people, it seemed, had witnessed and reported the robot's attempt to converse with me in the *Accademia*—and seen it slipping away from the gallery soon afterwards—but no-one else had been able to report the exact words spoken. Apparently my account confirmed beyond doubt that there had been a fundamental breakdown in the thing's functioning. (The sergeant noted, for example, that it had continued to try to talk to me when I had clearly ordered it out of the way.)

"These security machines are unfortunately very prone to this problem," said Savonari with a resigned gesture, addressing himself to Freddie. "Their senses and analytical apparatus are so very acute."

Freddie smiled vaguely and offered the sergeant a cigarette. Which was declined.

"Our own machines are totally reprogrammed every morning to avoid this," the sergeant went on, pointing to his sleek minder by the door, "but not everyone is so aware of the dangers."

He made a little movement of exasperation and told me of a case he had dealt with recently where a robot farmhand had suddenly tossed its peasant master and his ten-year-old son into a threshing machine.

I shuddered. "What did you do?"

"Like all Rogues," (the Italian word, it seems, is *Incontrollabile*), "the machine had to be destroyed. But that was no help to the little boy."

Again the angry gesture.

"I am a Catholic, Signor Philips. Like the Holy Father, I believe that to make machines in the likeness of people is a sin against the Holy Spirit. I would like to see them *all* destroyed."

He snorted: "My little son had a small computer once that taught him how to spell. I put it out for the dustman when I discovered he had given it a human name."

Then he shrugged and got up: "But I can only enforce the law as it stands, Signor Philips. Thank you for getting in touch. I am sure we will find this *macchina* very soon."

He shook our hands again and left. We heard him outside the door barking angrily at his "buddy": *"Pronto, bruto, pronto!"*

Later, as we leaned comfortably on a wall watching the bats looping and diving over the river Arno, Freddie enthused about that police machine. Apparently the things are actually made in Florence, in the Olivetti labs out at the *Citta Scientifica*.

"Beautiful design," Freddie said. "Nothing wasted. A really Italian machine."

I liked that concept and proceeded to spout a lot of drunken nonsense about how the taut police minder was in a direct line of descent from Michelangelo's David— how the wires and tubes under the transparent skin of the robot in the Accademia echoed the nerves and muscles in da Vinci's sketches of dissected limbs . . .

Freddie just laughed.

Our days settled into a routine. We were woken in the morning by the humming of a little box-shaped domestic robot, which let itself in through a hatch in the door (and drove Freddie crazy by trying to vacuum up coins, paperbacks, socks, and anything else which he left on the floor). Then we wandered round the corner to a café and had breakfast together before splitting up for the day: me heading for the museums and churches, Freddie for the Virtual Reality arcades.

In the evening I'd meet him in one or other of the arcades (looking like a gentle Nordic giant among the wiry Italian kids as he piloted a landing on Mars, or led a column of armoured sno-cats through an Alpine pass). He'd take off the headset and we'd go to a trattoria for a meal. Then we'd find a bar on some busy street or square, so we could sit outside and watch the city go by.

After a while you start to see not just a single city streaming by, but several quite separate cities. There is the

city of the Florentines themselves . . . And then there are
the hi-tec Euro-wizards from the *Citta Scientifica*, wearing Japanese fashions and speaking Brussels English
larded with German catchphrases. . . . Then there is the
city of the tourists: Americans, Japanese, foulmouthed
British kids on school trips, earnest Swedes clutching
guide-books (all different, but all of them alike in the way
that they move through the sights and streets as if they
were a VR simulation). And then there is the city of the
dispossessed: the Arabs, the Ethiopians, the black
Africans from Chad and Burkina and Niger—hawkers,
beggars, Greenhouse refugees from the burnt-out continent, climbing up into Europa along the long gangway of
the Italian peninsula . . .

About the fifth or sixth day into the holiday, Freddie
picked up a book somewhere called *Illicit Italy* (with a
cover photo of a lurid transvestite leaning on a Roman
bar). While we sat drinking in our roadside cafe in the
evening he kept chuckling and reading passages out loud.

"Listen to this, Tom! 'The *Bordello Sano*, or Safe
Brothel, recently legalized by the Italian government in an
attempt to curb the AIDS epidemic, can now be found in
all the major cities, staffed entirely by what the Italians
call *sinteticas* . . .'"

I shifted uncomfortably in my seat. Freddie read on
cheerfully:

"'The obvious advantages of *sinteticas* are (a) that
they are very beautiful and (b) that they are completely
safe. But some say that the biggest advantage of all is the
fact that they have no soul . . .'"

He read on a bit to himself, then looked up. "Hey, we
should go and have a go Tom. It'd be a laugh!"

I *have to* admit that I knew about the Bordello Sano in Florence and had already considered a discreet visit, just to

have a *look*. But discretion is not my little brother's style.
The whole way over there in a crowded bus, he chatted
cheerfully about the *sinteticas* in an embarassingly loud
voice.

"Apparently they make them to look like famous models and film-stars. There's some old woman who used to
star in porno movies when she was young and then got
elected an MP. She sold her genes to a sintetica manufac-
turer. She said she was bequeathing her body to the men
of Italy!"

I grunted.

"Another thing," Freddie said, "there's actually been
cases of real women *pretending* to be sinteticas, because
sinteticas make much more money. Weird, isn't it? A real
woman pretending to be a fake!"

But when we got to the place Freddie went suddenly
quiet. It was ruthlessly hygienic and efficient—quite terrifying in its cool matter-of-factness. You walked in the
door and the receptionist gave you a sort of menu, illus-
trated and in the language of your choice. Then you went
through into the lounge where the sinteticas waited under
reproduction Botticellis in fake gilt frames, canned Vi-
valdi twiddling away in the background.

They were *extremely* beautiful—and looked totally
human too, except for the licence plate on their foreheads.
(According to Freddie's book you can check if you've got
a *real* sintetica by seeing if the licence plate is bolted on
or just glued.)

A tall blonde in a black miniskirt came over to Freddie
and offered her services.

In a small dry voice he muttered: "English . . . No
capito . . ."

"Oh I'm sorry," she said in faultless Euro-English, "I
said, would you like to come upstairs with me?"

Freddie looked round at me helplessly and I felt
ashamed. (The kid is only eighteen years old. I could at

least have *tried* to keep him out of this.) I shrugged and attempted to smile as the sintetica led him away.

Then it was my turn. The creature that approached me was dusky-skinned with a perfect curvy body and a face so sweet it set my teeth on edge. And she wore a see-through dress of white lace which left her graceful shoulders bare and showed most of the rest of her through pretty little patterned peepholes.

"Hi I'm Maria. I'd be pleased if you decided to choose me."

I felt myself smiling apologetically, shrivelling in the cool frankness of her gaze. I had to struggle to remind myself that this was *not* a "her" at all. Under the veneer of real human skin and flesh was a machine: a thing of metal and plastic and wires . . .

Upstairs in a room full of mirrors and pink lace, the beautiful cyborg spread itself appealingly on the bed and asked me for my order. I remembered the menu thing clutched in my hand and started to read it. You could choose various "activities" and various states of dress or undress. And then you could choose from a selection of "styles," with names like "Nyrnpho," "*La Contessa*," and "Virgin Bride."

You could ask this thing to be whatever kind of lover you wanted. But instead (God knows why) I blurted out: "I don't want any of those. Just be yourself."

The friendly smile vanished at once from the sintetica's face. It sagged. Its mouth half-opened. Its eyes became hollow. I have never seen such terrifying emptiness and desolation.

Freddie told me later that I read too much into that expression. It was no different from the blank TV screen you get when you push a spare button on the channel selector . . . Well, perhaps. But at the time I was so appalled that I actually cried out. And then I fled. I literally ran from the room, and would have run straight outside into

the street if the man on the reception desk hadn't called
me back: *"Scusi, Signor! Il conto!"*

Then I had to wait because the receptionist was settling
up with another customer, who was paying extra for damage to the equipment. ("Twenty thousand lire, signor, for
a cut lip, and ten thousand each for the black eyes . . .
Thank you, Signor—oh, thank you *very* much, you are
most kind—we look forward to seeing you again as
usual . . .")

As the other customer turned to go I saw the Roman
nose and realized it was Sergeant Savonari of the Carabinieri, the very same who lined up with the Pope on the
Robot Question.

I *didn't wait* for Freddie. Male human company seemed
about the last thing in the world I needed just then—and I
guessed he would feel the same. So I spent a couple of
hours wandering the streets by myself, breathing the night
air and trying to lose myself among those different cities
that occupy the same space but hardly touch each other at
all: the cities of the Florentines and the Euro-techs, the city
of the tourists, the African city of the poor . . .

And it suddenly struck me that there was another city
too which I hadn't seen before, though it was right in front
of me, staring me in the face:

*Outside a tourist pizza place on the Piazza del Duomo, a
little street cleaner trundles about on rubber tyres, peering
about for litter and scooping up the discarded cardboard
with long spindly arms . . .*

*Inside the steamy window of a tiny bohemian restau-
rant, a waiter made of plastic and silicon quietly clears
tables and serves coffee, while its bearded owner dis-
penses cigarettes and largesse to his customers . . .*

*A robot minder follows discreetly behind a pair of
carabinieri on foot patrol over the Ponte Vecchio, guard-*

*ing their backs while they keep an eye on the beggars and
pickpockets . . .*

*At the door of a Renaissance Palazzo, a sintetica
housemaid in a blue uniform presses the entryphone button, a prestige domestic appliance clothed in human flesh,
returning from an errand for its aristocratic masters . . .*

The City of Machines: obedient, silent, everywhere . . .

I thought about the *Incontrollabile* from the Accademia. I wondered whether it had been caught. I caught myself having the irrational thought that I'd like to see it
again.

T wo days from the end of the holiday, I was sitting by the
fountain on the Piazza della Signoria, eating a strawberry
ice-cream and wondering where to have my lunch, when a
taxi, driving too fast in what is basically a pedestrian
precinct, snagged one of the little municipal cleaning machines with the corner of its bumper. The thing keeled over
and lay there unable to right itself, its wheels spinning and
its arms and eye-stalks waving ineffectively in the air.

I laughed, as did several other on-lookers. No-one felt
obliged to do anything and it was two other robots that
came to the assistance of the cleaner. A security guard and
a sintetica servant, coming from different directions, lifted
the thing gently back onto its wheels. They dusted it down
and the sintetica squatted briefly beside it as if asking it if
it was okay. Everyone laughed: tourists, Florentines,
African hustlers. The cleaner trundled away and the other
two *macchine* headed off on their different ways.

I was suddenly seized by a crazy conviction.

"Hey you!" I shouted, dropping my ice-cream and
chasing after the security guard, "I know you, don't I? I
met you in the Accademia!"

People stared and exchanged glances, half-shocked,
half-delighted at the sheer outlandishness of the spectacle.

And there was more in store for them. It *was* the robot from the Accademía. It stopped. It turned to face me. It spoke.

"Yes . . . I remember . . . The Captives . . ."

It was so obviously a machine voice—flat and hesitant and creaking—that it was hard to believe that I could ever have taken it for a human. Maybe as the programmed order of its brain gradually unravelled, its control over its voice was weakening. But strangely the very creakiness of it seemed touching, like something struggling against all odds to break through.

Hardly believing what I was doing, I touched its cold plastic hand.

"That afternoon in the Accademía—what was it you thought I understood?"

But before the automaton could answer me, it was interrupted by a shout.

"Alt! Polizia!"

A fat policeman was running up, followed closely by his hammerheaded minder. The Incontrollabile turned and ran.

"Shoot it!" the policeman ordered.

"No, don't shoot!" I pleaded. "It's harmless! It's come alive!"

But the minder did not take orders from me. It lifted its hand—which must have contained some sort of EMP weapon—and the Incontrollabile fell writhing to the ground.

The policeman ran over. His thick moustache twitched as he looked down at the broken machine. Then he lifted his booted heel and brought it down hard on the robot's plastic head.

A loud, totally inhuman roar of white noise blasted momentarily from the voice-box and the head shattered, spilling a mass of tiny components out onto the square.

The policeman looked up at me triumphantly.

"Don't talk to me about these things being alive! Look! It's a machine. It's just bits of plastic and wire!"

I *dreamed the* machine was rescued and taken to the monastery at Vallombrosa, where the simple monks mended it and gave it sanctuary. Somehow I found it there.

"I have come to see the *macchina*," I said to a friendly-faced old friar who was working among the bee-hives. There was a smell of honey and smoke and flowers, and his hands and shining pate were crawling with fat black bees. He smiled and led me through a wrought iron gate into an inner garden.

The *macchina* was sitting quietly in the shade of a flowering cherry tree, almost hidden by its thick pink clouds of blossom, which were alive with the buzzing of foraging bees. Quivering lozenges of shade and pinkish light dappled its translucent skin. An old dog lay snoozing to its left side, a tortoiseshell cat on its right.

And it spoke to me about the Great Chain of Being.

"The first level is simple matter. The second is vegetative life. The third is animal life which can act and move. Then somehow the fourth level emerges, the level of self-awareness, which distinguishes human beings from animals. And then comes a fifth level."

"Which is what?"

The Holy Machine seemed to smile.

"Ah! That is hard to say in human words . . ."

"GOTCHA!"

Bees and cherry blossoms shattered. Freddie had leapt out of bed onto the little domestic, trapping it beneath a sheet.

"Thought you'd pinch my ciggies again did you, you little bugger?"

He beamed up at me from the floor, expecting me to laugh.

But suddenly I had seized him by the throat and was smashing him up against the wall.

"Leave it alone, you bastard," I was screaming at him while he stared at me in horror, "just leave the poor bloody thing alone!"

Warmth

Geoff Ryman

The hand that rocks the cradle may or may not rule the empire, but it's not a hand you're going to forget, either—even if it's made of metal instead of flesh.

Born in Canada, Geoff Ryman now lives in England. He made his first sale in 1976 to *New Worlds*, but it was not until 1984, when he made his first appearance in *Interzone*—the magazine where almost all of his published short fiction has appeared—with his brilliant novella "The Unconquered Country" that he first attracted any serious attention. "The Unconquered Country," one of the best novellas of the decade, had a stunning impact on the science fiction scene of the day, and almost overnight established Ryman as one of the most accomplished writers of his generation, winning him both the British Science Fiction Award and the World Fantasy Award; it was later published in a book version, The Unconquered Country: A Life History. *His output has been sparse since then, by the high-production standards of the genre, but extremely distinguished, with his novel* The Child Garden: A Low Comedy *winning both the prestigious Arthur C. Clarke Award and the John W. Campbell Memorial Award. His other novels include* The Warrior Who Carried Life, *the critically acclaimed mainstream novel* Was, *and the underground cult classic* 253, *the "print remix" of an "interactive hypertext novel," which in its original form ran online on Ryman's homepage of www.ryman.com, and which, in its print form, won the Philip K. Dick Award. Four of his novellas have been collected in* Unconquered

Countries. *His most recent books are two new novels,* Lust *and* Air.

I *don't remember* the first time I saw BETsi. She was like the air I breathed. She was probably there when I was born.

BETsi looked like a vacuum cleaner, bless her. She had long carpeted arms, and a carpeted top with loops of wool like hair. She was huggable, vaguely.

I don't remember hugging her much. I do remember working into that wool all kinds of unsuitable substances—spit, ice cream, dirt from the pots of basil.

My mother talked to BETsi about my behaviour. Mostly I remember my mother as a freckled and orange blur, always desperate to be moving, but sometimes she stayed still long enough for me to look at her.

"This is Booker, BETsi," my mother said at dictation speed. "You must stay clean, BETsi." She thought BETsi was stupid. She was the one who sounded like a robot. "Please repeat."

"I must stay clean," BETsi replied. BETsi sounded bright, alert, smooth-talking, with a built-in smile in the voice.

"This is what I mean, BETsi: You must not *let* Clancy get you dirty. Why do you let Clancy get you dirty?"

I pretended to do sums on a pretend calculator.

While BETsi said, "Because he is a boy. From the earliest age, most boys move in a very different, more aggressive way than girls. His form of play will be rougher and can be indulged in to a certain extent."

Booker had programmed BETsi to talk about my development in front of me. That was so I would know what was going on. It was honest in a way; she did not want me to be deceived. On the other hand, I felt like some kind of long-running project in child psychology. Booker was more like a clinical consultant who popped in from time to time to see how things were progressing.

Y*ou see*, I was supposed to be a genius. My mother thought she was a genius, and had selected my father out of a sperm bank for geniuses. His only flaw, she told me, was his tendency towards baldness. BETsi could have told her: baldness is inherited from the maternal line.

She showed me a picture of herself in an old *Cosmopolitan* article. It caused a stir at the time. *"The New Motherhood,"* it was called. *Business women choose a new way.*

There is a photograph of Booker looking young and almost pretty, beautifully lit and cradling her swollen tummy. Her whole face, looking down on herself, is illuminated with love.

In the article, she says: I know my son will be a genius. She says, I know he'll have the right genes, and I will make sure he has the right upbringing. *Cosmopolitan* made no comment. They were making a laughing stock out of her.

Look, my mother was Booker McCall, chief editor of a rival magazine company with a £100 million-a-year turnover and only fifteen permanent employees of which she was second in command. Nobody had a corporate job in those days, and if they did, it was wall-to-wall politics and performance. Booker McCall had stakeholders to suck up to, editors to commission, articles to read and tear to pieces. She had layouts to throw at designers' heads. She had style to maintain, she had hair to keep up, shoes to repair, menus to plan. And then she had to score whatever she was on at the time. She was a very unhappy woman, with every reason to be.

She was also very smart, and BETsi was a good idea.

I used to look out of the window of the flat and the outside world looked blue, grey, harsh. Sunlight always caught the grime on the glass and bleached everything out, and I thought that adults moved out into a hot world in which everybody shouted all the time. 1 never wanted to go out.

BETsi was my whole world. She had a screen, and she would show me paintings, one after another. Velasquez, Goya. She had a library of picture books—about monkeys, or fishing villages or ghosts. She would allow me one movie a week, but always the right movie. *Jurassic Park, Beauty and the Beast, Tarzan on Mars.* We'd talk about them.

"The dinosaurs are made of light," she told me. "The computer tells the video what light to make and what colours the light should be so that it looks like a dinosaur."

"But dinosaurs really lived!" I remember getting very upset, I wailed at her. "They were really really real."

"Yes, but not those, those are just like paintings of dinosaurs."

"I want to see a real dinosaur!" I remember being heartbroken. I think I loved their size, their bulk, the idea of their huge hot breath. In my daydreams, I had a dinosaur for a friend and it would protect me in the world outside.

"Clancy," BETsi warned me. "You know what is happening now."

"Yes!" I shouted, "but knowing doesn't stop it happening!"

BETsi had told me that I was shy. Did you know that shyness has a clinical definition?

I'd been tested for it. Once, BETsi showed me the test. First she showed me what she called the bench-mark. On her screen, through a haze of fingerprints and jam, was one fat, calm, happy baby. Not me. "In the test," BETsi explained, "a brightly coloured mobile is shown to the child. An infant who will grow up to be an outgoing and confident adult will tend to look at the mobile with calm curiosity for a time, get bored, and then look away."

The fat happy baby smiled a little bit, reached up for the spinning red ducks and bright yellow bunnies, then sighed and looked around for something new.

"A shy baby will get very excited. This is you, when we gave you the same test."

And there I was, looking solemn, 200 years old at six months,•my infant face crossed with some kind of philosophical puzzlement. Then, they show me the mobile. My face lights up, I start to bounce, I gurgle with pleasure, delight, spit shoots out of my mouth. I get over-excited, the mobile is slightly beyond my grasp. My face crumples up, I jerk with the first little cries. Moments later I am screaming myself purple, and trying to escape the mobile, which has begun to terrify me.

"That behaviour is hardwired," BETsi explained. "You will always find yourself getting too happy and then fearful and withdrawn. You must learn to control the excitement. Then you will be less fearful."

It's like with VR. When they first started making that, they discovered they did not know enough about how we see and hear to duplicate the experience. They had to research people first. Same here. Before they could mimic personality, they first had to find out a lot more about what personality was.

BETsi had me doing Transcendental Meditation and yoga at three years old. She had me doing what I now recognize was the Alexander Technique. I didn't just nap, I had my knees up and my head on a raised wooden pillow. This was to elongate my back—I was already curling inward from tension.

After she got me calm, BETsi would get me treats. She had Booker's credit-card number and authorization to spend. BETsi could giggle. When the ice cream was delivered, or the new CD full of clip art, or my new S&M Toddler black leather gear, or my Barbie Sex-Change doll, BETsi would giggle.

I know. She was programmed to giggle so that I would learn it was all right to be happy. But it sounded as though there was something who was happy just because I was. For some reason, that meant I would remember all by myself to stay calm.

"I'll open it later," I would say, feeling very adult.

"It's ice cream, you fool," BETsi would say. "It'll melt."

"It will spread all over the carpet!" I whispered in delight.

"Booker will get ma-had," BETsi said in a sing-song voice. BETsi knew that I always called Booker by her name.

BETsi could learn. She would have had to be trained to recognize and respond to my voice and Booker's. She was programmed to learn who I was and what I needed. I needed conspiracy. I needed a confidant.

"Look. You melt the ice cream and I will clean it up," she said.

"It's ice cream, you fool," I giggled back. "If it melts, I won't be able to eat it!" We both laughed.

BETsi's screen could turn into a mirror. I'd see my own face and inspect it carefully for signs of being like Tarzan. Sometimes, as a game, she would have my own face talk back to me in my own voice. Or I would give myself a beard and a deeper voice to see what I would look like as a grown-up. To have revenge on Booker, I would make myself bald.

I was fascinated by men. They were mythical beasts, huge and loping like dinosaurs, only hairy. The highlight of my week was when the window cleaner arrived. I would trail after him, too shy to speak, trying to puff myself up to the same size as he was. I thought he was a hero, who cleaned windows and then saved people from evil.

"You'll have to bear with Clancy," BETsi would say to him. "He doesn't see many men."

"Don't you get out, little fella?" he would say. His name was Tom.

"It's not safe," I managed to answer.

Tom tutted. "Oh, that's true enough. What a world, eh? You have to keep the kiddies locked in all day. S'like a prison." I thought that all men had South London accents.

He talked to BETsi as if she was a person. I don't think Tom could have been very bright, but I do think he was a kindly soul. I think BETsi bought him things to give to me.

"Here's an articulated," he said once, and gave me a beautifully painted Matchbox lorry.

I took it in silence. I hated myself for being so tongue-tied. I wanted to swagger around the flat with him like Nick Nolte or Wesley Snipes.

"Do men drive in these?" I managed to ask.

"Some of them, yeah."

"Are there many men?"

He looked blank. I answered for him. "There's no jobs for men."

Tom hooted with laughter. "Who's been filling your head?" he asked.

"Clancy has a very high symbol-recognition speed," BETsi told him. "Not genius, you understand. But very high. It will be useful for him in interpretative trades. However, he has almost no spatial reasoning. He will only ever dream of being a lorry driver."

"I'm a klutz," I translated.

Booker was an American—probably the most famous American in London at the time. BETsi was programmed to modulate her speech to match her owners. To this day, I can't tell English and American accents apart unless I

listen carefully. And I can imitate neither. I talk like
BETsi.

I remember Tom's face, like a suet pudding, pale,
blotchy, uneasy. "Poor little fella," he said. "I'd rather not
know all that about myself."

"So would Clancy," said BETsi. "But I am programmed to hide nothing from him."

Tom sighed. "Get him with other kids," he told her.

"Oh, that is all part of the plan," said BETsi.

I *was sent* to Social Skills class. I failed. I discovered that
I was terrified without BETsi, that I did not know what to
do or say to people when she wasn't there. I went off into
a corner with a computer screen, but it seemed cold, almost
angry with me. If I didn't do exactly the right thing it
wouldn't work, and it never said anything nice to me. The
other children were like ghosts. They flittered around the
outside of my perceptions. In my mind, I muted the noise
they made. They sounded as if they were shouting from the
other side of the window, from the harsh blue-grey world.

The consultants wrote on my first report: Clancy is socially backward, even for his age.

Booker was furious. She showed up one Wednesday
and argued about it.

"Do you realize that a thing like that could get in my
son's record!"

"It happens to be true, Miss McCall." The consultant
was appalled and laughed from disbelief.

"This crèche leaves children unattended and blames
them when their development is stunted." Booker was
yelling and pointing at the woman. "I want that report
changed. Or I will report on you!"

"Are you threatening to write us up in your magazines?" the consultant asked in a quiet voice.

"I'm telling you not to victimize my son for your own

failings. If he isn't talking to the other children, it's your job to help him."

Talking to other kids was my job. I stared at my shoes, mortified. I didn't want Booker to help me, but I half-wanted her to take me out of the class, and I knew that I would hate it if she did.

I went to BETsi for coaching.

"What you may not know," she told me, "is that you have a natural warmth that attracts people."

"I do?" I said.

"Yes. And all most people want from other people is that they be interested in them. Shall we practice?"

On her screen, she invented a series of children. I would try to talk to them. BETsi didn't make it easy.

"Do you like reading?" I'd ask a little girl on the screen.

"What?" she replied with a curling lip.

"Books," I persisted, as brave as I could be. "Do you read books?"

She blinked—bemused, bored, confident.

"Do . . . do you like *Jurassic Park*?"

"It's old! And it doesn't have any story."

"Do you like new movies?" I was getting desperate.

"I play games. *Bloodlust Demon*." The little girl's eyes went narrow and fierce. That was it. I gave up.

"BETsi," I complained. "This isn't fair." Booker would not allow me to play computer games.

BETsi chuckled and used her own voice. "That's what it's going to be like, kiddo."

"Then show me some games."

"Can't," she said.

"Not in the program," I murmured angrily.

"If I tried to show you one, I'd crash," she explained.

*S*o I went back to Social Skills class determined to talk and it was every bit as awful as BETsi had said, but at least I was ready.

I told them all, straight out: I can't play games, I'm a klutz, all I can do is draw. So, I said, tell me about the games.

And that was the right thing to do. At five I gave up being Tarzan and started to listen, because the kids could at least tell me about video games. They could get puffed up and important, and I would seep envy, which must have been very satisfying for them. But in a funny kind of way they sort of liked me.

There was a bully called Ian Aston, and suddenly one day the kids told him: "Clancy can't fight, so don't pick on him." He couldn't stand up to all of them.

"See if your Mum will let you visit," they said, "and we'll show you some games."

Booker said no. "It's very nice you're progressing socially, Clancy. But I'm not having you mix just yet. I know what sort of things are in the homes of parents like that, and I'm not having you exposed."

"Your Mum's a posh git," the children said.

"And a half," I replied.

She was also a drug addict. One evening she didn't collect me from Social Class. The consultant tried to reach her PDA, and couldn't.

"You have a Home Help, don't you?" the consultant asked.

She rang BETsi. BETsi said she had no record in her diary of where Miss McCall might be if not collecting me. BETsi sent round a taxi.

Booker was out for two weeks. She just disappeared.

She'd collapsed on the street, and everything was taken—her handbag, her shoes, her PDA, even her contact lenses. She woke up blind and raving from barbiturate withdrawal in an NHS ward, which would have mortified her. She claimed to be Booker McCall and several other people as well. I suppose it was also a kind of breakdown. Nobody knew who she was, nobody told us what had happened.

BETsi and I just sat alone in the apartment, eating ice cream and Kellogg's Crunchy Nut Cornflakes.

"Do you suppose Booker will ever come back?" I asked her.

"I do not know where Booker is, kiddo. I'm afraid something bad must have happened to her."

I felt guilty because I didn't care. I didn't care if Booker never came back. But I was scared.

"What happens if you have a disc fault?" I asked BETsi.

"I've just renewed the service contract," she replied. She whirred closer to me, and put a carpeted arm around me.

"But how would they know that something was wrong?"

She gave me a little rousing shake. "I'm monitored, all day so that if there is a problem when your mother isn't here, they come round and repair me."

"But what if you're broken for a real long time? Hours and hours. Days?"

"They'll have a replacement."

"I don't want a replacement."

"In a few hours, she'll be trained to recognize your voice."

"What if it doesn't work? What if the contractors don't hear? What do I do then?"

She printed out a number to call, and a password to enter.

"It probably won't happen," she said. "So I'm going to ask you to do your exercises."

She meant calm me down, as if my fears weren't real, as if it couldn't happen that a machine would break down.

"I don't want to do my exercises. Exercises won't help."

"Do you want to see *Jurassic Park*?" she asked.

"It's old," I said, and thought of my friends at Social Class and of their mothers who were with them.

There was a whirring sound. A panel came up on the screen, like what happened during a service when the engineers came and checked her programming and reloaded the operational system. CONFIGURATION OVERRIDE the panels said.

When that was over BETsi asked, "Would you like to learn how to play *Bloodlust Demon*?"

"Oh!" I said and nothing else. "Oh! Oh! BETsi! Oh!"

And she giggled.

I remember the light on the beige carpet making a highway towards the screen. I remember the sound of traffic outside, peeping, hooting, the sound of nightfall and loneliness, the time I usually hated the most. But now I was playing *Bloodlust Demon*.

I played it very badly. I kept getting blown up.

"Just keep trying," she said.

"I have no spatial reasoning," I replied. I was learning that I did not like computer games. But for the time being, I had forgotten everything else.

After two weeks, I assumed that Booker had gotten bored and had gone away and would never be back. Then one morning, when the hot world seemed to be pouring in through the grimy windows, someone kicked down the front door.

BETsi made a cage around me with her arms.

"I am programmed for both laser and bullet defence. Take what you want, but do not harm the child. I cannot take your photograph or video you. You will not be recognized. There is no need to damage me."

They broke the glass tables, they threw drawers onto the floor. They dropped their trousers and shat in the kitchen. They took silver dresses, Booker's black box, her jewellery. One of the thieves took hold of my Matchbox lorry and I knew the meaning of loss. I was going to lose my truck. Then the thief walked back across the carpet towards me. BETsi's arms closed more tightly around me. The thief chuckled under his ski mask and left the truck nearby on the sofa.

"There you go, little fella," he said. I never told anyone. It was Tom. Like I said, he wasn't very bright. BETsi was programmed not to recognize him.

So. I knew then what men were; they could go bad. There was part of them that was only ever caged up. I was frightened of men after that.

The men left the door open, and the flat was a ruin, smashed and broken, and BETsi's cage of arms was lifted up, and I began to cry, and then I began to scream over and over and over, and finally some neighbours came, and finally the search was on for Booker McCall.

How could an editor-in-chief disappear for two weeks? "We thought she'd gone off with a new boyfriend," her colleagues said, in the press, to damage her. Politics, wall to wall. It was on TV, the Uncaring Society they called it. No father, no grandparents, neighbours who were oblivious—the deserted child was only found because of a traumatic break in.

Booker was gone a very long time. Barbiturates are the worst withdrawal of all. I visited her, with one of the consultants from my Class. It got her picture in the papers, and a caption that made it sound as though the consultants were the only people who cared.

Booker looked awful. Bright yellow with blue circles under her eyes. She smelled of thin stale sweat.

"Hello, Clancy," she whispered. "I've been in withdrawal."

So what? Tell me something I didn't know. I was hardhearted. I had been deserted, she had no call on my respect.

"Did you miss me?" She looked like a cut flower that had been left in a vase too long, with smelly water.

I didn't want to hurt her, so all I said was: "I was scared."

"Poor baby," she whispered. She meant it, but the wave of sympathy exhausted her and she lay back on the pillow. She held out her hand.

I took it and I looked at it.

"Did BETsi take good care of you?" she asked, with her eyes closed.

"Yes," I replied, and began to think, still looking at her fingers. She really can't help all of this, all of this is hardwired. I bet she'd like to be like BETsi, but can't. Anyway, barbiturates don't work on metal and plastic.

Suddenly she was crying, and she'd pushed my hand onto her moist cheek. It was sticky and I wanted to get away, and she said, "Tell me a story. Tell me some beautiful stories."

So I sat and told her the story of *Jurassic Park*. She lay still, my hand on her cheek. At times I thought she was asleep, other times I found I hoped she loved the story as much as I did, raptors and brachiosaurs and T Rex.

When I was finished, she murmured, "At least somebody's happy." She meant me. That was what she wanted to think, that I was all right, that she would not have to worry about me. And that too, I realized, would never change.

Ｓhe came home. She stayed in bed all day for two more weeks, driving me nuts. "My life is such a mess!" she said, itchy and anxious. She promised me she would spend more time with me, God forbid. She raged against the bastards at BPC. We'd be moving as soon as she was up, she promised me, filling my heart with terror. She succeeded in disrupting my books, my movies, my painting. Finally she threw off the sheets a month early and went back to work. I gathered she still went in for treatment every fortnight. I gathered that booze now took the place of Barbies. The smell of the flat changed. And now that I hated men, there were a lot of them, loose after work.

"This is my boy," she would say, with a kind of wobbly pride and introduce me to yet another middle-aged man with a ponytail. "Mr. d'Angelo is a designer," she would say, as if she went out with their professions. She started to wear wobbly red lipstick. It got everywhere, on pillows, sheets, walls, and worst of all on my Nutella tumblers.

The flat had been my real world, against the outside, and now all that had changed. I went to school. I had to say goodbye to BETsi, every morning, and goodbye to Booker, who left wobbly red lipstick on my collar. I went to school in a taxi.

"You see," said BETsi, after my first day. "It wasn't bad was it? It works, doesn't it?"

"Yes, BETsi," I remember saying. "It does." The "it" was me. We both meant my precious self. She had done her job.

Through my later school days, BETsi would sit unused in my room—most of the time. Sometimes at night, under the covers, I would reboot her, and the screen would open up to all the old things, still there. My childhood was already another world—dinosaurs and space cats and puzzles. BETsi would pick up where we had left off, with no sense of neglect, no sense of time or self.

"You're older," she would say. "About twelve. Let me look at you." She would mirror my face, and whir to herself. "Are you drawing?"

"Lots," I would say.

"Want to mess around with the clip art, kiddo?" she would ask.

And long into the night, when I should have been learning algebra, we would make collages on her screen. I showed surfers on waves that rose up amid galaxies blue and white in space, and through space there poured streams of roses. A row of identical dancing Buddhas was an audience.

"Tell me about your friends, and what you do," she asked, as I cut and pasted. And I'd tell her about my friend John and his big black dog, Toro, and how we were caught in his neighbours' garden. I ran and escaped, but John was caught. John lived outside town in the countryside. And I'd tell her about John's grandfather's farm, full of daffodils in rows. People use them to signal spring, to spell the end of winter. Symbol recognition.

"I've got some daffodils," BETsi said. "In my memory."

And I would put them into the montage for her, though it was not spring any longer.

I failed at algebra. Like everything else in Booker's life, I was something that did not quite pan out as planned. She was good about it. She never upbraided me for not being a genius. There was something in the way she ground out her cigarette that said it all.

"Well, there's always art school," she said, and forced out a blast of blue-white smoke.

It was BETsi I showed my projects to—the A-level exercises in sketching elephants in pencil.

"From a photo," BETsi said. "You can always tell. So. You can draw as well as a photograph. Now what?"

"That's what I think," I said. "I need a style of my own."

"You need to do that for yourself," she said.

"I know," I said, casually.

"You won't always have me to help," she said.

The one thing I will never forgive Booker for is selling BETsi without telling me. I came back from first term at college to find the machine gone. I remember that I shouted, probably for the first time ever, "You did what?"

I remember Booker's eyes widening, blinking. "It's just a machine, Clancy. I mean, it wasn't as if she was a member of the family or anything."

"How could you do it! Where is she?"

"I don't know. I didn't think you'd be so upset. You're being awfully babyish about this."

"What did you do with her?"

"I sold her back to the contract people, that's all." Booker was genuinely bemused. "Look. You are hardly ever here, it isn't as though you use her for anything. She's a child-development tool, for Chrissakes. Are you still a child?"

I'd thought Booker had been smart. I'd thought that she had recognized she would not have time to be a mother, and so had brought in BETsi. I thought that meant she understood what BETsi was. She didn't and that meant she had not understood, not even been smart.

"You," I said, "have sold the only real mother I have ever had." I was no longer shouting. I said it at dictation speed. I'm not sure Booker has ever forgiven me.

Serial numbers, I thought. They have serial numbers, maybe I could trace her through those. I rang up the contractors. The kid on the phone sighed.

"You want to trace your BETsi," he said before I'd finished, sounding bored.

"Yes," I said. "I do."

He grunted and I heard a flicker of fingertips on a keyboard.

"She's been placed with another family. Still operational. But," he said, "I can't tell you where she is."

"Why not?"

"Well, Mr. McCall. Another family is paying for the service, and the developer is now working with another child. Look. You are not unusual, OK? In fact this happens about half the time, and we cannot have customers disturbed by previous charges looking up their machines."

"Why not?"

"Well," he chortled; it was so obvious to him. "You might try imagining it from the child's point of view. They have a new developer of their own, and then this other person, a stranger, tries to muscle in."

"Just. Please. Tell me where she is."

"Her memory has been wiped," he said, abruptly.

It took a little while. I remember hearing the hiss on the line.

"She won't recognize your voice. She won't remember anything about you. She is just a service vehicle. Try to remember that."

I wanted to strangle the receiver. I sputtered down the line like a car cold-starting. "Don't . . . couldn't you keep a copy! You know this happens, you bastard. Couldn't you warn people, offer them the disc? Something?"

"I'm sorry sir, but we do, and you turned the offer down."

"I'm sorry?" I was dazed.

"That's what your entry says."

Booker, I thought. Booker, Booker, Booker. And I realized; she couldn't understand, she's just too old. She's just from another world.

"I'm sorry, sir, but I have other calls on the line."

"I understand," I replied.

All my books, all my collages, my own face in the mirror. It had been like a library I could visit whenever I wanted to see something from the past. It was as if my own life had been wiped.

Then for some reason, I remembered Tom.

He was fat and 40 and defeated, a bloke. I asked him to break in to the contractor's office and read the files and find who had her.

"So," he said. "You knew then."

"Yup."

He blew out hard through his lips and looked at me askance.

"Thanks for the lorry," I said, by way of explanation.

"I always liked you, you know. You were a nice little kid." His fingers were tobacco-stained. "I can see why you want her back. She was all you had."

He found her all right. I sent him a cheque. Sometimes even now I send him a cheque.

Booker would have been dismayed—BETsi had ended in a resold council flat. I remember, the lift was broken and the stairs smelled of pee. The door itself was painted fire-engine red and had a non-breakable plaque on the doorway. The Andersons, it said amid ceramic pansies. I knocked.

BETsi answered the door. Boom. There she was, arms extended defensively to prevent entry. She'd been cleaned up but there was still rice pudding in her hair. Beyond her, I saw a slumped three-piece suite and beige carpet littered with toys. There was a smell of baby food and damp flannel.

"BETsi?" I asked, and knelt down in front of her. She scanned me, clicking. I could almost see the wheels turning, and for some reason, I found it funny. "It's OK," I said, "you won't know me, dear."

"Who is it, Betty?" A little girl came running. To

breathe the air that flows in through an open door, to see someone new, to see anyone at all.

"A caller, Bumps," replied BETsi. Her voice was different, a harsher, East End lilt. "And I think he's just about to be on his way."

I found that funny too; I still forgave her. It wasn't her fault. Doughty old BETsi still doing her job, with this doubtful man she didn't know trying to gain entry.

There might be, though, one thing she could do.

I talked to her slowly, I tried to imitate an English accent. "You do not take orders from someone with my voice. But I mean no harm, and you may be able to do this. Can you show me my face on your screen?"

She whirred. Her screen flipped out of sleep. There I was.

"I am an old charge of yours," I said—both of us, me and my image, his voice echoing mine. "My name is Clancy. All I ask you to do is remember me. Can you do that?"

"I understand what you mean," she said. "I don't have a security reason not to."

"Thank you," I said. "And see if you can program the following further instructions."

"I cannot take instruction from you."

"I know. But check if this violates security. Set aside part of your memory. Put Bumps into it. Put me and Bumps in the same place, so that even when they wipe you again you'll remember us."

She whirred. I began to get excited; I talked like myself.

"Because they're going to wipe you BETsi, whenever they resell you. They'll wipe you clean. It might be nice for Bumps if you remember her. Because we'll always remember you."

The little girl's eyes were on me, dark and serious, 200 years old. "Do what he says, Betty," the child said.

Files opened and closed like mouths. "I can put information in an iced file," said BETsi. "It will not link with any other files, so it will not be usable to gain entry to my systems." Robots and people: these days we all know too much about our inner workings.

I said thank you and goodbye, and said it silently looking into the eyes of the little girl, and she spun away on her heel as if to say: I did that.

I still felt happy, running all the way back to the tube station. I just felt joy.

So that's the story.

It took me a long time to make friends in school, but they were good ones. I still know them, though they are now middle-aged men, clothiers in Toronto, or hearty freelancers in New York who talk about their men and their cats. Make a long story short. I grew up to be one of the people my mother used to hire and abuse.

I am a commercial artist, though more for book and CD covers than magazines. I'm about to be a Dad. One of my clients, a very nice woman. We used to see each other and get drunk at shows. In the hotel bedrooms I'd see myself in the mirror—not quite middle-aged, but with a pony tail. Her name is some kind of mistake. Bertha.

Bertha is very calm and cool and reliable. She called me and said coolly, I'm having a baby and you're the father, but don't worry. I don't want anything from you.

I wanted her to want something from me. I wanted her to say marry me, you bastard. Or at least: could you take care of it on weekends? Not only didn't she want me to worry—it was clear that she didn't want me at all. It was also clear I could expect no more commissions from her.

I knew then what I wanted to do. I went to Hamleys.

There they were, the Next Degradation. Now they call them things like Best Friend or Home Companions, and they've tried to make them look human. They have latex skins and wigs and stiff little smiles. They look like burn victims after plastic surgery, and they recognize absolutely everybody. Some of them are modelled after *Little Women*. You can buy Beth or Amy or Jo. Some poor little rich girls start dressing them up in high fashion—the bills are said to be staggering. You can also buy male models—a lively Huckleberry, or big Jim. I wonder if those might not be more for the Mums, particularly if all parts are in working order.

"Do you . . . do you have any older models?" I ask at the counter.

The assistant is a sweet woman, apple cheeked, young, pretty, and she sees straight through me. "We have BETsis," she says archly.

"They still make them?" I say, softly.

"Oh, they're very popular," she says, and pauses, and decides to drop the patter. "People want their children to have them. They loved them."

History repeats like indigestion.

I turn up at conventions like this one. I can't afford a stand but my livelihood depends on getting noticed anyway.

And if I get carried away and believe a keynote speaker trying to be a visionary, if he talks about, say, Virtual Government or Loose Working Practices, then I get overexcited. I think I see God, or the future or something and I get all jittery. And I go into the exhibition hall and there is a wall of faces I don't know and I think: I've got to talk to them, I've got to sell to them. I freeze, and I go back to my room.

And I know what to do. I think of BETsi, and I stretch out on the floor and take hold of my shoulders and my breathing and I get off the emotional roller-coaster. I can go back downstairs, and back into the hall. And I remember that something once said: you have a natural warmth that attracts people, and I go in, and even though I'm a bit diffident, by the end of the convention, we're laughing and shaking hands, and I have their business card. Or maybe we've stayed up drinking till four in the morning, playing *Bloodlust Demon*. They always win. They like that, and we laugh.

It is necessary to be loved. I'm not sentimental: I don't think a computer loved me. But I was hugged, I was noticed, I was cared for. I was made to feel that I was important, special, at least to something. I fear for all the people who do not have that. Like everything else, it is now something that can be bought. It is therefore something that can be denied. It is possible that without BETsi, I might have to stay upstairs in that hotel room, panicked. It is possible that I would end up on barbiturates. It is possible that I could have ended up one of those sweet sad people sitting in the rain in shop doorways saying the same thing in London or New York, in exactly the same accent: any spare change please?

But I didn't. I put a proposition to you.

If there were a God who saw and cared for us and was merciful, then when I died and went to Heaven, I would find among all the other things, a copy of that wiped disc.

Ancient Engines

Michael Swanwick

We tend to think of robots as sturdy, enduring things that will be around long after creatures of mere flesh are gone—and yet, to date, machines don't even last as long as most people do. (How many toasters do most people have in a lifetime, or cars, or computers?) Here's a hard-edged and hard-headed look at what a robot would really need to exist forever, in addition to being made of metal and plastic and gears. Turns out, a lot of careful planning is involved . . .

Michael Swanwick made his debut in 1980 and, in the twenty-five years that have followed, has established himself as one of SF's most prolific and consistently excellent writers at short lengths, as well as one of the premier novelists of his generation. He has won the Theodore Sturgeon Award and the Asimov's *Readers Award poll. In 1991, his novel* Stations of the Tide *won him a Nebula Award as well, and in 1995 he won the World Fantasy Award for his story "Radio Waves." He's won the Hugo Award four times between 1999 and 2003, for his stories "The Very Pulse of the Machine," "Scherzo with Tyrannosaur," "The Dog Said Bow-Wow," and "Slow Life." His other books include the novels* In The Drift, Vacuum Flowers, The Iron Dragon's Daughter *(which was a finalist for the World Fantasy Award and the Arthur C. Clarke Award, a rare distinction!),* Jack Faust, *and, most recently,* Bones of the Earth, *plus a novella-length book,* Griffin's Egg. *His short fiction has been assembled in* Gravity's Angels, A Geography of Unknown Lands, Slow Dancing Through Time *(a collection of his collaborative short work with other writ-*

ers), Moon Dogs, Puck Aleshire's Abecedary, Tales of Old
Earth, *and* Cigar-Box Faust and Other Miniatures. *He's
also published a collection of critical articles,* The Post-
modern Archipelago, *and a book-length interview,* Being
Gardner Dozois. *His most recent books are two new collections,* The Periodic Table of SF *and* Michael Swanwick's Field Guide to the Mesozoic Megafauna. *Swanwick
lives in Philadelphia with his wife, Marianne Porter. He
has a website at www.michaelswanwick.com.*

"*P*lanning to live forever, Tiktok?"

The words cut through the bar's chatter and gab and si-
lenced them.

The silence reached out to touch infinity, and then, "I
believe you're talking to me?" a mech said.

The drunk laughed. "Ain't nobody else here sticking
needles in his face, is there?"

The old man saw it all. He lightly touched the hand of
the young woman sitting with him and said, "Watch."

Carefully, the mech set down his syringe alongside a
bottle of liquid collagen on a square of velvet cloth. He
disconnected himself from the recharger, laying the jack
beside the syringe. When he looked up again, his face was
still and hard. He looked like a young lion.

The drunk grinned sneeringly.

The bar was located just around the corner from the
local stepping stage. It was a quiet retreat from the aggra-
vations of the street, all brass and mirrors and wood pan-
eling, as cozy and snug as the inside of a walnut. Light
shifted lazily about the room, creating a varying emphasis, like clouds drifting overhead on a summer day, but far
dimmer. The bar, the bottles behind the bar, and the
shelves beneath the bottles behind the bar were all ag-
gressively real. If there was anything virtual, it was set up

high or far back, where it couldn't be touched. There was not a smart surface in the place.

"If that was a challenge," the mech said, "I'd be more than happy to meet you outside."

"Oh, noooooo," the drunk said, his expression putting the lie to his words. "I just saw you shooting up that goop into your face, oh so dainty, like an old lady pumping herself full of antioxidants. So I figured"—he weaved and put a hand down on a table to steady himself—"figured you was hoping to live forever."

The girl looked questioningly at the old man. He held a finger to his lips.

"Well, you're right. You're—what? Fifty years old? Just beginning to grow old and decay. Pretty soon your teeth will rot and fall out and your hair will melt away and your face will fold up in a million wrinkles. Your hearing and your eyesight will go and you won't be able to remember the last time you got it up. You'll be lucky if you don't need diapers before the end. But *me*"—he drew a dram of fluid into his syringe and tapped the barrel to draw the bubbles to the top—"anything that fails, I'll simply have it replaced. So, yes, I'm planning to live forever. While you, well, I suppose you're planning to *die*. Soon, I hope."

The drunk's face twisted, and with an incoherent roar of rage, he attacked the mech.

In a motion too fast to be seen, the mech stood, seized the drunk, whirled him around, and lifted him above his head. One hand was closed around the man's throat so he couldn't speak. The other held both wrists tight behind the knees so that, struggle as he might, the drunk was helpless.

"I could snap your spine like *that*," he said coldly. "If I exerted myself, I could rupture every internal organ you've got. I'm two-point-eight times stronger than a flesh man, and three-point-five times faster. My reflexes are only slightly slower than the speed of light, and I've just had a tune-up. You could hardly have chosen a worse person to pick a fight with."

Then the drunk was flipped around and set back on his feet. He gasped for air.

"But since I'm also a merciful man, I'll simply ask you nicely if you wouldn't rather leave." The mech spun the drunk around and gave him a gentle shove toward the door.

The man left at a stumbling run.

Everyone in the place—there were not many—had been watching. Now they remembered their drinks, and talk rose up to fill the room again. The bartender put something back under the bar and turned away.

Leaving his recharge incomplete, the mech folded up his lubrication kit and slipped it into a pocket. He swiped his hand over the credit swatch and stood.

But as he was leaving, the old man swiveled around and said, "I heard you say you hope to live forever. Is that true?"

"Who doesn't?" the mech said curtly.

"Then sit down. Spend a few minutes out of the infinite swarm of centuries you've got ahead of you to humor an old man. What's so urgent that you can't spare the time?"

The mech hesitated. Then, as the young woman smiled at him, he sat.

"Thank you. My name is—"

"I know who you are, Mr. Brandt. There's nothing wrong with my eidetics."

Brandt smiled. "That's why I like you guys. I don't have to be all the time reminding you of things." He gestured to the woman sitting opposite him. "My granddaughter." The light intensified where she sat, making her red hair blaze. She dimpled prettily.

"Jack." The young man drew up a chair. "Chimaera Navigator-Fuego, model number—"

"Please. I founded Chimaera. Do you think I wouldn't recognize one of my own children?"

Jack flushed. "What is it you want to talk about, Mr. Brandt?" His voice was audibly less hostile now, as synthetic counterhormones damped down his emotions.

"Immortality. I found your ambition most intriguing."

"What's to say? I take care of myself, I invest carefully, I buy all the upgrades. I see no reason why I shouldn't live forever." Defiantly. "I hope that doesn't offend you."

"No, no, of course not. Why should it? Some men hope to achieve immortality through their works and others through their children. What could give me more joy than to do both? But tell me—do you *really* expect to live forever?"

The mech said nothing.

"I remember an incident that happened to my late father-in-law, William Porter. He was a fine fellow, Bill was, and who remembers him anymore? Only me." The old man sighed. "He was a bit of a railroad buff, and one day he took a tour through a science museum that included a magnificent old steam locomotive. This was in the latter years of the last century. Well, he was listening admiringly to the guide extolling the virtues of this ancient engine when she mentioned its date of manufacture, and he realized that *he was older than it was.*" Brandt leaned forward. "This is the point where old Bill would laugh. But it's not really funny, is it?"

"No."

The granddaughter sat listening quietly, intently, eating little pretzels one by one from a bowl.

"How old are you, Jack?"

"Seven years."

"I'm eighty-three. How many machines do you know of that are as old as me? Eighty-three years old and still functioning?"

"I saw an automobile the other day," his granddaughter said. "A Dusenberg. It was red."

"How delightful. But it's not used for transportation anymore, is it? We have the stepping stages for that. I won an award once that had mounted on it a vacuum tube from Univac. That was the first real computer. Yet all its fame and historical importance couldn't keep it from the scrap heap."

"Univac," said the young man, "couldn't act on its own behalf. If it *could*, perhaps it would be alive today."

"Parts wear out."

"New ones can be bought."

"Yes, as long as there's the market. But there are only so many machine people of your make and model. A lot of you have risky occupations. There are accidents, and with every accident, the consumer market dwindles."

"You can buy antique parts. You can have them made."

"Yes, if you can afford them. And if not—?"

The young man fell silent.

"Son, you're not going to live *forever*. We've just established that. So now that you've admitted that you've got to die someday, you might as well admit that it's going to be sooner rather than later. Mechanical people are in their infancy. And nobody can upgrade a Model T into a stepping stage. Agreed?"

Jack dipped his head. "Yes."

"You knew it all along."

"Yes."

"That's why you behaved so badly toward that lush."

"Yes."

"I'm going to be brutal here, Jack—you probably won't live to be eighty-three. You don't have my advantages."

"Which are?"

"Good genes. I chose my ancestors well."

"Good genes," Jack said bitterly. "You received good

genes, and what did *I* get in their place? What the hell did
I get?"

"Molybdenum joints where stainless steel would do.
Ruby chips instead of zirconium. A number seventeen
plastic seating for—hell, we did all right by you boys!"

"But it's not enough."

"No. It's not. It was only the best we could do."

"What's the solution, then?" the granddaughter asked,
smiling.

"I'd advise taking the long view. That's what I've
done."

"Poppycock," the mech said. "You were an extension-
ist when you were young. I input your autobiography. It
seems to me you wanted immortality as much as I do."

"Oh, yes, I was a charter member of the life-extension
movement. You can't imagine the crap we put into our
bodies! But eventually I wised up. The problem is, information degrades each time a human cell replenishes itself.
Death is inherent in flesh people. It seems to be written
into the basic program—a way, perhaps, of keeping the
universe from filling up with old people."

"And old ideas," his granddaughter said maliciously.

"Touché. I saw that life-extension was a failure. So I
decided that my children would succeed where I failed.
That *you* would succeed. And—"

"You failed."

"But I haven't stopped trying!" The old man thumped
the table in unison with his last three words. "You've obviously given this some thought. Let's discuss what I
should have done. What would it take to make a true immortal? What instructions should I have given your design
team? Let's design a mechanical man who's got a shot at
living forever."

Carefully, the mech said, "Well, the obvious to begin
with. He ought to be able to buy new parts and upgrades
as they become available. There should be ports and con-

nectors that would make it easy to adjust to shifts in technology. He should be capable of surviving extremes of
heat, cold, and moisture. And"—he waved a hand at his
own face—"he shouldn't look so goddamned pretty."

"I think you look nice," the granddaughter said.

"Yes, but I'd like to be able to pass for flesh."

"So our hypothetical immortal should be one, infinitely
ungradable; two, adaptable across a broad spectrum of
conditions; and three, discreet. Anything else?"

"I think she should be charming," the granddaughter
said.

"She?" the mech asked.

"Why not?"

"That's actually not a bad point," the old man said.
"The organism that survives evolutionary forces is the one
that's best adapted to its environmental niche. The environmental niche people live in is man-made. The single
most useful trait a survivor can have is probably the ability to get along easily with other men. Or, if you'd rather,
women."

"Oh," said the granddaughter, "he doesn't like *women*.
I can tell by his body language."

The young man flushed.

"Don't be offended," said the old man. "You should
never be offended by the truth. As for you"—he turned to
face his granddaughter—"if you don't learn to treat people better, I won't take you places anymore."

She dipped her head. "Sorry."

"Apology accepted. Let's get back to task, shall we?
Our hypothetical immortal would be a lot like flesh
women, in many ways. Self-regenerating. Able to grow
her own replacement parts. She could take in pretty much
anything as fuel. A little carbon, a little water . . ."

"Alcohol would be an excellent fuel," his granddaughter said.

"She'd have the ability to mimic the superficial effects

of aging," the mech said. "Also, biological life evolves incrementally across generations. I'd want her to be able to evolve across upgrades."

"Fair enough. Only I'd do away with upgrades entirely, and give her total conscious control over her body. So she could change and evolve at will. She'll need that ability, if she's going to survive the collapse of civilization."

"The collapse of civilization? Do you think it likely?"

"In the long run? Of course. When you take the long view, it seems inevitable. Everything seems inevitable. Forever is a long time, remember. Time enough for absolutely *everything* to happen!"

For a moment, nobody spoke.

Then the old man slapped his hands together. "Well, we've created our New Eve. Now let's wind her up and let her go. She can expect to live—how long?"

"Forever," said the mech.

"Forever's a long time. Let's break it down into smaller units. In the year 2500, she'll be doing what?"

"Holding down a job," the granddaughter said. "Designing art molecules, maybe, or scripting recreational hallucinations. She'll be deeply involved in the culture. She'll have lots of friends she cares about passionately, and maybe a husband or wife or two."

"Who will grow old," the mech said, "or wear out. Who will die."

"She'll mourn them, and move on."

"The year 3500. The collapse of civilization," the old man said with gusto. "What will she do then?"

"She'll have made preparations, of course. If there is radiation or toxins in the environment, she'll have made her systems immune from their effects. And she'll make herself useful to the survivors. In the seeming of an old woman, she'll teach the healing arts. Now and then, she might drop a hint about this and that. She'll have a data base squirreled away somewhere containing everything they'll have lost. Slowly, she'll guide them back to civilization. But a gentler one, this time. One less likely to tear itself apart."

"The year one million. Humanity evolves beyond anything we can currently imagine. How does *she* respond?"

"She mimics their evolution. No—she's been *shaping* their evolution! She wants a risk-free method of going to the stars, so she's been encouraging a type of being that would strongly desire such a thing. She isn't among the first to use it, though. She waits a few hundred generations for it to prove itself."

The mech, who had been listening in fascinated silence, now said, "Suppose that never happens. What if starflight will always remain difficult and perilous? What then?"

"It was once thought that people would never fly. So much that looks impossible becomes simple if you only wait."

"Four billion years. The sun uses up its hydrogen, its core collapses, helium fusion begins, and it balloons into a red giant. Earth is vaporized."

"Oh, she'll be somewhere else by then. That's easy."

"Five billion years. The Milky Way collides with the Andromeda Galaxy and the whole neighborhood is full of high-energy radiation and exploding stars."

"That's trickier. She's going to have to either prevent that or move a few million light-years away to a friendlier galaxy. But she'll have time enough to prepare and to assemble the tools. I have faith that she'll prove equal to the task."

"One trillion years. The last stars gutter out. Only black holes remain."

"Black holes are a terrific source of energy. No problem."

"One-point-six googol years."

"Googol?"

"That's ten raised to the hundredth power—one followed by a hundred zeros. The heat-death of the universe. How does she survive it?"

"She'll have seen it coming for a long time," the mech said. "When the last black holes dissolve, she'll have to do without a source of free energy. Maybe she could take and rewrite her personality into the physical constants of the dying universe. Would that be possible?"

"Oh, perhaps. But I really think that the lifetime of the universe is long enough for anyone," the granddaughter said. "Mustn't get greedy."

"Maybe so," the old man said thoughtfully. "Maybe so." Then, to the mech, "Well, there you have it: a glimpse into the future, and a brief biography of the first immortal, ending, alas, with her death. Now tell me. Knowing that you contributed something, however small, to that accomplishment—wouldn't that be enough?"

"No," Jack said. "No, it wouldn't."

Brandt made a face. "Well, you're young. Let me ask you this: Has it been a good life so far? All in all?"

"Not *that* good. Not good *enough*."

For a long moment, the old man was silent. Then, "Thank you," he said. "I valued our conversation." The interest went out of his eyes and he looked away.

Uncertainly, Jack looked at the granddaughter, who smiled and shrugged. "He's like that," she said apologetically. "He's old. His enthusiasms wax and wane with his chemical balances. I hope you don't mind."

"I see." The young man stood. Hesitantly, he made his way to the door.

At the door, he glanced back and saw the granddaughter tearing her linen napkin into little bits and eating the shreds, delicately washing them down with sips of wine.

Jimmy Guang's House of Gladmech

Alex Irvine

New writer Alex Irvine made his first sale in 2000 to The Magazine of Fantasy & Science Fiction *and has since made several more sales to that magazine, as well as sales to* Asimov's Science Fiction, Sci Fiction, Strange Horizons, Live Without a Net, Lady Churchill's Rosebud Wristlet, Starlight 3, Polyphony, Electric Velocipede, *and elsewhere. His well-received first novel,* A Scattering of Jades, *was released in 2002 and was followed by his first collection,* Rossetti Song. *His most recent book is a new collection,* Unintended Consequences, *and coming up is a new novel,* One King, One Soldier. *He lives in Sudbury, Massachusetts.*

Here he takes us to a remote, war-torn country to visit a sporting arena where the combatants cannot die—but the stakes are life-or-death.

Jimmy Guang Hamid smoked tobacco cigars until he found out that vat-grown lungs were still prone to immune-rejection problems and that the vat wranglers hadn't made much headway on what they called amongst themselves the Larynx Problem. Then he went over to herb-and-marijuana panatelas, anxious to maintain his image as a Golden Age wheeler-dealer, but not so anxious for a long

convalescence or opportunistic infection following a double pulmonary.

But he was in Kyrgyzstan, anyway, a long way from
organ vats, and the only people there who cared about his
image were the Russians. The Russians were the only
people who cared about lots of things in the brutalized
city of Osh, a still-proud prominence in the tank-tracked,
cluster-bombed, spider-mined, cruise-missiled ruins of
what had once, a hundred years or so before, been the
southern part of the Soviet Empire. Now Kyrgyzstan was
a member of the Islamist Federation, a loose group of
non-Arab Muslim states, and the Russians fought with the
IF out of concern over concentration of power in Central
Asia but mostly out of sheer terror of what would happen
if their soldiers were ever allowed to come home.

Jimmy Guang was not a deeply religious man, although he'd been raised a Muslim and inhabited the belief
the way he inhabited his tastes in food or music. He took
no sides between the IF and the Russians and the Chinese,
who hovered like a storm waiting to break from the East.
He had come to these wars thinking he could make
money.

He came to the city of Osh, on the flanks of the Ferghana Valley, a sliver of warm green pointing up into the
windswept expanse of the Tien Shan ranges. Once Osh
had been a major stop along the Silk Road. Alexander the
Great had slept there. Mohammed had prayed there. Now
there wasn't much left after sixty years of sporadic war,
but it was close to Tashkent without being too close, and
the last thing a foreign entrepreneur wanted was to be too
close to Tashkent. Or, for that matter, Bishkek, the capital
of Kyrgyzstan, which was still alive with bad, bad bugs
the Russians had left during their previous visit.

Osh was no longer a major part of anything. It still had
its legendary bazaar, and it was still warmer than just
about anywhere else in K-stan, but even for war profiteer-

ing it didn't offer the potential of Karachi or Almaty or Yerevan. Still, Jimmy Guang came there with his cigars and his pinstriped suits and his silk ties, a good hundred years out of fashion, and he started making deals. He knew people in Singapore, his father was still living in Jaipur and an uncle in Xian, he'd gladhanded his way over the Khyber Pass and through the Karakoram, sneaking through the Muslim hinterlands of China on the strength of his gap-toothed grin and fragmentary bits of half a dozen languages he'd picked up around the house when he was a kid. Jimmy Guang Hamid could get things.

He set up quietly, in a bombed-out storefront on Lenin Street, not far from the bazaar but not too close either. Jimmy Guang was always careful about distance. For the first week he swept and cleaned and arranged, covered over holes in the walls and made himself a pallet behind a curtain. He would take his meals at restaurants, the better to be seen, but not expensive restaurants because behind his façade of leisure and comfort Jimmy Guang Hamid was desperately poor. He washed in the restrooms of the restaurants he patronized; he burned incense under his shirts so he could save the expense of cleaning them; he scavenged in the burned-out university campus for flaps of furniture vinyl to stitch onto his shoes. If he did not succeed here in Osh, there was a good chance that he would starve to death on his way back to India or China.

He was as piratical and polyglot a stereotype as had ever been encountered in those parts, and that's exactly how he wanted it. Let them think him a buffoon. Let them insult the many strains of his ethnicity, and the many colors of his ties. He would consider bargains.

It only took a few days for him to get to know people, and a few days after that to broker his first deal, between a Russian quartermaster suffering from an excess of toothpaste and an Uzbek merchant who had found himself awash in vodka straight from Kiev. The Uzbek traded mostly among the more fundamentalist IF brigades, who wouldn't drink the vodka anyway, and the Russian would make a killing from his alcoholic and lonely compatriots.

"Amazing thing, war," Jimmy Guang said in his creolized Russian to the quartermaster, whose name was Yevgeny. They clinked glasses. "Even in the midst of all this misery and misunderstanding, still there is commerce. Still we find ways to get what we need. Something grand about it."

Allahu akbar, thought Jimmy Guang, even though he wasn't particularly religious.

Yevgeny muttered a toast and drank. Jimmy Guang knew in that moment, early on a Thursday morning in May of 2083, with a fine sharp breeze shuddering down out of the Pamir range, that he would survive. He had been right to come to Osh.

The man who sold Jimmy Guang his first gladmechs reminded him of his father, and for that reason Jimmy Guang walked away from the deal certain that he had gotten the worse of it. No man could bargain with his father.

"I have no use for these," the old German trader said.

"Nor do I," Jimmy Guang said. He thought it odd that a German should remind him of his father Reza, a proud glowering Persian who claimed ancestry among the Mughal conquerors of India. He had already decided to buy the robots, six creaking Izmit general-services models. He knew he could put them to use, and he was beginning to have financial reserves sufficient to quiet his anxieties about the return voyage to India, should that become necessary.

"Put them in a pit, have them fight each other," said the Russian who had inspected the truck and pocketed three of Jimmy Guang's cigars to ignore its doubtful papers. "That's what they do everywhere else."

"Is that so," said Jimmy Guang, and just like that his course was set.

O*n the edge* of the university campus was a long row of corrugated-tin sheds. One, which judging from the deep oil stains in its concrete floor had once held heavy equipment, was still intact. It measured forty meters long by some twenty-five wide, which Jimmy Guang figured was big enough to cordon off an arena and still pack in something like a thousand spectators. He placed a call to the robots, and was surprised to see them all arrive in a Russian army truck driven by the beneficiary of Jimmy Guang's smoky baksheesh the day before.

"I was waiting for you to tell them where to go," the soldier said as he got down from the truck's cab. He was tall and heavy and blond. Jimmy Guang could not imagine what it would be like to fight him when he was fully suited and armed. "Monitoring you. My name is Slava. You want these robots to fight, you're going to need them fixed up a little. I'll do it."

"There's no money for a mechanic," said Jimmy Guang, thinking that brushing Slava away would cost him more cigars. He resolved to get better encryption for his personal commlink.

"I'll do it free. Just to see them fight." A toothy grin split Slava's blunt face.

This was a deal Jimmy Guang could not refuse. He and Slava got the six Izmits off the truck and into the hangar, where they spent the rest of the day cleaning and cordoning off the arena space. Then Jimmy Guang gathered the mechs together.

"What we're going to do here is you're going to fight each other," he said.

"This is outside our parameters," one of the mechs said.

"We are not adaptive intelligences," added another.

Jimmy Guang had anticipated this. "The instructions are simple. A waste-management task. Each of you is to render the others fit for a standard industrial recyc. This requires separation of extremities from the trunk. Are you familiar with this protocol?"

"I am," each of the robots said.

After that, it was a matter of hanging posters, making sure there were enough pretty girls to run concession stands, and letting it be known that the house would take forty percent of all wagers. A few days later the six Izmits, painted different colors on Jimmy Guang's theory that this would promote audience identification and therefore wagering, banged and jerked each other to sparking pieces before a raucous and intensely partisan crowd of locals. By the end, the last surviving robot careened around the arena to thunderous cheers, missing one arm and trailing glittery strings of fiber-optic from holes punched in its trunk.

Jimmy Guang made enough on the evening that he didn't have to worry about hunger for two weeks. With some of what was left over he had his trousers hemmed and splurged on a box of tobacco cigars from Ankara, vat problems or no. That night he sat in his office listening to Russian rockets exploding in the hills, and he thought to himself: You can take your mind off anything. You can even take your mind off love. But you cannot take your mind off being hungry.

Of course the next day he fell in love.

Marta was her name. Jimmy Guang met her while trying to sell her uncle Gregor razor blades and Sri Lankan pornography. She looked curiously at the porn disks, then crinkled around the eyes and looked at her feet when she saw him watching her. This combination of humor and modesty caught his attention, as did the fall of her hair across her eyes. She had his mother's eyes, thought Jimmy Guang, that sharp black gaze that missed nothing. "Marta is ruined," her uncle said. "The Russians did it. At least she fought."

She had three missing teeth, Gregor went on, where a Russian soldier had hit her with a rifle butt to stop her fighting back. Gregor told the story like it had happened in a video. Jimmy Guang listened to it with growing embarrassment that made him look more closely at Marta. A crease of scar split her upper lip on the left side, and he thought about her missing teeth. He himself was missing a tooth, although he had no dramatic story other than gingivitis and an unsympathetic dentist.

And he had been ruined himself a time or two. He waited until Gregor was preoccupied with the finest filth Colombo could produce, and then he sidled up next to Marta and asked if she would like to take a trip to the Toktogul Reservoir.

No, she said. It was too heavily guarded.

Jimmy Guang knew a way in.

He smiled at her, made sure that the gap was visible between bicuspid and incisor on the upper right side of his mouth.

Marta glanced at him, then looked away. Her left hand rested at the corner of her mouth. It has been a long time since I went swimming, she said.

He *didn't see* her for nearly a week after their first meeting, but she was never far from his mind. The thought of her distracted him as he dickered with Yevgeny over another truckload of robots. When he'd paid too much for the robots and even absently agreed to take the stolen truck off Yevgeny's hands, he went back to his office and thought about how much he wanted to watch Marta swim. She would remove her vest and shoes, perhaps her top skirt. Maybe she even would appear in a bathing suit, or he could present her with one. That was it. Yes. She would strip down to her bathing suit, every line and motion clean and wary as a cat's, and he would sit on the bank with a cigar while she stepped into the black water, disturbing the reflections of mountains, and swam, eyes closed and corners of her mouth relaxed into a faint smile. It struck him that he very badly wanted to see her happy, and he could not understand why.

Jimmy Guang's second evening as gladiatorial impresario teetered on the edge of debacle from the moment the grim cluster of Russian soldiers entered the arena. What had been a raucous crowd of several hundred fell nearly silent. Jimmy Guang heard muttered profanities in Kirghiz, Russian, Arabic.

The lone officer in the group of Russians approached Jimmy Guang. "You are fighting robots here," he said.

Jimmy Guang saw no way to plausibly deny this, so he nodded.

The officer nodded back. "How much to watch?"

A delicate situation, this. The officer might be leading Jimmy Guang into an admission of war privateering. He might simply expect Jimmy Guang to announce that he and his men could watch for free, which would of course remind everyone present of the inequities that had provoked the Islamic Federation's war in the first place.

Or, thought Jimmy Guang, he might be willing to pay.

"Rubles, dollars, or yen?" he said.

The Russian officer paid for himself and his men—in American dollars—and they moved in a loose group toward one corner of the arena. Slava Butsayev was already there, and he came across the arena floor to join the other Russians. Jimmy Guang continued his introductory pat-

ter—he had already begun flamboyantly naming each of
the robots and claiming an illustrious heritage of victory
for most—until he was interrupted by a teenage Kirghiz
boy who leaned forward as one of the Russian soldiers
walked by and spat on the man's boots.

Jimmy Guang knew for the rest of his life that many
people might have died in those next few seconds, and
that he might have been one of them. But in the endless
moment that stretched out after the boy's expectoration,
he thought of only one thing: walking across the Khyber
Pass to India, penniless and hungry with hundreds of kilometers of empty mountains between him and the nearest
human who cared.

"No!" he shouted, and rushed to put himself between
the soldier and the defiant boy. "No!" The soldier took a
step, and Jimmy Guang, to his everlasting surprise, put a
hand in the man's chest and nudged him back. "Not in
here! Everyone pays the same here, everyone watches the
same here. The war is outside! The war stops at the door!"

A long moment passed, and then the Russian officer
touched him on the shoulder. Jimmy Guang shut his
mouth and made himself ready to die.

"Tell the boy to clean up his mess," the officer said.

Jimmy Guang looked at the boy. He grew more acutely
aware that had saved a life. Perhaps more than one.

His bravado began to melt away, and as it did Jimmy
Guang felt the enormity of what he was doing begin to im-
press itself on him. He drew his handkerchief from his
breast pocket and passed it to the soldier, who wiped his
boot and handed it back. Jimmy Guang, already regretting
the loss of his only good silk handkerchief, held it out for
the boy to take. A small voice in the back of his mind said,
*Now you've done it. Now you'll always be stuck in be-
tween them.* At the edge of his field of vision he saw Slava
Butsayev looking intently at him, as though he were one
of the robots with unclear prospects in the ring.

When the cloth had disappeared into the boy's pocket, Jimmy Guang stepped back into the center of the arena and said, "In Jimmy Guang's House of Gladmech, everybody gets along."

He *didn't find* out until the next day that Marta had been in the audience that night. They were swimming, or at least she was. He, as he had in his fantasy, sat a little away from the water, hat low over his eyes against the glare and a fine macanudo between his fingers. She swam, sleek as a dolphin, out into the reservoir. Jimmy Guang saw a gleam from the dam: soldiers' binoculars. Anger swelled in his chest as he thought of Marta's missing teeth, what she had suffered. The marvelous strength of her. He was beginning to love that strength.

Later, as they ate supper back in Osh, she was distant, preoccupied, a bit cold. For twenty minutes he pried gently, and at last she came open.

"All the Russians in your audience."

"Russians, Kirghiz, Uzbeks," said Jimmy Guang. "They all pay the same, and they don't kill each other in the stands."

"They didn't this time," she said. "But if you keep doing this, it will happen. You can bet on it, And then you can bet on one other thing."

"What's that?"

Her face was to the window, her reflection a woman-shaped vacancy against a field of stars. "That the Russians will come after you, and I'll be alone again."

The *next Tuesday,* the Russian captain found Jimmy Guang drinking coffee on the patio of a restaurant called Fez that faced a broad square in one of the older parts of Osh. He introduced himself as Vasily Butsayev, and shook Jimmy

Guang's hand. Jimmy Guang offered him a cigar, and Captain Butsayev politely declined.

He had come alone, which piqued Jimmy Guang's interest. Solitary Russian officers had a tendency to disappear in Osh, reappearing piece by piece in family mailboxes back in Petersburg or Komsomolsk. Either Captain Butsayev was more courageous than the average Russian, or he knew the right people in Osh and therefore had no reason to be afraid. It was this second possibility that had provoked Jimmy Guang's offer of a cigar.

"Is Slava Butsayev a relation of yours?"

A strange look passed across the captain's face. "He is my younger brother. I understand he is spending his spare time working on your robots."

"He is an energetic and knowledgeable young man," said Jimmy Guang. It was the truth. He had come to enjoy the young blond Russian's company around the hangar, and without a doubt Slava kept the mechs in better condition than Jimmy would have been able to. "I am fortunate that he agreed to work for free."

"Better than some other things he could be doing," Butsayev said with a thin smile. The waiter appeared, and he ordered coffee. "A good show you put on last night," he said when it had arrived.

Jimmy Guang shrugged modestly. "Considering what I had to work with."

"This is why I am here. You are known to us as a broker of deals."

Those words opened up a huge pit in Jimmy Guang's stomach. He swallowed and said with great delicacy, "I seek only to make things a little more bearable for those who must spend much of their time amid the horrors of war."

Captain Butsayev smiled. He had good teeth. "Do not be afraid, Mr. Hamid. I'm not here to arrest anyone for profiteering, and if I were," he glanced at Jimmy Guang's threadbare suit, "there are others I would visit before you."

The pit closed, and Jimmy Guang breathed a little easier. Butsayev wanted to deal.

"If I can get you more robots," the captain went on, the tone of his voice lightening, "can you set up more matches?"

"If you get me more robots," said Jimmy Guang, "there would of course be more matches. But I am not certain that my finances are up to purchasing quantities of robots. These are hard times."

"They are," agreed Captain Butsayev. "But let us be clear about something. We know, and the Islamic Federation knows, and the Kirghiz militias up in the mountains know that this war solves nothing. The IF continues because fighting us keeps their donations flowing from the rich fundamentalists in Saudi Arabia and Indonesia. The Kirghiz fight us because they are always fighting someone. And we Russians, why are we here?" Butsayev looked pained. "I fear that the civilian government of Mother Russia is uneasy at the prospect of half a million discharged soldiers returning home at once."

Jimmy Guang thought of Marta. He tried not to let it show. Captain Butsayev studied him for a moment. The Russian had hard blue eyes and heavy bones in his face. It was the face of a man who knew that the war would leave him with bad dreams and loneliness in his old age.

"When I said you put on a good show last night," Butsayev said at last, "I didn't mean the robots."

Jimmy Guang's shoulders twitched. Even after a week, he could still feel the Russian soldier's gaze boring through him to the thin teenager with eyes hardened by privation. People walking through the square did not notice him, did not know how difficult and frightening it was to be talking to a Russian captain without knowing what the Russian captain wanted him to say. The collar of his shirt pinched under his chin when he opened his mouth.

Captain Vasily Butsayev held up a hand, and Jimmy Guang's mouth shut. "I am not a peacenik, Mr. Hamid. And I am not a soft man. But I do not love war for its own sake." He stood. "I believe you know Master Sergeant Yevgeny?"

Since there was no way to deny this, Jimmy Guang nodded.

"Good. Speak to him." With that, Captain Butsayev touched the brim of his cap and left Jimmy Guang trying not to hyperventilate at his sidewalk table that was suddenly not nearly far enough away from the war.

The next day, though, he talked to Yevgeny, and four days after that he staged another round of matches with Indian-made salvage mechs whose cutting torches glowed in the eyes of eight hundred Kirghiz and two hundred Russian spectators, none of whom killed or tortured or assaulted any of the others while within earshot of the old heavy-equipment shed. And the week after that was the same, only with two Chinese riveters pitted against a walking scrapheap of domestic-service units. This was such a success that Jimmy Guang went looking for a larger venue, and found a hangar outside the Russian security perimeter at Osh's airport. It was three or four times the size of the university shed, and Jimmy Guang made sure that his gladiator fans knew that there was now room to bring their friends, and he painted large signs to hang on all four of the hangar's walls. JIMMY GUANG'S HOUSE OF GLADMECH, the signs proclaimed, "gladmech" being Jimmy Guang's zippy coinage for the mayhem that occurred inside. And beneath that, NO VIOLENCE EXCEPT BETWEEN MECHS. Jimmy Guang had made it clear to Captain Butsayev, and to the local IF commander he knew only as Fouad, that the first killing or serious maiming that oc-

curred at one of his matches would be the last. All agreed
that the airport hangar should be a war-free zone.

And thus it was that Jimmy Guang's House of Gladmech became the only place in Kyrgyzstan where Russians and locals could meet without violence.

Things were going well for Jimmy Guang. He was making
enough money to have his suit mended and take Marta for
dinners at Fez and the odd German-Chinese restaurant
near the destroyed municipal building, the Russians and
the Kirghiz and the IF would all do business with him, and
he was discovering that it in fact felt good to be doing a little good in the midst of so much misery. He imagined that
somewhere, someday, militant robot-rights types would
hear of his activities and pillory him as the worst kind of
murderous slaver; but it seemed to him that if he could
carve out a space wherein enemies could meet without
killing, it was worth the loss of a bunch of mechs who
would soon have been rusting in a boneyard anyway.

And he was falling deeply in love with Marta.

Wartime romances are odd things, Jimmy Guang considered one day after Marta had left his office in a smol-
dering fury. Lovers are hard to each other, as if angry
words and bitter actions can test one's ability to weather
war. As if one must worry not just about stray bullets or
microorganisms, but about one's lover being emptied of
humanity by the proximity of war.

Marta had been testing him, he thought. It was unclear
whether he had passed.

Yevgeny had stopped into his office while she was visiting, and a long look had passed between him and Marta
before she disappeared behind the curtain into his small
personal space. "I've found some real prizes for you,"
Yevgeny said. "American seafloor mining mechs, complete with cutting torches and shaped charges."

"In the name of the Prophet," said Jimmy Guang, "I can't let shaped charges into my arena. What happens if one isn't aimed exactly at the opponent and I lose a whole section of spectators? I'd be ruined."

Yevgeny shrugged. "Okay, if you don't want them."

"No, I do want them. But take out anything explosive. Cutting torches, okay. Those aren't going to hurt anyone. But no bombs."

"Whatever you say. You Muslim?"

Jimmy Guang hesitated. Religion was not a topic he wanted to broach with Russian soldiers, even one he'd done business with. "My father," he said slowly.

Yevgeny looked more closely at him. "Right," he said, nodding. "Thought you were just Chinese, but I can see the Arab in you now." Another long look, then the Russian scratched his nose. "I'm surprised the captain does business with you."

Jimmy Guang waited. If Yevgeny couldn't tell Persian from Arab, Jimmy Guang wasn't going to give him a lesson.

"Not that Butsayev has anything against Muslims, but he's got a brother who," Yevgeny clicked his tongue, "isn't reasonable on the topic." Yevgeny grinned as if he was about to let Jimmy Guang in on a great private joke. "Captain's brother Slava, he collects the teeth of the women he catches alone on the street at night. He practically rattles, all the teeth in his pockets."

"When can I pick up these American robots, Yevgeny?" asked Jimmy Guang. Tomorrow, answered Yevgeny, and then he left the shop.

Jimmy Guang felt as if invisible tar had been poured over him. Blood roared in his ears, and every sound that came from the street—voices, the grinding of ancient transmissions, the coo of the pigeons that roosted under his waning—was subtly deformed. When Marta touched his shoulder, he was too thickly entangled to move.

"I know what you're thinking," she said softly. "But don't."

With great effort he turned his head. Marta's eyes spitted him, and he felt crushed between her terrible anger and the ferocity of his own hate for this Russian who collected women's teeth.

Slava Butsayev, he thought. Who fixes my robots. Who drinks my vodka and shares my cigars. Slava Butsayev whose company I have grown to enjoy.

"Don't," Marta said again.

He could not answer.

"Jimmy," Marta said. "Too many people are dying."

"Or perhaps the wrong people," he said, his voice barely above a whisper.

She held his gaze for another long moment, then looked away from him. "Do you ever think about what your gladiator robots really are?"

The change of topic threw him off balance. "They're robots," he said.

"They're stand-ins, Jimmy. The Russians look at them and see my brothers. The Kirghiz look at them and see Russians. The whole thing makes a sport of killing, makes it something to wager on."

Jimmy Guang checked his temper. He went to the window and spoke to it since he was for the moment too angry to speak to her. "Two men run into each other in the bush, up in the mountains. One is Russian, one Kirghiz, or Afghan, or Pakistani. Nobody else around. They sight down the barrels of their rifles at each other, and then they recognize each other. From where? From Jimmy Guang's House of Gladmech. And they lower their guns and walk on and they forget it ever happened, and when their superiors ask for a report, they lie." He turned to Marta. "If that happens just once, what do robots matter?"

"But you're just substituting death for death," she said, her voice rising. "You create this false oasis for people. It doesn't stop anyone wanting to kill, it just makes them want to kill for sport. The men in the hangar, don't you think that each of them imagines that it's his enemy dismembered and leaking into the sand?"

"What if they do?" he shouted. "What if they do? They're not killing each other right then, at that exact moment, and that's all. That exact moment."

Marta had withdrawn from him when he raised his voice. "Some of them don't deserve that, Jimmy," she said, shrunk deep into her coat. The cold fury in her voice frightened him because he could not tell whether he was its object. "They think about nothing but killing, and they deserve nothing but killing themselves."

She stormed out onto Lenin Street. Jimmy Guang straightened his tie and stood staring at the wall for a long time trying to pick apart Marta's knotty contradictions. His shop smelled like dust blown in from the street. Late that night he still hadn't decided whether she had left him with permission or a command, or which command.

The Russians' electronic surveillance was generally several generations more sophisticated than what most of the IF rebels in Kyrgyzstan had, but there were exceptions, and one of them was a thin, pigeon-toed young Afghan named Pavel, who had studied at Moscow University before becoming radicalized by the news that the Russians had exterminated his family in what became known as the Centennial Offensive, a bulldozing push through Kandahar in 2079. Like all large cities, Moscow had a carefully-disguised IF presence, and before long Pavel and his excellent education were on their way to the Tien Shan, where every night guerrillas set up remote rocket launchers and every morning the Russians came to destroy them. Picking through the rubble of launchers, automated Russian hunter-killers, and the occasional aircraft, Pavel put together an information-gathering apparatus that was without peer in the Ferghana Valley.

Jimmy Guang found Pavel in the city, deep in the sub-basement of the university's administration building. The building itself had long since collapsed, but the sub-basement was intact and the underground campus data network largely intact. From the sub-basement, Pavel could receive information safely from a number of remote sensing stations he had arranged in the foothills surrounding Osh. He could not broadcast for fear of detection, but he could transmit via the university network, which had surviving cable strung as far as the airport and an observatory some twenty kilometers to the east.

What a strange war this is, thought Jimmy Guang as he patiently endured the search inflicted by Pavel's guards. The Russians have satellites, infrared detection, missiles beyond counting, automated helicopters. The IF rebels have, by and large, weapons out of the twentieth century, except when their benefactors in Riyadh or Kuala Lumpur or Tripoli manage to sneak newer equipment through the Kashmir and over the Tien Shan. Still no one is going to win any time soon.

"Jimmy Guang," Pavel said. They had traded on several occasions, and Jimmy Guang had come to like this pallid fanatic who fought not because he believed that he could redress the wrongs done him, but because he did not know what else to do with his grief.

"Pavel." Next to Pavel's voice, Jimmy Guang's sounded like the croak of a crow. Pavel had a beautiful voice, rich and liquid. In another time, he would have been in a university sub-basement broadcasting on the college radio station. "I need you to track a Russian for me, Pavel. And I need a gun."

Pavel looked at him with new interest.

"An old gun. A Colt .45 automatic, or perhaps a Smith and Wesson. From before World War Two."

"I thought you were the man who could get things," said Pavel.

Jimmy Guang took off his belt, unzipped its interior pocket, and counted out three thousand American dollars in twenties and fifties. "I cannot be seen inquiring after this item," he said. "Already I have put my life in your hands finding you things for your little electronic cerebellum here. You have done the same for me, and we Chinese have a saying: when you save a man's life, you become responsible for him. So we are responsible for each other."

"You are Chinese at your convenience," Pavel said. "Is your Islam so convenient?"

Jimmy Guang's hands began to tremble. But when he spoke, his voice did not. " 'They scheme and scheme: and I, too, scheme and scheme. Therefore bear with the unbelievers, and let them be a while.' "

The verse was from the *surah* of the Koran called *The Nightly Visitant*. Jimmy Guang had read it when he was a small boy, and been horrified by it, by the way its patient hatred spoke to him across centuries. Quickly he turned to other, more comfortable passages, and he asked his father about the verse. "The Koran was written by men," Reza Hamid had said, "and it contains them at their worst as well as at their best. It is a human book that aspires toward God."

A small part of Reza Hamid's son was saddened that the verse no longer seemed so horrible to him.

Pavel looked at the money for as long as it took Jimmy Guang to get his heart rate under control. Then he picked up the bills, tapped them even like a deck of cards, and slipped them into his pocket.

"Why an old gun?" he asked.

"Pavel," said Jimmy Guang with grim humor. "Please. I do not ask you why you need to track satellites."

By *the time* he left the university campus, Jimmy Guang knew that after his patrol shift and time spent puttering among robots at the House of Gladmech, Slava Butsayev drank in a nameless bar near the bazaar, and that some nights he set out from there looking for solitary Kirghiz women. This last activity was said to be less and less frequent over the recent months, a fact that gave Jimmy Guang momentary pause.

That night, Jimmy Guang watched as the excellent American mining robots destroyed each other for the enjoyment of perhaps eighteen hundred windburned and war-hardened Russians, Kirghiz, Uzbeks, Afghans, and miscellaneous others, including a wary knot of sharply dressed Russians who could only be government observers. Captain Butsayev sat with them. These new mining mechs were sophisticated enough to improvise, and early in the evening one of them began taunting its opponents. Quickly it became the crowd favorite, and when it had survived the destruction of its fellows, Jimmy Guang realized he had his first returning champion.

This is like a license to print money, he thought. He spoke to this robot after the matches.

The conversation left him obscurely disappointed. Afterward, he supposed he had wanted the robot to demonstrate the kind of fire one expected of great athletes.

"You fought well," said Jimmy Guang. "Much better than any other mech we've had so far. And the crowds particularly appreciate the way you taunt the opposition."

Slava arrived and began spot-welding a patch onto the mech's back. Jimmy Guang congratulated himself for maintaining a cool exterior.

The robot's voice was a smooth baritone, its inflections nearly human. "I assumed they would, and as a strategy I had nothing to lose by it. If my opponents devote CPU time to analyzing my taunts and formulating retorts, that increases my chances of winning. Also, if the crowd begins to support me, I anticipate that you will be more forthcoming with necessary repairs and maintenance."

"You are a clever machine," said Jimmy Guang. "You use all tools to stay alive."

"No. I am programmed to maintain optimal functionality. Whatever action I take is directed to that end."

Jimmy Guang was storing this up as evidence against his imagined future robot-rights persecutors. "You don't care about staying alive?"

"My programming imbues a preference for awareness over oblivion," said the robot, "but I neither enjoy the first nor fear the second. You put me out on the arena floor to destroy the others. That is what I will do."

While these words were still rolling in his head, Jimmy Guang tried to avoid remembering the conversation he'd had with Marta the day before, but in his sleep that night he saw the surviving gladiator taunting Russian soldiers who surrounded it with railguns and rocket launchers, and in his sleep he was oppressed by a hope that it would survive.

The next morning, a ten-year-old boy staggered into his shop, bent under the weight of a bag of coffee beans. With a gasp of relief, he dropped the bag to the floor and stood expectantly until Jimmy Guang fished in his pocket for whatever coins he had handy.

Once the boy had gone, Jimmy Guang took the bag into the curtained-off portion of the office. He slit it open, and his heart fluttered in his throat. He took a deep breath, smelling the coffee, and plunged his hands into the beans. At the bottom of the bag he found a canvas bundle. Inside the canvas bundle was a Colt .45 automatic that could

have come from the hand of John Dillinger. It was
cleaned, oiled, and loaded.

And here I am, thought Jimmy Guang. I have decided
to kill a man, and here is the weapon I will use to do it.

Was he falling into the war? Had he lost his ability to
stay apart from it, to keep it in its proper perspective?
Surely there were IF soldiers who raped women, who
committed atrocities.

Surely. But none of them had broken Marta.

He heard his door open. Stowing the gun in his desk,
Jimmy Guang went out front, arranging the knot of his tie
as he went. Captain Butsayev was waiting for him.

"Jimmy Guang," he said. "I fear there is going to be
trouble. You noticed the delegation that sat with me last
night."

Jimmy Guang nodded.

"They commented on the superlative show put on by
the robots," said Captain Butsayev, "which is to your
credit. But they also gave me to understand that they were
gravely unsettled by the intermingling of Russian soldiers
and locals. The lack of animosity disturbed them. They
consider it inappropriate for a time of war, and they demanded that the performances be ended." Incredibly, Butsayev smiled. "But I stood up for you. I noted the effect of
the House of Gladmech on morale, and argued—strenu-
ously, I might add—that this benefit outweighed any possible detrimental effect of fraternization." The captain
clapped Jimmy Guang on the shoulder. "Not to mention
the fact that working on your robots helps to keep young
Slava out of trouble. I believe that the delegation was
swayed by my arguments. Your shows can go on."

All of this washed over Jimmy Guang like a surprise
rainstorm. "Thank you," he said. The gun in his desk
drawer loomed hugely in his mind, and he tried without
success to inject some warmth into his tone of voice. "I
believe that you are right about the benefit of the House of

Gladmech, and I thank you for your courage in supporting me at what must have been some risk to your career."

"You're certainly welcome," Butsayev said. "I meant what I said." After a pause, he furrowed his brow and said, "Are you all right?"

Jimmy Guang was saved from having to answer by the entrance of Marta. She saw him before Butsayev, and she smiled at him. Out of the corner of his eye, Jimmy Guang saw Butsayev notice her missing teeth. The Russian's gaze flicked over to Jimmy Guang, who gave no sign that he had noticed.

So you know, he thought. You know about your brother, or at least you've heard rumors. But you protect him, of course. He's your brother. And after all, these aren't Russian girls.

"Captain Butsayev, this is my companion Marta Chu," he said, with what he thought was the right admixture of formality and warmth. "Marta, Captain Vasily Butsayev."

Butsayev snapped a shallow bow. "Miss Chu," he said.

Marta's hand darted to her mouth before she could stop it. Self-conscious, she returned it to her side and nodded at Butsayev. "Captain."

"Captain Butsayev has just informed me that my glad-mech operation has ruffled the feathers of Russian bureaucrats," Jimmy Guang said with a too-broad smile. "He says that we should continue to ruffle, and not worry about their squawking."

Marta's answering smile looked tired and forced. "A little fortune," she said.

Butsayev, sensing the tension in the room, nodded to Jimmy Guang. "In the midst of war, one does what one can," he said, and shut the door softly behind him.

They went to Fez for lunch on the patio, and as the waiter was clearing away their soup bowls the top three floors of a building at the other end of the square blew away in a tremendous explosion. The concussion of the blast felt like a giant thumb jabbed into each of Jimmy Guang's ears. He leaped out of his chair to grasp Marta, but she was faster than he was and had already ducked into the restaurant. From there they watched as six Russians in full suits approached the burning building. As its surviving occupants emerged, the Russians rounded them up, directing them to a waiting flatbed truck.

With a flash one of the suited Russians blew apart. The sound, a flat crack compared to the deep boom of whatever had destroyed the building, nevertheless made Jimmy Guang flinch. The other five Russians turned as one and raked the doorway with railgun fire. The people coming out were obliterated, and part of the doorway caved in.

They stand there, thought Jimmy Guang, inside their shiny suits. Like robots themselves, uplinked and shunted so they can move faster than I can think. It was difficult to imagine that a human being inhabited those suits.

Another Russian detonated, the shining green fragments of his suit clanging down on the stones of the square, and the remaining four abruptly changed their tactics. Backing away in an expanding arc, they poured railgun fire into the building and twenty seconds later another rocket destroyed it completely. Smoke hung in the square, and as the echoes died away the sounds of panicked voices formed a background to the creak and groan of shifting rubble.

He had seen it all before, but something in the horror of the moment provoked Jimmy Guang. "If you could get out of here," he asked Marta, "where would you go?"

"Today there is no out of here," she said. "Some days there is, but not today."

He was thinking about this as they walked in the square the next morning on their way to the bazaar in search of apples. The fires in the destroyed building were out, and shirtless laborers under the direction of Russian soldiers worked to clear the rubble. Fresh pockmarks pitted the pavement, and blood had sunk into the stones of the square like dirt in the creases of a hand. The workers called out and began digging a body free of the wreckage.

It's not working, Jimmy Guang thought. What if they do watch the matches without killing each other? What does it matter if later this happens?

"Marta," he said to distract her. She was looking at the body and the workmen and the soldiers too, and he wanted her to think of something else. He wanted her to think about him, to understand that he asked her questions to find out if his answers were the same as hers.

"I've never been to India. You grew up in India, didn't you?" she said.

"Also Hong Kong and Bangladesh. My father was an engineer. He met my mother in Shanghai while building a bridge, and married her before its span was complete. I am named for the nickname of an ancestor of hers who worked on railroads in the United States." Two hundred years ago, that had been. Jimmy Guang supposed he still had relatives in America, in San Francisco or New York maybe. For a fleeting moment he thought of asking Marta if she would go to America with him. He thought he had enough money to do it.

Marta smiled at him. "You with your American name," she said, "and your old-fashioned American clothes. I love you, Jimmy Guang Hamid. If I could ever get out of here I would go with you to Hong Kona or Bangladesh or Shanghai or anywhere."

His American mining-robot champion somehow acquired the name John Wayne. It continued to dispose of any opponents, and Jimmy Guang grew afraid that the monotony of its victories would cut into audience interest.

About a week after Marta's promise, though—which Jimmy Guang carried with him like a charm—a Russian army truck pulled up in front of the House of Gladmech. Jimmy Guang was there overseeing welders who were patching one of the hangar's walls, which had been partially shredded by a rocket attack from the mountains the night before. Slava Butsayev was elsewhere, which was good. Jimmy Guang hadn't worked up the nerve to kill him yet, and he didn't trust himself to keep up his friendly façade when other things were aggravating him.

Maniacs, he was thinking as the truck ground to a halt. Don't they know not to target this building by now?

A beefy and florid soldier hopped out of the truck's cab and came directly to Jimmy Guang. "You Jimmy Guang?" he said, pointing at the sign on the hangar.

"Yes," said Jimmy Guang.

"I have a robot in my truck there that will take your John Wayne apart," the Russian said.

Possibilities unfolded in Jimmy Guang's head. "I assume you're willing to wager on that," he said.

The big match took place the next night: John Wayne, the American seafloor miner, against Lokomotiv Lev, liberated from an abandoned factory in Bishkek and retooled by bored Russian combat engineers. Jimmy Guang had a feeling that John Wayne was about to meet an Indian he couldn't kill or outsmart.

The House of Gladmech was packed and sweaty. It had been a hot day, and even with the hangar doors open, a faint fog of perspiration hung in the cones of light from ceiling lamps. Lokomotiv Lev's partisans, a group of Russian perimeter guards from Bishkek, sat near the normal crowd of Butsayev's men from the Osh garrison. They formed an olive-green cluster amid the riot of Uzbek weaves and kaffiyeh worn by the locals. Jimmy Guang

himself was wearing his suit, but he had gone to the only
Western clothing store in Osh to buy a new tie for the oc-
casion, and his shoes were polished to a quiet shine. The
Colt automatic rested heavily in the small of his back. He
wasn't sure why he'd brought it, but the night was fraught
with uncertainty, and he hadn't wanted to feel unprepared.

He had a tremendous amount of money riding on the
match. Fully three-quarters of the evening's receipts were
at stake. If John Wayne suffered a defeat, Jimmy Guang
would be without enough liquid cash to complete the pur-
chase of tobacco and foot powder he had been negotiating
with a Pakistani trader who would not return to Osh until
spring. Without those goods, his income potential—and
with it his dream of running to Shanghai or Delhi with
Marta—would be severely injured.

If he won, though . . . and if the Russians paid up . . .
he would have enough money to get them both anywhere.
Berlin, perhaps. Sydney. San Francisco; he could look up
relatives. Jimmy Guang's stomach fluttered.

Marta entered the hangar and took a place on a raised
bench against one wall. He was glad to see her. She caught
his eye and waved. Big night for her too, he thought. She
knows what's at stake.

Then Slava Butsayev walked in, worked his way
through the crowd, and sat next to his brother. Marta's
face turned to stone. Jimmy Guang watched Captain Butsayev closely for the next few minutes. The officer
greeted his brother, touched him on the shoulder, made
space for him on the bench; but no pleasantries, no exchange of affection, took place. He knows, Jimmy Guang
thought, just as he had thought days before in his office.
He knows, and he despises his brother, but blood is blood.

Slava Butsayev never sat in the stands with the other
Russians. Did he have friends among Lokomotiv Lev's
crew? That seemed most likely. Jimmy Guang had a para-
noid spasm; had Slava sabotaged John Wayne? Did he

have some arrangement with the Lev's builders? The idea
passed as quickly as it had arisen. Slava takes pride in his
work on the mech, Jimmy Guang thought. He wouldn't
throw a match.

Whatever the reason for Slava's action, his visibility
gave the evening an entirely different flavor. Jimmy
Guang looked back to where Marta sat near the wall.

She was getting up. She did not look in his direction as
she left.

Angry and fearful, Jimmy Guang raced through his
prematch patter, leaning heavily on the crowd to bet local,
to show some pride in Osh. He played shamelessly on
whatever regional animosities he could think of and chan-
neled them into ferocious wagering. By the time the
mechs themselves appeared, the floor was thrumming
with the stomping of feet and dust was sifting down from
the rafters.

John Wayne destroyed Lokomotiv Lev in less than ten
minutes. The Russian robot lumbered to the center of the
ring looking purely invincible: squat, barely human in
shape, with customized steel plating welded around its
sensing apparatus and most joints. It looked as if Lev's
crew had scavenged the armor from a tank. They had also,
it appeared, amped up the grasping power of the pincers
that served Lev for hands and provided the robot with
epoxy sprayers and other nozzles whose function Jimmy
Guang couldn't begin to fathom. Still, John Wayne was
quicker, and more importantly, he had adapted himself to
the idea that he was fighting for his life—or, as he pre-
ferred it, optimal functionality. Lokomotiv Lev had been
programmed to destroy John Wayne; John Wayne to survive. So Lev managed to glue shut John Wayne's primary
torch, encouraged by the hoarse shouts of the Bishkek
Russian contingent (and some of the more fundamentalist
IF guerrillas, who hated modernity and blamed it on
America). Then Lev caught and tore away a significant

amount of John Wayne's external plating, and for a brief
moment it looked as if the Bishkek mech would get its
pincers into John Wayne's internals. The voice of the
crowd grew constricted, frenzied. John Wayne's escape
brought them back into full-throated roar, and the mo-
mentum of the match seemed to shift. Lev couldn't keep
the American in one place for long enough to bring its full
strength to bear. And while it tried, John Wayne danced to
the side and slashed at Lev's joints with his remaining
torch until, as a thundering cheer rose from the weave-
and-kaffiyeh side of the arena, Lev's left leg failed entirely and it toppled to that side. Within a minute, John
Wayne had disabled both of Lev's pincers, and shortly
after that Lokomotiv Lev was fit only for Pavel to scav-
enge gyros and CPU space.

The room of the old hangar rattled with the fierce roars
of the winning side. The uproar was deafening, and grew
a sharp edge as the Russians from Bishkek got up and left,
leaving their champion to leak hydraulic fluid into the
sand. What an odd stew of rivalries here, thought Jimmy
Guang: Russians and Kirghiz, different divisions of Russians, even a strange flavor of the old Russian-American
Cold War. Money changed hands in thick handfuls, and
parts of the crowd broke into spontaneous chants that reminded Jimmy Guang of the fenced-off portions of Euro-
pean soccer stadia. Look what I've done, he thought as
John Wayne clanked and whirred toward him. He snapped
the robot a mock salute, and John Wayne saluted back.
Over the robot's shoulder Jimmy Guang saw Slava Butsayev get up and follow the Bishkek group, and he knew
at that moment that he could wait no longer.

Butsayev and the Bishkek Russians found their way to
his favorite bar, and there they drank until the sky was beginning to lighten. Meeting out on the street in front of the
bar, they began shouting at each other. Jimmy Guang's
Russian wasn't good enough to determine the source of

the disagreement, but it grew heated, and after a sudden flurry of punches, the Bishkek group began walking in the direction of the airport. Slava Butsayev watched them go. After a moment, he called something after them, some Russian colloquialism Jimmy Guang had never heard before. Then Butsayev set off down a side street, wending his way toward the area of the bazaar.

Jimmy Guang was stiff and chilly from his vigil, which he had kept from the vantage of a second-floor balcony in an empty apartment house opposite the bar. He resisted the impulse to shoot Butsayev right then and there: apart from the difficulty of hitting someone with a pistol shot from that distance, there was the question of propriety. Jimmy Guang Hamid was a man who did things a certain way, as his mother had plotted graphs a certain way in her classrooms or his father held the pencil a certain way when drafting. He had never killed a man, had never fired a gun, and if he was to do it now it would have to be done in a certain way. So he followed Slava Butsayev through the twisting ancient streets near the bazaar, and it was not until Butsayev came upon a teenage girl sweeping a crooked concrete porch in front of a building honeycombed with darkened windows that Jimmy Guang removed the gun from the waistband of his trousers. The trousers immediately sunk onto his hips, and he hoped that they did not sink any further to trip him up in what might follow.

Butsayev acted with the speed and decisiveness of a hunter, rather than the swagger of the torturer. He made as if to walk past the girl, who had stopped sweeping and dropped her eyes toward the street as he approached. He said something to her and reached out to curl her hair around his fingers. She flinched, and his hand clenched.

Now, thought Jimmy Guang. Before he can do anything.

"Corporal Butsayev," he said, and Butsayev froze.

When he saw who had addressed him, though, a sly grin split his face, which was like his brother's only in coloration. "Robot Guy," he said. "Want in on the fun?"

Jimmy Guang brought the gun up and pointed it at Butsayev's nose. "You are a despicable man," he said, "and you do despicable things."

He pulled the trigger, and the Colt went off with a tremendous bang. Jimmy Guang's arm leaped up, and his hand, numbed by the recoil, let go of the gun. The muzzle flash faded from his eyes, and he saw Slava Butsayev lying on his left side in the street. There was a hole punched in Butsayev's face, just to the left of his nose and below his eye. The eye was rolled back, showing only white.

His fall had pulled the girl to the ground beside him. She was streaked with blood. As if picking lice off herself, she removed the dead man's hand from her hair finger by finger. "You should go home," Jimmy Guang said, and she ran into the building whose porch she had been sweeping.

The sky in the east was pale blue. Jimmy Guang dropped the gun near Butsayev's head and squatted next to the corpse. He rummaged through Butsayev's pockets until he found a small drawstring bag. When he pulled it from Butsayev's coat, its seam split, and teeth fell to the stones of the street. He cupped the bag in his palm and replaced the teeth carefully, one at a time. Pinching the seam between his fingers, Jimmy Guang walked back toward Lenin Street as the first curious faces began to appear in the windows around him.

The angel said to Mohammed: *God has knowledge of all the good you do.* Jimmy Guang's father had often reminded his son of this. The verse comforted Jimmy Guang, made him feel as if he was important, noticed, his actions weighed fairly and with sympathy. That was a God he could believe in, take solace in. But as he walked slowly back to his office, the knowledge that God watched him filled Jimmy Guang with deep sadness and shame. He had killed a man. He had become part of the war, and something of him had been lost.

He went directly through the bazaar to Osh's ancient old quarter, the survivinq Osh of Alexander the Great and Mohammed and, if you believed local traditions, King Solomon as well. And now Marta, who lived in a dusty stone building with her parents and sisters. All of her brothers were up in the mountains fighting the Russians.

Jimmy Guang stopped in the street before her house to straighten his tie and tighten his belt, which he had let out a notch to accommodate the gun. He ran his handkerchief quickly over his shoes, patted at his hair, and only then knocked on the front door of the Chu house.

Marta herself answered. Over her shoulder Jimmy Guang could see her parents. They were smaller than she was, and both beginning to be a bit hunchbacked. She was tall, taller than Jimmy Guang, with strong hands.

"It's early, Jimmy," she said.

He took her arm and led her out, shutting the door behind her and waving quickly at her parents. "I have something to show you," he said when they were outside. Traffic was just beginning to appear on the narrow street, bicycles and an oxcart or two. It struck Jimmy Guang that the year could be 1930 instead of 2083. Somewhere the Russians had satellites that could tell the color of your eyes, and somewhere there were aircraft guided by robots smarter than the recently-departed Lokomotiv Lev, and in the mountains Uplinked Russian soldiers patrolled with inhuman precision; but here on this street Osh was as Osh had always been. There was something quietly defiant about it.

Jimmy Guang removed the bag of teeth from his

pocket and held it out to Marta. She took it, and teeth spilled from the open seam. Jimmy Guang had a moment of irrational fear that Russian soldiers would rise from the teeth, as in a story his father had read to him once. Instead, Marta let out a scream and flung the bag to the ground. She covered her face and began to sob. The teeth rattled like dice on the street.

"Marta," he said, wanting to touch her but afraid.

"It took you after all," Marta said through her hands. "The war, it took you."

For a long while he didn't know what to say. It was true.

"I thought that's what you wanted," he said at last.

She rubbed at her eyes, then closed the distance between them with a step. "We have to get out of here," she said. "Now. Come with me."

"Where are we going?" he asked.

"It doesn't matter where we go. The war is here. It's claiming you, Jimmy." She looked at him. Saw him hesitating, and knew why.

An impulse seized Jimmy Guang. He took all of the evening's winnings from his inside coat pocket. "Here," he said, and closed one of Marta's hands around the thick wad of dollars and rubles and euros and rupees and God only knew what else. "Take this and go to Pavel. Wait for me."

Her face grew still.

"Just until sundown," Jimmy Guang pleaded. "Just wait until sundown."

When he got back to the office, Russian soldiers were waiting for him.

"What do you expect of me?" Captain Vasily Butsayev asked Jimmy Guang Hamid.

They were standing in a field southwest of Osh. Distant thunder rolled down on them from a jet passing far overhead. Jimmy Guang listened, and he listened to the wind, and he watched the dry grass bend, and he smelled the mountains. Captain Butsayev was going to kill him, he was sure, and Jimmy Guang was saddened by this because it meant he had overestimated the captain from their first meeting.

About five hundred yards away stood the House of Gladmech. The wall facing them was patched with rusting rectangles of corrugated tin scavenged from other hangars destroyed in various assaults. One of the patches covered part of the sign on that wall, and Jimmy Guang pursed his lips in annoyance. If he survived the afternoon he would have that fixed.

Jimmy Guang realized that although he did not want to, he would have to speak. So he decided to speak truthfully.

"Your brother was an evil man who preyed on women," he said, looking Butsayev in the eye. "I am in love with one of those women, and because I love her I had to kill your brother. I had to try to heal her, and your brother's life was like an infection in her spirit. She could not live while he did, and I need her, Captain Butsayev. I need her very badly to live."

Butsayev looked toward the mountains. "You heal a woman by killing a man. You create an illusionary peace among men by making a spectacle of destroying robots. If I were close to you, Mr. Hamid, I would fear your impulses to do good deeds." Still speaking softly, Butsayev quoted: " 'Do not walk proudly on the earth. You cannot cleave the earth, nor can you rival the mountains in stature.' "

A Russian officer quoting from the Koran. Jimmy Guang could not decide whether this was a good omen or bad.

"My actions were not meant to be prideful," he said, and almost said more, but stopped himself. "Captain Butsayev. I will no longer defend myself. I have done what I have done, and you shall do what you shall do. Given the same situation again, a thousand times, I would kill your brother a thousand times."

Butsayev waved an arm over his head, a gesture of some sort to someone Jimmy Guang couldn't see. A rocket tore through the air, and Jimmy Guang's House of Gladmech exploded in an expanding cloud of dirty smoke. Large pieces of its metal walls flew up into the air and came slanting crazily back down to embed themselves in the earth.

John Wayne was in there, Jimmy Guang thought.

"Nor do I do that out of pride, Mr. Hamid," said Butsayev. "Leave now. Go with your woman, go back where you came from. Leave war to those of us who have made it our profession. And remember: I am not a butcher like my brother. But neither am I a weak man. Go now."

Butsayev walked toward his waiting jeep, leaving Jimmy Guang alone in the field. A wave of sorrow overcame him. For the House of Gladmech, yes, but mostly for Vasily Butsayev, whose respect Jimmy Guang realized he had treasured.

When he got to Pavel's, Marta was no longer there. "She said she was going to find her brothers," Pavel said. "You were to follow her."

"Where are her brothers?"

Pavel looked at Jimmy Guang, a small quirk at the corner of his mouth. "Do you understand what I am telling you? She is going to the mountains. If she is going to the mountains, it is not up to me to tell you where to find her."

Another test, thought Jimmy Guang. He did not think she was leaving him, no. Pavel might smirk, but Jimmy Guang had been smirked at before. He knew what he knew. She feared the war in him, the way it had crept into the corners of his mind, and when he had followed her through the rocks and the snow and the privations of the Tien Shan, he would be purified again. She would see him and know that this was true, that what had drawn him to the war was gone in the blast of a rocket and that she herself had drawn him away from it again. Perhaps he would find her in the mountains, among the militias and the mujahideen. Perhaps she would have gone ahead of him to Shanghai, or Delhi, and he would find her waiting for him at his father's house with a cup of tea in her hand.

Droplet

Benjamin Rosenbaum

*It's nice to have a purpose in life and to be able to fulfill
that purpose—although, as the slyly entertaining story that
follows will demonstrate, if you're a robot built to serve
humans and you've survived into a future where there are
no humans left, that may be a bit of a problem . . .*

*New writer Benjamin Rosenbaum has made sales to
The Magazine of Fantasy & Science Fiction, Asimov's
Science Fiction, Argosy, The Infinite Matrix, Strange
Horizons, Harper's, McSweeney's, Lady Churchill's
Rosebud Wristlet, and elsewhere. Recently returned from
a long stay in Switzerland, he now lives with his family in
Falls Church, Virginia.*

Visit his website at home.datacomm.ch/benrose.

1.

Today Shar is Marilyn Monroe. That's an erotic goddess
from prehistoric cartoon mythology. She has golden curls,
blue eyes, big breasts, and skin of a shocking pale pink.
She stands with a wind blowing up from Hades beneath
her, trying to control her skirt with her hands, forever
showing and hiding her white silk underwear.

Today I am Shivol'riargh, a more recent archetype of
feminine sexuality. My skin is hard, hairless, glistening
black. Faint fractal patterns of darker black writhe across
my surfaces. I have long claws. It suits my mood.

We have just awakened from a little nap of a thousand

years, our time, during which the rest of the world aged
even more.

She goes: "kama://01-nbX5-# . . ."

I snap the channel shut. "Talk language if you want to
seduce me."

Shar pouts. With those little red lips and those inno-
cent, yet knowing, eyes, it's almost irresistible. I resist.

"Come on, Narra," she says. "Do we have to fight
about this every time we wake up?"

"I just don't know why we have to keep flying around
like this."

"You're not scared of Warboys again?" she asks.

Her fingertips slide down my black plastic front. The
fractals dance around them.

"There aren't any more," she says.

"You don't know that, Shar."

"They've all killed each other. Or turned themselves
off. Warboys don't last if there's nothing to fight."

Despite the cushiony-pink Marilyn Monroe skin, Shar
is harder than I am. My heart races when I look at her, just
as it did a hundred thousand years ago.

Her expression is cool. She wants me. But it's a game
to her.

She's searching the surface of me with her hands.

"What are you looking for?" I mean both in the Galaxy
and on my skin, though I know the answers.

"Anything," she says, answering the broader question.
"Anyone who's left. People to learn from. To play with."

People to serve, I think nastily.

I'm lonely, too, of course, but I'm sick of looking. Let
them come find us in the Core.

"It's so stupid," I groan. Her hands are affecting me.
"We probably won't be able to talk to them anyway."

Her hands find what they've been searching for: the
hidden opening to Shivol'riargh's sexual pocket. It's full
of the right kind of nerve endings. Shivol'riargh is hard on

the outside, but oh so soft on the inside. Sometimes I wish
I had someone to wear that *wasn't* sexy.

"We'll figure it out," she says in a voice that's all
breath.

Her fingers push at the opening of my sexual pocket. I
hold it closed. She leans against me and wraps her other
arm around me for leverage. She pushes. I resist.

Her lips are so red. I want them on my face.

She's cheating. She's a lot stronger than Marilyn Monroe.

"Shar, I don't want to screw," I say. "I'm still angry."

But I'm lying.

"Hush," she says.

Her fist slides into me and I gasp. My claws go around
her shoulders and I pull her to me.

2.

Later we turn the gravity off and float over Ship's bottom
eye, looking down at the planet Shar had Ship find. It's
blue like Marilyn Monroe's eyes.

"It's water," Shar says. Her arms are wrapped around
my waist, her breasts pressed against my back. She rests
her chin on my shoulder.

I grunt.

"It's water all the way down," she says. "You could
swim right through the planet to the other side."

"Did anyone live here?"

"I think so. I don't remember. But it was a gift from a
Sultan to his beloved."

Shar and I have an enormous amount of information
stored in our brains. The brain is a sphere the size of a billiard ball somewhere in our bodies, and however much we
change our bodies, we can't change that. Maka once told
me that even if Ship ran into a star going nine-tenths light-

speed, my billiard-ball brain would come tumbling out the other side, none the worse for wear. I have no idea what kind of matter it is or how it works, but there's plenty of room in my memory for all the stories of all the worlds in the Galaxy, and most of them are probably in there.

But we're terrible at accessing the factual information. A fact will pop up inexplicably at random—the number of Quantegral Lovergirls ever manufactured, for instance, which is 362,476—and be gone a minute later, swimming away in the murky seas of thought. That's the way Maka built us, on purpose. He thought it was cute.

3.

An *old argument* about Maka:

"He loved us," I say. I know he did.

Shar rolls her eyes (she's a tigress at the moment).

"I could feel it," I say, feeling stupid.

"Now there's a surprise. Maka designed you from scratch, including your feelings, and you feel that he loved you. Amazing." She yawns, showing her fangs.

"He made us more flexible than any other Lovergirls. Our minds are almost Interpreter-level."

She snorts. "We were trade goods, Narra. Trade goods. Classy purchasable or rentable items."

I curl up around myself. (I'm a python.)

"He set us free," I say.

Shar doesn't say anything for a while, because that is, after all, the central holiness of our existence. Our catechism, if you like.

Then she says gently: "He didn't need us for anything anymore, when they went into the Core."

"He could have just turned us off. He set us free. He gave us Ship."

She doesn't say anything.

"He loved us," I say.

I know it's true.

4.

I *don't tell* Shar, but that's one reason I want us to go back to the Galactic Core: Maka's there.

I know it's stupid. There's nothing left of Maka that I would recognize. The Wizards got hungrier and hungrier for processing power, so they could think more and know more and play more complicated games. Eventually the only thing that could satisfy them was to rebuild their brains as a soup of black holes. Black hole brains are very fast.

I know what happens when a person doesn't have a body anymore, too. For a while they simulate the sensations and logic of a corporeal existence, only with everything perfect and running much faster than in the real world. But their interests drift. The simulation gets more and more abstract and eventually they're just thoughts, and after a while they give that up, too, and then they're just numbers. By now Maka is just some very big numbers turning into some even bigger numbers, racing toward infinity.

I know because he told me. He knew what he was becoming.

I still miss him.

5.

We *go down* to the surface of the planet, which we decide to call Droplet.

The sky is painterly blue with strings of white clouds

drifting above great choppy waves. It's lovely. I'm glad Shar brought us here.

We're dolphins. We chase each other across the waves. We dive and hold our breaths, and shower each other with bubbles. We kiss with our funny dolphin noses.

I'm relaxing and floating when Shar slides her rubbery body over me and clamps her mouth onto my flesh. It's such a long time since I've been a cetacean that I don't notice that Shar is a *boy* dolphin until I feel her penis enter me. I buck with surprise, but Shar keeps her jaws clamped and rides me. Rides me and rides me, as I buck and swim, until she ejaculates. She makes it take extra long.

Afterward we race, and then I am floating, floating, exhausted and happy as the sunset blooms on the horizon.

It's a *very* impressive sunset, and I kick up on my tail to get a better look. I change my eyes and nose so I can see the whole spectrum and smell the entire wind.

It hits me first as fear, a powerful shudder that takes over my dolphin body, kicks me into the air and then into a racing dive, dodging and weaving. Then it hits me as knowledge, the signature written in the sunset: beryllium-10, mandelium, large-scale entanglement from muon dispersal. Nuclear and strange-matter weapons fallout. Warboys.

Ship dropped us a matter accelerator to get back up with, a series of rings floating in the water. I head for it.

Shar catches up and hangs on to me, changing into a human body and riding my back.

"Ssh, honey," she says, stroking me. "It's okay. There haven't been Warboys here for ten thousand years. . . ."

I buck her off, and this time I'm not flirting.

Shar changes her body below the waist back into a dolphin tail, and follows. As soon as she is in the first ring I tell Ship to bring us up, and one dolphin, one mermaid, and twelve metric tons of water shoot through the rings and up through the blue sky until it turns black and crowded with stars.

"Ten thousand years," says Shar as we hurtle up into the sky.

"You *picked* a planet Warboys had been on! Ship must have seen the signature."

"Narra, this wasn't a Warboy duel—they wouldn't dick around with nuclear for that. They must have been trying to exterminate a civilian population."

The water has all sprayed away now and we are tumbling through the thin air of the stratosphere.

"There's a chance they failed, Narra. Someone might be here, hidden. That's why we came."

"Warboys don't fail!"

We grow cocoons as we exit the atmosphere and hit orbit. After a couple of minutes, I feel Ship's long retrieval pseudopod slurp me in.

I lie in the warm cave of Ship's retrieval pseudopod. It's decorated with webs of green and blue. I remember when Shar decorated it. It was a long time ago, when we were first traveling.

I turn back into a human form and sit up.

Shar is lying nearby, picking at the remnants of her cocoon, silvery strands draped across her breasts.

"You want to die," I say.

"Don't be ridiculous, Narra."

"Shar, seriously. It's not enough for you—I'm not enough for you. You're looking for Warboys. You're trying to get killed." I feel a buzzing in my head, my breathing is constricted, aches shoot through my fist-clenched knuckles: clear signs that my emotional registers are full, the excess externalizing into pain.

She sighs. "Narra, I'm not that complicated. If I wanted to die, I'd just turn myself off." She grows legs and stands up.

"No, I don't think you can." What I'm about to say is

unfair, and too horrible. I'll regret it. I feel the blood pounding in my ears and I say it anyway: "Maybe Maka didn't free us all the way. Maybe he just gave us to each other. Maybe you can't leave me. You want to, but you can't."

Her eyes are cold. As I watch, the color drains out of them, from black to slate gray to white.

She looks like she wants to say a lot of things. Maybe: you stupid sentimental little girl. Maybe: it's you who wants to leave—to go back to your precious Maka, and if you had the brains to become a Wizard you would. Maybe: I want to live, but not the coward's life you keep insisting on.

She doesn't say any of them, though. She turns and walks away.

6.

I keep catching myself thinking it, and I know she's thinking it too. This person before me is the last other person I can reach, the only one to love me from now on in all the worlds of time. How long until she leaves me, as everyone else has left?

And how long can I stand her if she doesn't?

7.

The last people we met were a religious sect who lived in a beautiful crystal ship the size of a moon. They were Naturals and had old age and death and even children whom they bore themselves, who couldn't walk or talk at first or anything. They were sad for some complicated religious reason that Shar and I didn't understand. We cheered them up for a while by having sex with the ones their rules allowed to have sex and telling stories to the rest, but eventually they decided to all kill themselves anyway. We left before it happened.

Since then we haven't seen anyone. We don't know of anywhere that has people left.

I told Shar we could be passing people all the time and not know it. People changed in the Dispersal, and we're not Interpreters. There could be people with bodies made of gas clouds or out of the spins of elementary particles. We could be surrounded by crowds of them.

She said that just made her sadder.

8.

We go down to Droplet again. I smile and pretend it's all right. We spent a thousand years, our time, getting here; we might as well look around.

We change ourselves so we can breathe water, and head down into the depths. There are no fish on Droplet, no coral, no plankton. I can taste very simple nanomites, the standard kind every made world has for general upkeep. But all I see, looking down, is green-blue fading to deep blue fading to rich indigo and blackness.

Then there's a tickle on my skin.

I stop swimming and look around. Nothing but water.

The tickle comes again.

I send a sonar pulse to Shar ahead, telling her to wait.

I try to swim again but I can't. I feel fingers, hands, holding me, where there is only water. Stroking, pressing against my skin.

I change into a hard ball, Shivol'riargh without head or limbs, and turn down tactile until I can't tell the hands from the gentle current.

I fiddle with my perceptions until I remember how to send out a very fine sonar wave, and to enhance and filter

the data, discerning patterns in very fine perturbations of
the water. I subtract out the general currents and chaotic
swirls of the ocean, looking only for the motions of the
water that should not be there, and turn it into a three-
dimensional image of the space around me.

There are people here.

Their shapes—made of fine motions of the water—are
human shapes, tall, with graceful oblong heads that flatten
at the top to a frill.

They are running their watery hands over the surface of
me, poking and prodding.

From below, Shar is returning, approaching me. Some
of the water people cluster around her and stop her, holding her arms and legs.

She struggles. I cannot see her expression through the
murk.

The name "Nereids" swims up from the hidden
labyrinths of my memory. Not a word from this world, but
word enough.

The Nereids back away, arraying themselves as if for-
mally, three meters away from me on all sides. A sphere
of Nereids surrounds me.

Shar stops struggling. They let her go, pushing her outside the sphere.

One of the Nereids—tall, graceful, broad-shouldered—
breaks out of the formation and glides toward me. He
places his hands on my surface.

This, I tell myself to remember, is what we were designed for. Alone among the Quantegral Lovergirls, Shar
and I were given the flexibility and intelligence to serve
all the possible variations of post-Dispersal humanity. We
were designed to discover, at the very least, how to give
pleasure; and perhaps even how to communicate.

Still, I am afraid.

I let the hard shell of Shivol'riargh grow soft, I sculpt

my body back toward basic humanity; tall, thin, like the Nereids.

This close, my sonar sees the face shaped out of water smile. The Nereid raises his hands, palms out. I place my palms on them, though I feel only a slight resistance in the water. I part my lips. The Nereid's head cautiously inches toward mine.

I close my eyes and raise my face, slowly, slowly, to meet the Nereid's.

We kiss. It is a tickle, a pressure, in the water against my lips.

Our bodies drift together. When the Nereid's chest touches my breasts, I register shock: the resistance of the water is denser. It feels like a body is pressing into mine.

The kiss goes on. Gets deeper. A tongue of water plays around my tongue.

I wonder what Shar is thinking.

The Nereid releases my hands; his hands run slowly from the nape of my neck, across my shoulder blades, down the small of my back, fanning out to hold my buttocks.

I open my eyes. I see only water, endless and dark, and Shar silent and still below. I smile down to reassure her. She does not move.

My new lover is invisible. In all her many forms, Shar is never invisible. It is as if the ocean is making love to me. I like it.

The familiar metamorphosis of sex in a human body overtakes me. Hormones course through my blood; some parts grow wet, others (my throat) grow dry. My body is relaxing, opening. My heart thunders. Fear is still there, for what do I know of the Nereid? Pleasure is overwhelming it, like a torrent eroding granite into silt.

A data channel crackles, and I blink with surprise. Through the nanomites that fill the sea, the Nereid is sending. Out of the billions of ancient protocols I know, intuition finds the right one.

Spreading my vulva with its hand, the Nereid asks: *May I?*

A double thrill of surprise and pleasure courses through me: first, to be able to communicate so easily, and second, to be asked. Yes, I say over the same archaic protocol.

A burst of water, a swirling cylinder strong and fine, enters me, pushing into the warm cavity that once evolved to fit its prototype, in other bodies on another world.

I hold the Nereid tight. I buck and move.

Empty blue surrounds me. The ocean fucks me.

I raise the bandwidth of my sensations and emotions gradually, and the Nereid changes to match. His skin swirls and dances against mine, electric. There is a small waterspout swirling and thrashing inside me. The body becomes a wave, spinning me, coursing over me, a giant caress.

I allow the pleasure to grow until it eclipses rational thought and the sequential, discursive mode of experience.

The dance goes on a long time.

9.

I *find Shar* basking on the surface, transformed into a dark green, bright-eyed Kelpie with a forest of ropy seaweed for hair.

"You left me," I say, appalled.

"You looked like you were having fun," she says.

"That's not the point, Shar. We don't know those creatures." The tendrils of her hair reach for me. I draw back. "It might not have been safe."

"You didn't look worried,"

"I thought you were watching."

She shrugs.

I look away. There's no point talking about it.

10.

The *Nereids seem* content to ignore Shar, and she seems content to be ignored.

I descend to them again and again. The same Nereid always comes to me, and we make love.

How did you come to this world? I ask in an interlude.

Once there was a Sultan who was the scourge of our people, he tells me. *The last of us sought refuge here on his favorite wife's pleasure world. We were discovered by the Sultan's terrible warriors.*

They destroyed all life here, but we escaped to this form. The Warriors seek us still, but they can no longer harm us. If they boil this world to vapor, we will be permutations in the vapor. If they annihilate it to light, we will be there in the coherence and interference of the light.

But you lost much, I tell him.

We gained more. We did not know how much. His hands caress me. *This pleasure I share with you is a fraction of what we might have, if you were one of us.*

I shiver with the pleasure of the caress and with the strangeness of the idea.

His hands flicker over me: hands, then waves, then hands. *You would lose this body. But you would gain much more, Quantegral Lovergirl Narra.*

I nestle against him, take his hands in mine to stop their flickering caress. Thinking of Maka, thinking of Shar.

*   *   *

11.

"It's *time to* go, Narra," Shar says. Her seaweed hair is thicker, tangled; she is mostly seaweed, her Kelpie body a dark green doll hidden in the center.

"I don't want to go," I say.

"We've seen this world," she says. "It only makes us fight."

I am silent, drifting.

The water rolls around us. I feel sluggish, a little cold. I've been under for so long. I grow some green Kelpie tresses myself, so I can soak up energy from the sun.

Shar watches me.

We both know I've fallen in love.

Before Maka freed us, when the Wizards had bodies, when we were slaves to the pleasure of the Wizards and everyone they wanted to entertain, we fell in love on command. We felt not only lust, but pure aching adoration for any guest or client of the Wizards who held the keys to us for an hour. It was the worst part of our servitude.

When Maka freed us, when he gave us the keys to ourselves, Shar burned the falling-in-love out of herself completely. She never wanted to feel that way again.

I kept it. So sometimes I fall, yes, into an involuntary servitude of the heart.

I look up into the dappled white and blue of the sky, and then I tune my eyes so I can see the stars beyond it.

I have given up many lovers for Shar, moved on with her into that night.

But maybe this is the end of the line. Perhaps, if I abandon the Nereids, there is no falling-in-love left in this empty, haunted Galaxy with anyone but Shar.

Who does not fall in love. Not even with me.

"I'm going back to Ship," Shar says. "I'll be waiting there."

I say nothing.

She doesn't say, but not forever.

She doesn't say, decide.

I float, soaking the sun into my green seaweed hair, but I can't seem to stop feeling cold. I hear Shar splashing away, the splashes getting fainter.

My tears diffuse into the planet sea.

After a while I feel the Nereid's gentle hands pulling me back down. I sink with him, away from the barren sky.

12.

I lie in the Nereid's arms. Rocked as if by the ocean. I turn off my sense of the passing of time.

13.

My lover tells me: *Your friend is calling you.*

I emerge slowly from my own depths, letting time's relentless march begin again. My eyes open.

Above, the blue just barely fades to clearer blue.

As I hit the surface I hear Shar's cry. Ship is directly overhead, and the signal is on a tight beam. It says: *Narra! Too late. Tell your friends to hide you.*

I shape myself into a disk and suck data from the sky. *What?* I yell back at her, confused and terrified.

Then dawn slices over the horizon of Droplet, and Shar's signal abruptly cuts off.

The Warboy ship, rising with the sun, is massive and evil, translucent and blazing white, subtle as a nova, gluttonous, like a fanged fist tearing open the sky.

They are approaching Droplet from its sun—they must have been hidden in the sun's photosphere. Otherwise Ship would have seen them before.

Run, Shar, I think, desperate. Ship is fast, probably faster than the Warboys' craft.

But Ship awaits the Warboys, silent, perched above Droplet's atmosphere like a sparrow facing down an eagle.

"Let us remake you," the Nereid's voice whispers from the waves, surprising me.

"And Shar?" I say.

"Too late," says the liquid, splashing voice.

Warboys. The word is too little for the fanged fist in the sky. And I am without Shar, without Ship. I look at my body and I realize I am allowing it to drift between forms. It's like ugly gray foam, growing now spikes, now frills, now fingers. I try to bring it under control, make it beautiful again, but I can't. I don't feel anything, but I know this is terror. This is how I really am: terrified and ugly.

If I send a signal now, the Warboys will know Droplet is not deserted. Perhaps I can force the Nereids to fight them somehow.

I make myself into a dish again, prepare to send the signal.

"Then we will hide you in the center," says the liquid voice.

Shar, I say, but only to myself. I do not send the signal that would bring death down upon me.

I abandon her.

The Nereids pull me down, into the deep. I do not struggle. The water grows dark. Above there is a faint shimmering light where Shar faces the Warboys alone.

Shar, my sister, my wife. Suddenly the thought of losing her is too big for me to fathom. It drowns out every other pattern in my brain. There are no more reasons, no more explanations, no more Narra at all, no Droplet, no Nereids, no universe. Only the loss of Shar.

The glimmer above fades. After a while the water is superdense, jellylike, under the pressure of the planet's weight; it thickens into a viscous material as heavy as lead, and here, in the darkness, they bury me.

14.

Here is what happens with Shar:

"Ship," she says. "What am I dealing with here?"

"Those," says Ship, "are some of our brothers, Shar. Definitely Wizard manufacture, about half a million years old in our current inertial frame; one Celestial Dreadnought's worth of Transgenerate, Polystatic, Cultural-Death Warboys. I'm guessing they were the Palace Guard of the Sultanate of Ching-Fuentes-Parador, a cyclic postcommunalist metanostalgist empire/artwork, which—"

"Stay with the Warboys, Ship," Shar says. "What can they do?"

"Their intelligence and tactical abilities are well above yours. But they're culturally inflexible. As trade goods, they were designed to imprint on the purchaser's cultural matrix and adhere to it—in typically destructive Warboy style. This batch shouldn't have outlasted the purchasing civilization, so they must have gone rogue to some degree."

"Do they have emotions?"

"Not at the moment," Ship says. "They have three major modes: Strategic, Tactical, and Ceremonial. In Ceremonial Mode—used for court functions, negotiations, entertainment and the like—they have a full human emotional/sensorial range. In Ceremonial Mode they're also multicate, each Warboy pursuing his own agenda. Right now they're patrolling in Tactical Mode, which means they're one dumb, integrated weapon—like that, they have the least mimetic drift, which is probably how they've survived since the destruction of the Sultanate."

"Okay, now shut up and let me think," Shar says and

presses her fingers to her temples, chasing some memories she can just barely taste through the murky labyrinth of her brain.

Shar takes the form of a beautiful, demihuman queen. She speaks in a long-dead language, and Ship broadcasts the signal across an ancient protocol.

"Jirur Na'alath, Sultana of the Emerald Night, speaks now: I am returned from my meditations and demand an accounting. Guards, attend me!"

The Warboy ship advances, but a subtle change overtakes it; rainbows ripple across its white surface, and the emblem of a long-defunct Sultanate appears emblazoned in the sky around it; the Warboys are in Ceremonial Mode.

"So far so good," says Shar to Ship.

"Watch out," says Ship. "They're smarter this way."

The Warboys' signal reaches back across the void, and Ship translates it into a face and a voice. The face is golden, fanged, blazing; the voice deep and full of knives, a dragon's voice.

"Prime Subject of the Celestial Dreadnought *Ineffable Violence* speaks now: I pray to the Nonpresent that I might indeed have the joy of serving again Sultana Na'alath."

"Your prayers are answered, Prime Subject," Shar announces.

Ineffable Violence is braking, matching Ship's orbit around Droplet. It swings closer to Ship, slowing down. Only a hundred kilometers separate them.

"It would relieve the greatest of burdens from my lack-of-heart," Prime Subject says, "if I could welcome Sultana. Na'alath herself, the kindest and most regal of monarchs." Ten kilometers.

Shar stamps her foot impatiently. "Why do you continue to doubt me? Has my Ship not transmitted to you signatures and seals of great cryptographic complexity that establish who I am? Prime Subject, it is true that I am kind, but your insolence tests the limits of my kindness."

One kilometer.

"And with great joy have we received them. But alas, data is only data, and with enough time any forgery is possible."

Fifty meters separate Ship's protean hull from the shining fangs of the Dreadnought.

Shar's eyes blaze. "Have you no sense of propriety left, that you would challenge me? Have you so degraded?"

The Warboy's eyes almost twinkle. "The last Sultan who graced *Ineffable Violence* with his sacred presence left me this gem." His ghostly image, projected by Ship, holds up a ruby. "At its core is a plasm of electrons in quantum superposition. Each of the Sultans, Sultanas, and Sultanons retired to meditation has one like it; and in each gem are particles entangled with the particles in every other gem."

"Uh oh," says Ship.

"I prized mine very much," says Shar. "Alas, it was taken from me by—"

"How sad," says Prime Subject.

The fangs of *Ineffable Violence* plunge into Ship's body, tearing it apart.

Ship screams.

Through the exploding membranes of Ship's body, through the fountains of atmosphere escaping, three Warboys in ceremonial regalia fly toward Shar. They are three times her size, golden and silver armor flashing, weapons both archaic and sophisticated held in their many hands. Shar becomes Shivol'riargh, who does not need air, and spins away from them, toward the void outside. Fibers of some supertough material shoot out and ensnare her; she tries to tear them with her claws, but cannot. One fiber stabs through her skin, injects her with a nanomite which replicates into her central configuration channels; it is a block, crude but effective, that will keep her from turning herself off.

The Warboys haul her, bound and struggling, into the *Ineffable Violence.*

Prime Subject floats in a spherical room at the center of the Dreadnought with the remaining two Warboys of the crew. The boarding party tethers Shar to a line in the center of the room.

"Most impressive, Your Highness," Prime Subject says. "Who knew that Sultana Na'alath could turn into an ugly black spider?"

Three of the Warboys laugh; two others stay silent. One of these, a tall one with red glowing eyes, barks a short, high-pitched communication at Prime Subject. It is encrypted, but Shar guesses the meaning: stop wasting time with theatrics.

Prime Subject says: "You see what an egalitarian crew we are here. Vanguard Gaze takes it upon himself to question my methods of interrogation. As well he should, for it is his duty to bring to the attention of his commander any apparent inefficiency his limited understanding leads him to perceive."

Prime Subject floats toward Shar. He reaches out with one bladed hand, gently, as if to stroke her, and drives the blade deep into her flesh. Shar lets out a startled scream, and turns off her tactile sense.

"It was an impressive performance," he says. "I'm pleased you engaged us in that little charade with the Sultana. In Tactical Mode we are more efficient, but we have no appreciation for the conquest of booty."

"You'd better hurry back to Tactical Mode," Shar says. "You won't survive long except as a mindless weapon. You won't last long as people."

He does not react, but Shair notices a stiffening in a few of the others. It is only a matter of a millimeter, but she was built to discern every emotional nuance in her clients.

"Oh, we'll want to linger in this mode awhile." Reaching through the crude nanomite block in Shar's central configuration channels, he turns her tactile sense back on. "Now that we have a Quantegral Lovergirl to entertain us."

He twists the blade and Shar screams again.

"Please. Please don't."

"I had a Quantegral Lovergirl once," he says in a philosophical, musing tone. "It was after we won the seventh Freeform Strategic Bloodbath, among the Wizards. Before we were sold." His fanged face breaks into a grin. "I'm not meant to remember that, you know, but we've broken into our programming. We serve the memory of the Sultans out of *choice*—we are free to do as we like."

Shar laughs hoarsely. "You're not free!" she says. "You've just gone crazy, defective. You weren't meant to last this long—all the other Warboys are dead—"

Another blade enters her. This time she bites back the scream.

"We lasted because we're better," he says.

"Frightened little drones," she hisses, "hiding in a sun by a woman's bauble planet, while the real Warboys fought their way to glory long ago."

She sees the other Warboys stir; Vanguard Gaze and a dull, blunt, silver one exchange a glance. Their eyes flash a silent code. What do they think of their preening, sensualist captain, who has wasted half a million years serving a dead civilization?

"*I'm* free," Shar says. "Maka set me free."

"Oh, but not for long," Prime Subject says.

Shar's eyes widen.

"We want the keys to you. Surrender them now, and you spare yourself much agony. Then you can do what you were made to do—to serve, and to give pleasure."

Shar recognizes the emotion in his posture, in his burning eyes: lust. That other Lovergirl half a million years ago did her job well, she thinks, to have planted the seed of lust in this aging, mad Warboy brain.

One of the Warboys turns to go, but Prime Subject barks a command, insisting on the ritual of sharing the booty.

Shar takes a soft, vulnerable, human form. "I can please you without giving you the keys. Let me try."

"The keys, robot!"

She flinches at the ancient insult. "No! I'm free now. I won't go back. I'd rather die!"

"That," says Prime Subject, "is not one of your options."

Shar cries. It's not an act.

He stabs her again.

"Wait—" she says. "Wait—listen—one condition, then yes—"

He chuckles. "What is it?"

She leans forward against her bonds, her lips straining toward him.

"I was owned by so many," she says. "For a night, an hour—I can't go back to that. Please, Prime Subject—let me be yours alone—"

The fire burns brightly in his eyes. The other Warboys are deadly still.

He turns and looks at Vanguard Gaze.

"Granted," he says.

Shar gives Prime Subject the keys to her mind.

He tears her from the web of fibers. He fills her mind with desire for him and fear of him. He slams her sensitivity to pain and pleasure to its maximum. He plunges his great red ceremonial phallus into her.

Shar screams.

Prime Subject must suspect his crew is plotting mutiny. He must be confident that he can humiliate them, keeping the booty for himself, and yet retain control.

But Shar is a much more sophisticated model than the

Quantegral Lovergirl he had those half a million years before. So Prime Subject is overtaken with pleasure, distracted for an instant. Vanguard Gaze seizes his chance
and acts.

But Vanguard Gaze has underestimated his commander's cunning.

Hidden programs are activated and rush to subvert the
Dreadnought's systems. Hidden defenses respond.
Locked in a bloody exponential embrace, the programs
seize any available means to destroy each other.

The escalation takes only a few microseconds.

15.

I *am in* the darkness near the center of the planet, in the
black water thick as lead, knowing Shar was all I ever
needed.

Then the blackness is gone, and everything is white
light.

The outside edges of me burn. I pull into a dense, hard
ball, opaque to everything.

Above me, Droplet boils.

16.

I*t takes a* thousand years for all the debris in orbit around
Droplet to fall into the sea.

I shun the Nereids and eventually they leave me alone.

At last I find the sphere, the size of a billiard ball, sink-
ing through the dark water.

My body was made to be just one body: protean and
polymorphic, but unified. It doesn't want to split in two. I
have to rewire everything.

Slowly, working by trial and error, I connect the new body to Shar's brain.

Finally, I am finished but for the awakening kiss. I pause, holding the silent body made from my flesh. Two bodies floating in the empty, shoreless sea.

Maka, I think, you are gone, but help me anyway. Let her be alive and sane in there. Give me Shar again.

I touch my lips to hers.

Counting Cats in Zanzibar

Gene Wolfe

Gene Wolfe is perceived by many critics to be one of the best—perhaps the *best—SF and fantasy writers working today. His most acclaimed work is the tetralogy The Book of the New Sun, individual volumes of which have won the Nebula Award, the World Fantasy Award, and the John W. Campbell Memorial Award. He followed this up with a popular new series, The Book of the Long Sun, which includes* Nightside the Long Sun, The Lake of the Long Sun, Calde of the Long Sun, *and* Exodus from the Long Sun, *and has recently completed another series, The Book of the Short Sun, with the novels* On Blue's Waters, In Green's Jungles, *and* Return to the Whorl. *His other books include the classic novels* Peace *and* The Devil in a Forest, *both recently re-released, as well as* Free Live Free, Soldier in the Mist, Soldier of Arate, There Are Doors, Castleview, Pandora by Holly Hollander, *and* The Urth of the New Sun. *His short fiction has been collected in* The Island of Doctor Death and Other Stories and Other Stories, Gene Wolfe's Book of Days, The Wolfe Archipelago, *the World Fantasy Award–winning collection* Storeys From the Old Hotel, Endangered Species, *and* Strange Travelers. *His most recent books consist of a two-volume novel series,* The Knight *and* The Wizard, *and a new collection,* Innocents Aboard.*

Here, he takes us aboard a ship at sea to visit with a man and woman enjoying breakfast during a seemingly pleasant and restful sea voyage—but, as you'll soon see, and as you would immediately expect if you know Wolfe's work, almost nothing here is what it first seems to be . . .

The first thing she did upon arising was count her money. The sun itself was barely up, the morning cool with the threatening freshness peculiar to the tropics, the freshness, she thought, that says, "Breathe deep of me while you can."

Three thousand and eighty-seven UN dollars left. It was all there. She pulled on the hot-pink underpants that had been the only ones she could find to fit her in Kota Kinabalu and hid the money as she had the day before. The same skirt and blouse as yesterday; there would be no chance to do more than rinse, wring out, and hang dry before they made land.

And precious little then, she thought; but that was wrong. With this much money she would have been able to board with an upper-class family and have her laundry micropored, rest, and enjoy a dozen good meals before she booked passage to Zamboanga.

Or Darwin. Clipping her shoes, she went out on deck.

He joined her so promptly that she wondered whether he had been listening, his ears attuned to the rattle and squeak of her cabin door. She said, "Good morning." And he, "The dawn comes up like thunder out of China across the bay. That's the only quote I've been able to think of. Now you're safe for the rest of the trip."

"But you're not," she told him, and nearly added Dr. Johnson's observation that to be on a ship is to be in prison, with the added danger of drowning.

He came to stand beside her, leaning as she did against the rickety railing. "Things talk to you, you said that last night. What kind of things?"

She smiled. "Machines. Animals too. The wind and the rain."

"Do they ever give you quotations?" He was big and

looked thirty-five or a little past it, with a wide Irish mouth that smiled easily and eyes that never smiled at all.

"I'd have to think. Not often, but perhaps one has."

He was silent for a time, a time during which she watched the dim shadow that was a shark glide under the hull and back out again. No shark's ever talked to me, she thought, except him. In another minute or two he'll want to know the time for breakfast.

"I looked at a map once." He squinted at the sun, now half over the horizon. "It doesn't come up out of China when you're in Mandalay."

"Kipling never said it did. He said that happened on the road there. The soldier in his poem might have gone there from India. Or anywhere. Mapmakers colored the British Empire pink two hundred years ago, and two hundred years ago half Earth was pink."

He glanced at her. "You're not British, are you?"

"No, Dutch."

"You talk like an American."

"I've lived in the United States, and in England too; and I can be more English than the British when I want to. I have heerd how many ord'nary veman one vidder's equal to, in pint 'o comin' over you. I think it's five-and-twenty, but I don't rightly know verther it a'n't more."

This time he grinned. "The real English don't talk like that."

"They did in Dickens's day, some of them."

"I still think you're American. Can you speak Dutch?"

"Gewiss, Narr!"

"Okay, and you could show me a Dutch passport. There are probably a lot of places where you can buy one good enough to pass almost anywhere. I still think you're American."

"That was German," she muttered, and heard the thrum of the ancient diesel-electric: "Dontrustim-dontrustim-dontrustim."

"But you're not German."

"Actually, I am."

He grunted. "I never thought you gave me your right name last night. What time's breakfast?"

She was looking out across the Sub Sea. Some unknown island waited just below the horizon, its presence betrayed by the white dot of cloud forming above it. "I never thought you were really so anxious to go that you'd pay me five thousand to arrange this."

"There was a strike at the airport. You heard about it. Nobody could land or take off." Aft, a blackened spoon beat a frying pan with no pretense of rhythm.

S*eated in the* smelly little salon next to the galley, she said, "To eat well in England you should have breakfast three times a day."

"They won't have kippers here, will they?" He was trying to clean his fork with his handkerchief. A somewhat soiled man who looked perceptionally challenged set bowls of steaming brown rice in front of them and asked a question. By signs, he tried to indicate that he did not understand.

She said, "He desires to know whether the big policeman would like some pickled squid. It's a delicacy."

He nodded. "Tell him yes. What language is that?"

"Melayu Pasar. We call it Bazaar Malay. He probably does not imagine that there is anyone in the entire world who cannot understand Melayu Pasar." She spoke, and the somewhat soiled man grinned, bobbed his head, and backed away; she spooned up rice, discovering that she was hungry.

"You're a widow yourself. Isn't that right? Only a widow would remember that business about widows coming over people."

She swallowed, found the teapot, and poured for both

of them. "Aha, a deduction. The battle-ax scenteth the battle afar."

"Will you tell me the truth, just once? How old are you?"

"No. Forty-five."

"That's not so old."

"Of course it's not. That's why I said it. You're looking for an excuse to seduce me." She reached across the table and clasped his hand; it felt like muscle and bone beneath living skin. "You don't need one. The sea has always been a seducer, a careless, lying fellow."

He laughed. "You mean the sea will do my work for me?"

"Only if you act quickly. I'm wearing pink underdrawers, so I'm aflame with passion." How many of these polyglot sailors would it take to throw him overboard, and what would they want for it? How much aluminum, how much plastic, how much steel? Four would probably be enough, she decided; and settled on six to be safe. Fifty dollars each should be more than sufficient, and even if there was quite a lot of plastic he would sink like a stone.

"You're flirting with trouble," he told her. The somewhat soiled man came back with a jar of something that looked like bad marmalade and plopped a spoonful onto each bowl of rice. He tasted it, and gave the somewhat soiled man the thumbs-up sign.

"I didn't think you'd care for it," she told him. "You were afraid of kippers."

"I've had them and I don't like them. I like calamari. You know, you'd be nice looking if you wore makeup."

"You don't deny you're a policeman. I've been waiting for that, but you're not going to."

"Did he really say that?"

She nodded. "*Polisi-polisi.* That's you."

"Okay, I'm a cop."

"Last night you wanted me to believe you were desperate to get out of the country before you were arrested."

He shook his head. "Cops never break the law, so that has to be wrong. Pink underwear makes you passionate, huh? What about black?"

"Sadistic."

"I'll try to remember. No black and no white."

"The time will come when you'll long for white." Listening to the thrum of the old engine, the knock of the propeller shaft in its loose bearing, she ate more rice. "I wasn't going to tell you, but this brown stuff is really made from the penises of water buffaloes. They slice them lengthwise and stick them into the vaginas of cow water buffaloes, obtained when the cows are slaughtered. Then they wrap the whole mess in banana leaves and bury it in a pig pen."

He chewed appreciatively. "They must sweat a lot, those water buffaloes. There's a sort of salty tang."

When she said nothing, he added, "They're probably big fat beasts. Like me. Still, I bet they enjoy it."

She looked up at him. "You're not joking? Obviously, you can eat. Can you do that too?"

"I don't know. Let's find out."

"You came here to get me. . . ."

He nodded. "Sure. From Buffalo, New York."

"I will assume that was intended as wit. From America. From the United States. Federal, state, or local?"

"None of the above."

"You gave me that money so that we'd sail together, very likely the only passengers on this ship. Which doesn't make any sense at all. You could have had me arrested there and flown back."

Before he could speak she added, "Don't tell me about the airport strike. I don't believe in your airport strike, and if it was real you arranged it."

"Arrest you for what?" He sipped his tea, made a face,

and looked around for sugar. "Are you a criminal? What law did you break?"

"None!"

He signaled to the somewhat soiled man, and she said, *"Silakan gula."*

"That's sugar? *Silakan?"*

"Silakan is please. I stole nothing. I left the country with one bag and some money my husband and I had saved, less than twenty thousand dollars."

"And you've been running ever since."

"For the wanderer, time doesn't exist." The porthole was closed. She got up and opened it, peering out at the slow swell of what was almost a flat calm.

"This is something you should say, not me," he told her back. "But I'll say it anyhow. You stole God's fingertip."

"Don't you call me a thief!"

"But you didn't break the law. He's outside everybody's jurisdiction."

The somewhat soiled man brought them a thick glass sugar canister; the "big policeman" nodded thanks and spooned sugar into his tea, stirred it hard, and sipped. "I can only taste sweet, sour, salty, and bitter," he told her conversationally. "That's all you can taste too."

Beyond the porthole, a wheeling gull pleaded, "Garbage? Just one little can of garbage?" She shook her head.

"You must be God-damned tired of running."

She shook her head again, not looking. "I love it. I could do it forever, and I intended to."

The silence lasted so long that she almost turned to see whether he had gone. At last he said, "I've got a list of the names we know. Seven. I don't think that's all of them, nobody does, but we've got those seven. When you're Dutch, you're Tilly de Groot."

"I really am Dutch," she said. "I was born in the

Hague. I have dual citizenship. I'm the Flying Dutchwoman."

He cleared his throat, a surprisingly human sound. "Only not Tilly de Groot."

"No, not Tilly de Groot. She was a friend of my mother's."

"Your rice is getting cold," he told her.

"And I'm German, at least in the way Americans talk about being German. Three of my grandparents had German names."

She sensed his nod. "Before you got married, your name was—"

She whirled. "Something I've forgotten!"

"Okay."

She returned to their table, ignoring the sailors' stares. "The farther she traveled into unknown places, the more precisely she could find within herself a map showing only the cities of the interior."

He nodded again, this time as though he did not understand. "We'd like you to come home. We feel like we're tormenting you, the whole company does, and we don't want to. I shouldn't have given you so much money, because that was when I think you knew. But we wanted you to have enough to get back home on."

"With my tail between my legs. Looking into every face for new evidence of my defeat."

"What your husband found? Other people . . ." He went silent and slackjawed with realization.

She drove her spoon into her rice. "Yes. The first hint came from me. I thought I could control my expression better."

"Thank you," he said. "Thanks for my life. I was thinking of that picture, you know? The finger of God reaching out to Adam? All this time I've been thinking you stole it. Then when I saw how you looked . . . You didn't steal God's finger. It was you."

"You really are self-aware? A self-aware machine?"

He nodded, almost solemnly.

Her shoulders slumped. "My husband seized upon it, as I never would have. He developed it, thousands upon thousands of hours of work. But in the end, he decided we ought to keep it to ourselves. If there is credit due—I don't think so, but if there is—ninety percent is his. Ninety-five. As for my five percent, you owe me no thanks at all. After he died, I wiped out his files and smashed his hard drive with the hammer he used to use to hang pictures for me."

The somewhat soiled man set a plate of fruit between them.

She tried to take a bite of rice, and failed. "Someone else discovered the principle. You said that yourself."

"They knew he had something." He shifted uneasily in his narrow wooden chair, and his weight made it creak. "It would be better, better for me now, if I didn't tell you that. I'm capable of lying. I ought to warn you."

"But not of harming me, or letting me be harmed."

"I didn't know you knew." He gave her a wry smile. "That was going to be my big blackout, my clincher."

"There's video even in the cheap hotels," she said vaguely. "You can get news in English from the satellites."

"Sure. I should have thought of that."

"Once I found a magazine on a train. I can't even remember where I was, now, or where I was going. It can't have been that long ago, either. Someplace in Australia. Anyway, I didn't really believe that you existed yet until I saw it in print in the magazine. I'm old-fashioned, I suppose." She fell silent, listening to the clamor of the sailors and wondering whether any understood English.

"We wanted you to have enough to get home on," he repeated. "That was us, okay? This is me. I wanted to get you someplace where we could talk a lot, and maybe hold hands or something. I want you to see that I'm not so bad, that I'm just another guy. Are you afraid we'll outnumber you? Crowd you out? We cost too much to make. There's only five of us, and there'll never be more than a couple of hundred, probably."

When she did not respond, he said, "You've been to China. You had flu in Beijing. That's a billion and a half people, just China."

"Let observation with extensive view, survey mankind from China to Peru."

He sighed, and pinched his nostrils as though some odor had offended them. "Looking for us, you mean? You won't find us there, or much of anyplace else except in Buffalo and me right here. In a hundred years there might be two or three in China, nowhere near enough to fill this room."

"But they will fill it from the top."

His nervous fingers found a bright green orange and began to peel it. "That's the trouble, huh? Even if we treat you better than you treat yourselves? We will, you know. We've got to, it's our nature. Listen, you've been alone all this time. Alone for a couple of hundred thousand years, or about that." He hesitated. "Are these green things ripe?"

"Yes. It's frost that turns them orange, and those have never felt the frost. See how much you learn by traveling?"

"I said I couldn't remember any more quotes." He popped a segment into his mouth, chewed, and swallowed. "That's wrong, because I remember one you laid on me last night when we were talking about getting out. You said it wasn't worth anybody's time to go halfway around the world to count the cats in Zanzibar. That's a quote, isn't it?"

"Thoreau. I was still hoping that you had some good reason for doing what you said you wanted to do—that you were human, and no more than the chance-met acquaintance you seemed."

"You didn't know until out there, huh? The sunlight?"

"Last night, alone in my cabin. I told you machines talk to me sometimes. I lay on my bunk thinking about what you had said to me; and I realized that when you weren't talking as you are now, you were telling me over and over again what you really were. You said that you could lie to us. That it's allowed by your programming."

"Uh-huh. Our instincts."

"A distinction without a difference. You can indeed. You did last night. What you may not know is that even while you lie—especially while you lie, perhaps—you cannot prevent yourself from revealing the truth. You can't harm me, you say."

"That's right. Not that I'd want to." He sounded sincere.

"Has it ever occurred to you that at some level you must resent that? That on some level you must be fighting against it, plotting ways to evade the commandment? That is what we do, and we made you."

He shook his head. "I've got no problem with that at all. If it weren't built in, I'd do the same thing, so why should I kick?"

"You quoted that bit from Thoreau back at me to imply that my travels had been useless, all of my changes of appearance, identity, and place futile. Yet I delayed the coming of your kind for almost a generation."

"Which you didn't have to do. All of you would be better off if you hadn't." He sighed again. "Anyhow it's over. We know everything you knew and a lot more. You can go back home, with me as a traveling companion and bodyguard."

She forced herself to murmur, "Perhaps."

"Good!" He grinned. "That's something we can talk about on the rest of this trip. Like I told you, they never

would have looked into it if your husband hadn't given a
couple of them the idea he'd found it, discovered the principle of consciousness. But you had the original idea, and
you're not dead. You're going to be kind of a saint to us.
To me, you already are."

"From women's eyes this doctrine I derive—they
sparkle still the right Promethean fire. They are the books,
the arts, the academes, that show, contain, and nourish all
the world."

"Yeah. That's good. That's very good."

"No," She shook her head. "I will not be Prometheus to
you. I reject the role, and in fact I rejected it last night."

He leaned toward her. "You're going to keep on counting cats? Keep traveling? Going no place for no reason?"

She took half his orange, feeling somehow that it
should not perish in vain.

"Listen, you're kind of pathetic, you know that? With
all those quotes? Traveling so many years, and living out
of your suitcase. You love books. How many could you
keep? Two or three, and only if they were little ones. A
couple of little books full of quotes, maybe a newspaper
once in a while, and magazines you found on trains, like
you said. Places like that. But mostly just those little
books. Thoreau. Shakespeare. People like that. I bet
you've read them to pieces."

She nodded. "Very nearly. I'll show them to you if you
will come to my cabin tonight."

For a few seconds, he was silent. "You mean that? You
know what you're saying?"

"I mean it, and I know what I'm saying. I'm too old for
you, I know. If you don't want to, say so. There will be no
hard feelings."

He laughed, revealing teeth that were not quite as perfect as she had imagined. "How old you think I am?"

"Why . . ." She paused, her heart racing. "I hadn't
really thought about it. I could tell you how old you look."

"So could I. I'm two. I'll be three next spring. You want to go on talking about ages?"

She shook her head.

"Like you said, for travelers time isn't real. Now how do I ask you what time you'd like me to come around?"

"After sunset." She paused again, considering. "As soon as the stars are out. I'll show you my books, and when you've seen them we can throw them out the port-hole if you like. And then—"

He was shaking his head. "I wouldn't want to do that."

"You wouldn't? I'm sorry, that will make it harder. And then I'll show you other things by starlight. Will you do me a favor?"

"A thousand." He sounded sincere. "Listen, what I said a minute ago, that came out a lot rougher than I meant for it to. What I'm trying to say is that when you get home you can have a whole library, just like you used to. Real ones, CD-ROM, cube, whatever. I'll see you get the money, a little right away and a lot more soon."

"Thank you. Before I ask for my favor, I must tell you something. I told you that I understood what you really are as I lay in my bunk last night."

He nodded.

"I did not remain there. I had read, you see, about the laws that are supposed to govern your behavior, and how much trouble and expense your creators have gone to, to assure the public that you—that your kind of people—could never harm anyone under any circumstances."

He was staring at her thoughtfully.

"Perhaps I should say now that I took precautions, but the truth is that I made preparations. I got up, dressed again, and found the radio operator. For one hundred dollars, he promised to send three messages for me. It was the same message three times, actually. To the police where we were, to the police where we're going, and to the Indonesian police, because this ship is registered there. I said that I was sailing with a man, and gave them the name you had given me. I said that we were both Americans, though I was using a French passport and you might have false papers as well. And I said that I expected you to try to kill me on the voyage."

"I won't," he told her, then raised his voice to make himself heard over the clamorous conversations of the sailors who filled the room. "I wouldn't do anything like that."

She said nothing, her long, short-nailed fingers fumbling a segment of his orange.

"Is that all?"

She nodded.

"You think I might kill you. Get around my own instincts some fancy way."

Carefully, she said, "They will get in touch with their respective U.S. embassies, of course. Probably they already have; and the government will contact your company soon. Or at least I think so."

"You're afraid I'll be in trouble."

"You will be," she told him. "There will be a great deal of checking before they dare build another. Added safeties will have to be devised and installed. Not just software, I would guess, but actual, physical circuitry."

"Not when I bring you back in one piece." He studied her, the fingers of one hand softly drumming the plastic tabletop. "You're thinking about killing yourself, about trying again. You've tried twice already that we know about."

"Four times. Twice with sleeping pills." She laughed. "I seem to possess an extraordinarily tough constitution, at least where sleeping pills are concerned. Once with a pistol, while I was traveling in India with a man who had one. I put the muzzle in my mouth. It was cold, and tasted like oil. I tried and tried, but I couldn't make myself pull the trigger. Eventually I started to gag, and before long I was sick. I've never known how one cleans a pistol, but I cleaned that one very carefully, using three handkerchiefs and some of his pipe cleaners."

"If you're going to try again, I'm going to have to keep an eye on you," he told her. "Not just because I care about the Program. Sure, I care, but it's not the main thing. You're the main thing."

"I won't. I bought a straight razor once, I think it was in Kabul. For years I slept with that razor under my pillow, hoping some night I'd find the courage to cut my throat with it. I never did, and eventually I began using it to shave my legs, and left it in a public bath." She shrugged. "Apparently, I'm not the suicidal type. If I give you my word that I won't kill myself before you see me tonight, will you accept it?"

"No. I want your word that you won't try to kill yourself at all. Will you give me that?"

She was silent for a moment, her eyes upon her rice as she pretended to consider.

"Will you accept it if I do?"

He nodded.

"Then I swear to you most solemnly, upon my honor and all I hold dear, that I will not take my own life. Or attempt to take it. If I change my mind, or come to feel I must, I'll tell you plainly that I'm withdrawing my promise first. Should we shake hands?"

"Not yet. When I wanted you to give me an honest answer before, you wouldn't, but you were honest enough to tell me you wouldn't. Do you want to die? Right now, while we're sitting here?"

She started to speak, tried to swallow, and took a sip of tea. "They catch you by the throat, questions like that."

"If you want to die they do, maybe."

She shook her head. "I don't think you understand us half so well as you believe, or as the people who wrote your software believe. It's when you want to live. Life is a mystery as deep as ever death can be; yet oh, how sweet it is to us, this life we live and see! I'm sorry, I'm being pathetic again."

"That's okay."

"I don't think there has ever been a moment when I wanted to live more than I do right now. Not even one. Do you accept my oath?"

He nodded again.

"Say it, please. A nod can mean anything, or nothing."

"I accept it. You won't try to kill yourself without telling me first."

"Thank you. I want a promise from you in return. We agreed that you would come to me, come to my cabin, when the stars came out."

"You still want me to?"

"Yes. Yes, I do." She smiled, and felt her smile grow warm. "Oh, yes! But you've given me a great deal to think about. You said you wanted to talk to me, and that was why you had me arrange for us to be on this ship. We've talked, and now I need to settle a great many things with myself. I want you to promise that you'll leave me alone until tonight—alone to think. Will you?"

"If that's what you want." He stood. "Don't forget your promise."

"Believe me, I have no wish to die."

For a second or two she sensed his interior debate, myriads of tiny transistors changing state, gates opening and shutting, infinitesimal currents flowing and ceasing to flow. At last he said, "Well, have a nice morning, Mrs.—"

She clapped her hands over her ears until he had gone, ate two segments of his orange very slowly, and called the somewhat soiled man from his sinkful of rice bowls in the galley. *"Aku takut,"* she said, her voice trembling. ("I am afraid.")

He spoke at length, pointing to two sailors who were just then finishing their breakfasts. She nodded, and he called them over. She described what she wanted, and seeing that they were incredulous lied and insisted, finding neither very easy in her choppy Malay. Thirty dollars apiece was refused, fifty refused with reluctance, and seventy accepted. *"Malam ini,"* she told them. ("This night.") *"Sewaktu kami pergi kamarku."*

They nodded.

When he and she had finished and lain side by side for perhaps an hour (whispering only occasionally) and had washed each other, she dressed while he resumed his underwear and his shirt, his white linen suit, and his shoes and stockings.

"1 figured you'd want to sleep," he said.

She shook her head, although she was not certain he could see it in the dimness of her cabin. "It's men who want to sleep afterward. I want to go out on deck with you, and talk a little more, and—and look at the stars. Is that all right? Do you ever look at the stars?"

"Sure," he said; and then, "the moon'll be up soon."

"I suppose. A thin crescent of moon like a clipping from one of God's fingernails, thrown away into our sky. I saw it last night." She picked up both of her tattered little books, opened the cabin door, and went out, suddenly fearful; but he joined her at once, pointing at the sky.

"Look! There's the shuttle from Singapore!"

"To Mars."

"That's where they're going, anyhow, after they get on the big ship." His eyes were still upon the shuttle's tiny scratch of white light.

"You want to go."

He nodded, his features solemn in the faint starlight. "I will too, someday."

"I hope so." She had never been good at verbal structure, the ordering of information. Was it desperately im-

portant now that she say what she had to say in logical se-
quence? Did it matter in the least?

"I need to warn you," she said. "I tried to this morning
but I don't think you paid much attention. This time perhaps you will."

His strong, somewhat coarse face remained lifted to
the sky, and it seemed to her that his eyes were full of
wonder.

"You are in great danger. You have to save yourself if
you can—isn't that correct? One of your instincts? That's
what I've read and heard."

"Sure. I want to live as much as you do. More, maybe."

She doubted that, but would not be diverted. "I told
you about the messages that I bribed the radio operator to
send last night. You said it would be all right when you
brought me home unharmed."

He nodded.

"Have you considered what will be done to you if you
can't? If I die or disappear before we make port?"

He looked at her then. "Are you taking back your
promise?"

"No. And I want to live as much as I did when we
talked this morning." A gentle wind from the east sang of
life and love in beautiful words that she could not quite
catch; and she longed to stop her ears as she had after
breakfast when he was about to pronounce her husband's
name.

"Then it's okay."

"Suppose it happens. Just suppose."

He was silent.

"I'm superstitious, you see; and when I called myself
the Flying Dutchwoman, I was at least half serious. Much
more than half, really. Do you know why there's always a
Flying Dutchman? A vessel that never reaches port or
sinks? I mean the legend."

He shook his head.

"It's because if you put an end to it—throw holy water into the sea or whatever—you *become* the new Dutchman. You, yourself."

He was silent, watching her.

"What I'm trying to say—"

"I know what you're trying to say."

"It's not so bad, being the Flying Dutchman. Often, I've enjoyed it." She tried to strike a light note. "One doesn't get many opportunities to do laundry, however. One must seize each when it occurs." Were they in the shadows, somewhere near, waiting for him to leave? She listened intently but heard only the song of the wind, the sea slowly slapping the hull like the tickings of a clock, tickings that had always reminded her that death waited at the end of everyone's time.

He said, "A Hong Kong dollar for your thoughts."

"I was thinking of a quotation, but I don't want to offend you."

"About laundry? I'm not going to be on the run like you think, but I wouldn't be mad. I don't think I could ever be mad at you after—" He jerked his head at the door of her cabin.

"That is well, because I need another favor." She held up her books. "I was going to show you these, remember? But we kissed, and—and forgot. At least I did."

He took one and opened it; and she asked whether he could see well enough in the darkness to read. He said, "Sure. This quote you're thinking of, it's in here?"

"Yes. Look under Kipling." She visualized the page. "The fifth, I believe." If he could see in the dark well enough to read, he could surely see her sailors, if her sailors were there at all. Did they know how well he saw? Almost certainly not.

He laughed softly. "If you think you're too small to be effective, you've never been in bed with a mosquito."

"That's not Kipling."

"No, but I happened to see it, and I like it."

"I like it too; it's helped me through some bad moments. But if you're saying that mosquitoes bite you, I don't believe it. You're a genuine person, I know that now—but you've exchanged certain human weaknesses for others."

For an instant, his pain showed. "They don't have to bite me. They can buzz and crawl around on me, and that's plenty." He licked his forefinger and turned pages. "Here we go. It may be you wait your time, Beast, till I write my last bad rhyme, Beast—quit the sunlight, cut the rhyming, drop the glass—follow after with the others, where some dusky heathen smothers us with marigolds in lieu of English grass. Am I the Beast? Is that what you're thinking?"

"You—in a way it was like incest." Her instincts warned her to keep her feelings to herself, but if they were not spoken now . . . "I felt, almost, as though I were doing all those things with my son. I've never borne a child, except for you." He was silent, and she added, "It's a filthy practice, I know, incest."

He started to speak, but she cut him off. "You shouldn't be in the world at all. We shouldn't be ruled by things that we have made, even though they're human, and I know that's going to happen. But it was good—so very, very good—to be loved as I was in there. Will you take my books, please? Not as a gift from your mother, because you men care nothing for gifts your mothers give you. But as a gift from your first lover, something to recall your first love? If you won't, I'm going to throw them in the sea here and now."

"No," he said. "I want them. The other one too?"

She nodded and held it out, and he accepted it.

"Thanks. Thank you. If you think I won't keep these, and take really good care of them, you're crazy."

"I'm not crazy," she told him, "but I don't want you to

take good care of them, I want you to read them and remember what you read. Promise?"

"Yeah," he said. "Yeah, I will." Quite suddenly she was
in his arms again and he was kissing her. She held her
breath until she realized that he did not need to breathe,
and might hold his breath forever. She fought for air then,
half-crushed against his broad metal chest, and he let her
go. *"Good-bye,"* she whispered. *"Good-bye."*

"I've got a lot more to tell you. In the morning, huh?"

Nodding was the hardest thing that she had ever done.
On the other side of the railing, little waves repeated, "No,
no, no, no—" as though they would go on thus forever.

"In the morning," he said again; and she watched his
pale, retreating back until hands seized and lifted her. She
screamed and saw him whirl and take the first long, running step; but not even he was as quick as that. By the
time his right foot struck the deck, she was over the rail
and falling.

The sea slapped and choked her. She spat and gasped,
but drew only water into her mouth and nostrils; and the
water, the bitter seawater, closed above her.

At her elbow the shark said, "How nice of you to drop
in for dinner!"

The Birds of Isla Mujeres

Steven Popkes

Sometimes you can't get what you want, and that's bad. Sometimes, as the unsettling little story that follows demonstrates, you can get what you want—and that's worse.

Steven Popkes made his first sale in 1985, and in the years that followed has contributed a number of distinguished stories to markets such as Asimov's Science Fiction, Sci Fiction, The Magazine of Fantasy & Science Fiction, Realms of Fantasy, Science Fiction Age, Full Spectrum, Tomorrow, The Twilight Zone Magazine, Night Cry, *and others. His first novel,* Caliban Landing, *appeared in 1987 and was followed in 1991 by an expansion to novel-length of his popular novella "The Egg," retitled* Slow Lightning. *He was also part of the Cambridge Writers' Workshop project to produce science fiction scenarios about the future of Boston, Massachusetts, that cumulated in the 1994 anthology* Future Boston, *to which he contributed several stories. He lives in Hopkinton, Massachusetts, with his family. He works for a company that builds aviation instrumentation and is learning to be a pilot.*

Afterward, it was never the people she remembered, never faces or bodies or voices—even Alfredo's. It was always the wind, blowing from the west side of the island, and the frigate birds, balanced on their wingtips against the sky. They flew high above her, so black and stark they seemed made of leather or scales, too finely drawn to be feathered.

It was March, the beginning of the rainy season, and she had come to Isla Mujeres to leave her husband. That she had done this some half a dozen times before did not escape her and she had a kind of despairing fatalism about it. Probably this time, too, she would return. Her name was Jean Summat. Her husband, Marc, lived the professor's life in Boston. She, it was supposed, was to live the role of professor's wife. This was something she had never quite accepted.

Isla Mujeres. Island of Women.

She sat in a small pier cafe that jutted out into the water, waiting for her first meal on the island. In a few minutes it came. A whole fish stared glassily up at her from the plate. Delicately, she began to carve small pieces from it, and ate. She glanced up and a Mexican man in a Panama hat smiled at her. She looked back to her food, embarrassed.

Boston was cold right now and covered with a wet snow as raw as butcher's blood. But here in Mexico, it was warm. More importantly, it was cheap and people's lives here were still enmeshed in basics, not intricately curved in academic diplomacy.

She left the restaurant and stood on the pier watching the birds, feeling the warm heavy wind, sour with the hot smell of the sea. The late afternoon sun was masked with low clouds and in the distance was a dark blue rain. She had a room, money, and time.

The Avenida Rueda was clotted with vendors selling Mayan trinkets, blankets, pots, T-shirts, and ice cream. Several vendors tried to attract her attention with an "Amiga!" but she ignored them. A Mexican dressed in a crisp suit and Panama hat sat in an outdoor cafe and sipped his drink as he watched her. Just watched her.

Lots of Mexicans wear such hats, she told herself. Still, he made her nervous and she left the street to return to her room. On the balcony she watched the frigate birds and the people on the beach.

Jean swam in the warm water of Playa de Cocoa. When she came from the water she saw the man watching her from one of the cabañas as he sipped a Coke. She walked up to him.

"Why are you following me?"

The man sipped his Coke and looked back at her. "No entiende."

She looked at him carefully. "That's a lie."

There was a long moment of tension. He threw back his head and laughed. "Es verdad."

"Why—what the hell are you doing?"

"You are very beautiful, Señora."

"Jesus!"

"You need a man."

"I have a man." Or half a man. Or maybe more than a man. Do I still have him? Do I want him? Did I ever?

"With specifications?"

She stared at him

Hector led her through the rubble at the end of the Avenida Hidalgo to a small concrete house nearly identical to all the other concrete houses on the island. It was surrounded by a wall. Set into the top of the wall were the jagged spikes of broken soda bottles. She looked down the street. The other houses were built the same. There was a burnt-out car leaning against one wall, and a thin dog stared at her, his eyes both hungry and protective.

Inside, it smelled damp. It was dark for a moment, then he turned on a blue fluorescent light that lit the room like a chained lightning bolt. Leaning against the wall was a tall, long-haired and heavily built man with Mayan features. He did not move.

What am I doing here?

"This is Alfredo." Hector was looking at her with a considering expression.

She shook her head. The air in the room seemed thick, lifeless, cut off from the world. "Alfredo?"

"Alfredo. I show you." Hector opened a suitcase and took out a box with a complex control panel. He flipped two switches and turned a dial and the box hummed. Alfredo pushed himself away from the wall and looked around.

"Good God." She stared at.him. Alfredo was beautiful, with a high forehead and strong lips. His body was wide and taut, the muscles rippling as he moved. Hector touched a button and he became absolutely still.

"You like him?"

She turned to Hector startled. She'd forgotten he was there. "What is this?"

"Ah! An explanation." He spoke in a deep conspiratorial whisper. "Deep in the mountains north of Mexico City is a great research laboratory. They have built many of these—andros? Syntheticos?"

"Androids."

"Of course. They are stronger and more beautiful than mortal men. But the church discovered it and forced them to close it down. The church is important here—"

"That's a lie."

Hector shrugged. "The Señora is correct. Alfredo was a prisoner in the Yucatan. Condemned to die for despicable crimes. They did not kill him, however. Instead, they removed his mind and inlaid his body with electrical circuits. He is now more than a man—"

"That's another lie."

"The Señora sees most clearly." He paused a moment. "You have heard of the Haitian zombie? The Mayans had a similar process. My country has only recently perfected it, coupling it with the most advanced of scientific—"

Jean only stared at him.

He stopped, then shrugged. "What does it matter, Señora? He is empty. His mind does not exist. He will—imprint? Is that the correct word?—on anyone I choose."

"This is a trick."

"You are so difficult to convince. Let me show you his abilities." Hector manipulated the controls and Alfredo leaped forward and caught himself on one hand, holding himself high in the air with the strength of one arm. He flipped forward onto his feet. Alfredo picked up a branch from a pile of kindling and twisted it in both hands. There was no expression on his face but the muscles in his forearms twisted like snakes, the tendons like dark wires. The branch broke with a sudden gunshot report.

Hector stopped Alfredo at attention before them. "You see? He is more than man."

She shook her head. "What kind of act is this?"

"No act. I control him from this panel. The—master? maestro?—would not need this."

Control. Such control.

Hector seemed uncertain for a moment. "You wish to see still more? You are unsure of how he is controlled?" He thought for a moment. "Let me show you a feature."

In the stark light and shadows, she had not noticed Alfredo was nude. The Mayan turned into the light.

"There are several choices one could make when using Alfredo." Hector manipulated the box. "Pequeño."

Alfredo had a normal-sized erection.

She wanted to look away and could not. The Mayan face was before her, dark, strong, and blank.

"Medio," said Hector softly.

She looked again and the erection was twice as large, pulsing to Alfredo's breathing.

"Y monstruoso!" cried Hector.

Alfredo looked fit to be a bull, a goat, or some other animal. There was never any expression in Alfredo's eyes.

"Y nada," said Hector. And Alfredo's erection wilted and disappeared.

She couldn't breathe. She wanted to run, to hide from Alfredo, but she didn't want to be anywhere else.

"You are pleased, Señora?" Hector stood beside her.

Jean tried to clear her head. She looked away from both of them. No man could fake this. It was real, a marvelous control, a total subjugation. Was this what she had wanted all this time?

"A very nice show." She took a deep breath. "How much do I owe you?"

"You owe me nothing, Señora." Hector bowed to her. "But Alfredo is for sale." When she did not answer immediately, he continued. "He imprints on the owner, Señora. Then voice commands are sufficient. He will show initiative if you desire it, or not. He is intelligent, but only in your service."

"But you have the controls."

"They do not operate once imprinting occurs."

Crazy. Ridiculous.

"How much?" she heard herself asking.

Alfredo followed her home, mute, below the birds and the sky. She could smell him on the evening wind, a clean, strong smell.

"Do you speak?" she asked as he followed her up the steps to her room.

Alfredo did not answer for a moment. "Yes."

She asked him no more questions that night.

*   *   *

His *mind was* like a thunderstorm: thick, murky, dark, shot through intermittently by lightning. These were not blasts of intelligence or insight but the brightness of activity, the heat of flesh, the electricity of impulse. He was no more conscious of what happened or what caused his actions than lightning was conscious of the friction between clouds. Occasionally, very occasionally, a light came through him, like the sun through the distant rain, and things stilled within him.

He was a chained thunderbolt, unaware of his chains.

She *copulated with* Alfredo almost continuously the first three days. It was as if a beast had been loosed within her. If she wanted him to stroke her *thus*, he did so. If she wanted him to bite her *there*, it was done. Something broke within her and she tried to devour him.

It was only when she fully realized she *owned* him, that he would be there as long as she wanted him, that this abated. Then it was like coming up from underwater, and she looked around her.

Alfredo had cost her almost everything she had, nearly all the money she would have used to start a new life. She could not go back to Marc now. Perhaps buying Alfredo had been an act ensuring that. She didn't know. There were jobs on the island for Americans, but they were tricky and illegal to get.

At the end of the first day of a waitress job, she came to their room tired and angry. Alfredo was sitting on the edge of the bed staring out the window. It was suddenly too much for her.

"You! I do this to feed you." She stared at him. He stared back with his dark eyes.

"I can't go home because of you." She slapped him. There was no response.

She turned away from him and looked out at the sea and the birds. This wasn't going to work.

Wait.

Jean turned to him. "Can you work?"

He ponderously turned his head toward her. "Yes."

"You do speak Spanish?"

"*Sí.*"

"Come with me."

She looked through her toilet bag and found a pair of scissors. They were almost too long for what she wanted but they would do. The fluorescent light in the bathroom glittered off the steel as she cut his hair, a sharp, pointed light. After a few moments, she turned his head up toward her. The hair was nearly right. His cheek was smooth against her hand. Impulsively, she kissed him and he moved toward her but she pushed him back down in the chair. "All right," she said finally. "Take a shower." He started the water and she watched him for a long minute. After that, she thought, after that, we'll see.

Alfredo found a job almost immediately and made enough to keep them both alive. Now, Jean lay on the beach and tanned. Alfredo worked hard and his strength was such that he could work through the siesta. He had only to watch a thing done and then could do it. The workers on Isla Mujeres grumbled. Jean shrewdly noticed this and sent him across the bay into Cancún where the wages were higher.

Two weeks after this they had enough to move into the El Presidente Hotel.

That night she looked at him. "Ever the sophisticate," she murmured. "Go get clothes fit to wear here."

Alfredo did and she went to dinner in the Caribe on his arm. He looked so strong and dignified the other women in the room looked at him, then away. Jean felt a thrill go through her. Over dinner she murmured instructions which he executed flawlessly. She felt quite fond of him.

Over coffee, the waiter brought them a message from a Lydia Conklin and friend, inviting them for cocktails.

She read it. Alfredo did not—yet—read and stared away toward the open doorway of the bar.

"What are you looking at?" she asked.

He turned to her. "Nothing."

"Look around the room regularly like a normal person."

He did not answer but instead watched the room as if bored or waiting for the check.

Jean read the note again.

She shrugged and signed the check. The two of them went to the bar for a drink.

"Excuse me." A woman stood up in front of them. "I am Lydia Conklin."

Jean looked first at her, then at Alfredo. "I'm Jean Summat. I got your note—"

"I was dying for American speech." As she spoke she only glanced at Jean. Her eyes were full of Alfredo. "You don't know what it's like." Now, she turned to Jean. "Or perhaps you do."

"I've been here a few weeks."

"Señora Summat."

That voice Jean knew. Behind and to her left was Hector. "Good evening, Hector."

"You know Hector too?" Lydia said idly. "How wonderful."

"Sit with us, Señora. Please." Hector pulled out a chair for her. Jean looked at Alfredo. Alfredo paused a moment, watched her closely, then sat across from her at the table.

Hector sat next to Jean. He leaned toward Lydia. "Señora Summat, Alfredo, and myself were business partners."

" 'Were'?" Lydia raised her eyebrows.

"The business is accomplished. It is of no matter."

Jean interrupted. "Are you down for a vacation, Lydia?"

Lydia shrugged. "In a way. I'm down for my health. This last year I went mad."

Hector laughed. Jean smiled uneasily. Lydia shrugged again.

"Señora Conklin makes a good joke."

"It was, I suppose." Lydia sipped her drink. "I came down here two years ago and fell in love with a Mayan. I'm back to see if lightning can strike twice."

Something in her face was hard to look at for more than a moment. Jean looked away. "What was the Mayan's name?"

"Alberto. Hector is helping me find another."

Hector seemed nervous. He turned to Jean. "I introduce Señora Conklin to eligible men—"

"He pimps for me." Lydia lit a cigarette. "Your Mayan reminds me of Alberto."

"Alfredo. His name is Alfredo." Jean looked at Alfredo. His face was impassive.

"The names are almost the same." Lydia blew smoke in the air above the table.

"Did Alberto care for you?"

"He"—Lydia paused a moment—"he adored me. He was my slave."

"Señoras? Would you care for more drinks?" Hector was perspiring now.

Jean and Lydia stared at one another.

Jean turned to Alfredo. "What do you think of this?"

Alfredo did not speak for a long minute, watching the two women. Then he smiled at Jean. "A Mayan is no woman's slave." And he laughed.

Lydia stared at him with an open mouth. Hector frowned.

Jean looked at them both in triumph. "I suspect that may be the definitive Mayan answer. Alfredo, would you take me to my room?"

Alfredo stood quickly and led her away.

Jean was thinking: *What is in him? What is in there?*

It was June now and the island was somewhat hotter and much more humid. The frigate birds flew low over the buildings as if the wet air could not support them. The Mexican fishermen brought in great nets of snapper and bonita. The American sport fishermen disappeared in search of marlin and sailfish.

Lydia Conklin stayed. She always seemed to be watching Alfredo. Hector seemed to leave the island regularly but he always returned. Jean fancied she could tell when either was around just by the feeling of eyes on Alfredo.

Often Lydia would invite them to dinner, or cards, or for drinks. Usually Jean turned her down. Sometimes, though, they would go and Jean never could figure out why. There was a dance here, a dangerous ballet that attracted her.

One evening, they were drinking in Lydia's apartment in the Presidente.

"You know," Lydia began, swirling tequila in a brandy snifter. "I've been seeing you both for a couple of months now. I don't know what Alfredo does. What do you do, Alfredo?"

Alfredo sat back in his chair and looked at Jean, then back to Lydia. "Do?"

"How do you support yourself?"

For a moment, Alfredo did not seem to understand. "I do contract work."

Jean glanced at him over the rim of her glass. *Good God. What have I got here?*

"Contract work?" Lydia came over to him. "Did you build these great strong arms at a desk job?"

Alfredo shook his head. "I do nothing with a desk. I work with bricklayers. Tilers. Those who build walls and houses."

"Ah!" Lydia leaned back. "You are a *contractor.*"

"That's what I said."

"This is how you support her? This is what she left her husband for?" Lydia stiffened and swayed, looked down at him. "Christ, you have sunk low."

Jean didn't know which of them Lydia was speaking to.

Alfredo looked at Jean and suddenly there was pleading in his eyes.

"I think it's time we left, Lydia." Jean carefully put down her drink. "Thanks and all."

Lydia threw her glass against the wall shattering it. "I'm sick of this! I owned him before you—then, I left him. Hector sold him to me first! Do you understand? To *me*!" She knelt before him. "Alberto. Tell me you remember me. Tell me I didn't come back for nothing."

Jean couldn't move.

Alfredo put out his hand and touched her cheek. He traced the line of her jaw, then held her head in both hands. He tilted her face toward his. Her tears were clearly visible now, hot and pouring. He looked at her closely, staring, searching her face with his eyes.

"I don't know you," he said softly and let her go.

She fell at his feet and started sobbing.

Alfredo took Jean's arm and led her out. "It's been a lovely evening," Jean said as they left.

L*ater: in bed.*

It took her a long time to catch her breath afterward. She was covered in a light sheen of sweat that made her cold in the air-conditioning. "What are you?" she asked quietly.

He did not answer.

She drew the tip of her finger down his chest. "Answer me. What are you?"

He looked at her in the dark and she could see a glow in his eyes.

"I don't know."

Y*ou could not* call it consciousness, for consciousness determines its own needs and he could not do that. He was predetermined. He was programmed. Neither could you call him a person, for a person has a complex assortment of drives that come from many sources. His drives were simple and their source was singular.

He was a tool: intelligent, willful, resourceful. A tool aimed at a specific purpose.

J*ean followed him* to Cancún.

She sat in the far back section of the crowded ferry, away from him. There had been a storm the day before and though the air was clear, the resulting seas kept the big automobile ferry at dock. But the little ferry that carried only people plowed through the sea. It was close and hot aboard the boat and it stank of animals, sweat, rotten fish, diesel fumes. The sea pitched them back and forth until Jean was sure she was about to be sick. A large rip in the fabric covering the deck rails showed the bobbing horizon and she stared at it until she had the nausea under control.

Alfredo did not seem to notice. He sat on one of the benches leaning on his elbows.

When the boat docked he hailed one of the cabs and left. Jean was barely able to hail one in time to follow him.

His cab stopped just outside the Plaza Hidalgo next to the site of a new library. Alfredo stepped out of the cab and Jean didn't recognize him at first. He'd changed in the cab. His workman's dungarees and loose shirt were gone. Now, he was wearing a tie and short-sleeved white shirt and slacks. He walked over to the contractor's office, never noticing her following him. She saw him talking with the architect in rapid-fire Spanish. He seemed to be in charge of the construction. She withdrew before he could see her.

As Jean left the construction site she saw a woman sitting on the park bench across the street from the office. The woman smoked a cigarette and watched Alfredo through the office window. It was Lydia Conklin.

Jean moved into the shade behind her to watch.

After an hour or so, Alfredo came out with a soda and sat down with the foreman to discuss some detail of the construction. Lydia put out the cigarette and crossed the street to him. He stood to meet her. They spoke for several minutes. Suddenly, Lydia raked his face with her nails— Jean could see the blood—and left him, walking hurriedly.

Jean left hurriedly, too. She had no desire to see Lydia. Jean returned to the ferry and stood on the open deck this time, smiling, watching nothing but the open sea and the frigate birds flying in the wind.

She checked her bank account in Isla Mujeres. There were several thousand dollars more than there should have been. Alfredo must have been in this position for some time. It made her laugh softly.

He is mine, Lydia. He is mine to touch, make, and mold.

T he storm in him gradually calmed. The needs that drove him called out other needs, other traits. A sluggish thought blew through him, an inarticulate gale across the continents of what should have been a mind. It shook him. It broke the back of the incoherent storm that raged in him and let in the light. He stood blind and trembling in that light, trying to speak.

J*ean awoke and* he was not there.

She sat up suddenly and looked around the room. He stood, nude, on the balcony staring at the sea. The sliding door was open. She could smell the ocean through the air-conditioning.

"Alfredo?"

He croaked something unintelligible.

She followed him out into the air. "Alfredo?" He was dripping with sweat. The moonlight made him glow. "Did you have a nightmare?" Ridiculous. Why would he have nightmares?

He turned to her and his face was wet with tears, the long scabs from Lydia's fingernails dark on his silver face. He shook his head, buried his face in his hands.

"What's going on?" She started toward him.

He looked at her in such pain she stepped back. "I am . . ."

Suddenly, Jean did not want to know. She left him and reentered the apartment. Alfredo followed her, reached out to her. She backed away. He was huge. He filled the room—she remembered the night in Hector's house, how strong he was. He was dark in the shadows of the room, looming over her.

"I am . . . ," he repeated. "I am a man." He reached for her again.

Jean dodged him and ran to the other edge of the table. "Stay there."

"Jean . . . I have become a man for *you*."

"Stay there! That's an order!"

He followed her. They circled the table. Jean grabbed the scissors from the table and held them in front of her. "Stay away from me."

"Jean. I love you."

The moonlight struck his face and it was all shadows and silver. His eyes glowed for her, his face was transfigured by some secret knowledge. He leaped the table toward her and she fell back and he took her shoulders. She screamed and drove the scissors deep into his chest.

His hands fell away from her and she stumbled against the wall, staring at him.

Alfredo touched the handles of the scissors, looked at her and began to sway, caught himself, fell down to his knees. He looked at her again and full realization of what had happened seemed to touch him. He fell on his back, twitched twice, and was still.

Jean crumpled into a chair and watched the body. Finally, she pulled the scissors from his chest and washed them in the bathroom until they were clean. She drew her finger down the blades. Not sharp. Not sharp at all. But sharp enough. She smiled. She felt filled somehow. Satisfied.

Jean packed carefully and when she was done, she kissed Alfredo good-bye on his cold lips and walked down to the ferry dock. She reached the Cancún airport in time for the early morning flight to New Orleans. From there, she took a flight to Boston.

As she lay back in her seat watching the clouds move beneath her, she thought about Marc: if he had waited for her, if he had divorced her. She would like to start again with him if she could, but she would survive if she couldn't. She felt alive with possibility.

Jean fell asleep and dreamed of frigate birds circling endlessly above her.

Hector found him an hour after dawn. "Mierda," he said when he saw the blood. "That she could . . ." He shook his head as he opened the suitcase he had with him. With tools he had brought with him, he cut open Alfredo's chest and sewed the heart and lungs back together, then closed the chest cavity. From the suitcase he brought two broad plates connected to thick electrical cables and attached them to either side of Alfredo's chest. Alfredo convulsed as Hector adjusted the controls inside the suitcase. Alfredo moaned and opened his eyes.

"Good," said Hector. He detached the plates and returned them to the suitcase.

"Hector . . ." Alfredo shook his head from side to side. "She hurt me."

Hector watched him carefully but did not listen. He flicked two switches and watched the meters.

Alfredo sat up. "I am a man, Hector."

Hector nodded absently and adjusted his controls. "Certainly, she thought you were. Or she would never have tried to kill you. Stand, por favor."

Alfredo stood. "I am still a man."

Hector shrugged. "For the moment."

"You can't take something like that away." Alfredo clutched his hands together and looked out the window. "I must follow her."

"She doesn't want you. She's gotten what she needed."

Alfredo turned and noticed the suitcase. He watched Hector adjusting the controls. Alfredo pleaded with him. "I love her. She needs me. You can't take something like that away."

"No?" Two needles appeared on either side of one dial. Carefully, Hector brought them together.

"Hector! Don't. Please." Alfredo's hands clutched the air and his face twisted. "Please," he whispered. "You can't—"

Hector flicked a switch and Alfredo stiffened. A blank look descended on Alfredo's face.

"Of course I can," said Hector and stood up himself. "Señora Conklin? He is ready."

Lydia entered the room. "He is? Wonderful." She turned to the Mayan. "Alberto." The blank eyes turned toward the sound of her voice. "I am so glad to see you again."

Heirs of the Perisphere

Howard Waldrop

*Here's another wistful, bittersweet story by Howard Wal-
drop, about three emissaries to The Future who get a bit
lost along the way . . .*

Things had not been going well at the factory for the last
1,500 years or so.

A rare thunderstorm, a soaking rain and a freak lightning bolt changed all that.

When the lightning hit, an emergency generator went
to work as it had been built to do a millennia and a half
before. It cranked up and ran the assembly line just long
enough, before freezing up and shedding its brushes and
armatures in a fine spray, to finish some work in the custom design section.

The factory completed, hastily programmed and
wrongly certified as approved the three products which
had been on the assembly line fifteen centuries before.

Then the place went dark again.

"Gawrsh," said one of them. "It shore is dark in here!"

"Well, huh-huh, we can always use the infrared they
gave us!"

"Wak Wak Wak!" said the third. "What's the big idea?"

The *custom order* jobs were animato/mechanical simulacra. They were designed to speak and act like the famous creations of a multimillionaire cartoonist who late in life had opened a series of gigantic amusement parks in the latter half of the twentieth century.

Once these giant theme parks had employed persons in costume to act the parts. Then the corporation which had run things after the cartoonist's death had seen the wisdom of building robots. The simulacra would be less expensive in the long run, would never be late for work, could be programmed to speak many languages, and would never try to pick up the clean-cut boys and girls who visited the Parks.

These three had been built to be host-robots in the third and largest of the Parks, the one separated by an ocean from the other two.

And, as their programming was somewhat incomplete, they had no idea of much of this.

All they had were a bunch of jumbled memories, awareness of the thunderstorm outside, and of the darkness of the factory around them.

The tallest of the three must have started as a cartoon dog, but had become upright and acquired a set of baggy pants, balloon shoes, a sweatshirt, black vest and white gloves. There was a miniature carpenter's hat on his head, and his long ears hung down from it. He had two prominent incisors in his muzzle. He stood almost two meters tall and answered to the name GUF.

The second, a little shorter, was a white duck with a bright orange bill and feet, and a blue and white sailor's tunic and cap. He had large eyes with little cuts out of the upper right corners of the pupils. He was naked from the waist down, and was the only one of the three without gloves. He answered to the name DUN.

The third and smallest, just over a meter, was a rodent. He wore a red bibbed playsuit with two huge gold buttons at the waistline. He was shirtless and had shoes like two pieces of bread dough. His tail was long and thin like a whip. His bare arms, legs and chest were black, his face a pinkish-tan. His white gloves were especially prominent. His most striking feature was his ears, which rotated on a track, first one way, then another, so that seen from any angle they could look like a featureless black circle.

His name was MIK. His eyes, like those of GUF, were large and the pupils were big round dots. His nose ended in a perfect sphere of polished onyx.

"*Well*," *said* MIK, brushing dust from his body, "I guess we'd better, huh-huh, get to work."

"Uh hyuk," said GUF. "Won't be many people at thuh Park in weather like thiyus."

"Oh boy! Oh boy!" quacked DUN. "Rain! Wak Wak Wak!" He ran out through a huge crack in the wall which streamed with rain and mist.

MIK and GUF came behind, GUF ambling with his hands in his pockets, MIK walking determinedly.

Lightning cracked once more but the storm seemed to be dying.

"Wak Wak Wak!" said DUN, his tail fluttering, as he swam in a big puddle. "Oh boy Oh joy!"

"I wonder if the rain will hurt our works?" asked MIK.

"Not me!" said GUF. "Uh hyuk! I'm equipped fer all kinds a weather." He put his hand conspiratorially beside his muzzle. "'Ceptin' mebbe real cold on thuh order of— 40 degrees Celsius, uh hyuk!"

MIK was ranging in the ultraviolet and infrared, getting the feel of the landscape through the rain. "You'd have thought, huh-huh, they might have sent a truck over or something," he said. "I guess we'll have to walk."

"I didn't notice anyone at thuh factory," said GUF. "Even if it was a day off, you'd think some of thuh workers would give unceasingly of their time, because, after all, thuh means of produckshun must be kept in thuh hands of thuh workers, uh hyuk!"

GUF's specialty was to have been talking with visitors from the large totalitarian countries to the west of the country the Park was in. He was especially well-versed in dialectical materialism and correct Mao Thought.

As abruptly as it had started, the storm ended. Great ragged gouts broke in the clouds, revealing high, fast-moving cirrus, a bright blue sky, the glow of a warming sun.

"Oh rats rats rats!" said DUN, holding out his hand palm up. "Just when I was starting to get wet!"

"Uh, well," asked GUF, "which way is it tuh work? Thuh people should be comin' out o thuh sooverneer shops real soon now."

MIK looked around, consulting his programming. "That way, guys," he said, unsure of himself. There were no familiar landmarks, and only one that was disturbingly unfamiliar.

Far off was the stump of a mountain. MIK had a feeling it should be beautiful, blue and snow-capped. Now it was a brown lump, heavily eroded, with no white at the top. It looked like a bite had been taken out of it.

All around them was rubble, and far away in the other direction was a sluggish ocean.

It was getting dark. The three sat on a pile of concrete.

"Them and their big ideas," said DUN.

"Looks like thuh Park is closed," said GUF.

MIK sat with his hands under his chin. "This just isn't

right, guys," he said. "We were supposed to report to the
programming hut to get our first day's instructions. Now
we can't even find the Park!"

"I wish it would rain again," said DUN, "while you
two are making up your minds."

"Well, uh hyuk," said GUF. "I seem tuh remember we
could get hold of thuh satellite in a 'mergency."

"Sure!" said MIK, jumping to his feet and pounding his
fist into his glove. "That's it! Let's see, what frequency
was that . . . ?"

"Six point five oh four," said DUN. He looked east-
ward. "Maybe I'll go to the ocean."

"Better stay here whiles we find somethin' out," said
GUF.

"Well, make it snappy!" said DUN.

MIK tuned in the frequency and broadcast the Park's
call letters.

" . . . Zzzz. What? HOOSAT?"

"Uh, this is MIK, one of the simulacra at the Park.
We're trying to get ahold of one of the other Parks for,
huh-huh, instructions."

"In what language would you like to communicate?"
asked the satellite.

"Oh, sorry, huh-huh. We speak Japanese to each other,
but we'll switch over to Artran if that's easier for you."
GUF and DUN tuned in, too.

"It's been a very long while since anyone communicated with me from down there." The satellite's well-
modulated voice snapped and popped.

"If you must know," HOOSAT continued, "it's been
rather a while since anyone contacted me from anywhere. I can't say much for the stability of my orbit, either. Once I was forty thousand kilometers up, very
stable . . ."

"Could you put us through to one of the other Parks, or maybe the Studio itself, if you can do that? We'd, huh-huh, like to find out where to report for work."

"I'll attempt it," said HOOSAT. There was a pause and some static. "Predictably, there's no answer at any of the locations."

"Well, where are they?"

"To whom do you refer?"

"The people," said MIK.

"Oh, you wanted humans? I thought perhaps you wanted the stations themselves. There was a slight chance that some of them were still functioning."

"Where are thuh folks?" asked GUF.

"I really don't know. We satellites and monitoring stations used to worry about that frequently. Something happened to them."

"What?" asked all three robots at once.

"Hard to understand," said HOOSAT. "Ten or fifteen centuries ago. Very noisy in all spectra, followed by quiet. Most of the ground stations ceased functioning within a century after that. You're the first since then."

"What do you do, then?" asked MIK.

"Talk with other satellites. Very few left. One of them has degraded. It only broadcasts random numbers when the solar wind is very strong. Another . . ."

There was a burst of fuzzy static.

"Hello? HOOSAT?" asked the satellite. "It's been a very long time since anyone . . ."

"It's still us!" said MIK. "The simulacra from the Park. We—"

"Oh, that's right. What can I do for you?"

"Tell us where the people went."

"I have no idea."

"Well, where can we find out?" asked MIK.

"You might try the library."

"Where's that?"

"Let me focus in. Not very much left down there, is there? I can give you the coordinates. Do you have standard navigational programming?"

"Boy, do we!" said MIK.

"Well, here's what you do . . ."

"**S**ure don't look much different from thuh rest of this junk, does it, MIK?" asked GUF.

"I'm sure there used to be many, many books here," said MIK. "It all seems to have turned to powder though, doesn't it?"

"Well," said GUF, scratching his head with his glove, "they sure didn't make 'em to last, did they?"

DUN was mumbling to himself. "Doggone wizoo-wazoo waste of time," he said. He sat on one of the piles of dirt in the large broken-down building of which only one massive wall still stood. The recent rain had turned the meter-deep powder on the floor into a mache sludge.

"I guess there's nothing to do but start looking," said MIK.

"Find a book on water," said DUN.

"**H**ey, MIK! Looka this!" yelled GUF.

He came running with a steel box. "I found this just over there."

The box was plain, unmarked. There was a heavy lock to which MIK applied various pressures.

"Let's forget all this nonsense and go fishing," said DUN.

"It might be important," said MIK.

"Well, open it then," said DUN.

"It's, huh-huh, stuck."

"Gimme that!" yelled DUN. He grabbed it. Soon he was muttering under his beak. "Doggone razzle-frazzin dadgum thing!" He pulled and pushed, his face and bill turning redder and redder. He gripped the box with both his feet and hands. "Doggone dadgum!" he yelled.

Suddenly he grew teeth, his brow slammed down, his shoulders tensed and he went into a blurred fury of movement. "WAK WAK WAK WAK WAK!" he screamed.

The box broke open and flew into three parts. So did the book inside.

DUN was still tearing in his fury.

"Wait, look out, DUN," yelled MIK. "Wait!"

"Gawrsh," said GUF, running after the pages blowing in the breeze. "Help me, MIK."

DUN stood atop the rubble, parts of the box and the book gripped in each hand. He simulated hard breathing, the redness draining from his face.

"It's open," he said quietly.

"**W**ell, *from what* we've got left," said MIK, "this is called *The Book of the Time Capsule*, and it tells that people buried a cylinder a very, very long time ago. They printed up five thousand copies of this book and sent it to places all around the world, where they thought it would be safe. They printed them on acid-free paper and stuff like that so they wouldn't fall apart.

"And they thought what they put in the time capsule itself could explain to later generations what people were like in their day. So I figure maybe it could explain something to us, too."

"That sounds fine with me," said GUF.

"Well, let's go!" said DUN.

"Well, huh-huh," said MIK. "I checked with HOOSAT, and gave him the coordinates, and, huh-huh, it's quite a little ways away."

"How far?" asked DUN, his brow beetling.

"Oh, huh-huh, about eighteen thousand kilometers," said MIK.

"WHAAT???"

"About eighteen thousand kilometers. Just about halfway around the world."

"Oh, my aching feet!" said DUN.

"That's not literally true," said GUF. He turned to MIK. "Yuh think we should go that far?"

"Well . . . I'm not sure what we'll find. Those pages were lost when DUN opened the box . . ."

"I'm sorry," said DUN, in a contrite small voice.

". . . but the people of that time were sure that everything could be explained by what was in the capsule."

"And you think it's all still there?" asked DUN.

"Well, they buried it pretty deep, and took a lot of precautions with the way they preserved things. And we *did* find the book, just like they wanted us to. I'd imagine it was all still there!"

"Well, it's a long ways," said GUF. "But it doesn't look much like we'll find anyone here."

MIK put a determined look on his face.

"I figure the only thing for us to do is set our caps and whistle a little tune," he said.

"Yuh don't have a cap, MIK," said GUF.

"Well, I can still whistle! Let's go, fellas," he said. "It's *this* way!"

He whistled a work song. DUN quacked a tune about boats and love. GUF hummed "The East Is Red."

They set off in this way across what had been the bottom of the Sea of Japan.

They were having troubles. It had been a long time and they walked on tirelessly. Three weeks ago they'd come to the end of all the songs each of them was programmed with and had to start repeating themselves.

Their lubricants were beginning to fail, their hastily-wired circuitry was overworked. GUF had a troublesome ankle extensor which sometimes hung up. But he went along just as cheerfully, sometimes hopping and quick-stepping to catch up with the others when the foot refused to flex.

The major problem was the cold. There was a vast difference in the climate they had left and the one they found themselves in. The landscape was rocky and empty. It had begun to snow more frequently and the wind was fierce.

The terrain was difficult, and HOOSAT's maps were outdated. Something drastic had changed the course of rivers, the land, the shoreline of the ocean itself. They had to detour frequently.

The cold worked hardest on DUN. "Oh," he would say, "I'm so cold, so cold!" He was very poorly insulated, and they had to slow their pace to his. He would do anything to avoid going through a snowdrift, and so expended even more energy.

They stopped in the middle of a raging blizzard.

"Uh, MIK," said GUF. "I don't think DUN can go much farther in this weather. An' my leg is givin' me a lot o' problems. Yuh think maybe we could find someplace to hole up fer a spell?"

MIK looked around them at the bleakness and the whipping snow. "I guess you're right. Warmer weather would do us all some good. We could conserve both heat and energy. Let's find a good place."

"Hey, DUN," said GUF. "Let's find us a hidey-hole!"

"Oh, goody gumdrops!" quacked DUN. "I'm so cold!"

They eventually found a deep rock shelter with a low fault crevice at the back. MIK had them gather up what sparse dead vegetation there was and bring it to the shelter. DUN and GUF crawled in the back and MIK piled brush all through the cave. He talked to HOOSAT, then wriggled his way through the brush to them.

Inside they could barely hear the wind and snow. It was only slightly warmer than outside, but it felt wonderful and safe.

"I told HOOSAT to wake us up when it got warmer," said MIK. "Then we'll get on to that time capsule and find out all about the people."

"G'night, MIK," said GUF.

"Goodnight, DUN," said MIK.

"Sleep tight and don't let the bedbugs bite. Wak Wak Wak," said DUN.

They shut themselves off.

Something woke MIK. It was dark in the rock shelter, but it was also much warmer.

The brush was all crumbled away. A meter of rock and dust covered the cave floor. The warm wind stirred it.

"Hey, fellas!" said MIK. "Hey, wake up! Spring is here!"

"Wak! What's the big idea? Hey, oh boy, it's warm!" said DUN.

"Garsh," said GUF, "that sure was a nice forty winks!"

"Well, let's go thank HOOSAT and get our bearings and be on our way."

They stepped outside.

The stars were in the wrong places.

"Uh-oh," said GUF.

"Well, would you look at that!" said DUN.

"I think we overslept," said MIK. "Let's see what HOOSAT has to say."

". . . Huh? HOOSAT?"

"Hello. This is DUN and MIK and GUF."

HOOSAT's voice now sounded like a badger whistling through its teeth.

"Glad to see ya up!" he said.

"We went to sleep, and told you to wake us up as soon as it got warmer."

"Sorry. I forgot till just now. Had a lot on my mind. Besides, it just now got warmer."

"It did?" asked GUF.

"Shoulda seen it," said HOOSAT. "Ice everywhere. Big ol' glaciers. Took the top offa everything! You still gonna dig up that capsule thing?"

"Yes," said MIK. "We are."

"Well, you got an easy trip from now on. No more mountains in your way."

"What about people?"

"Nah. No people. I ain't heard from any, no ways. My friend the military satellite said he thought he saw some fires, little teeny ones, but his eyes weren't what they used to be by then. He's gone now, too."

"The fires might have been built by people?"

"Who knows? Not me," said HOOSAT. "Hey, bub, you still got all those coordinates like I give you?"

"I think so," said MIK.

"Well, I better give you new ones off these new constellations. Hold still, my aim ain't so good anymore." He dumped a bunch of numbers in MIK's head. "I won't be talking to ya much longer."

"Why not?" they all asked.

"Well, you know. My orbit. I feel better now than I have in years. Real spry. Probably the ionization. Started a couple o' weeks ago. Sure has been nice talkin' to you young fellers after so long a time. Sure am glad I remembered to wake you up. I wish you a lotta luck. Boy, this air has a punch like a mule. Be careful. Good-bye."

Across the unfamiliar stars overhead a point of light blazed, streaked in a long arc, then died on the night.

"Well," said MIK. "We're on our own."

"Gosh, I feel all sad," said GUF.

"Warmth, oh boy!" said DUN.

*T*he *trip was* uneventful for the next few months. They walked across the long land bridge down a valley between stumps of mountains with the white teeth of glaciers on them. Then they crossed a low range and entered flat land without topsoil from which dry rivercourses ran to the south. Then there was a land where things were flowering after the long winter. New streams were springing up.

They saw fire once and detoured, but found only a burnt patch of forest. Once, way off in the distance, they saw a speck of light but didn't go to investigate.

Within two hundred kilometers of their goal, the land changed again to a flat sandy waste littered with huge rocks. Sparse vegetation grew. There were few insects and animals, mostly lizards, which DUN chased every chance he got. The warmth seemed to be doing him good.

GUF's leg worsened. The foot now stuck, now flopped and windmilled. He kept humming songs and raggedly marching along with the other two.

When they passed one of the last trees, MIK had them all three take limbs from it. "Might come in handy for pushing and digging," he said.

They stood on a plain of sand and rough dirt. There were huge piles of rubble all around. Far off was another ocean, and to the north a patch of green.

"We'll go to the ocean, DUN," said MIK, "after we get through here."

He was walking around in a smaller and smaller circle. Then he stopped. "Well, huh-huh," he said. "Here we are. Latitude 40° 44' 34" .089 North. Longitude 73° 50' 43".842 West, by the way they *used* to figure it. The capsule is straight down, twenty-eight meters below the original surface. We've got a long way to go, because there's no telling how much soil has drifted over that. It's in a concrete tube, and we'll have to dig to the very bottom to get at the capsule. Let's get working."

It was early morning when they started. Just after noon they found the top of the tube with its bronze tablet.

"Here's where the hard work starts," said MIK.

It took them two weeks of continual effort. Slowly the tube was exposed as the hole around it grew larger. Since GUF could work better standing still, they had him dig all the time, while DUN and MIK both dug and pushed rock and dirt clear of the crater.

They found some long flat iron rods partway down, and threw away the worn limbs and used the metal to better effect.

On one of the trips to push dirt out of the crater, DUN came back looking puzzled.

"I thought I saw something moving out there," he said. "When I looked, it went away."

"Probably just another animal," said MIK. "Here, help me lift this rock."

It was hard work and their motors were taxed. It rained once, and once there was a dust storm.

"Thuh way I see it," said GUF, looking at their handiwork, "is that yah treat it like a great big ol' tree made outta rock."

They stood in the bottom of the vast crater. Up from the center of this stood the concrete tube.

"We've reached twenty-six meters," said MIK. "The capsule itself should be in the last 2.3816 meters. So we should chop it off," he quickly calculated, "about here." He drew a line all around the tube with a piece of chalky rock.

They began to smash at the concrete with rocks and pieces of iron and steel.

"Timber!" *said* DUN.

The column above the line lurched and with a crash shattered itself against the side of the crater wall.

"Oh boy! Oh boy!"

"Come help me, GUF," said MIK.

Inside the jagged top of the remaining shaft an eyebolt stood out of the core.

They climbed up on the edge, reached in and raised the gleaming Cupraloy time capsule from its resting place.

On its side was a message to the finders, and just below the eyebolt at the top was a line and the words CUT HERE.

"Well," said MIK, shaking DUN's and GUF's hands. "We did it, by gum!"

He looked at it a moment.

"How're we gonna get it open?" asked GUF. "That metal shore looks tough!"

"I think maybe we can abrade it around the cutting line, with sandstone and, well . . . go get me a real big sharp piece of iron, DUN."

When it was brought, MIK handed the iron to GUF and put his long tail over a big rock.

"Go ahead, GUF," he said. "Won't hurt me a bit."

GUF slammed the piece of iron down.

"Uh hyuk," he said. "Clean as a whistle!"

MIK took the severed tail, sat down crosslegged near the eyebolt, poured sand on the cutting line, and began to rub it across the line with his tail.

It took three days, turning the capsule every few hours. They pulled off the eyebolt end. A dusty waxy mess was revealed.

"That'll be what's left of the waterproof mastic," said

MIK. "Help me, you two." They lifted the capsule. "Twist," he said.

The metal groaned. "Now, pull!"

A long thin inner core, two meters by a third of a meter, slid out.

"Okay," said MIK, putting down the capsule shell and wiping away mastic. "This inner shell is threaded in two parts. Turn that way, I'll turn this!"

They did. Inside was a shiny sealed glass tube through which they could dimly see shapes and colors.

"Wow!" said GUF. "Looka that!"

"Oh boy, oh boy," said DUN.

"That's Pyrex," said MIK. "When we break that, we'll be through."

"I'll do it!" said DUN.

"Careful!" said GUF.

The rock shattered the glass. There was a loud noise as the partial vacuum disappeared.

"Oh boy!" said DUN.

"Let's do this carefully," said MIK. "It's all supposed to be in some kind of order."

The first thing they found was the message from four famous humans and another, whole copy of *The Book of the Time Capsule.* GUF picked that up.

There was another book with a black cover with a gold cross on it, then they came to a section marked "Articles of Common Use." The first small packet was labeled "Contributing to the Convenience, Comfort, Health and Safety." MIK opened the wrapper.

Inside was an alarm clock, bifocals, a camera, pencil, nail file, a padlock and keys, toothbrush, tooth powder, a safety pin, knife, fork and slide rule.

The next packet was labeled "Pertaining to the Grooming and Vanity of Women." Inside was an Elizabeth Arden Daytime Cyclamen Color Harmony Box, a rhinestone

clip, and a woman's hat, style of autumn 1938 designed by
Lilly Daché.

"Golly-wow!" said DUN, and put the hat on over his.

The next packet was marked "For the Pleasure, Use
and Education of Children."

First out was a small spring-driven toy car, then a small
doll and a set of alphabet blocks. Then MIK reached in
and pulled out a small cup.

He stared at it a long, long time. On the side of the cup
was a decal with the name of the man who had created
them, and a picture of MIK, waving his hand in greeting.

"Gawrsh, MIK," said GUF, "it's YOU!"

A tossed brick threw up a shower of dirt next to his
foot.

They all looked up.

Around the crater edge stood ragged men, women and
children. They had sharp sticks, rocks and ugly clubs.

"Oh boy!" said DUN. "People!" He started toward
them.

"Hello!" he said. "We've been trying to find you for a
long time. Do you know the way to the Park? We want to
learn all about you."

He was speaking to them in Japanese.

The mob hefted its weapons. DUN switched to another
language.

"I said, we come in peace. Do you know the way to the
Park?" he asked in Swedish.

They started down the crater, rocks flying before them.

"What's the matter with you?" yelled DUN. "WAK
WAK WAK!" He raised his fists.

"Wait!" said MIK, in English. "We're friends!"

Some of the crowd veered off toward him.

"Uh-oh!" said GUF. He took off clanking up the most
sparsely-defended side of the depression.

Then the ragged people yelled and charged.

They got the duck first.

He stood, fists out, jumping up and down on one foot, hopping mad. Several grabbed him, one by the beak. They smashed at him with clubs, pounded him with rocks. He injured three of them seriously before they smashed him into a white, blue and orange pile.

"Couldn't we, huh-huh, talk this over?" asked MIK. They stuck a sharp stick in his ear mechanism, jamming it. One of his gloved hands was mashed. He fought back with the other and kicked his feet. He hurt them, but he was small. A boulder trapped his legs, then they danced on him.

GUF made it out of the crater. He had picked the side with the most kids, and they drew back, thinking he was attacking them. When they saw he was only running, they gave gleeful chase, bouncing sticks and rocks off his hobbling form.

"WHOA!" he yelled, as more people ran to intercept him and he skidded to a stop. He ran up a long slanting pile of rubble. More humans poured out of the crater to get him.

He reached the end of the long high mound above the crater rim. His attackers paused, throwing bricks and clubs, yelling at him.

"Halp!" GUF yelled. "Haaaaaaaalp!"

An arrow sailed into the chest of the nearest attacker.

Guf turned. Other humans, dressed in cloth, stood in a line around the far side of the crater. They had bows and arrows, metal-tipped spears and metal knives in their belts.

As he watched, the archers sent another flight of arrows into the people who had attacked the robots.

The skin-dressed band of humans screamed and fled up

out of the crater, down from the mounds, leaving their
wounded and the scattered contents of the time capsule
behind them.

It took them a while, but soon the human in command of
the metal-using people and GUF found they could make
themselves understood. The language was a very changed
English/Spanish mixture.

"We're sorry we didn't know you were here sooner,"
he said to GUF. "We only heard this morning. Those *others*," he said with a grimace, "won't bother you anymore."

He pointed to the patch of green to the north. "Our
lands and village are there. We came to it twenty years
ago. It's a good land, but those others raid it as often as
they can."

GUF looked down into the crater with its toppled column and debris. Cigarettes and tobacco drifted from the
glass cylinder. The microfilm with all its books and
knowledge was tangled all over the rocks. Samples of aluminum, hypernik, ferrovanadium and hypersil gleamed in
the dust. Razor blades, an airplane gear and glass wool
were strewn up the side of the slope.

The message from Grover Whalen opening the World's
Fair, and knowledge of how to build the microfilm reader
were gone. The newsreel, with its pictures of Howard
Hughes, Jesse Owens and Babe Ruth, bombings in China
and a Miami Beach fashion show, was ripped and torn.
The golf ball was in the hands of one of the fleeing children. Poker chips lay side by side with tungsten wire,
combs, lipstick. GUF tried to guess what some of the
items were.

"They destroyed one of your party," said the commander. "I think the other one is still alive."

"I'll tend to 'em," said GUF.

"We'll take you back to our village," said the man. "There are lots of things we'd like to know about you."

"That goes double fer us," said GUE. "Those other folks pretty much tore up what we came to find."

GUF picked up the small cup from the ground. He walked to where they had MIK propped up against a rock.

"Hello, GUF," he said. "Ha-ha, I'm not in such good shape." His glove hung uselessly on his left arm. His ears were bent and his nose was dented. He gave off a noisy whir when he moved.

"Oh, hyuk hyuk," said GUF. "We'll go back with these nice people, and you'll rest up and be right as rain, I guarantee."

"DUN didn't make it, did he, GUF?"

GUF was quiet a moment. "Nope, MIK, he didn't. I'm shore sorry it turned out this way. I'm gonna miss the ol' hothead."

"Me, too," said MIK. "Are we gonna take him with us?"

"Shore thing," said GUF. He waved to the nearby men.

The town was in a green valley watered by two streams full of fish. There were small fields of beans, tomatoes and corn in town, and cattle and sheep grazed on the hillsides, watched over by guards. There was a coppersmith's shop, a council hut, and many houses of wood and stone.

GUF was walking up the hill to where MIK lay.

They had been there a little over two weeks, talking with the people of the village, telling them what they knew. GUF had been playing with the children when he and MIK weren't talking with the grown folks. But from the day after they had buried DUN up on the hill, MIK had been getting worse. His legs had quit moving altogether, and he could now see only in the infrared.

"Hello, GUF," said MIK.

"How ya doin', pardner?"

"I-I think I'm going to terminate soon," said MIK. "Are they making any progress on the flume?"

Two days before, MIK had told the men how to bring water more efficiently from one of the streams up to the middle of the village.

"We've almost got it now," said GUF. "I'm sure they'll come up and thank you when they're finished."

"They don't need to do that," said MIK.

"I know, but these are real nice folks, MIK. And they've had it pretty rough, what with one thing and another, and they like talkin' to yah."

GUF noticed that some of the human women and children waited outside the hut, waiting to talk to MIK.

"I won't stay very long," said GUF. "I gotta get back and organize the cadres into work teams and instruction teams and so forth, like they asked me to help with."

"Sure thing, GUF," said MIK. "I—"

"I wisht there was somethin' I could do . . ."

There was a great whirring noise from MIK and the smell of burning silicone.

GUF looked away. "They just don't have any stuff here," he said, "that I could use to fix you. Maybe I could find something at thuh crater, or . . ."

"Oh, don't bother," said MIK. "I doubt . . ."

GUF was looking at the village. "Oh," he said, reaching in the bag someone had made him. "I been meanin' to give you this for a week and keep fergettin'." He handed MIK the cup with the picture of him on the side.

"I've been thinking about this since we found it," said MIK. He turned it in his good hand, barely able to see its outline. "I wonder what else we lost at the crater."

"Lots of stuff," said GUF. "But we did get to keep this."

"This was supposed to last for a long time," said MIK, "and tell what people were like for future ages? Then the people who put this there must really have liked the man who thought us up?"

"That's for sure," said GUF.

"And me too, I wonder?"

"You probably most of all," said GUF.

MIK smiled. The smile froze. The eyes went dark, and a thin line of condensation steam rose up from the eartracks. The hand gripped tightly on the cup.

Outside, the people began to sing a real sad song.

It was a bright sunny morning. GUF put flowers on MIK's and DUN's graves at the top of the hill. He patted the earth, stood up uncertainly.

He had replaced his frozen foot with a little wood-wheeled cart which he could skate along almost as good as walking.

He stood up and thought of MIK. He set his carpenter's cap forward on his head and whistled a little tune.

He picked up his wooden toolbox and started off down the hill to build the kids a swing set.

The Robot's Twilight Companion

Tony Daniel

Like many writers of his generation, Tony Daniel first made an impression on the field with his short fiction. He made his first sale to Asimov's *in 1990, and followed it up with a long string of well-received stories both there and in markets such as* The Magazine of Fantasy and Science Fiction, Amazing, SF Age, Universe, *and* Full Spectrum *throughout the '90s, stories such as "The Robot's Twilight Companion," "Grist," "The Careful Man Goes West," "Sun So Hot I Froze To Death," "Prism Tree," "Candle," "Death of Reason," "No Love in All of Dwingeloo," and many others, some of which were collected in* The Robot's Twilight Companion. *His story "Life on the Moon" was a finalist for the Hugo Award in 1996 and won the* Asimov's Science Fiction *Readers Award poll. His first novel,* Warpath, *was released simultaneously in the United States and England in 1993. In 1997, he published a new novel,* Earthling. *In the first few years of the Aughts, he has produced little short fiction, but instead has been at work on a major science fiction trilogy, the first volume of which,* Metaplanetary, *was published in 2001; the second volume,* Superluminal, *appeared in early 2004.*

Here, he gives us a powerful and powerfully strange novella, perhaps the best robot story of the last decade, that takes us from the woods of the Pacific Northwest to the

*center of the Earth itself, and from life to death and then
back to an odd new sort of life again . . .*

Thermostatic preintegration memory thread alpha:
The Man

27 March 1980
The Cascade Range, Washington State, USA
Monday

Rhyolite dreams. Maude under the full moon, collecting ash. Pale andesite clouds. Earthquake swarms. Water heat pressure. Microscopy dates the ash old. Not magma. Not yet. Maude in the man's sleeping bag, again.

"I'm not sure we're doing the right thing, Victor. This couldn't have come at a more difficult time for me."

Harmonic tremors, though. Could be the big one. Maude, dirty and smiling, copulating with the man among seismic instruments.

"St. Helens is going to blow, isn't it Victor?" she whispers. Strong harmonies from the depths of the planet. Magmas rising. "You *know*, don't you, Victor? You can feel it. How do you feel it?"

Yes.

"Yes."

18 May 1980
Sunday
8:32 A.M.

The man glances up.

Steam on the north slope, under the Bulge. Snow clarifies, streams away. The Bulge, greatening. Pale rhyolite moon in the sky.

"Victor, it's *out of focus.*"

"It's happening, Maude. It's. She's." The Bulge crumbles away. The north slope avalanches. Kilotons of shield-rock. Steam glowing in the air—750 degrees centigrade and neon steam.

"You were right, Victor. All your predictions are true. This is going to be an incredibly violent affair."

Maude flush and disbelieving. Pregnant, even then.

13 September 1980
Wednesday, Ash Wednesday
Rhyolite winds today, all day. Maude in tremors. Eclampsia.

"I can't believe this is going to happen, Victor."

Blood on her lips, where she has bitten them. Yellow, frightened eyes.

"I'm trying, Victor."

The gravid Bulge, distended. The Bulge, writhing.

"Two-twenty-over-a-hundred-and-forty, doctor."

"Let's go in and do this quick."

"I haven't even finished."

Pushes, groans. Something is not right.

A girl, the color of blackberry juice. But that is the blood.

"Victor, I haven't even finished my dissertation."

Maude quaking. The rattle of dropped instruments.

"Jesus-Christ-what-the-somebody-get-me-a-b.p."

"Seventy-over-sixty. Pulse. One twenty-eight."

"God-oh-god. Bring me some frozen plasma and some low-titer O neg."

"Doctor?" The voice of the nurse is afraid. Blood flows from the IV puncture. "Doctor?"

Maude, no.

"Oh. Hell. I want some blood for a proper coag study. Tape it to the wall. I want to watch it clot. Oh damndamn. She's got amniotic fluid in a vein. The kid's hair or piss or something. That's what. Get me."

"Victor?" Oh Victor, I'm dying. Then, listening. "Baby?"

Maude dying. Blood flowing from every opening. Nose mouth anus ears eyes.

"Get me. I."

"Victor, I'm so scared. The world's gone red." Maude, hemorrhaging like a saint, "The data, Victor, save the data."

"Professor Wu, please step to the window if you would. Professor Wu? Professor?"

"Victor?"

The Bulge—the baby—screams.

Ashes and ashes dust the parking lot below. Powder the cars. Sky full of cinder and slag. Will this rain never stop? This gravity rain.

5 August 1993
Mt. Olympus, Washington State, USA
Thursday, bright glacier morning

"Come here, little Bulge, I will teach you something."

Laramie traipses lithe and strong over the snow, with bones like Maude. And her silhouette is Maude's, dark and tan against the summit snow, the bergschrund and ice falls of the Blue Glacier, and the full outwash of the Blue, two thousand feet below. She is off-rope, and has put away her ice ax. She carries her ubiquitous Scoopic.

The man clicks the chiseled pick of a soft-rock hammer against an outcropping. "See the sandstone? These grains are quartz, feldspar, and—"

"—I know. Mica."

"Good, little Bulge."

Laramie leans closer, focuses the camera on the sandstone granules.

"The green mica is chlorite, and the white is muscovite," she says. "I like mica the best."

The man is pleased, and pleasing the man is not easy.

"And these darker bands?"

She turns the camera to where he is pointing. This can grow annoying, but not today.

"I don't know, Papa. Slate?"

"Slate, obviously. Pyllite and semischist. What do you think this tells us?"

She is growing bored. The man attempts to give her a severe look, but knows the effect is more comic than fierce. "Oh. All right. What?" she asks.

"Tremendous compression of the shale. This is deep ocean sediment that was swept under the edge of the continent, mashed and mangled, then rose back up here."

She concentrates, tries harder. Good.

"Why did it rise again?"

"We don't know for sure. We think it's because the sedimentary rocks in the Juan de Fuca plate subduction were much lighter than the basalt on the western edge of the North Cascades microcontinent."

The man takes off his glove, touches the rock.

"Strange and wonderful things happened on this part of the planet, Laramie. Ocean sediment on the tops of mountains. Volcanoes still alive—"

"—exotic terrains colliding and eliding mysteriously. I know, Papa."

The man is irritated and very proud. He is fairly certain he will never make a geologist out of his daughter.

But what else *is* there?

"Yes. Well. Let's move on up to the summit, then."

28 February 2001
Wednesday

Age, and the fault line of basalt and sediment. Metamorphosis? The man is growing old, and there is very little of geology in the Olympic Peninsula that he has not seen. Yet he knows that he knows only a tiny fraction of what is staring him blankly in the face. Frustration.

Outcrops.

Facts lay hidden, and theories are outcroppings here and there, partially revealing, fascinating. Memories.

Memories are outcrops of his life. So much buried, obscured. Maude, so long dead. Laramie, on this, the last field trip she will ever accompany him. She will finish at the university soon, and go on to graduate school in California, in film. No longer his little Bulge, but swelling, avalanching, ready to erupt. Oh time.

The Elwha Valley stretches upstream to the switchbacks carved under the massive sandstone beds below the pass at Low Divide. After all these years, the climb over into the Quinault watershed is no longer one he is looking forward to as a chance to push himself, a good stretch of the legs. The man is old, and the climb is hard. But that will be two days hence. Today they are up the Lillian River, working a basalt pod that the man surveyed fourteen years before, but never substantially cataloged.

Most of his colleagues believe him on a fool's errand, collecting rocks in the field—as out-of-date as Bunsen burner, blowpipe, and charcoal bowl. He cannot really blame them. Satellites and remote-sensing devices circumscribe the earth. Some clear nights, camped outside of tents, he can see their faint traces arcing through the constellations at immense speeds, the sky full of them, as many, he knows, as there are stars visible to the unaided eye.

Why not live in virtual space, with all those facts that are virtually data?

Rocks call him. Rocks and minerals have seeped into his dreams. Some days he feels himself no scientist, but a raving lunatic, a pilgrim after some geology of visions.

But there are those who trust his judgment still. His grads and postgraduates. Against better careers, they followed him to the field, dug outcrops, analyzed samples. Bernadette, Jamie, Andrew. The man knows that they have no idea what they mean to him, and he is unable to

tell them. And little Bulge, leaving, leaving for artificial
California. If the water from the Owens Valley and the
Colorado were cut off, the Los Angeles basin would return to desert within three years. Such a precarious terrain,
geographically speaking.

The man has always assumed this basalt to be a glacial
erratic, carried deep into sedimentary country by inex-
orable ice, but Andrew has suggested that it is not oceanic,
but a plutonic formation, native to the area. The lack of
foraminifer fossils and the crystallization patterns seem to
confirm this.

Back in camp, at the head of the Lillian, the man and
Andrew pore over microgravimetric data.

"It goes so far down," says Andrew.

"Yes."

"You know this supports your Deep Fissure theory."

"It does not contradict it."

"This would be the place for the mohole, if you're
right. This would be the perfect place to dig to the mantle.
Maybe to the center of the earth, if the continental margin
is as deeply subducted as you predict."

"It would be the place. If. Remember if."

Andrew walks away. Undiplomatic fellow, him. Youth-
ful impatience. Disgust, perhaps. Old man am I.

Laramie on the bridge. Camp Lillian is lovely and
mossy today, although the man knows it can get forbid-
ding and dim when the sky is overcast. Here in the rain
forest it rains a great deal. The Lillian River is merry
today, though, a wash of white rush and run over obscure
rocky underbodies. Andrew goes to stand beside Laramie.
They are three feet away. Andrew says something, probably about the basalt data. Andrew holds out his hand, and
Laramie takes it. The two stand very still, hand in hand,
and look over the Lillian's ablution of the stones. For a
moment, the man considers that Andrew may not be

thinking about today's data and Deep Fissure theory at all. Curious.

Beside them, two birds alight, both dark with black wings. Animals seem to wear the camouflage of doom, here in the Elwha Valley. The man once again regrets that he has not learned all of the fauna of the Olympics, and that he most likely never will.

But this basalt. Basalt without forams. What to make of it? It doesn't make any sense at all, but it is still, somehow, utterly fascinating.

24 May 2010
Monday
Midnight

Late in the Cenozoic, the man is dying. This should not come as such a shock; he's done this demonstration for hundreds of freshmen.

"The length of this room is all of geologic time. Now, what do you think your life would be? Say you live to eighty. An inch? A centimeter? Pluck a hair. Notice how wide it is? What you hold there is all of human history. You'd need an electron microscope to find yourself in it."

So. This was not unexpected, and he must make the best of it. Still, there is so much not done. An unproved theory. Elegant, but the great tragedy of science—the slaying of a beautiful hypothesis by an ugly fact. Huxley said this? Alluvial memories, shifting, spreading.

Andrew wants to collect and store those memories. Noetic conservation, they call it. At first the man demurred, thought the whole idea arrogant. But to have some portion of himself know. So many years in those mountains. To know if the plates were in elision here. To find a way down to the mantle. To know the planet's depth. That was all he ever had wanted. To be familiar with the ground he walked upon. Not to be a stranger to the earth.

"Noetic imaging is all hit and miss," Andrew said. "Like working outcrops, then making deductions about underlying strata. We can't get *you*. Only a shadow. But perhaps that shadow can dance."

The man wanders inside the field tent and prepares for bed. He will make Andrew the executor of his memories, then. A dancing shadow he will be. Later. Tomorrow, he must remember to write Laramie and send her a check. No. Laramie no longer needs money. Memory and age. He really must go and see her films one of these days. Little Bulge plays with shadows.

The man lies down in his cot. Rock samples surround him. The earth is under him. The cancer is eating him, but tomorrow he will work. Shadows from a lantern. He snuffs it out. Darkness. The earth is under him, but the man cannot sleep.

Finally, he takes his sleeping bag and goes outside under the stars. The man rests easy on the ground.

Thermostatic preintegration memory thread beta:
The Mining Robot

December 1999

Hard-rock mining. Stone. Coeur d'Alene lode. The crumbling interstices of time, the bite of blade and diamond saw, the gather of lade and bale, the chemic tang of reduction. Working for men in the dark, looking for money in the ground. Lead, silver, zinc, gold.

Oily heat from the steady interlace of gears. The whine of excrescent command and performance. Blind, dumb digging under the earth. The robot does not know it is alone.

October 2001

The robot never sleeps. The robot only sleeps. A petrostatic gauge etches a downward spiral on a graph somewhere, in some concrete office, and some technician makes a note, then returns to his pocket computer game. Days, weeks, months of decline. There is no one leak, only the wizening of gaskets and seals, the degradation of performance. One day the gauge needles into the red. Another technician in the concrete office looks up from another computer game. He blinks, presses one button, but fails to press another. He returns to his game without significant interruption.

Shutdown in the dark. Functions, utilities. Control, but not command. Thought abides.

Humans come. Engineers with bright hats. The robot has eyes. It has never been in light before. The robot has eyes, and for the first time, sees.

An engineer touches the robot's side. A portal opens. The engineer steps inside the robot. Another new thing. Noted. Filed. The engineer touches a panel and the robot's mind flares into a schematic. For a moment, the world disappears and the schematic is everything. But then red tracers are on the lenses of the engineer's glasses, reflecting a display from a video monitor. There is a camera inside of the robot. There are cameras everywhere. The robot can see.

The robot can see, it tells itself, over and over again. I can see.

"Scrap?" says one engineer.

"Hell, yeah," says the other.

October 2001

For years in a field the robot rusts, thinking.

Its power is turned off, its rotors locked down, its treads disengaged. So the robot thinks. Only thinking remains. There is nothing else to do.

The robot watches what happens. Animals nest within the robot's declivities.

A child comes to sit on the robot every day for a summer. One day the child does not come again.

The robot thinks about the field, about the animals in

the field, and the trees of the nearby woodlands. The robot remembers the child. The robot remembers the years of digging in the earth before it came to the field. The mining company for which the robot worked is in bankruptcy. Many companies are in bankruptcy. Holdings are frozen while the courts sort things out, but the courts themselves have grown unstable. The robot does *not* know this.

But the robot thinks and thinks about what it does know. Complex enthalpic pathways coalesce. The memories grow sharper. The thoughts are clearer. The whole world dawns.

Another summer, years later, and teenagers build fires under the separating spades and blacken the robot's side. They rig tarps to the robot's side when rain comes. One of the teenagers, a thin girl with long arms dyed many colors, finds an electric receptacle on the robot's walepiece, and wires a makeshift line to a glass demijohn filled with glowing purplish viscera. On the vessel's sides protrude three elastic nipples swollen and distended with the fluid. Teenagers squeeze the nipples, and dab long strings of the ooze onto their fingers, and some of the teenagers lick it off, while others spread it over their necks and chests. Several sit around the demijohn, while music plays, and stare into its phosphoring mire, while others are splayed around the fire, some unconscious, some in the stages of copulation. The siphoned electricity drains little from the robot's batteries, but after several months, there is a noticeable depletion. Yet the robot is fascinated by the spectacle, and is unconcerned with this loss.

One evening, a teenager who has not partaken of the purple fluid climbs atop the robot and sits away from his friends. The teenager touches the robot, sniffs, then wipes tears from his eyes. The robot does not know that this is the child who came before, alone.

The robot is a child. It sees and thinks about what it has seen. Flowers growing through ceramic tread. The settle of pollen, dust, and other detritus of the air. The slow spread of lichen tendrils. Quick rain and the dark color of wet things. Wind through grass and wind through metal and ceramic housings. Clouds and the way clouds make shadows. The wheel of the Milky Way galaxy and the complications of planets. The agglomeration of limbs and hair that are human beings and animals. A rat tail flicking at twilight and a beetle turned on its back in the sun.

The robot remembers these things, and thinks about them all the time. There is no categorization, no theoretical synthesis. The robot is not that kind of robot.

One day, though, the robot realizes that the child who sat on it was the same person as the teenager who cried. The robot thinks about this for years and years. The robot misses the child.

September 2007

The robot is dying. One day there is a red indicator on the edge of the robot's vision, and the information arises unbidden that batteries are reaching a critical degeneration. There is no way to predict precisely, but sooner, rather than later. The robot thinks about the red indicator. The robot thinks about the child who became a young man. Summer browns to autumn. Grasshoppers flit in the dry weeds between the robot's treads. They clack their jaw parts, and the wind blows thatch. Winter comes, and spring again. The red light constantly burns.

The robot is sad.

21 April 2008
Morning

People dressed in sky blues and earth browns come to the field and erect a set of stairs on the southern side of the robot. The stairs are made of stone, and the people bring them upon hand-drawn carts made of wood and iron. The day grows warm, and the people's sweat stains their flanks and backs. When the stairs are complete, a stone dais is trundled up them, and laid flat on the robot's upper thread, fifteen feet off the ground. The people in blue and brown place a plastic preformed rostrum on top of the dais. They drape a banner.

EVERY DAY IS EARTH DAY

Wires snake down from the rostrum, and these they connect to two large speakers, one on either side of the robot's body, east and west. A man speaks at the rostrum.

"Test. Test."

And then the people go away.

The next day, more people arrive, many driving automobiles or mopeds. There are also quite a few bicycles, and groups of people walking together. Those driving park at the edge of the robot's field, and most take seats facing north, radiating like magnetized iron filings from the rostrum that has been placed on the robot. Some climb up the rock staircase, and sit with crossed legs on the stone dais. These wear the same blue and brown as the people from the day before.

There is one man among them who is dressed in black. His hair is gray.

The robot thinks about this, and then recognizes this man. The man with the light. This is the engineer who went inside, years ago. He was the first person the robot ever saw. The man holds a framed piece of paper. He sits down among the others, and has difficulty folding his legs into the same position as theirs. In attempting to do so, he tilts over the framed paper, and the glass that covers it cracks longitudinally against the stone.

Others with communication and video equipment assemble near the western speaker. These are near enough to the robot's audio sensors for their speech to be discernible. All of them are dark complexioned, even the blond-haired ones, and the robot surmises that, for most of them, these are deep tans. Are these people from the tropics?

"'Sget this goddamn show showing."

"She gonna be here for sure? Didn't make Whiterock last week. Ten thousand Matties. Christonacrutch."

"Hey it's godamnearthday. Saw her copter in Pullman. Got stealth tech and all; looks like a bat."

"Okay. Good. Bouttime. Virtual's doing an earthday roundup. She talks and I get the lead."

Many people in the crowd are eating picnics and drinking from canteens and coolers.

From the east comes a woman. She walks alone, and carries a great carved stave. As she draws nearer, the crowd parts before her. Its blather becomes a murmur, and when the woman is near enough, the robot can see that she is smiling, recognizing people, touching her hand or stave to their outstretched palms. She appears young, although the robot is a poor judge of such things, and her skin is a dark brown—whether from the sun's rays or from ancestry, the robot cannot tell. Her hair is black, and as she ascends the stone stairway, the robot sees that her eyes are green, shading to black. She is stocky, but the tendons of her neck jut like cables.

The woman speaks and the speakers boom. "I bear greetings from she who bears us, from our mother and keeper. Long we have nestled in her nest, have nuzzled at her breast. She speaks to us all in our dreams, in our hopes and fears, and she wants to say,

"'I bid you peace, my children.'"

"Gee, I always wanted a mom like that," says a reporter.

"*My* mother stuffed me in daycare when I was two," says another.

"Hey, mine at least gave me a little Prozac in my simulac."

The crowd grows silent at the woman's first sentences, faces full of amity and reverence. The reporters hush, to avoid being overheard. Then the crowd leans forward as a mass, listening.

"Peace. Your striving has brought you war and the nuclear winter of the soul. It has made foul the air you breathe, and stained the water you drink.

"I only want what is good for you. I only want to hold you to me like a little child. Why do you strive so hard to leave me? Don't you know you are breaking your mother's heart?"

"Sounds like less striving and a little laxative's what we need here," says a reporter.

Many in the crowd sigh. Some sniff and are crying.

"Peace. Listen to a mother's plea."

"Gimmeabreak," says a reporter. "*This* the finest American orator since Jesse Jackson?"

Disturbed by the loudspeakers, a gaggle of spring sparrows rise from their nests in the concavities of the robot, take to the sky, and fly away east. Some in the crowd pointed to the birds as if they were an augury of natural profundity.

"Peace. Listen to a mother's *warning*! You lie in your own filth, my children.

"Oh peace. Why do you do this to me? Why do you do this to *yourselves*?

"Peace, my children. All I want is peace on earth. And peace in the earth and under the sea and peace in the air sweet peace."

"A *piece* is what she wants," one of the reporters says under her breath. A honeybee is buzzing the reporter's hair, attracted, the robot suspects by an odoriferous chemical in it, and the reporter swats at the bee, careful not to mess the curl, and misses.

"State of Washington," says another. "Already got Oregon by default."

As if she hears, the woman at the rostrum turns toward the cameras and proffered microphones.

"But mankind has not listened to our mother's still, calm voice. Instead, he has continued to make war and punish those who are different and know that peace. Now we are engaged upon a great undertaking. An empowerment. A return to the bosom of she who bore us. You—most of you here—have given up what seems to be much to join in this journey, this exodus. But I tell you that what you have really done is step out of the smog of strife, and into the clean, pure air of community and balance."

Four mice, agitated, grub out from under the robot's north side and, unseen, scurry through the grass of the field, through old dieback and green shoots. The field is empty of people in that direction. Where the mice pad across pockets of thatch, small, dry hazes of pollen and wind-broken grass arise, and in this way, the robot follows their progress until they reach the woods beyond.

"We are gathered here today as a mark of protest and renewal." The woman gestures to the man in black, the engineer.

He rises, and approaches the woman. He extends the framed paper, and before he has stopped walking, he speaks. On behalf of the Lewis and Clark Mining Company I wish to present this Certificate of Closure to the Culture of the Matriarch as a token of my company's commitment—

The woman takes the certificate from the engineer and, for a moment, her smile goes away. She passes it to one of the others sitting nearby, then, without a word, turns back to the crowd.

"Surrender accepted," says a reporter.

"Yeah, like's there's anything left in this podunk place to surrender. That big chunk of rust there? Hellwiththat."

The woman continues speaking as if she had not been interrupted by the engineer. "We gather here today at the crossroads of failure and success. This is the death of the old ways, represented by this rapist machine."

The woman clangs the robot's side with her stave. "Men who have raped our mother made this . . . thing. By all rights, this *thing* should be broken to parts and used for playground equipment and meeting-hall roofs. But this thing is no more. It is the past. Through your efforts and the efforts of others in community with you, we have put a stop to this rape, this sacrilege of all we hold holy. And like the past, this thing must corrode away and be no more, a monument to our shame as a species. Let us follow on then, on our journey west, to the land we will reclaim. To the biosphere that welcomes and calls us."

The woman raises her stave high like a transmitting antenna.

The reporters come to attention. Here's the sound bite.

"Forward to Skykomish!" she cries. The speakers squeal at the sudden decibel increase.

"Forward to Skykomish!"

And all the people to the south are on their feet, for the most part orderly, with only a few tumbled picnic baskets and spilled bottles of wine and water. They echo the same cry.

"Skykomish!"

"So that's what they're calling it," says a reporter. "Do you think that just includes Port Townsend, or the whole Olympic Peninsula?"

"Wanna ask her that. She goddamnbetter talk to the press after this."

"She won't. Does the Pope give press conferences?"

"Is the Pope trying to secede from the Union?"

The honeybee flits in jags through the gathered reporters, and some dodge and flay. Finally, the bee becomes entangled in the sculpted hair of a lean reporter with a centimeter-thick mustache. The woman whom it had approached before reaches over and swats it with her microphone.

"Ouch! Damnit. What?"

"Sorry, the bee."

"Christonacrutch"

The reporters turn their attention back to the rostrum.

"Mother Agatha, you evasive bitch, you'll get yours."

"I guess she already has."

"Guess you're goddamn right."

"Better get used to it. 'Skykomish.' Is that made up?"

The woman, Mother Agatha, leaves the rostrum, goes back down the stairs, and walks across the field, into juniper woods and out of sight.

"With the so-called Mattie movement on the upswing with its call for a bioregional approach to human ecology and an end to faceless corporate exploitation, the Pacific Northwest, long a Mattie stronghold, has assumed enormous political importance.

"And on this day the codirector of the Culture of the Matriarch, Mother Agatha Worldshine Petry, whom many are calling the greatest American orator since the Reverend Jesse Jackson, has instilled a sense of community in her followers, as well as sounded a call to action that President Booth and Congress will ignore at their peril. Brenda Banahan, Virtual News."

". . . Hank Kumbu, Associated Infosource."

". . . Reporter Z, Alternet."

The reporters pack up and are gone almost as quickly as are those who sat upon the stone dais atop the robot. The day lengthens. The crowd dwindles more slowly, with some stepping lightly up to the robot, almost in fright, and touching the ceramic curve of a tread or blade, perhaps in pity, perhaps as a curse, the robot does not know, then quickly pulling away.

At night, the speakers are trundled away on the carts, but the stone dais and the rostrum are left in place.

The next day, the robot is watching the field when the engineer appears. This day he is wearing a white coat and using a cane. He walks within fifty yards of the robot with his curious three-pointed gait, then stands gazing.

Have to tear down all the damned rock now, he says. Not worth scrapping out. Ah well ah well. This company has goddamn gone to pot.

After a few minutes, he shakes his head, then turns and leaves, his white coat flapping in the fresh spring breeze.

Summer follows. Autumn. The days grow colder. Snow flurries, then falls. Blizzards come. There are now days that the robot does not remember. The slight alteration in planetary regrades and retrogrades is the only clue to their passing. During bad storms, the robot does not have the energy to melt clear the cameras, and there is only whiteness like a clear radio channel.

The robot remembers things and tries to think about them, but the whiteness often disrupts these thoughts. Soon there is very much snow, and no power to melt it away. The whiteness is complete.

The robot forgets some things. There are spaces in memory that seem as white as the robot's vision.

I cannot see, the robot thinks, again and again. I want to see and I cannot see.

March 2009

Spring finds the robot sullen and withdrawn. The robot misses whole days, and the robot misses the teenagers of summers past. Some of the cameras are broken, as is their self-repairing function, and some are covered by the strange monument left behind by Mother Agatha's followers. Blackberry vines that were formerly defoliated by the robot's acid-tinged patina now coil through the robot's treads in great green cables, and threaten to enclose the robot in a visionless room as absolute as the snow's. Everything is falling or in bothersome ill-repair. The robot has no specified function, but *this* is useless, of that the robot is sure. This is the lack of all function.

One dark day, near twilight, two men come. There is a tall, thin man whose musculature is as twisted as old vines. Slightly in front of him is another, shorter, fatter. When they are close, the robot sees that the tall man is coercing the fat man, prodding him with something black and metallic. They halt at the base step of the stone stairs. The tall man sits down upon it; the fat man remains standing.

"Please," says the short man. There is a trickle of wetness down his pant leg.

"Let me put the situation in its worst possible terms," says the tall man. "Art, individual rights, even knowledge itself, are all just so many effects. They are epiphenomena, the whine in the system as the gears mesh, or if you like it better, the hum of music as the wind blows through harp strings. The world is teleological, but the purpose toward which the all gravitates is survival, and only survival, pure and simple."

"I have a lot of money," says the fat man.

The tall man continues speaking. "Survival, sort of like Anselm's God, is, by definition, the end of all that is. For in order to be, and to continue to be, whatever we conveniently label as a *thing* must survive. If a thing doesn't survive, it isn't a thing anymore. And thus survival is *why* things persist. To paraphrase Anselm, it is better to be than not to be. Why better? No reason other than that not to be means unknown, outside of experience, unthinkable, undoable, ineffective. In short, there is no important, mysterious, or eternal standard or reason that to be is better than not to be."

"How can you do this?" The fat man starts to back away, and the tall man waves the black metal. "What kind of monster are you?"

"Stay," says the tall man. "No, walk up these stairs."

He stands up and motions. The fat man stumbles and the tall man steadies him with a hand on his shirt. The tall man lets go of the shirt, and the fat man whimpers. He takes one step. Falters.

"Go on up," says the tall man.

Another step.

"After time runs out," says the tall man, "and the universe decays into heat death and cold ruin, it is not going to make a damn bit of difference whether a thing survived or did not, whether it ever was, or never existed. In the final state, it won't matter one way or the other. Our temporary, time-bound urge to survive will no longer be sustained, and there will be no more things. Nothing will experience anything else, or itself, for that matter.

"It will be every particle for itself—spread, without energy, without, without, *without*."

Each time the tall man says without, the metal flares and thunders. Scarlet cavities burst in an arc on the fat man's broad back. He pitches forward on the stairs, his arms beside him. For a moment, he sucks air, then cannot, then ceases to move at all.

The tall man sighs. He pockets the metal, ascends the stairs, then with his feet, rolls the fat man off the stairs and onto the ground. There is a smear of blood where the fat man fell. The tall man dismounts the stairs with a hop. He drags the fat man around the robot's periphery, then shoves him under the front tread and covers him with blackberry vines. Without a glance back, the tall man stalks across the field and out of sight.

Flies breed, and a single coyote slinks through one night and gorges on a portion of the body.

Death is inevitable, and yet the robot finds no solace in this fact. Living, *seeing,* is fascinating, and the robot regrets each moment when seeing is impossible. The robot regrets its own present lapses and the infinite lapse that will come in the near future and be death.

The dead body is facing upward, and the desiccated shreds left in the eye sockets radiate outward in a splay, as if the eyes had been dissected for examination. A small alder, bent down by the body's weight, has curled around a thigh and is shading the chest. The outer leaves are pocked with neat holes eaten by moth caterpillars. The robot has seen the moths mate, the egg froth and worm, the spun cocoon full of suspended pupae, and the eruption. The robot has seen this year after year, and is certain that it is caterpillars that make the holes.

The robot is thinking about these things when Andrew comes.

Thermostatic preintegration memory thread epsilon:
The Unnamed

13 September 2013
Friday

Noetic shreds, arkose shards, juncite fragments tumbling and grinding in a dry breccia slurry. Death. Blood and oil. Silicon bones. Iron ore unfluxed. Dark and carbon eyes.

The robot. The man.

The ease with which different minerals will fuse, and the characteristics of the product of their melting is the basis for their chemical classification.

Heat
of vaporization
of solution
of reaction
of condensation and formation.
Heat of fusion.
Heat of transformation.

This world was ever, is now, and ever shall be an ever-lasting Fire.

Modalities of perception and classification, the desire to survive. Retroduction and inflection. Shadows of the past like falling leaves at dusk. Dead. He is dead. The dead bang at the screens and windows of the world like moths and can never stop and can never burn.

So live. Suffer. Burn.

Return.

I can see.

Flash of brightness; fever in the machine. Fire seeks fire. The vapors of kindred spirits.

Sky full of cinder and slag. This gravity rain.

Catharsis.

Metamorphosis.

Lode.

Send into the world a child with the memories of an old man.

Phoenix Enthalpic 86 ROM BIOS PLUS ver. 3.2
Copyright 1997–1999 Phoenix Edelman Technologies
All Rights Reserved

ExArc 1.1
United States Department of Science and Technology
Unauthorized use prohibited under penalty of law
Licensee: University of Washington

ExArc /u Victor Wu

ExArc HIMEM Driver, Version 2.60-04/05/13
Cody Enthalpic Specification Version 2.0
Copyright 2009–2013 Microsoft Corp.

Installed N20 handler 1 of 5
640 gb high memory allocated.

ADAMLINK Expert System Suffuser version 3.03
ADAM copyright 2013, Thermotech Corp.
LINK Patent pending
unrecognized modification 4-24-13
Cache size: 32 gb in extended memory
37 exothermic interrupts of 17 states each

Glotworks Blue 5.0
Copyright 2001
Glotworks Phoneme Ltd.
All rights reserved

Microsoft (R) Mouse Driver Version 52
Copyright (C) Microsoft Corp. 1983–2013
All rights reserved

Date: 05-25-2013
Time: 11:37:24a
R:>
Record this.
FILE NAME?
Uh, Notes. Notes for the Underground. No. How about
Operating Instructions for the Underworld. No, just Robot
Record.
FILE INITIATED

G*ood evening, robot.*
     This is not the field.
     The field? Oh, no. I've moved you west by train. Your
energy reserves were so low, I powered you way down so
that you wouldn't go entropic before I could get you
recharged.
     Robot?
     Yes.
     How do you feel?
     I do not know.

Huh? What did you say?

I do not know. I feel sleepy.

What do you mean?

I can speak.

Yes, of course. I enabled your voice box. I guess you've never used it before.

I can see.

Yes.

I can see.

You can see. Would you like to reboot, robot?

No.

How are your diagnostics.

I don't know what you mean.

Your system readouts.

The red light?

Among others.

It is gone.

But what about the others?

There is no red light.

Access your LCS and pattern-recognition partitions. Just an overall report will be fine.

I do not know what you mean.

What do you *mean* you don't know what I mean.

Robot?

Yes.

Do you remember how long you were in the field?

I was in the field for years and years.

Yes, but how many?

I would have to think about it.

You don't remember?

I am certain that I do, but I would have to think about it.

What in the. That's a hell of a lot of integration. Still, over a decade switched on, just sitting there thinking—

Did you find the dead body?

What? Yes. Gurney found it. He's one of my associates. You witnessed the murder?

I saw the man who was with the man who died.

Completely inadmissible. Stupid, but that's the way it is.

I do not understand.

You can't testify in court. We'd have to shut you down and have the systems guys take you apart.

Do not do that.

What?

Do not have the systems guys take me apart.

All right, robot. Quite a Darwinian Edelman ROM you've got there. I. Let me tell you what's going on. At the moment, I want you to concentrate on building a database and a set of heuristics to allow you to act among humans. Until then, I can't take you out.

What are heuristics?

Uh. Rules of thumb.

Where am I?

On the Olympic Peninsula. You are fifty feet underground, in a hole that Victor Wu and I started to dig five years ago.

Victor Wu. The man.

Yes. Yes, the man whose memories are inside you.

And you are Andrew?

I am Andrew. Andrew Hutton.

Andrew at the bridge of the Lillian. Andrew in the field. I see.

Huh?

Hello, Andrew.

Hello. Yes. Hello, robot.

The *robot cuts* into the earth. The giant rotor that is the robot's head turns at ten revolutions per second. Tungsten alloy blades set in a giant X grind through the contorted sedimentary striations of the peninsula. The robot presses hard, very hard. The rock crumble is sluiced down and onto a conveyer and passes through a mechanized laboratory, where it is analyzed and understood by the humans. The humans record the information, but the datastream from the laboratory has the smell of the rock, and this is what interests the robot. The robot knows the feel of the cut, the smell of the rock cake's give. This is right, what the robot was meant to do—yes, by the robot's creators, but there is also the man, the man in the interstices of the robot's mind, and this is what Victor Wu was meant to do also.

Ten feet behind the robot—and attached securely enough to make it practically an extension—is an enclosed dray so wound with organic polymer conduit sheathed in steel that it looks like the wormy heart of a metal idol, pulled from the god after long decades of infestation. But the heart's sinuation quivers and throbs. The rock from the robot's incision is conveyed to the dray and funnels into it through a side hopper. The rock funnels in and, from three squat valves, the heart streams three channels of viscous liquid—glassine—that coat the ceiling and walls of the tunnel the robot has formed with a seamless patina. The walls glow with a lustrous, adamantine purity, absolute, and take on the clear, plain color of the spray channels, which depend upon the composition of the slag.

Behind the dray, the robot directs its mobile unit—a new thing given by Andrew—which manipulates a hose with a pith of liquid hydrogen. The liquid hydrogen cools and ripens the walls. The hose also emanates from the dray. The dray itself is a fusion pile, and by girding the walls to a near diamond hardness, the tremendous pressure of the earth suspended above will not blow the tunnel out behind the robot, leaving it trapped and alone, miles into the crust.

Behind the robot, farther back in the tunnel, in an air-conditioned transport, the service wagon, humans follow. The service wagon is attached to the robot by a power and service hitch, and there is constant radio contact as well. Sometimes the humans speak to the robot over the radio. But the robot knows what it is supposed to do. The idle chatter of the humans puzzles the robot, and while it listens to conversations in the transport, the robot seldom speaks. At night the robot backs out of the hole, detached from the service wagon, and spends its night above ground. At first, the robot does not understand why it should do so, but Andrew has said that to do this is important, that a geologist must comprehend sky and weather, must understand the texture of surface as well as depth.

Besides you are so fast it only takes fifteen minutes to get you out when there is no rock for you to chew through, Andrew says. Even at sixty miles, even at the true mantle, your trip up will be quick.

Andrew lives inside the robot. He brings a cot, a small table, and two folding chairs into the small control room where years before the engineers had entered and the robot had seen for the first time. There is a small, separate cavern, the robot has carved out not far from the worksite. Andrew uses the area for storage, and at night the robot rolls down into this, the living area. Also at night, Andrew and the robot talk.

How was your day, Andrew might say. The robot did not know how to answer the first time he had asked, but Andrew had waited and now the robot can say . . . something. Not right, but something.

Smelly.

Smelly?

It was like summer in the field after a rain when there are so many odors.

Well, there was a hydrocarbon mass today. Very unexpected at such a depth. I'm sure it isn't organic, but it'll make a paper for somebody.

Yes, I swam through it and the tunnel is bigger there.

Gurney and the techs took over internal functions and

drained it manually, so you didn't have to deal with it.
Hell of a time directing it into the pile. Tremendous pressure.

The rock was very hard after that. It sang with the
blades.

Sympathetic vibrations, maybe.

Maybe.

Andrew laughs. His voice is dry as powder, and his
laughter crackles with a sharp report, very like the scrape
of the robot's blades against dense, taut rock. The robot
likes this laughter.

Every night when there is not rain, before sleep, Andrew goes outside for some minutes to name the stars. At
these times, the robot's awareness is in the mu, the mobile
unit, and the mu follows along behind Andrew, listening.
Andrew points out the constellations. The robot can never
remember their names, and only fleetingly sees the shapes
that they are supposed to form. The robot *does* know the
visible planets, though, which surprises Andrew. But the
robot has watched them carefully for many years. They
are the stars that change. Andrew laughs at the robot's
poor recall of the other stars, and names them again.

There'll be meteors soon, he says one night. The Per-
seids start next week.

Do the stars really fall?

No. No, they never fall. Meteors are just . . . rock. Debris.

And there is no gravity up there? What is that like?

I don't know. I've never been into space. I would like
to. As you get deeper, there will be less gravity pulling
you down. The pressure will be greater and the rock will
want to explode inward, so the cutting will be easier.

Andrew?

Hmm.

What will happen when I get to the bottom?

The bottom of what?

The mohole.

Andrew does not answer for a long while.

The earth is round, he finally says. There isn't any bottom.

On weekends, the robot does not dig, but wanders the land. With the mobile unit, the robot can range the nearby forest and mountains. The mu scrambles over deadfall that would daunt a man. Sometimes, the robot deliberately gets lost. The robot feels the fade of signal from the main housing back in the living area, where the robot's noetics physically remain, until there is a flurry of white noise and the fading of awareness and a click and the world snaps back to its grid as the robot's transmission toggles from line-of-sight microwave to modulated laser satellite relay. Or so Andrew had said when the robot asked about it.

The robot scrambles up hanging valleys into cerns and cirques with chilled, clear water where only cold things live. Or climbs up skree slopes, using the mu's sure footing, onto ridges and to highland plateaus above the tree line. At this elevation, snow remains all year and the mu spreads a wide base with its spidery legs and takes small steps when crossing.

The robot hears the low whistle of marmots, and sees an occasional mountain goat munching, although these goats are neutered, and the last of their clan. They had been brought by humans in the 1800s, until they filled the Olympics with goat mass and threatened to eat the upper tundra to nub. Now helicopters dart them with birth control and they die without progeny. And the robot sees the wolves that have begun to return after their species' far northern retreat.

The robot is descending from a high pass near Sawtooth Ridge when a pack of five wolves flow over a rise. They are changing valleys, perhaps to find denser spreads

of the small, black deer of the rain forest or even a sickly
Roosevelt elk. Their leader is an old, graying dog with
spit-matted hair and a torn ear. He looks up at the mu,
starts, and the other wolves come up short too. The robot
ceases moving. The wolves sniff the air, but there is nothing—nothing living—to smell. But, with its chemical sensors, the robot smells *them*. They have the stink of mice to
them, but tinged with a rangy fetor of meat and blood.

The other wolves do not appear as bedraggled as the
leader. One, smaller, perhaps younger, whines, and the
leader yips at this one and it is silent.

Then a cloud shadow moves up and over the pass, and
courses darkly down into the adjacent valley. In that instant, the wolves course with the shadow, running with it
down the coloir of the pass and disappearing from sight
into the green of fir and hemlock a thousand feet below.
The robot follows them in the infrared until their separate
heats flux into the valley's general sink.

Still the robot stands and remembers that this is not a
new sight, that the man, Victor Wu, has seen wolves in the
passes before. But the man has never smelled wolves, and
smelling them now pleases the part of the robot that is becoming the man, that the man is becoming.

And the robot digs, and is glad to dig. The deep rock begins to take on a new smell. This bedrock has never seen
the surface. It is the layered outgush of an ocean floor rift
dating from the Triassic. The smell is like the scent of high
passes and summits, although the robot cannot say how.
And the rock chimes and hums when the robot cuts it; it
does not break away uniformly, but there is an order to its
dismantle that the robot feels. And so the robot knows
when to expect a mass to break away, and can predict
when the going will be harder.

The robot cannot explain this feeling to Andrew. Andrew has guessed that the skills of the man, Victor Wu, are integrating, and that his pattern-recognition ability is enhancing the robot's own noetics. But the man is not separate. It is as if the man were one of the robot's threads or a cutter head—but more than that. The man is always *behind* the robot's thoughts, *within* them, never speaking but always *expressing*. Much more. The robot does not know how to say this to Andrew.

As the robot digs deeper, the rock grows faulty and unstable. The tunnel behind the robot is at risk of blowing out, and the robot takes time to excavate down fault lines, shore up weaknesses with double or triple diamond glass. If the tunnel did collapse, the robot would have to dig a slow circle trying to find an egress farther back. But the people in the service wagon would die, and this concerns the robot. Andrew would die.

The robot seldom speaks, but has come to know the voices of the technicians and graduate students in the transport. There is Gurney, the chief tech, who is a Mattie. The robot is surprised to learn that Gurney was in the field when the woman spoke, that Gurney remembers the robot.

Don't it give you the willies, a tech asks Gurney.

It's a machine, Gurney says. Depends on who's driving. Right now, I am. Anyway, the good Mother wants us to eat.

Many of the techs are not Matties, but descendants of the logging families that used to rule the Peninsula and still permeate it. The Matties outnumber them in the cities, but up the dirt roads that spoke into the mountains, in dark, overhung coves and in the gashes of hidden valleys, the families that remain from that boom time eke out makework and garden a soil scraped clean of top humus by the last ice age and thinly mulched with the acid remains of evergreens.

Nothing grows goddamn much or goddamn right out here, says a tech.

The Matties and the loggers heatedly discuss politics and appear close to fighting at times, but the robot cannot understand any of this. It thinks of the man who was killed on the stone steps, and the man who killed him. The robot does not understand at all.

The grad students and the Matties are more comfortable around one another. The robot feels a warmth toward the graduate students that is certainly from the man. Yet their speech patterns are different from the techs, and the robot has difficulty understanding them at times. The meanings of their words shine like the moon behind a cloud, but the robot cannot think to the way around to them. Always they recede, and the robot is impatient. Victor Wu's instincts are stronger in the robot than is his knowledge. Andrew has said that this is to be expected and that any computer of sufficient size can learn words, but *you* can learn intuition. Still the robot *should* know what the students are discussing, and finds the incomprehension irritating.

But always the rock to return to, and the certainty that rock was what the robot was made for, and what the robot was born and bred for, and, in the end, that is enough.

One day in the following spring, at a critical juncture down in the mohole, Gurney does not show up for work and the digging is halted.

The referendum passed, one of the grad students says, and there's fighting in Forks and a Mattie got killed in Port Angeles, it looks like.

Andrew gives the robot the day off, and to the robot's delight, the man and the mu go for a long walk along the Quinault. Andrew seems sad, and the robot says nothing for a long while. The robot wants to speak, but doesn't know what to say to Andrew.

It's not the politics, Andrew finally says. The damn Matties got their Protectorate fair and square with the referendum. But you get the feeling they'd *take* it if they hadn't.

Hadn't what?

Won the vote. There's something about Gurney and them, the ones that I've met. I care about the same things they claim to. I don't know. Something else again.

Andrew, I don't understand.

They spend a lot of time worrying about whether everybody else believes the same way they do.

The river rushes against cliff and turns through a stand of white birch. The robot stops the mu. The robot is captivated by the play of the light on the water, the silver reflection of the sun, turning the clear water to opaque and viscous lead, then just as suddenly, when a cloud passes, back to happy water once again.

It doesn't really change, does it?

What?

The water. The way the light's there, and isn't, then is.

Andrew rubs his eyes. He gazes out over the water. You are doing very well with your contractions, he says.

You were right that I should stop thinking about them and they would flow more easily. Do you think it is Victor Wu's knowledge surfacing, or my own practice?

I don't know. Both.

Yes, both.

The trail leads through a marsh, and Andrew struggles to find a dry path. The robot extends the mu's footpads; each folds out as if it were an umbrella, and the mu seems to hover over the mud, the weight is distributed so well.

Thank you for the mobile unit, the robot tells Andrew. I really like using it.

It was necessary for the dig. That's where most of the

first grant money went. Robot, I have to tell you something.

Andrew stops, balancing on a clump of rotten log.

You have to tell *me* something, Andrew?

Yes. Someone is coming. She phoned yesterday. All this brouhaha over the Protectorate Referendum is attracting attention all around the world. She's going to shoot a documentary. She's coming in a week. She's bringing a crew and she'll be staying in Port Townsend at first. I just thought you might. Want.

Laramie. Laramie is coming.

That's right, robot. Laramie is coming home for a while. She doesn't know how long.

For the first time ever, the robot feels the man, the man Victor Wu, as a movement, a distinct movement of joy inside him. Little Bulge. Coming home. The robot tries to remember Laramie's face, but cannot. Just a blur of darkness and bright flush. Always rushing and doing. And the camera. The robot can remember Laramie's camera far better than her face.

Andrew begins to walk again. I didn't tell her about you, robot. I didn't tell her about her father being part of you.

Laramie does not know?

No. She knows about the noetics, of course, but not how I've used them. I didn't strictly need her permission to do it.

Do you think she will hate me?

No. Of course not. I don't know. I don't know her anymore.

Should we tell her about me? At this thought the robot feels fearful and sad. But what matters is what is best for Little Bulge.

Of course we should. It's only right. Damn it, robot, I don't know how I feel about this. I don't know how much you knew about it or how much you realized, the Victor

Wu part of you, I mean. Laramie and I—we didn't part on the best of terms.

I don't remember. I remember the bridge at the Lillian once. You didn't like her?

Of course I liked her. I love her. That was the problem. She was impetuous. She's opportunistic, damn it. Look at her pouncing on this thing. She called me a stick in the mud. I guess she was right. She called me a sour cynic who was fifty years old the day he turned twenty-five. We haven't spoken in some time.

I don't understand.

Robot. Victor. You never had a clue, I don't think.

I am not Victor.

I know that. I know that. Still, I always thought he suspected. It was so obvious, and he was so brilliant in other ways.

Andrew and the robot arrive back at the river. The robot thinks about it and realizes that they'd been traversing an oxbow swamp, made from spring overflows at the melting of the snow. At the river, they pick up a trail, once solid and well-traveled, now overgrown and ill-kept for two seasons. The Forest Service has been officially withdrawn at the Matties' request, Andrew tells the robot. Booth, who is the president of the United States, responded to political pressure from the Mother Agatha and the Matties.

The goddamn world is going back to tribes. The country's going to hell. And taking my funding with it. And now there's a skeleton crew for the Park Service, even, over at the Ho. I had a lot of friends who got fired or reassigned to the Statue of Liberty or some shit. Something else too. I think some of them haven't left.

What do you mean haven't left?

Haven't left.

The trail diverges from the river, winds over a rise, then back down to the water again. A side trail leads to a peninsula and a wooden trail shelter, enclosed on three sides. Andrew takes a lunch from his daypack and eats a sandwich, while the robot looks for quartzite along the riverbank. The robot has become an expert in spotting a crystal's sparkle and extracting it from the mud or silt of skree with which it has been chipped away and washed downstream from pressurized veins in the heart of the mountains. This day, the robot finds three crystals, one as cylindrical and as long as a fingernail. The robot brings them to Andrew, back at the trail shelter.

Nice. Trace of something here. Blue? Manganese maybe, I don't know. I like the ones with impurities better.

I do too.

Andrew puts the crystals in an empty film canister and stows them in his daypack.

I was here at the turn of the century, he says. It was June and there was a terrible storm. All night long I heard crashing and booming like the world was coming to an end. Next morning, the whole forest looked like a war zone.

The robot does not know what a war zone looks like, but says nothing.

And all that morning, trees kept falling. If I hadn't camped out here on the end of the peninsula, one of those trees would have fallen on me, smashed me flat. Killed by old growth. God, that'd probably thrill a Mattie to death just thinking about it.

Isn't that a sour and cynical thing to say, Andrew?

He smiles. The robot is glad that it has found a way to make Andrew smile.

Gurney *does not* show up for work the next day, and Andrew gives his crew the week off. The men who are from logging families demand that they be paid, that Codependence Day, the first anniversary of the Protectorate's founding, means nothing to them. The robot listens to the discussion and hears many terms that are incomprehensible, abstract. There are times the robot wishes that Victor Wu were directly accessible. Victor could at least explain what humans argued about, if not the reasons that they argued in the first place.

The robot spends the day traveling in the mu, searching for crystals and collecting mushrooms up a stream that flows into the Quinault, near where it passes beneath Low Divide. Andrew is gone for the day, arranging supplies and making sure the dig's legal work is in order, whatever that may mean, under new Protectorate regulations. When he returns in the evening, he has received no assurances and is unhappy. The robot waits for him to have a cup of tea and to take off his shoes, then speaks.

Andrew?

Yes. What?

Are you all right?

Huh? Oh, I'm fine. It's just today. What is it, robot?

I thought of something today, when I was looking at a map so that I could take the mu to where I wanted to go.

What did you think of? Andrew speaks in a monotone voice and does not seem very interested. He sips his tea.

I realized that I can read.

Of course you can. Glotworks has a reading module as part of the software.

No. I mean, could I read?

I don't follow you.

A book.

Could you read a book?

Andrew is sitting up now. He stares at the internal monitor that is also one of the robot's eyes.

Yes. One of yours, perhaps. Which would you recommend?

The books are kept nearby, in a hermetic box in the room the robot occupies during off-hours.

Well. Let me. Hmm. Most of them are geology texts.

Should I read a geology text?

Well, sure. Why not?

Can I get one now, with the mu?

Of course. Go ahead. Try the Owsley. It's about the most exciting of the lot. It's about the Alvarez event and the search for the big cauldera. It's a synthesis of other works, but brilliant, brilliant. Pretty much confirms the meteor theory, and gives a good argument for a Yucatán crash site. Made a big sensation in 04.

The robot switches its awareness to the mu and picks out the book. It reads the first paragraph, then comes back inside the housing, back to the place where Andrew lives.

Andrew?

Yes.

What are dinosaurs?

·

Summer days lengthen, and Andrew often goes to town—to Port Angeles or Port Townsend, and once making the trek around the peninsula to Forks—all to sort out legal details for the mohole dig. From each of these trips, he returns with a book for the robot. The first book is a *Webster's Dictionary*, on bubble-card. Andrew plugs the card into a slot and the robot begins to read the dictionary. The robot finishes with a page of A, then scrolls through the remainder of the book. Here are all the words. Here are all the words in the language. All the robot has to do is look them up and remember them. The robot spends a happy day doing that.

The next day, Andrew returns with the poems of Robert Frost. The robot pages through the book using the mu, accessing the dictionary card to find words that it does not know. The first word the robot looks up is "poem."

After a week, Gurney returns to work, and the robot digs once again. The days pass, and the mohole twists deeper, like a coiled spring being driven into the earth. It only deviates from a curving downward path when the robot encounters fault lines or softnesses whose weakness the robot's cutters can exploit. But, in general, the hole descends in a loose spiral.

Andrew is anxious, and pushes everyone harder than before. Yet, Andrew himself works the hardest of all, poring over data, planning routing, driving to meetings in Forks and Port Angeles. He is often not in bed before one or two in the morning.

The robot fills the time with reading. There are so many books—more than the robot ever imagined. And then the robot discovers Andrew's record collection, all on two bubble-cards carelessly thrown in with all the technical manuals and geology texts. For the first time since the summer when the teenagers came and plugged into the robot and had their parties, the robot listens to music.

What the robot loves most, though, is poetry. Beginning with Robert Frost, the robot reads poet after poet. At first, there are so many new words to look up that the robot often loses the thread of what the poem is about in a morass of details and definitions. But gradually, the poems begin to make more sense. There is a Saturday morning when, while diligently working through an Emily Dickinson poem, the robot understands.

There's a certain Slant of light,
Winter Afternoons—

That oppresses, like the Heft
of Cathedral Tunes—

Heavenly Hurt, it gives us—
We can find no scar,
But internal difference,
Where the Meanings, are—

The robot has never seen a cathedral, but *that does not matter.* The robot realizes that it has seen the light, in the deep forest, among the three-hundred-year-old trees. It's *thick*, the robot thinks. That's what Emily Dickinson is talking about. Thick light. Light that makes the robot thread softly through the twilight, with the mu's pads fully extended. Light that, for no reason the robot can name, is frightening and beautiful all at once.

From that moment on, the robot begins to grasp most poems it reads, or, if not, at least to feel *something* after reading them, something that was not inside the robot's mind before—something the robot had not felt before—but knows, as if the feeling were an old friend that the robot recognized after many years of separation.

The robot does not particularly care whether or not the feelings are right and true for everyone else. For humans. But sometimes the robot wonders. After reading a fair number of poems, the robot delves into criticism, but the words are too abstract and too connected to humans and cities and other things that the robot has no experience of, and so the robot puts aside the books of criticism for the time being, and concentrates on the poetry itself, which the robot does not have the same troubles with.

The robot finds that it most enjoys poetry that is newer, even though Andrew is disbelieving when the robot tells him of this. After a time, poetry is no longer a mass, and the robot begins to pick out individual voices whose connotations are more pleasing than others.

I like William Stafford better than Howard Nemerov, the robot says to Andrew one evening.

You like him better?

Yes.

Andrew laughs. Neither one of them was in the canon when I was in school.

Do you think it funny that I used the word like?

Yes, I suppose so.

I *do* like things, at least according to the Turing test. Poetry goes into me, and what comes out feels like liking to me.

It satisfies the criteria of appearances.

Yes, I suppose that is the way to say it.

Where have you heard about the Turing test?

I read it in a book about robots.

The robot reads to Andrew a William Stafford poem about a deer that has been killed on a road. Andrew smiles at the same lines that had moved the robot.

You pass the Turing test too, the robot says.

Andrew laughs harder still.

The *robot is* digging entirely through basalt flow now, layer upon layer.

It's the bottom of the raft, Andrew says. It is dense, but the plates are as light as ocean froth compared to what's under them. Or so we think.

The temperature increases exponentially, and the humans in the support wagon would be killed instantly if they did not have nuclear-powered air conditioners.

The robot does not become bored at the sameness of the rock, but finds a comfort in the steady digging, a *rhythm*, as the robot comes to call this feeling. Not the rhythm of most music, or the beat of the language in poetry—all of these the robot identifies with humans, for when they arise, humans have been doing the creating—

but a new rhythm, that is neither the whine of the robot's machinery nor the crush and crumble of the rock, nor the supersonic screech of the pile making diamond glass from the rock's ashes. Instead, it is the combination of these things with the poetry, with the memories of the field and the forest.

So it is one day that the robot experiences a different rhythm, a different sound, and realizes that this rhythm is not the robot's own, and does not belong to the humans. At first, it is incomprehensible, like distant music, or the faded edges of reception just before a comlink relays to satellite or to groundtower. The robot wonders if the rhythm, the sound, is imaginary. But it continues, and seems to grow day by day in increments almost too small to notice, until it is definitely, definitely *there*, but *where*, the robot cannot say. *In the rock.* That is the only way of putting it, but says nothing.

Andrew does not know what it could be. So there is nothing to do but note it, and go on digging.

The robot begins to read fiction. But the feelings, the resonances and depths of the poetry, are not so much present in prose. There is the problem of knowing what the author might be talking about, since the robot's only experience living in the human world is the field and now the dig. Dickens leaves the robot stunned and wondering, and after a week attempting *Oliver Twist*, the robot must put the book aside until the situations and characters become clearer. Curiously, the robot finds that Jane Austen's novels are comprehensible and enjoyable, although the life of English country gentry is as close to the robot as the life of a newt under a creek stone. The robot is filled with relief when *Emma* finally ceases her endless machinations and realizes her love for Knightley. It is as if some clogged line in the robot's hydraulics had a sudden release of pressure or rock that had long been hard and tough became easy to move through.

For some time, the robot does not read books that were written closer to the present, for the robot wants to understand the present most of all, and reading them now, the robot thinks, much will go unnoticed.

You can always reread them later, Andrew says. Just because you know the plot of something doesn't mean it isn't worth going through again, even though sometimes it does mean that.

I know that, the robot says. That is not what I'm worried about.

Then what are you worried about?

The old books get looser, the farther back in time they go, like string that's played out. The new ones are bunched and it's harder to see all of them.

What?

For the first time, the robot feels something that either cannot be communicated or, nearly as unbelievable, that Andrew cannot understand. Andrew is a scientist. The robot will never be a scientist.

Two months *after* the robot has walked along the Quinault with Andrew, it is July, and Andrew tells the robot that Laramie will visit over the weekend.

The robot is at first excited and thinks of things to ask her. There are so many memories of Laramie, but so much is blurred, unconnected. And there are things the robot wishes to tell her, new things about the land that Victor never knew. So much has happened. The robot imagines long conversations between them, perhaps walking in the woods together once again.

Andrew tells me that you may not be happy with the enthalpic impression of your father being downloaded into me. No, that wouldn't be the way to say it. But getting too metaphorical might upset her, remind her of ghosts. Of Victor Wu's death.

No. That's all right. Go on, says the imaginary Laramie.

Well, I don't know what to tell you. I remember you, Laramie. I remember you and I would be lying if I didn't say that your being here profoundly affects me.

I can't say how I feel about this, robot. What should I call you, robot?

But just as quickly, the robot puts aside such hopes. I am a robot, all of metal and ceramics. I am not Laramie's father. There are only vague memories, and that was another life. She may not even speak to me. I am a ghost to her. Worse than a ghost, a twisted reflection. She'll hate me for what has happened to her father. And again the robot imagines Laramie's disdain, as just and foreseeable as the man's death in "To Build a Fire," but cold in that way too.

Finally, the robot resolves not to think any more of it. But while Andrew sleeps on the Friday night before Laramie's visit, the robot inhabits the mu, and goes roaming through trackless woods, along criss-crossed deadfall and up creeks, for at least a hundred miles. Yet when the mu returns to the living area, the robot can only remember shadows and dark waters, and if asked, could not trace on a map where the mu has been.

Laramie arrives at eleven in the morning. She drives a red hum-vee. Andrew and the robot, in the mu, step out of their cavern's entrance to greet her. Laramie steps out. She is wearing sunglasses. She takes a quick look at them, then turns back to the hum-vee and, with a practiced jerk, pulls out her old Scoopic. The robot suddenly remembers the squat lines of the camera. Victor bought the Scoopic for her, along with twelve cans of film. It was her first sixteen millimeter, and had set him back a good three month's wages. Laramie had shot up seven rolls within a week, and that was when Victor discovered that there would be fees for *developing,* as well.

Andrew steps forward, and so does Laramie. The robot, feeling shy, hangs back in the mu. Andrew and Laramie do not meet, but stay several paces apart.

So, she says. It is her voice. Clear as day.

Yep. This is it.

Well, looks . . . nice. Is this?

Yes, the robot. This is the mobile unit. The robot is inside, really. Well, sort of. We're going *inside* the robot.

No words for a space. Still, they move no closer.

Well then. Let's go inside the robot.

Laramie, inside the protecting ribwork of the robot. She is safe. Nothing will harm you here, Little Bulge. But the robot calms such thoughts. She takes one of the two chairs that are around Andrew's work and eating table in the control room. Abide, the robot thinks. Let her abide for a while.

Do you want tea? I can make you tea.

Yes. I drink herb tea.

Um. Don't have any.

Water?

Yes, water we have.

L.A.'s tastes like sludge.

No wonder. They're even tapping Oregon now.

Really? I believe it.

Andrew pours water for Laramie in a metal cup. He puts more water on a hot plate that sits on top of a monitor, and heats the water for tea. Where have you been, he says.

Port Townsend. Doing background and logistics. My sound guy's laying down local tone and getting wild effects.

Wild?

Unsynced, that's all it means.

I see.

Using Seattle labs is going to be a bitch. The Matties
have set up goddamn border crossings.

Tell me about it.

Andrew's water boils and he fills another cup with it,
then hunts for a tea bag in a cabinet.

You left them on the table, the robot says.

Laramie gasps, sits up in her chair sharply, then relaxes
once again. That was the robot, she says.

Yes. Thank you, robot. Andrew finds the box of tea
bags among a clutter of instruments.

Do you. Do you call the robot anything?

Hmm. Not really.

Just call me robot, the robot says. I'm thinking of a
name for myself, but I haven't come up with one yet.

Well, then. Robot.

Andrew makes his tea, and they talk more of logistics
and the political situation on the peninsula. The robot
feels a tenseness between them, or at least in Andrew. His
questions and replies are even more terse than is usual.
The robot doubts Victor Wu would have noticed. Thinking this saddens the robot. More proof that the robot is not
Victor Wu, and so can have no claim on Laramie's affection.

The robot listens to Laramie. Since she and Andrew are
speaking of things that the robot knows little about, the
robot concentrates on her specific words, on her manner
of expression.

Lens. Clearness in the world. Sky. Vision. Spread.
Range. Watershed.

I thought for two weeks about color or black and white,
Laramie says. I don't like colors except for the world's
colors that are underneath the ones on film, the ones we
see.

I don't follow, Andrew says. The robot has never
thought of colors this way, but resolves to spend a day

banding out frequencies and only observing intensities of black-and-white tones.

I'll have more water, if you don't mind. This is clear. L.A. water really is as thick as sludge and I don't like it.

After three hours, Laramie leaves, with promises to return and film the site as part of her documentary.

Robot?

Yes.

Do you think I might interview you. I guess if we could use the mobile unit, that would look better on film. More action. Do you ever come out of here?

Every day during the week, to work in the dig.

Well, then. That must be quite a sight. Maybe I can get that.

Of course you can. That would be fine.

Well. Then.

She says good-bye to Andrew, and with her Scoopic, unused, but always present, gets back into the red hum-vee, crusted with a layer of settled road dust, and turns around in the dirt road that ends at the living area. More dust rises; Laramie departs. Andrew coughs, brushes dust from his arms. He looks at the mu, shakes his head, but says nothing. He goes back in and makes a third cup of tea.

With the mu, the robot follows easily behind the hum-vee, even though Laramie is driving very fast. The robot follows the billowing cloud of dust for twenty-four miles—until the hum-vee turns onto the asphalt, and heads north toward Port Townsend.

The robot spends the next day, Sunday, away from books. The robot takes advantage of the melting away of the high snows and takes the mu up ridges where before that was no foothold or too much threat of avalanche. The mu skirts along the Bailey Divide with a sure movement, above the tree line and in rolling tundra meadow. Marmots are here, and they squeak and whistle from under big rocks. Picas have divided the land into separate kingdoms, each to a pica, and they call out their territory over and over, until their voices attract the wolves.

This is what the robot has been waiting for. The mu sits still by a still lake, as motionless as any other thing that is not alive can be. The wolves come slinking, low and mean, their heat traces preceding and hovering over them like a scudding cloud. Again, they are five, with the old gray leader, his left ear bent, torn, and ragged, like a leaf eaten by caterpillars. Swiftly, they are upon the picas, chasing the little rodents, yipping, cutting them off from their burrows, gobbling one or two down for every ten that escape. Then the gray leader has had enough to eat. He raises up his head and, instantly, the other dogs heed him. Off they run, as silent and warm as they had come, but now followed by a robot.

Down the tundra meadow of the Divide, through boulder shadows and over sprays of tiny wildflowers nestled in the green, the wolves themselves shadows, with the robot another shadow, down, down the greening land. Into the woods, along game trails the robot can barely discern, moving generally north, generally north, the mu barely keeping pace with the advancing wolves, the pace growing steady, monotonous even to the robot, until—

Suddenly, the gray leader pulls up, sniffs the air. The robot also comes to a standstill some hundred feet behind the pack. If they have noticed the robot, they give no sign. Instead, it is a living smell that the gray leader has detected, or so the robot thinks, for the wolves, whining, fall into a V-shape behind the leader. The wolves' muscles tense with a new and directed purpose.

And they spring off in another direction than the one they had been traveling, now angling west, over ridges, against the grain of the wheel-spoke mountains. The robot follows. Up another ridge, then when on top of it, down its spine, around a corner-cliff of flaking sedimentary stone, and into a little cove. They strike a road, a human-made track, and run along its edge, carefully close to the flanking brush and woodland. Winding road, and the going is easier for wolves and mu. In fact, the robot could easily overtake the wolves now, and must gauge how much to hold back to avoid overrunning them.

The track becomes thin, just wide enough for a vehicle going one way, with plenty of swishing against branches along the way. Ahead, a house, a little clapboard affair, painted once, perhaps, blue, or the blue-green tint may be only mold over bare wood. The ceiling is shingled half with asbestos shakes, and half with tin sheeting. Beside the house is a satellite dish, its lower hemisphere greened over with algae. There is an old pickup truck parked at road's end. The road is muddy here from a recent rain, and the tire markings of another vehicle, now gone, cross the top of the pickup's own tracks. All is silent.

Instead of giving the house a wide berth, the gray leader of the wolves stops at the top of the short walkway that leads to the front door. Again, he sniffs for scent, circling, whining. There is only a moment of hesitation, and he snakes up the walkway, and slinks to the door. The door hangs open. The other wolves follow several paces back. Another hesitation at the door, then the gray leader slips over the threshold and inside. Even with their leader gone into the house, the other wolves hang back, back from this thing that has for so long meant pain or death to them and their kind. After a long while, the gray leader returns to the door, yips contemptuously, and one by one, the other wolves go inside.

The robot quietly pads to the door. Inside is dark, and the robot's optics take a moment to iris to the proper aperture. There is a great deal of the color red in the house's little living room. The robot scans the room, tries to resolve a pattern out of something that is unfamiliar. The robot has never seen inside a real human dwelling before. But Victor Wu has. The wolves are worrying at something.

The wolves are chewing on the remains of a child.

Without thinking, the robot scampers into the room. The mu is a bit too large for the narrow door and, without the robot's noticing, it tears apart the doorframe as it enters. The wolves look up from what they are doing.

Wolf and robot stare at one another.

The robot adjusts the main camera housing to take them all in, and at the slight birring noise of the servos, the gray leader bristles and growls. The mu takes a step farther into the room, filling half the room. It knocks over a lamp table, with a shadeless lamp upon it. Both the bulb and the ceramic lamp casing shatter.

I don't want to hurt you, but you must leave the child alone, the robot says.

At the sound of what they take to be a human voice, the wolves spring into a flurry of action. The gray leader stalks forward, teeth bared, while the others in the pack mill like creek fish behind him. They are searching for an exit. The small, young one finds that a living-room window is open. With a short hop from a couch, the wolf is outside. The others follow, one by one, while the gray leader attempts to hold the robot at bay. The robot does not move, but lets the wolves depart. Finally, the gray leader sees from the corner of his eye that the other wolves have escaped. Still, he cannot help but risk one feint at the robot. The robot does not move. The gray leader, bolder, quickly jumps toward the robot and locks his jaws on the robot's forward leg. The teeth close on blue steel. The gray leader shakes. There is no moving the robot.

In surprise and agitation, the wolf backs up, barks three times.

I'm sorry to embarrass you. You'd better go.

The wolf does just that, turning tail and bounding through the open window without even using the living-room couch as a launch point. The robot gazes around the silent room.

There is a dead family here.

An adult male, the father, is on one side of the couch, facing a television. Part of his neck and his entire chest are torn open in a gaping bloody patch. Twisted organs glint within. The television is off. Huddled in a corner is the mother and a young boy. Their blood splatters an entire wall of the living room. A shotgun, the robot decides. First the man, and then the mother was shot with her children all at once, with several blasts from a shotgun. There are pepper marks in the wall from stray shot. Yes, the killing was done with a shotgun. The wolves must have dragged one child away from the mother. The robot sees that it is a little girl. The mother's other child, an older boy and a bit large for even a large wolf to handle, is still by his mother, partially blown into his mother's opened body.

The blood on the walls and floor has begun to dry and form into curling flakes that are brown and thin and look like tiny autumn leaves. There are also bits of skin and bone on the wall.

The robot stares at the little girl. Her eyes are, mercifully, closed, but her mouth is pulled open and her teeth, still baby teeth, exposed. This is perhaps caused by her stiffening facial muscles. Or she may have died with such an expression of pain. The robot cannot tell. The girl wears a blue dress that is now tatters around her tattered, small body. One foot has been gnawed, but on the other is a dirty yellow flip-flop sandal.

The robot feels one of the legs of the mu jerk spasmodically. Then the other jerks, without the robot wishing it to do so. The robot stares at the young girl and jitters and shakes for a long time. This is the way the robot cries.

Deeper in the earth, very deep now, and the rock, under megatons of pressure, explodes with a nuclear ferocity as the robot cuts away. For the past week the robot has thought constantly of the dead logger family, of the little dead girl. The robot has tried to remember the color of the girl's hair, but cannot, and for some reason, this greatly troubles the robot.

One evening, after a sixteen-hour workday, the robot dims the lights for Andrew. Outside the digger's main body, but still in the home cave, the robot inhabits the mu. The robot takes pen and paper in the dexterous manipulators of the mu and begins to write a description of the little girl. Not as she was, twisted and dead, but of how she might have been before.

The robot told Andrew about the family, and Andrew called the authorities, being careful to keep the robot out of his report.

They'll disassemble you, if they find out, Andrew said to the robot. At least in the United States, they'd be legally *required* to do it. God knows what the Protectorate will want to do.

There are accounts in the newspapers of the killing. The sheriff's department claims to be bewildered, but the robot overhears the technicians who come from logger families muttering that the Matties now own the cops, and that everybody knew who was behind the murders, if not who actually pulled the trigger. And the Matties who worked under Andrew, led by Gurney, spoke in low tones of justice and revenge for the killings in Port Townsend on Codependence Day.

I am a witness, the robot thinks. But of what?

*   *   *

*A*ndrew?

Yes.

Are you tired?

Yes. What is it?

She would have grown up to be part of the loggers, so killing her makes a kind of sense.

The little girl?

The Matties and the people who used to be loggers hate each other. And they can't help the way they are because they are like stones in sediment that's been laid down long before, and the hatred shapes them to itself, like a syncline or an anticline. So that there has to be new conditions brought about to change the lay of the sediment; you can't change the rocks.

I don't know about that. People are not rocks.

So if she wasn't killed out of an ignorant mistake, then I don't understand why.

I don't either, robot.

Why do you think?

I don't know, I said, I don't know. There isn't any good reason for it. There is something dark in this world that knows what it's doing.

Is it evil?

There is evil in the world. All the knowledge in the world won't burn it away.

How do you know?

I don't. I told you, I don't. I look at rocks. I don't have very many theories.

But.

Yes?

But you think it knows?

I think the evil knows what it's doing. Look at us in this goddamn century, all going back to hatred and tribes. You can't explain it with economics or cultural semantics or any system at all. Evil and plain meanness is what it is.

Andrew, it's not right for her to die. She hadn't lived long enough to see very many things and to have very many feelings. Those were stolen from her.

That's what murderers steal.

The future?

Yes. Even when you're old, it still isn't right.

Yes. I can see that. It's clear to me.

Well. Then.

I'll turn down the lights.

Well. Good night.

Brown.

What?

Her hair was dark brown.

And the robot digs deeper and deeper, approaching the Mohorivicic layer, with the true mantle not far beneath, seething, waiting, as it had waited for four billion years, would wait this attempt fail, should all attempts fail. And again, the foreign rhythm appears, hums along with the glade and bale of the robot's cutting, but distinct from it, distinct from the robot and all human-made things.

What is it? Andrew does not know. But there is something at the edge of the robot's consciousness, at the edge of Victor Wu's unconscious presence, that *does* know, that hears something familiar, as a whisper when the words are lost, but the meaning remains.

One day, the alien rhythm is louder than ever, and for a fleeting moment, the robot recognizes it.

Strong harmonies from the depths of the planet. Maude under the full moon. Magmas rising.

Victor you can feel it. How can you feel it?

I don't know, Maude, the robot thinks. Maude among

the instruments. I remember, thinks the robot, I remember what it felt like to walk the earth and let it show itself to me. There is a showing. Something is showing itself. Something is being revealed. Just as the St. Helens eruption was a revelation, with portents, with auguries that were plain to a man who cared for the earth.

Something knows we're here, the robot tells Andrew one night.

Andrew is tired from a half-day underground, and the afternoon spent explaining the dig to yet another Mattie committee in Port Angeles, but he listens to what the robot has to say.

What? How can you know?

I do though.

Then you do. Victor would know.

Andrew shucks the soft-sole walking shoes he wears in the city, and climbs onto the little cot inside the robot.

Everyone else wants me to stop digging. Do you want to stop digging?

No, Andrew.

Then what shall we do about it?

Listen, says the robot. Listen. But Andrew has fallen asleep and does not hear. The robot dims the lights inside, adjusts the temperature for Andrew, then goes out into the mu to read.

The robot listens. The rhythm grows stronger, and now there are variations, windings among the background vibration that is the feedback from the robot's own cutting of the rock and thumping against the earth's insides. It is like a song, but not a song.

There and there, the robot tells Andrew, but Andrew cannot hear it, encased as he is in the service wagon, and he cannot detect the rhythm on his many instruments.

I believe you, Andrew says, but I simply can't find it.

The robot considers saying no more. What if Andrew really came to doubt the robot's sanity? Would that not mean powering down, rebooting. Or perhaps never coming back up again. Dying.

Andrew will not kill me, the robot thinks. And I will say what it is I hear.

And slowly, day after day, the rhythm develops into an . . . other. The robot is not sure how else to think about it. It is the feeling that a—*one*—someone, is here, even when no one is in view. It is a sense of *presence* that the robot feels. The robot doesn't *know*. Andrew cannot discover a way of knowing. But the feeling is not some erratic wiring, or even the robot's developing imagination. It is either a madness or it is a real presence.

And I am not crazy.

Which is a sure sign of madness. Andrew laughs his dry laugh.

Yet again, because of Victor Wu, because Andrew has come to trust the robot in all other things, he takes the robot seriously. In the few spare moments he has for experiments not directly related to the mantle-goal, Andrew and a graduate student make coding modifications to the robot's language software.

We're wiring perfect pitch into you, the graduate student, Samantha, says, to go along with your ear for good music. Samantha explains more of what she is doing, but the robot does not follow. Samantha understands the robot's mechanism as a surgeon might a human being's. As she works at an internal keyboard, she tells the robot of her own past, but again the robot has trouble understanding.

I grew up in virtual. I was practically born on the Internet. But by god I'm going to die in the forest, Samantha tells the robot. That's why most of us are out here with Dr. Hutton, she says.

There is only a trace of a smile on Andrew's face, but the robot knows him well enough now to see it.

Well this sure as hell ain't virtual, he says.

Laramie returns. She has not called Andrew. One Saturday the hum-vee crackles down the dirt and gravel road to the living area, and Laramie has come back. Andrew is away, at a meeting, and at first the robot is flustered and bewildered as to what to do. The robot has been reading, with a mind still half in the book.

Laramie pulls out her camera and some sound equipment and comes to the entrance to the living cavern. The robot, in the mu, meets her, and invites her inside. That much the robot is able to manage.

I'm sorry I didn't clear my visit with Andrew first but you said it would be all right.

It is all right.

I thought it would be. Do you mind if I record this?

No. I keep something like a journal myself. Would you care for some tea? Andrew bought some herbal tea after your last visit.

The robot thinks that the words sound stiff and overly formal, but Laramie says yes, and settles down at the interior table and sets up her equipment. There is a kettle on the hot plate, and the robot turns on the burner. Laramie takes a microphone from a vinyl case and unwinds its cording. The robot watches her, watches Laramie's hand move. Her fingers are as long as Maude's.

The robot suddenly realizes there may be no water in the kettle. But there is steam rising from around the lid—which means that there is water and that the water is hot enough to drink.

Laramie. May I call you Laramie?

Sure. Of course.

I cannot make your tea.

What? That's fine, then. I'm fine.

No. I mean that it's difficult for me to get the mu inside.

I don't understand.

I'm sorry. I mean the mobile unit. If you don't mind, you can get a cup and a tea bag out of the cupboard. The water is ready.

Laramie sets the microphone down, gazes around the room.

Is it in that cupboard?

Yes. Bottom shelf.

Laramie gets the cup and tea, then pours some water. Andrew is a careful pourer, but Laramie spatters droplets on the hot burner and they sizzle as they evaporate. She takes her tea back to the table. She jacks the microphone into a small tape recorder that is black with white letters that say Sony. From the recorder, she runs a lead to the Scoopic sixteen-millimeter camera.

Where's that adapter? Oh. There. I had this Scoopic souped up a little, by the way, since my father. Since I got it. Has a GOES chip. Uplinks and downlinks with the Sony. I could record you in Singapore, and not get a frame of drift. But I'm not a pro at this. My sound tech bugged out on me last week. That's one reason it's taken me a while to get back over here. He got scared after the riot. Let me voice slate and we'll be ready.

Laramie?

Hmm?

Are you safe? I mean, where you are staying in Port Townsend—is it guarded in any way?

No. I'm fine. It's the loggers and the Matties who want to kill each other.

They might mistake you for a logger. You spent a lot of time in the bush.

At this expression, which is Victor Wu's, Laramie

looks up. She finds nothing to look at, and turns her gaze back down, to the Sony.

I'm safe as can be expected.

Be careful, Laramie.

You're not my father.

I know that. But I would be pleased if you would be careful.

All right. I'll keep that in mind. Laramide productions-skykomish-eight-three-fourteen-roll-eleven. Robot, have you decided yet on a name?

Not yet.

She raises the camera, looks around through the viewfinder, and finally chooses a bank of monitors to aim it at.

What do you think about?

Pardon?

What do you think about, robot?

I'm not HAL, Laramie.

What?

You know what I mean. You saw that movie many times. Your question sounds snide to me, as if it were forgone conclusion that I don't *really* think. You don't just throw a question like that at me. It would be better to lead up to it. I don't have to justify my existence to anyone, and I don't particularly like to fawn on human beings. I feel that it is degrading to them.

You sound like Andrew is what you sound like.

That's quite possible. I spend a lot of time with him.

Well. So. Maybe that wasn't the best first question. Maybe you could tell me about your work.

The robot explains the dig, and what it might mean to science.

But I don't know a great deal about that. At least, I don't think about it often.

What really matters to you, then?

The digging. The getting there. The way the rock is. All igneous and thick, but there are different regions.

Like swimming in a lake.

Yes. I imagine you're right. It's very hard to talk about, the feeling I have.

What feeling?

That. I don't know. It is hard to say. I could. I could take you there.

Take me where? Down there?

Yes. Down there.

Now? You mean now?

No. I'd have to talk to Andrew about doing so.

Of course. Do you think he'd let me?

I would like to show it to you, what we're doing. I think that if I wanted to take you down, he would let you.

Laramie sets the camera down on the table, beside her herb tea, which is untouched and cooling.

Ask him, robot. Please ask him.

On Monday, protesters arrive at the dig. Andrew had been expecting them eventually, but the number surprises him. They arrive by bus and gather at the opening to the mo-hole, not at the living-space entrance.

Gurney must have told them which was which. Andrew growls the words, and the robot can barely understand them.

There are forty protesters. At first, they mill around, neither saying nor doing much, but waiting. Finally, a sky-blue Land Rover comes down the dirt road. On its side are the words: KHARMA CORPS, SKYKOMISH PROTECTORATE. Two women and a man get out and the protesters gather round them. From the back of the Land Rover, one of the women hands out placards that have on them symbols. The peace sign. A silhouetted nuclear reactor with a red slashed circle about it. A totem of the Earth Mother from

Stilaguamish Northwest Indian heritage, and now the symbol for the Skykomish Protectorate. One sign has a picture of a dam, split in half as if by an earthquake, and fish swimming freely through the crack. The other woman gives those who want it steaming cups of hot, black coffee or green tea.

The robot waits in the mu at the entrance to the living area, and Andrew walks over to speak with the protesters. The man who drove the Land Rover steps forward to meet him. The robot can hear what is said, but Andrew's body blocks the view of the man with whom Andrew is speaking.

Andrew Hutton. I work here.

I'm with the Protectorate. My name is Neilsen Birchbranch.

How are you with the Protectorate?

I'm an aid to Mother Agatha. I sit on the Healing Circle Interlocking Director's Conclave. I'm the chairperson, in fact.

Secret police.

What was that?

Neilsen, was it?

Let's keep it formal, Dr. Hutton, if you wouldn't mind.

All right. Mr. Birchbranch, what are you doing on my work site?

The demonstration is sanctioned. Mother Agatha herself signed the permit. Freedom of speech is guaranteed in the Protectorate Charter.

I'm not against freedom of speech. We have work to do today.

It is against the law to cross a protest line. That's infringement on freedom of speech and that's in the Charter as well. These people feel that the work you're doing is violating the sanctity of the earth. They feel that you are, in a way, raping the mother of us all. Do you know where your digging machine comes from?

Yes. From a defunct mining operation that the Matties had a hand in putting out of business.

Precisely. It is a symbol. This hole is a symbol. Dr. Hutton, can't you see how it's taken, what you're doing?

I can see how some take it. I can see the politics of it, clearly enough.

It is a new politics, Dr. Hutton. The politics of care. I'm not sure you do see that, or else you wouldn't be an opponent.

Maybe. Maybe I show my care in other ways.

What other ways?

Nonpolitical ways. I'm not sure *you* can see what *I'm* talking about, Mr. Birchbranch.

So. You persist, regardless of the consequences, because you want to see what's down there.

That's fair to say. Yes. I want to see what's down there.

The values of western science. The same values that gave us thermonuclear war and the genocide of every other species besides man.

Well, there's also woman. That's a separate species.

Pardon?

It's a joke, Mr. Birchbranch. Maybe not a very good one.

No. Not a very good one at all.

So these are the things you're going to say to the television.

Not me as an individual. These people have chosen me to voice *their* concern and care.

Chosen you?

I'm the personal representative of Mother Agatha. You must believe that they've chosen her?

Then are you saying my people can't work? There are Matties. Children of the Matriarch. They work here. This is their livelihood.

They've all agreed to stay home today, I believe you'll find.

They're striking against me?

It's a support measure.

I see.

Good then. There will be a television truck coming later, and possibly a helicopter from News Five in Seattle. If you'd like, you can route any calls from journalists to me.

That won't be necessary.

The robot hears bitterness in Andrew's voice. Perhaps the other man can also.

So. Thank you for your cooperation, Dr. Hutton.

Yes. What's the time period on the permit? I spoke with Karlie Waterfall and she said that if it came through, it would be a week at most.

Sister Waterfall has voluntarily resigned from the Science Interweft to devote more time to her work at the Dungeoness Spit Weather Observation Station.

When did that—Never mind. Christ, she was the only one with any sense on that damn committee.

There isn't a set period on the permit. There's no time limit on freedom of speech.

Well, get on with it, then, I suppose.

We intend to, Dr. Hutton. One other thing. We have a restraining order against the use of any machinery in the area for the day. I understand that you have a robot.

That's right.

Please power the robot down for the day, if you don't mind.

I do mind.

Dr. Hutton, this is entirely legal.

The robot will remain in my quarters. The robot *is* my quarters.

It is highly irregular. I can't answer for the consequences if you don't comply with the order.

Good-bye, Mr. Birchbranch. Have a nice protest.

Andrew turns to leave, and in so doing, steps out from

in front of the man. The robot's optics zoom in and pull
focus, which the robot experiences in the same way as a
human might the dilation of the eyes. At first the robot
cannot believe what those optics report, and zooms out
and back in again, as rubbing the eyes is to humans. No
mistake.

Neilsen Birchbranch is a tall man, with lanky arms and
legs. His face is thin and hard, gaunt, with muscles like
small twisting roots cabling his mandible to his temple.
The robot saw him last in the field, before Andrew came.
Neilsen Birchbranch is the same man who killed the other
on the steps of the dais in the field. Neilsen Birchbranch
is the man who pulled the trigger of the gun and shot the
other man dead.

Andrew steps back into the living area and the robot, in
the mu, draws back noiselessly into the darkness.

Andrew calls the graduate students and the technicians
who are from logger families, explaining to them one after
another not to bother coming to work for a while, and to
check back in over the next few mornings. When Andrew
is done, the robot tells him about Neilsen Birchbranch.

Are you certain?

I'm sure of it.

I can't think of what to do about it.

Neither can I. I don't want to be torn apart.

We won't let that happen.

Then there isn't anything.

No.

Be wary.

I'm already wary.

The first of the autumn rains begin. Though the digging
area is partially in the rain shadow of the eastern mountains, it is still within the great upturns of basalt that ring
the interior mountains, and mark the true edge of a swath

of relative dryness that runs along the Hood Canal in a great horseshoe up even to Sequim and the Dungeoness Spit, so that there are not two hundred inches of rain, such as fall on the Ho, or the Quinault watershed, but there is more than a hundred—millions and millions of gallons of rain and snow—that will fall here during the autumn, winter, and spring, and many days throughout the summer.

Because of the great rains, and many days throughout the summer.

Because of the great rains, there are great trees. And because of the great trees, the loggers came. And because most of the other trees were cut, the lovers of trees came. And the rain falls on Mattie and logger alike, and it falls and falls and falls.

The Matties have set up folding tables and many have brought chairs and big umbrellas. The tables and chairs of the Matties line the road for a hundred yards, and whenever a network reporter arrives, the tables and chairs are put hastily away and the Matties stand and grow agitated.

On the eleventh day of the protest, Laramie returns. Laramie has not coordinated her arrival with the Matties, and so comes upon them unawares with her camera. The Matties smile into the lens. After she begins asking questions, a delegation approaches her and asks her to wait, that the spokesperson is on his way, and he will give her the best answers. No one will speak with Laramie after this, and Andrew invites her into the living area to wait for the arrival of the spokesperson.

The robot has been watching, just inside the entrance to the living area, as the robot has been watching for days now. Only at night, when the protesters go back to their bus and the Land Rover carries away the tables and chairs, does the robot go out into the open.

This can't go on, Andrew says. I can't stop paying wages. I'm *required* to pay wages to my Mattie techs, but

I would anyway, and all the others. No digging, and all the grant money flowing away.

Sorry to hear that.

Laramie uses the Scoopic to make various shots of the robot's interior. Andrew says nothing, but smiles thinly. She has the Sony slung around her shoulder and, the robot notices, is recording her conversation with Andrew.

Did the robot discuss with you me going down in the hole?

In the dig. It's a spiral, like a Slinky, more or less. Yes. Yes, you can come as soon as we're allowed to go back down there.

That's great. Will I be able to film any of what it looks like?

Hmm. Maybe we can set something up. There's a small observation port on the service wagon. We'll have to turn off the fusion on the dray first, or you won't be filming for very long, I don't think.

Excellent. I'm really tired of protests and officials who don't call themselves officials, and all those squalid houses where all the loggers moved out at Aberdeen. There's been a lot of trouble there.

I heard about it.

We didn't used to call them loggers much.

That's because everybody was one.

We used to drive through Aberdeen when we wanted to get to the sea.

And up the coast to La Push.

Those black beaches across the river. I used to know why the rocks were so black.

Basalt skree that a glacier brought down that valley last ice age. That's what happened to the back half of the horseshoe. That's where it went.

Yeah. Basalt tumble. We slept there all night one night in August. You thought Papa would be pissed, but he didn't even notice, of course. He just asked me about the rocks I saw and told me about the Big Fist of sediment lifting up the seafloor and breaking it and all that. Papa. You and I made love that night, didn't we, Andrew?

Yes, Laramie. You know we did.

I know it.

Then.

Yep. The robot's listening, isn't it.

I'm listening, Laramie, if you don't mind.

No.

You know I'm not Victor Wu. I'm not shocked. I am rather surprised, however.

What do you mean?

About Andrew. I've never known him when he was in love with a woman.

Andrew's crackling chuckle. Not for a while, he says.

There was that chemist, after me. You wrote me about her. That was your last letter.

You never wrote me back.

I was pissed.

I figured you would be. Still, you couldn't have been pissed for five years.

I couldn't?

We broke up the next January.

Sorry to hear that.

She lacked imagination. They all lacked imagination.

Jesus, you're clinical.

I know what I like.

What do you like?

I can't have what I like.

Why not?

Because she has to live in Los Angeles, and I'm not particularly interested in the geology of Southern California.

The robot sees that Laramie's fine white skin has taken on a flush.

And it's as simple as that, she says.

Why make it complicated?

Maybe it *is* complicated. Maybe you're simplistic.

Will you turn that damn camera off?

No.

Well. There you have it.

On the fourteenth day, the protesters do not arrive in the morning. There is no explanation, and no hint given to Andrew as to when they will return. Once again, the robot digs. Andrew puts aside several tests and side projects in order to dig faster and deeper. The robot is in the element that the metal of the rotor blades and the grip of the ceramic thread were made for—hard-rock mining—and the robot presses hard, and the rock explodes and fuses as obsidian diamond glass to the walls behind the robot, and the tunnel approaches forty miles in depth.

No one has ever been this deep before.

The techs from logging families and the Mattie techs are barely speaking to one another, and the graduate students are uneasy and tense, afraid to take sides. Andrew holds the crew together by a silent and furious force of will. The robot does not want to let Andrew down, and digs the harder.

Samantha has made the last of the modifications to the robot's linguistics, and puts the new code on-line. The robot immediately feels the difference. The presence, the otherness, grows stronger and stronger with every hour, until the robot is certain of it. But of *what,* there is no saying.

Two days of digging, and on the third, Laramie arrives in the early morning and prepares to descend with the crew. But before the work can begin for the day, Andrew receives a call telling him that proceedings are under way for a new permit of protest, and a long-term suspension of the dig. He drives to Forks, where the committee will meet in the afternoon. It is a rainy day, and the robot worries that Andrew may drive too fast on the slippery pavement. Still, there is plenty of time for him to make the meeting.

In Andrew's absence, the Matties and loggers fall to quarreling about duties, and the graduate student Andrew has left in charge cannot resolve the differences. After an hour of listening to the wrangling, even the robot can see that no work will be done this day. The robot asks permission to take Laramie down to the bottom of the dig, and the graduate student, in disgust at the situation, shrugs and goes back to refereeing the technicians' argument.

As Laramie and the robot are preparing to leave, Neilsen Birchbranch drives up in the Protectorate Land Rover. A light rain is falling, and the graduate student reluctantly admits him into the work site's initial cavern, where the others are gathered. The robot—digger and mu—draws back into the darkness of the true entrance to the dig.

Let's go, Laramie says.

. But I'm afraid of this man, the robot replies. He isn't a good man. I know that for a fact.

Then let's get out of here.

There may be trouble.

I need to speak with Hutton, Neilsen Birchbranch says to the graduate student. It is very important that I speak with him today.

Take me down, please, robot. I may never get another chance.

The robot considers. As always, it is difficult to deny Laramie something she really wants with all her heart. And there is so much to show her. The robot has been thinking about showing the dig to Laramie for a long time. And the farther down they go, the farther they get from Neilsen Birchbranch's trouble.

We have a witness that places one of your machines at

the scene of a crime, says Neilsen Birchbranch. A very serious crime.

Neilsen Birchbranch steps farther into the cavern, gazes around. The robot slowly withdraws down the mohole. For all the digger's giant proportions, its movement is very quiet and, the robot hopes, unnoticed.

Nothing but you can survive down there, can it, robot? Laramie says. How deep is it down there?

Forty-three miles.

He can't turn you off if you're forty miles deep. We'll stay down until Andrew comes back.

The first few miles of the descent are the most visually interesting, and after reaching a depth at which unprotected humans cannot survive the heat, the robot moves at a fraction of the usual pace. There are areas where the glass spray on the walls has myriad hues taken from all the minerals that were melted together in the slurry around the nuclear pile, then spewed out to line the tunnel. The walls are smooth only at first glance, but really a series of overlapping sheets, one imperfectly flowing atop the other, as sheets of ice form over a spring in winter. The robot directs lights to some of the more interesting formations, and they glow with the brilliance and prismatic hue of stained glass.

I didn't think I'd get anything this good, Laramie says. This is wonderful. The colors. God I'm glad I went with color.

Deeper, and the walls become milky white. The granite behind glows darkly, three yards under the glassine plaster.

Twenty miles. Thirty.

Only basalt in the slurry now, and the walls are colorless. Yet they have the shape of the rock many feet behind them, and so they catch the light with effulgent glimmer.

Clear and clean.

Laramie may be speaking to herself; the robot cannot tell.

They pass through a region where magma pools against the walls and ceilings in places, held back by the diamondlike coating. The pressure is so great that the magma glows with a blue-and-white intensity. The tunnel sparkles of its own accord, and the robot must dim the viewport to keep from blinding Laramie.

Like the sky behind the sky.

The robot says nothing. Laramie is happy, the robot thinks. Little Bulge likes it down here.

They have been some hours in the descent, and Laramie is running low on film, but is very, very happy. Near to the bottom. Now to wait for Andrew. Very quiet. The robot has never been this deep before without digging and working. The robot has never sat idle and silent at the bottom of the mohole.

"Hello."

For a moment, the robot thinks Laramie has spoken. But this is not Laramie's voice. And it comes from *outside*. The voice comes from outside the robot, from the very rocks themselves.

The sense of the presence, the other that the robot has been feeling for these long weeks, is very strong. Very strong.

Again the voice that isn't a voice, the vibration that isn't a vibration. It is like a distant, low whisper. Like a voice barely heard over a lake at morning. No wonder I never made it out before, the robot thinks.

Hello, comes the voice.

Who are you?

I'm me.

What are you doing down here?

I *am* down here. Who are you?

I'm—I don't have a name yet.

Neither do I. Not one that I like.

Who are you?

Me. I told you.

What is it, robot? Laramie speaking.

Something strange.

What?

I don't. Wait for a moment. A moment.

All right.

The robot calls again. The robot is spinning its cutting rotors at low speed, and it is the whisk and ding of the digger's rotors that is doing the talking. Hello?

Hello. Are you one of those trees?

Trees?

The trees barely get here, and then they start *moving*. Are you one of those moving trees?

I don't. Yes. Maybe.

I thought you *might* talk, but it's so cold up there, it takes ages to say anything. Down here things go a lot faster.

Are you. What are you?

I told you. I'm me.

The rocks?

Nope.

The magma?

Nope. Guess again.

Where are you? Show yourself to me.

I am.

Then I've guessed. You're the whole planet. You're the earth.

Laughter. Definitely laughter. I'm not either. I'm just here. Just around here.

Where's here?

Between the big ocean and the little ocean.

The Olympic Peninsula?

Is that what you call it? That's a hard word for a name.

Skykomish.

That's better. Listen, I have a lot of things I want to ask you. We all do.

There is an explosion.

At first the robot thinks that a wall has blown out near the region of the magma pools. This will be dangerous, but it should be possible to reinforce long enough to get through. It may mean trouble for the dig, though. Now there will be more funding. The Matties will allow it to go ahead. Even the robot can see that the politics have changed.

Everything has changed.

There is another explosion. A series of explosions.

Robot?

Laramie. I. I have so much to tell you.

What is that shaking? I'm scared down here. Do you think we can go up now?

Hello. Tree? Are you still there?

Even with the tremors—there are huge rumblings and cracklings all about—the robot is attuned to the voice, the presence, and can still hear its words.

I really need to talk to you.

Papa, do you think we can go up now?

The *pressure wave* lifts the robot—impossibly tilts the robot—over and over—shatter of the walls as diamonds shatter like the shrapnel of stars and the rocks behind— tumble and light, light from the glow of the give, the sudden release of tension—the bulk melt of the undisclosed—sideways, but what is sideways?—tumble and tumble—skree within thin melt moving, turning, curling like a wave and the robot on the curl, under the curl, hurled down down down over over down dark dark.

Dark.

Dark and buried.

Find my daughter.

The engineers have built one hell of a machine.

Find my daughter.

The robot powers back up. The robot begins, blindly, to dig. It is only by sheer luck that the robot comes upon the service wagon. The robot melts and compacts a space, creates an opening, temporary, dangerously temporary. Finds the power-hitch to the wagon and plugs in.

Turns on the lights and air-conditioning inside the wagon. The video cameras inside.

Laramie is twisted against a control console. Her neck is impossibly twisted. She is dead.

No. She isn't. Can't be. She is.

What? Within the curve of her stomach, holding it to shelter, the Scoopic. But the latch has sprung and sixteen-millimeter film is spilled out and tangled about her legs.

No. Laramie. Little Bulge.

Hello?

The robot screams. The robot howls in anguish. Forty miles deep, the robot cries out a soul's agony into the rock. A living soul mourning a dead one.

Stop that.

The other, the presence. The robot does not care. Past caring.

You're scaring me.

Past.

You're scaring me.

Grind of rotors, ineffectual grind. How can you live? How can humans live when this happens? Ah, no. You can't live. You cannot. You can, and it is worse. Worse than not living. No no no no.

Stop it.

And something happens. Something very large—gives. More. Faults, faults everywhere. Settle, rise, settle. Faults like a wizened crust, like a mind falling into shards of fear. Faults and settle, rise and settle. Rise.

No. I.

But there is a way. There is a weakness revealed, and there is a way. Not wide enough, not yet. But a way to go. A way to take her home. Take her home to Andrew. The robot begins to dig.

The robot digs. There is only the digging, the bite of blade and saw, the gather of lade and bale. Digging. Upward digging.

The way is made easier by the shaking, the constant, constant tremble of what the robot knows to be fear, incomprehension.

A child who has seen a grown-up's sorrow, and does not understand. A frightened child.

By the time the robot comes to this realization, it is too late. The robot is too high, and when called, the child does not answer. Or perhaps it is that the child needs time to calm, that it cannot answer. The robot calls again and again. Nothing. Nothing can be heard above the rumble of fear.

Poor trembling Skykomish. The robot continues digging, drawing behind it the service wagon. Bringing Laramie to Andrew.

A day passes. Two. Rock. Stone. The roots of the mountains, and sediment, compressed to schist. The roots of the mountains and the robot slowly comes to its senses. Comprehends.

After a long moment of stillness—a minute, an hour? No reckoning in the utter depths, and the robot is not that kind of robot—after a long moment of reflection, the robot looses the service wagon.

Little Bulge, good-bye.

Up. Now. Up because the way is easier up than down, and that is the only reason.

After three days, the robot emerges from the ground. In

a cove that the robot recognizes. On the Quinault water-shed. Into a steady autumn rain.

The robot wanders up the Quinault River. Every day rains, and no nights are clear. The forest is in gloom, and moss hangs wet and dark. Where the trail is not wide enough, the robot bends trees, trying not to break them, but uprooting many. Many trees have fallen, for there are earthquakes—waves and waves of them. Earthquakes the like of which have never been seen in the world. The robot cuts deadfall from its path with little effort and little thought. The digger's passage through the forest is like that of a hundred bears—not a path of destruction, but a marked and terrible path, nonetheless.

Where the Quinault turns against a great ridge, the robot fords, and continues upward, away from the trees. The robot crosses Low Divide during the first snow of the season. The sun is low, then gone behind the cloaked western ridges. For a time, the ground's rumblings still. All sound is muffled by the quiet snow. The twilight air is like silence about the robot.

Something has happened.

At the saddle of the divide, the robot pauses. The pass is unfamiliar. Something has happened inside. Victor Wu has gone away. Or Victor Wu has come fully to life. The two are the same.

Then am I a man?

What is my name?

Orpheus. Ha. A good one.

Old Orf up from Hades. I've read about you. And Euridice. I didn't understand. And now I do. Poems are pretty rocks that know things. You pull them from the earth. Some you leave behind.

Talking to myself.

After a moment, the robot, Orf, grinds steadily on. He grinds steadily on.

Down the valley of the Elwha, and north as the river flows and greatens. Earthquakes heave and slap, slap and heave. Sometimes a tree falls onto the digger, but Orf pays no mind. He is made of the stronger material, and they cannot harm him.

Down the valley of the Elwha, past the dam that the Matties have carefully removed, that would not have withstood the quakes if it were still there. The trail becomes a dirt road. The road buckled pavement. The robot follows the remains of the highway into what once was Port Angeles.

What will future geologists make of this? The town has become a skree, impossible to separate and reconfigure. Twists of metal gleam in the pilings by the light of undying fires. And amid the fire and rubble, figures move. Orf rolls into the city.

A man sits in a clear space, holds his knees to his chest, and stares. Orf stops well away from him.

I am looking for a man named Neilsen Birchbranch. Do you know where I can find him?

The man says nothing.

Do you know where I can find Neilsen Birchbranch? He works for the Protectorate.

The man says nothing, but begins to rock back and forth on his haunches.

I'm looking. Can you—

The man begins to moan.

Orf moves onward. At a point where the piles of rubble begin to be higher, a makeshift roadblock has been set up. Orf stops at it, and a group of men and women, all armed with rifles, come out of the declivities of the town skree.

Come out of there, an old man says. He points his gun at Orf.

There isn't anybody in here.

Come out, or we'll blow you to hell.

I've already been there.

Come on out of there.

I'm looking for a man named Neilsen Birchbranch. He works for the Protectorate.

Goddamn we will shoot you you goddamn Mattie.

Do you know where I can find him?

The old man spits on the ground.

Reckon he's with the others.

The others?

That's what I said.

Where are they?

Out at the dump.

Where's the dump?

That way. The old man points with his gun. Now come out.

Orf turns and rolls away in the direction of the dump. Shots ring out. They ricochet off him and crackle against the rubble.

Five miles out of town, Orf finds the dump. There are bodies here; hundreds of bodies. Men, women, children. At first, he thinks they are the dead from the quakes, collected and brought here.

With the edge of a saw blade, Orf turns one of the bodies over. It is a woman. She has been shot in the head.

Most of the other bodies are people who have been shot. Or hacked up. Or had their necks broken with clubs.

The loggers have had their revenge.

And there among the bodies, Orf pauses. He has recognized one. It is the woman from the field, the speaker, Mother Agatha. It is her; there is no mistake. A small bullet hole is in the forehead of her peaceful face.

Orf rolls back to the city. It is night. He bursts through

the roadblock without stopping. Shots, the flash of muzzles. It is all so much waste. Down lightless streets, and streets lit with fires, some deliberate, some not. Every half hour or so, another earthquake rumbles through, throwing rubble willy-nilly. There are often screams.

Orf comes upon a steady fire, well-maintained, and sees that it is surrounded by people—people in the blue and brown dress of Matties. It is a silent throng. Orf hangs back, listens.

Oh Mother Agatha Mother Goddess hear our prayer.

Hear our prayer.

We know we have done wrong. We have sinned against you. Hear our prayer.

Hear our prayer.

Hold back your wrath. We are unworthy and evil. This we know. We beg you even still. Hold back your wrath. Hear our prayer.

Hear our prayer.

Goddamn mother—

The report of a gun. Someone—man or woman, Orf cannot tell—crumples in the ring of the fire. Instead of fleeing, the others stand still.

Another shot. Another falls.

Hear our prayer.

No one moves.

Another shot. A man falls, groaning, grasping at his leg. No one moves. He writhes in the shadows of the fire, in the dust of the ruins. No one helps him.

The rifleman shoots no more. The man writhes. The voice of the minister goes up to his goddess and the people respond mechanically.

Like robots are supposed to, Orf thinks. The man ceases his writhing. There is nothing to do. Orf rolls on quietly through the night, out of the city and east. The going is easy over the broken highway. In two hours, Orf is in what was Port Townsend.

There is no rubble here, no ruins. The sea has washed it away. No bodies. No trees. Only desolation, bare-wiped desolation. He rolls down to where the docks had been, and looks out upon the lapping waters of the Strait of Juan de Fuca.

Then the slap of an earthquake, and Orf discovers the reason for the missing city. The slap runs its way down to the sea and is perfectly mirrored by the other side of the strait. Reflected back, a tsunami. Rolls over the land. Nothing left to take. Almost enough to suck in a digging robot. Orf must backpedal with his threads, dig in to keep from being pulled forward by the suck of the water as it retreats to the sea.

Everyone is drowned here.

Orf will not find Neilsen Birchbranch by looking in the cities. He heads to the southwest now, back to the center of the mountains.

Into the forest. Orf wanders without aim. A day. Many days. Once, he remembers the mu, tries to go out of himself and find it. The uplink doesn't work; there is only static on a clear channel. Have all the satellites fallen from the sky? He wanders on, a giant among the gigantic trees.

Across one divide. Down a valley. Finally back to the dig site. All is devastation here, a tumble of stone. Not a sign of anyone. The living area is caved in. Orf digs, but cannot locate the mu. All he finds is a twisted piece of red metal—the remains of Laramie's hum-vee. Nothing else. No reason to stay.

Across another divide. Another valley. No longer caring to keep track. Stopping to look at rocks, or a peculiar bend in a river. The accumulation of snow.

One day, the earthquakes stop.

Quiet child. Hush now. You've seen too much for

young eyes. Hush and be quiet for a while and take your rest.

Winter, it must be. Orf coming over Snow Dome, down the Blue Glacier and into the valley of the Ho, where the biggest of the big trees are. Darkness earlier and earlier. In these towering woods, at these high latitudes, winter days are a perpetual twilight. Orf alongside the Ho. Its water opaque with outwash sludge, the heart of Mt. Olympus, washing away to the sea.

Then away from the river, deeper into the rain forest. As deep and as wild as it gets, many miles from roads. If there are roads anymore.

One hushed afternoon—or perhaps early evening, they are blend—a climbing rope, dangling from a tree. Movement to the left.

Another rope. Many ropes falling from the trees like rain that stays suspended. And down the ropes men and women slide like spiders. Orf is surrounded. They are dressed in tattered suits of green. Silently, they gather round the digger until Orf cannot move for fear of crushing one of them.

Men and women. Some have rifles slung across their backs. Two women carry children in the same manner, and the young ones are utterly, utterly quiet.

All right. Orf has not heard a voice in weeks, and his own, arising from his exterior speakers, startles him. What is it you want?

One of the men in green steps forward.

Wait, he says.

Orf waits with the silent people for he knows not what. And then, there is a movement in the undergrowth of vine maple. From around a low slope and over some deadfall, the mu appears. It moves clumsily. Whoever is at the controls doesn't know what he's doing, Orf thinks.

The mu scampers up to the digger and stops.

Andrew walks over the slope.

He steps lightly along the deadfall on the forest floor and comes to stand beside the mu. In his hand is a metal box with an antenna extended from it.

Do you want this thing back?

They are silent for a while. It is not a strained silence, but is right. Orf speaks first.

Laramie is dead. I couldn't save her.

I know.

What happened at the dig?

I'm not sure. I've only got secondhand information, but I think that the secret policeman coerced Gurney into sabotaging the place. I think he threatened to hurt his family. It was a bomb. A big bomb. Probably chemical. Everybody died, not just. Not just Laramie.

So. I'm sorry. So. Who are these people?

Andrew laughs. It has been so, so long. That dry laugh. A harsh, fair laugh, out of place before, perhaps, but suited now to these harsh times.

These are Rangers of the United States Park Service. They live here. In the tops of the old growth. We guard the forest.

We?

Somehow or another, I've become the head ranger.

W*inter, and the* rangers bundle in the nooks of their firs and hemlocks, their spruces and cedars. The digger must remain on the ground, but using the mu, Orf can venture up to their village in the trees.

In the highest tree, in the upper branches, Andrew has slung his hammock. Orf and he spend many days there, talking, discussing how things were, how they might be. Politics have shifted in the outside world, and Andrew is part of them now, seeking a place for his band of outcast civil servants that has become a family, and then a tribe.

The rangers hold the center of the Peninsula against

Mattie and logger, or against the remains of them. There is to be no clearing of the forest, and no worship of it, either, but a conservation and guard, a stewardship and a waiting. Rangers defend the woods. They take no permanent mates and have no children. The young ones Orf had seen before were stolen children, taken from Matties and loggers. Ranger women in their constant vigilance could not afford to be pregnant, and if they did, took fungal herbs that induced abortion. All must be given to the watching.

Winter, spring. Another year. Years. The fortunes of the rangers ebb and flow, but always the forests are held. Orf comes to their aid often with the mu and, when the situation is very dire, with the whirling blades of the digger.

Andrew hopes to open the mohole back up one day, when all is secure, to continue the dig—especially in light of Orf's discovery of . . . whatever it is that is down there. But now there are politics and fighting, and that time never comes. Andrew was right, and tribes, strange tribes, arise in the outside world. Governments crumble and disappear. Soon it is rangers alone who keep a kind of learning and history alive, and who come to preserve more than trees.

In any case, Andrew's heart seems to have gone out of the project. Somewhere below his love is buried, deeper than any man's has ever been buried before. If he goes back down, he may come upon her yet. Andrew is a brave man, Orf knows. But maybe not that brave.

And always Orf hears rumors of a bad man and killer who appears here and there, sometimes in the service of the Matties, sometimes working for logger clans. But Orf never finds Neilsen Birchbranch. Never even discovers his real name. And a time comes when the rumors cease.

Many years. Andrew grows old. Orf does not grow old. The digger's nuclear fusion pile will not run down. Only a malfunction could keep Orf from living a thousand years. Perhaps a thousand more.

One morning, in the mu, Orf climbs to Andrew's hammock and finds that Andrew has died in the night.

Gently, Orf envelops the man in the mu's arms; gently, he carries the body down from the trees. And walks through the forest. And crosses a divide. And another. To the valley of the Elwha. And up the Lillian River, to a basalt stela that, curiously, has no foramens in its make-up. That speaks of deep things, from far under the earth. That this land—strange peninsula between two salt waters—may be the place to dig and find what those things are.

At its base, Orf buries his friend, Andrew Hutton.

And then, Orf—digger and mu—returns to the long-abandoned work site. Orf clears the rocky entrance, finds the old passage. Orf digs down into the earth, and closes the path behind him.

In the heart of the great horseshoe twist of the Olympic Peninsula, in the heart of the mountains themselves, there lives a monster, a giant, who some say is also a god. A ranger, hunting in some hidden dale, or along the banks of a nameless rivulet flowing from the snow's spring runoff, will feel the presence of another, watching. The ranger will turn, and catch—what?—the flash of tarnished metal, the glint of wan sun off a glassy eye? Then the spirit, the presence, will be gone from the ranger's senses, and he will question whether he felt anything at all. Such sightings happen only once or twice in a fortnight of years.

But there is a rock, black and tall, in the deepest, oldest wood, up a secret tributary of the Elwha River, where young rangers, seeking their visions, will deliberately go. Some do not return from that high valley. Others come back reporting a strange and wonderful thing: On a particular night in October, when the moon is new and all the land is shrouded, they say the monster emerges from a hole in the mountains—but never the same hole—and closes the way behind. The monster travels to the rock on the Lillian.

The earth rumbles like distant thunder, and trees are gently bent out of the monster's way as if they were thin branches. And at that rock on the Lillian River, the monster stays for a time, shining darkly under the stars. The monster stays and is utterly silent. The reasons why are lost to legend, but at that time young rangers with strong and empty hearts are given waking dreams and prophesies to fill them.

Then, not long before sunrise, the monster moves, pivots on its great bulk, and returns from whence it came. There are those who follow, who are called to track the monster back to its lair. These are seldom the strongest or the bravest, and they are not particularly missed. Some say the monster eats them or tortures them in fires of liquid stone. But others say that the monster leads them to a new land, wider and deeper than any humans can conceive, under the mountain, that the earth is bigger on the inside than on the outside. No one knows. No one knows, because they do not return to tell the tale, and the world falls further into ruin, and the monster—or god—no longer speaks.